What people are saying about

Twice

Dark and dazzling, with mesmeric twists and much to say about where we are today.
Anna Minton, Ground Control, Big Capital

Drawn breathlessly into a nightmare world in which the usual conventions do not apply, there is no reprieve until one insecurely draws near to the conclusion. Written with skilful pace and polished art, we are presented with a first-rate fantasy and something that is more than mere fantasy. Here is a dextrously woven tale with deftly drawn characters that will cause as much intellectual stimulus as it does readership enjoyment. One is left gasping.
Peter Tremayne, Sister Fidelma mysteries

T0168514

Twice

A Novel

Twice

A Novel

Susanna Kleeman

zer0
books

Winchester, UK
Washington, USA

JOHN HUNT PUBLISHING

First published by Zero Books, 2021
Zero Books is an imprint of John Hunt Publishing Ltd., No. 3 East St., Alresford,
Hampshire SO24 9EE, UK
office@jhpbooks.com
www.johnhuntpublishing.com
www.zero-books.net

For distributor details and how to order please visit the 'Ordering' section on our website.

Text copyright: Susanna Kleeman 2020

ISBN: 978 1 78904 621 2
978 1 78904 622 9 (ebook)
Library of Congress Control Number: 2020936363

A CIP catalogue record for this book is available from the British Library.

Design: Stuart Davies

UK: Printed and bound by CPI Group (UK) Ltd, Croydon, CR0 4YY
Printed in North America by CPI GPS partners

We operate a distinctive and ethical publishing philosophy in
all areas of our business, from our global network of authors to
production and worldwide distribution.

For Eddie and Hazie

I

My phone went dead the night he came back twice. It did this weird beep and then powered off. I pressed, bashed, charged it: nothing—and now they don't let you get at the batteries. 11pm, a wet Sunday in late November, all help desks closed. I was researching this crisis on my laptop, watching some pap on my tablet, when my doorbell rang: five rings, a pause, six more.

The five and the six, the shed code. Souvenir of our childhood in crank camp. I didn't think it was Chris. I never thought it was Chris. I thought it was Tal, because it was always poor mad Tal out on a jolly, come to tell me more about the spiders who ruled the world. I'd get this twice a year maybe: eleven rings in the middle of the night, eleven more if I didn't move fast enough, to the fury of downstairs. So I was quick: paused things, braced for a couple of hours of sweet tea and nonsense, tiptoed down, opened the front door.

Nothing, then a curl of cold breath and into the frame moved Christopher Kipp doing a lopsided grin like it had been two hours instead of eleven years. The same, older, jeans, hooded sweatshirt, hands stuffed into jacket pockets. His flecked eyes giving me the stare.

My old mucker himself, large and in charge. Blow me down.

'Hey sorry, wrong doorbell. Wow it's you, who'd have thunk it? No seriously, hello, can I come in?' he said, smiling past me over the threshold into the hallway. 'Nim. How lovely. Looking just the same. Do you know?'

'Do I know what?' I said, to say something.

'How fantastic you look,' already bounding upstairs. 'Second floor? Not disturbing anything? Boyfriend? Husband?'

'Chris?'

'Nim,' swinging his head down round the banisters, locking eyes with me.

Get stuffed, I didn't say. Because I was up for it and had new muscles, I thought. Because I was curious. Why not.

'Ten minutes,' I said. 'Tiptoe,' I told him. 'This better be good,' following him up the stairs.

2

'Nice pad you got here, Nimmywim,' he said, scanning the dinge of my North London flat, opening my bedroom door, peeping into the cramped bathroom, checking out the tiny airing cupboard. A few months back on a tech gossip website I'd seen leaked plans of the latest proposed campus for a company he funded: a desert eco ranch with three square miles of underground robot labs.

You're bound to feel a pang, seeing someone like that again, a body you once knew so well, its little forgotten ways.

'How did you find me?'

'Tal. I'm starving. Got anything to eat?' heading for my fridge, stopping by my desk to admire my laptop. 'Nice, light,' hefting it, closing it, an American lilt now. 'But battery issues I hear? And if you don't mind,' snapping the tablet cover down over the paused image: 'I'm only up to Season Three, don't want to spoil things.'

The brass balls on this clown. Still thinking his sham worked, here for what? *Careful Chris, I might bite.* I settled in to enjoy this.

'How's Tal?' I hadn't seen Tal for ages, was due a visit.

'Fine. Nuts. The usual. Lots of product development ideas. Got any cheese?'

I leant against the window sill and let him find cheese in my fridge. Then he was darting about opening cupboards, locating plates, crackers, condiments, ferreting out chutney. Then he was holding his platter and scanning my bookshelves, admiring my textbooks, marvelling that I'd gone so conventional, and did I enjoy it, and how he could just see me in gown and wig, telling judge and jury what for.

A slight paunch but still fleet and spry. Casual but luxurious clothes reeking of discrete software zillions. The white face, the bitten nails. The single tear trickling down his face on our last day: 'Is that what you wanted?'

Time to take charge.

'So Chris. What's up?'

'Well,' flopping into my sofa with his mini feast. 'Nim. Nimmywimmy. Minnymoo. Nim Wynn. Or Nim *Burdock*, as it seems to be these days. Been a while now. Been thinking of you. Got a few things to say. But first,' balancing plate on sofa arm, running his right index finger down the length of his nose. This gesture meant: focus. I'd adopted it myself after we split, part of my widow's weeds.

'Nim,' hands spread out in his lap now, staring down, talking in this high holy voice: 'I don't know why it's taken so long for me to come here and say this. I want you to know how much I love, esteem and cherish you and our long strange history together, and will forever. How much I feel your absence and wish you were still part of my story, somehow. Above all, how sorry I am about…how things were left and how I behaved…at the end.'

He paused, to scan my face and reach for his plate. Over the years a possible apology scene had played out many different ways in my head, but never this…*smirking* version. In town and curious if his twist still worked?

Go for it, sweet cheeks. You gad away.

'Not a day goes past,' he went on, munching a cracker, 'that I don't think back on our time together, our special cherished history, all the strangeness we went through that we should be so proud of, and so proud of surviving, and know how much I owe it all to you, and would be nothing and not here without you, and how very bitterly I regret my fear and immaturity in treating you as I did. Call it a testament to your very great power over me. Leaving you is the hardest thing I've ever had to do and I knew the break had to be total, so very powerful were my feelings for you. But so deep was my immaturity that the only way I knew how to accomplish this was to behave badly and make you hate me and make you end it, instead of talking it through, honouring you and our time together. And I have suffered for my cowardice ever since.'

This template of a speech, possibly downloaded from the internet or purchased from a therapist, was such a calculated insult that perhaps he was in self-loathing mode and wanted a rise, a slap across the face. I saw him when he was twelve on top of the bus, throwing rocks at rocks, shouting singsong apologies for deeds he felt no guilt for.

Should have known then. Alan always told you.

Cut yourself the slack. We all learn in the end.

'Thanks Chris,' I said, noting new eye crinkles, clipped nasal hair. He looked very *washed*, probably did deep whatever high-tech skin treatments. His sweatshirt wasn't quite grey, it was dark charcoal, an unusual colour that brought out the green-brown of his eyes, probably swatched by experts, a database of outfits. I remembered something I hadn't in ages: a New York meltdown just after his first big pay cheque. Coming home from buying him pricey fashion gear in shops we never went to: he tried the new clothes on again and hated them, and hated me for letting him buy them. And hated me for my high-waisted jeans, not the fashion then: 'Don't you have a fucking clue?'

You let him, my dear.

'That's the problem with young love,' flicking a large crumb from his lap to my floor, launching into a small sermon about the problem with young love, specially ours: mad pash in the middle of total craziness, the first time those hormones flood through you, us really and truly against the world, feeling it would last forever, all those promises, when in the end we were children, and very sheltered children at that, who didn't know anything and hadn't met anyone.

'I'm sure you feel the same.'

I told him I did. Then I moved off the sill, to start escorting him off the premises, but he got in there first: 'I've brought you something,' before I could stop him, putting his plate back on the sofa arm, standing up, patting some inner jacket pocket, pulling out an envelope, walking the few paces it took to cross the room and hand it over, brushing my hand, returning to his cheeses on the sofa, watching my face.

The envelope was light and thin. One of his top secret machines, maybe, that the internet told me one of his companies was making out of utterly new materials, foldable things as weightless as feathers. Inside though were Polaroids, of me, from Scritchwood and everywhere, as a teen in the hollow, at ten up a tree. New York in the first days, one from the redwoods. But mainly Scritchwood Covert Motorhome Park and the woods and mud of South Bucks where we grew up and all the things I never thought about: me outside *Merriweather*, the static home I lived in with Ann Wynn and Clarice, me outside the bus Chris lived in with Alan, the broken house, the shed, the washing, me by the gilt quartz carriage clock on the bus mantelpiece. Me on a fallen beech dangling my legs over the water with my hair swept over me, smiling at him behind the lens.

'Was tidying up, found them, didn't know what to do with them. Thought you might want them.'

In the first years of him gone an image would come to me sometimes when I thought of him: he was a white hot metal bar I grabbed for and dropped, taking with it seared pieces of hand.

The squatter. Taint and blight. Using me all those years, stringing me along as a mirror for his preen. Till I saw clear and shone his dirt back instead and was no longer convenient and got bundled out the back door.

'How kind,' I said, putting the photos back into the envelope, putting that down on the side to chuck out later, 'for you to find these and think of me and go to all the trouble of tracking me down to deliver them in person and say…all this. And now, if you've finished your refreshments, I think it's time to go.'

'OK,' snack done, crumbs gone, plate to floor, running his finger down his nose. 'You're too good and I've imposed too long. It's been great to be here with you and have the chance to say...things to you. But I'd better get down to it. I'm actually here for something. Apart from all the rest of it.'

'Oh really?' I said, very suspicious. 'What?'

'Well. The book.'

It seemed weird at the time, so random. 'The book?'

He nodded. 'All those fun games. The slovenly elephant, the sly magpie.'

'The sly jackdaw.' I couldn't help myself.

'Right. Always needed your help. Anyway. The book. Turns out I need it. That's why I'm here. Dreadful I know.'

He waited, for me to ask why he wanted the book I guessed. 'It's a long story,' he went on when I wouldn't play. 'As you know it belonged to my mum and it's the one thing I have from her and I'm getting married and it would mean a lot.'

Watching me, slipping it in.

Poor woman, if she even existed. But I couldn't help myself:

'Congratulations. You're getting married and you want to... share the book with your fiancée? It's inscribed to me with your eternal love, you might remember.'

'I do. But ink can be removed. Names can be changed.'

I had to laugh. 'Romantic.'

But he didn't seem to share the joke: 'I think you can let me worry about all that. I don't know that it's any of your business. After all, morally, the book *is* mine.'

'I see.' I apologised, for thinking it was a gift, for not understanding it as a licensing agreement. Something in my tone must have irked. He got up, started pacing the room.

'Considering who you are, or who you were, or who I thought you were, plus what we both went through and what you know about my mum, I thought you might be a bit more understanding. Plus does it really have that much emotional value to you these days? Apart from the Alan stuff, of course. But you have lots of Alan stuff. Or you did.'

He actually seemed angry. He paused, sat back down, watched me, spoke again, soft and clear:

'It's a very rare edition, though, I know. A certain market value I'd be happy to reimburse you for if I didn't think you'd be insulted.'

This wheeler-dealer. He really did seem desperate for it. 'How much were you thinking?'

'Whatever you want. Three thousand, let's say?'

'Three thousand bitcoins?'

'Very current. I was thinking dollars. Or pounds. Or bitcoins, though I hear there are issues. Whatever you want. Though considering the circumstances I was hoping for a mate's rate. For old times' sake.'

'Didn't one of yours just float for three point eight billion?' Some digital games company bewitching commuters with matching lines of gems.

'Flattered you've been following. Three point nine but who's counting. If you need help, I'm here, any time, it's yours.'

This suave jousting. How well he'd adapted to the world. How well I had in the end. Perhaps I was being awful to him. Perhaps he actually wanted the book for real. And I suddenly felt sorry for him, this cavalcade of ticks wonking into town.

'I don't want money. You can have it,' I said.

'Nim. I knew...'

His face changed, he looked genuinely grateful.

'But it's not here,' I said. 'I'll have to get it. Give me an address, I'll post it. Now go.'

'So many thanks, you can't know, but things are actually super-urgent. Tell me where and I'll go get it myself, or we can go together.'

'It's midnight. I've got work tomorrow. Don't push it.'

'I really have to insist. It's...an event I'm planning. Tomorrow. The book...figures. Everything's...booked. People are...flying in.'

This entitled loon, what kind of 'event'? Some new Scritch game for his engagement party? Clues in the woods from the book like the old days? What a freak but I already knew that. '"People" might have to wait. You should've factored-in a bit more leeway.' The nerve: turning up in the middle of the night for the book on the off-chance. 'I might have been out. I might have sold it, burnt it, ripped it to shreds.'

'As usual: correct. But since I've planned no leeway and have always relied on you to get me out of everything, I'm begging. I'm down on my knees.'

'Except you're not.'

'If that's what it takes.'

He got off the sofa, came over and knelt in front of me. Meaningless but strangely satisfying. He really did want that book for some reason.

'Get up,' I said after a while. 'Whatever you're up to I can't get it right now. Maybe tomorrow. It's with Flora. It's hard to contact her.'

'Flora. How's she doing? You didn't burn it, did you? Why's it with Flora?'

Lots of our stuff was with Flora. I couldn't quite bring myself to burn it.

'Where is she?'

'Wales. I'll get her to send it. I can't promise by tomorrow but I'll do my best. And after that Chris? Never contact me again. Never think of me. Any other skeezy begs, get them in now, cos if you come here again I won't know you, I won't answer the door to you.'

'You're wonderful but can't you just call her right now, see if I can come over? Wake her up, explain it's an emergency? Or just give me her address?'

No I couldn't. It was midnight and even if I'd wanted to I couldn't contact her. She didn't have a computer or a phone.

'Oh doesn't she?' he said, and started pacing the room again, walking up and down in front of my bookshelves, scanning for the book, I now supposed. 'She has a landline though.'

'She doesn't.' Flora didn't have electricity or running water. 'She lives off-grid in the Brechfa Forest.'

'I bet she does. So how d'you contact her?'

You wrote, or called the farm shop in the village two miles away and left a message asking her to call back from the phone box.

'What's the village called?'

I said I couldn't remember, would dig it out in the morning, get her to call back, tell her it was an emergency, money no object, he might send a private jet to Swansea if that was OK. The private jet was a joke but he nodded perfectly seriously.

'Or you could just give me her address.'

I shook my head. 'If you turn up she won't give you anything.'

'Why not?'

'Why d'you think?'

'A good friend. Protective. *You* don't hate me, though, do you?' almost batting his eyelashes at me.

'I'm off to bed now,' I said. 'Leave me your contact details and go.' I'd email him the next day with an update, I said. Any more pestering and I'd get Flora to feed the book to the sheep.

He hemmed and hawed but that was it. He tried for my whole contact slew but settled for scrawling down his personal email. Then I escorted him downstairs and said goodbye at the front door.

'Nim,' he said there, flaring his nostrils, bending down to brush his lips against my hair.

We're just animals, slaves to learnt reflex. Even then I had to bolster my innards against his scent. But he helped out: 'You can't know how grateful I am, or how much this reconnection means. I'll wait to hear tomorrow and then from now on let's be in touch from time to time, shall we? I'd like that: telling each other the important things, the big life moments. I'm not saying regular contact, my fiancée won't like that...'

'I'll email tomorrow. Good luck, Christopher. Best wishes for your marriage and...event.'

'Nim?'

But I pushed him out the door and closed it behind him. Then I stood on tiptoes and put my eye to the top keyhole and watched him. He stood facing the house for a while eyeing my flat, the ground floor, the basement flat. Then he came back to my door and put his own eye right up to the keyhole too so it went black. I froze and didn't breathe.

Then he stood back, pulled up his hood, turned and seemed to walk away, up the curve of the road, to some driverless limo lurking there for him no doubt.

He didn't look back.

Then I was sitting on the floor of the hall with my back to the door feeling the cold draught, hugging my legs. Was that always him underneath? Or was it the ice of the world?

Who cared. Good luck to him. Time for self-care. I should feel proud: I'd behaved with grace and compassion, and that's all you can do. You can't best such creatures—if you could you'd be as bad as them. And there was no point kicking myself for falling for it and putting up with it for so long once upon a time. I'd been young and dumb and desperate then, an easy mark, desperate for any crumbs of affection, thinking I deserved no better. Now I was older and over it. It was bound to feel weird for a while, seeing it up front again, but I'd be fine.

In fact I'd been finally set free. That's what happens when your worst fears turn out true. There was no better Chris after all, no matter what I sometimes nursed inside me. He really was as bad as all that, vaporware.

I'd go upstairs, have a bath, go to bed. In the morning I'd sort my phone, call Flora's farm shop, speak to her, email Chris, arrange a drop-off point, never see him again, forget about it, build my new wondrous.

I sat on the doormat thinking about the broken house.

After a while of this it felt like the stairs were watching me and having a laugh. I stretched, was about to get up to go upstairs and have that bath when my doorbell rang: five rings, a pause, six more.

3

Various possibilities. Him back different and sorry: unlikely, unwanted. Him back to twist worse for immediate book action: very likely indeed. Tal popping in for a late-night cuppa: a nice world irony I was in no mood for. Someone else for something else: didn't cross my mind.

I'd been clear with him—and courteous. I was now furious: utter cheek, me as pure means. Zero boundaries, zero respect—I wasn't going to open the door. But if I moved he'd hear me, start opening the letterbox to spew more poison. Perhaps he was already peeping through the keyhole. If so he wouldn't be able to see me down on the doormat. I froze.

My light upstairs was on, he'd know I was still up. Sure enough he rang his eleven times again, followed by another eleven. And then next to me the door to the downstairs flat opened: my neighbour Glen in red silk dressing gown all furious: did I have the slightest consideration, did I know the time?

My visitor, aware I was in the hall due to Glen's commotion, was indeed pushing open the letterbox trying to talk to me.

'Nim. I know you're there. Are you OK? Please. I'm begging you. It's me, Chris. Christopher Kipp. Open the door, I got to talk to you. Do you know?'

Many apologies, Glen. Give me one minute, I'd sort this.

Glen shuffled back muttering into his flat.

I'd been majestic for more than an hour now, vast provocations shrugged off. Limits reached I stood up, put the door chain on, yanked the chained door open as far as it would go. Into the sliver once more moved Christopher Kipp in his posh jacket and million-dollar hoodie, pushing his face close to me.

'Chris,' I hissed quietly for Glen's sake. 'Fuck off. Forget about the book. Just manage your "event" without it, you precious dick, cos it is now feed for the sheep of the Brechfa Forest.'

'Nim,' he said, all fake-shocked now. 'What are you talking about?'

So lost, really thinking he could play this. For the first time I saw him as he was: someone who just knew a bit less than me. No point. What a release.

'Just go,' I said, like I was talking to a child. 'I'll email, get you the book tomorrow. Now leave. No matter what I won't give you the address.'

'What address? What are you talking about?'

'What are *you* talking about?'

'Nim. I just got here. I don't understand anything you're saying.'

I gaped at him. He gaped right back.

'Oh God,' he said, and his face changed. 'Do you mean..? Has someone…was I just here? Before? Have I been here earlier tonight?'

Wow. I raised my eyebrows at him. 'Enjoying your work, Chris. Admiring your stylings. Keen to see where this is going. Whole new territories you're mapping out here. Good luck down this road mateykins.'

'I…OK, I thought I'd do this slowly but this is bad. There's…a lot of freaky stuff. OK. So I came here earlier tonight and wanted something?'

'You came here earlier tonight and wanted something. Weak. Are you on drugs? You sound like Tal.'

'What did I want?'

'A soul. Goodbye, Chris.' I was closing the door but he jammed it open with a filthy trainer, pushed his face in close over the chain.

'It's totally freaky, I know,' he said, much too close, bad breath, the top of his right index finger missing now, the finger he ran down his nose. 'But the one who was here before? He wasn't me, Nim. It's so fucked up, Nim. I know how crazy this sounds. He's…let me in and I'll explain.'

4

'He's my...brother,' he said from behind the chain because I still wouldn't let him in, his rotten shoe jamming open the door. 'Yup, I got a...brother now. Identical. Twins, let's call it. I didn't know. I found out. We look the same, almost, outside. Inside we're different. But there's two of us and I'm the real one,' gabbling over the chain, running fingers through messy hair, grabbing his roots, his right index fingertip gone now, the top joint missing, running this stump down his nose again, a stump topped by a bobble of flesh. 'I just turned up, this is the first time I've seen you in eleven years, I wasn't here before, haven't seen you since New York. The one before's my double, pretending to be me, fake.'

Stone-cold effrontery. Off-the-scale gaslighting and contempt. I couldn't speak. The stump seemed new. I hadn't noticed it up in my flat before and I'd have noticed. His face looked the same, kind of: dirtier, more stubble, but it was Chris Kipp's face. But the Chris in my flat, in my hall twenty minutes before had been finger-perfect, I was pretty certain.

'I'm Chris Kipp,' this stump one was saying from behind the chain. *He* was my old love from Scritchwood who I'd grown up with, the one who'd behaved poorly in New York and elsewhere. 'That other one,' the first one, who'd just left: clean and shaven Mr Finger-Perfect who I'd let through the door and upstairs to my flat? 'He's someone else,' this stump Chris was saying: someone called Sean, someone bad and dangerous who'd pretended to be Chris, to gain access to me and entrance to my flat under false pretences—for what reason? Chris and Sean. What had Sean been up to? 'We're kind of twins, it's a long story, what did he want? What was all that about books and sheep?'

Then I shouted at him for a bit and he didn't blame me—'It *is* crazy,' he said, nodding away. 'Just undo the chain and let me in so I can explain properly, five minutes. In fact, undo the chain and leave with me right now, we're in terrible danger. You got to know: if Sean's been here we're fucked, you and me, like you can't believe. You're fucked, your flat's fucked—did he touch you, your walls, your machines, your computers and phones? Did he go into your fridge, your cupboards and jars? They've planted stuff, that's what they do: smear things, listen in, leave messages for each other. They're listening in right now, leaving messages, coming for us, me and you right now, they'll know I'm here now, they're after me, maybe they're here already, maybe you're one of them. Are you? Oh god are you, Nim? Are you Nim at all or something else?' staring deep into my eyes from different angles. 'I'm so paranoid, I can't trust anything, even you, that's what they've done to me. Where's your phone? I got to have your phone, I can't have phones. The world's so fucked up, do you realise? It's all a front. Nothing's what it seems.'

Pure nutty Tal. I stared at him, rattling the chain, babbling on for me to open up right now, get out right now, with him, into the street, into his car parked not far away, so he could explain properly about the fucked world. A psycho in full punishment meltdown, because I'd dared to show he could no longer control me?

Or was it all to get his hands on the book?

'Why was Sean here, what did he want, why was he pretending to be me, what book, what sheep, what event, where's the Brechfa Forest, what did he want to know, what did you tell him, where's Sean now? I got to know.'

That stump. White now, gripping the door frame along with the rest of his fingers, stopping me from closing the door on him, the force of his hand plus his forehead and the jammed-in foot. Bad old trainers now, battered things, not the box-fresh luxe-casual of his first visit. Him and all his clothes, the charcoal: dirty and frayed. His face seemed more gaunt. Now he had stubble and blackheads, no clean pores. He had sprouting nostril hair. His nails were longer: less bitten, more filthy. But you could change clothes and filth your face and fingers, and glue-on stubble and nose hair and nails, and contour cheekbones: a quick session behind bushes up Holmesdale Road, no probs. It meant a planned operation, though, the opposite of crazy, nothing Tal could come up with: make-up kit, costume-changes, this whole loony twin yarn in reserve as an encore if I wouldn't play ball, wouldn't give him back his precious book—all for the book, what was it with the sodding book?

But. Possible. You could change clothes. You could put on foundation, stubble, nose hair, put dirt under nails, bloody eyes, spray on stink. The voice and gestures were the same. The aura felt different: caffeinated, desperate. When I'd known him he'd never been a good actor, too self-conscious, but maybe acting yourself was easier, specially if you really wanted something.

He seemed thinner, though it was hard to tell from the sliver of him I could see. Something about the eyes felt different.

A bad actor but a good liar.

Not crazy at all.

But could you change fingers, remove tips?

The bobbled stump was smooth, aged, healed, nothing recent. Nothing bloody, nothing hacked off behind trees five minutes ago.

'What happened to your finger?'

'Docked. Punishment. Undo the chain.'

Unless the stump had been disguised the first time, always there but topped off with a bit of sculpted silicon or—who knew?—real flesh, stuck on with art so the finger looked whole. Weird bother for no clear purpose but not impossible. Who knew how much he wanted the book, for what event or purpose? Who knew what they were up to in their robot labs?

Not for the first time I wanted that machine we'd all get shortly that would record everything, the lifelog with playback. So I could get a good look at that whole index finger up in my flat before. Freeze-frame, zoom, search for seams, scan face and clothes.

My dead phone.

But it was crazy to think my phone dying was part of this. It was Tal-like: massive connections, nonsense, everything I'd given up, everything I hated. Solid foundations, I'd built my new life on. I didn't go big any more. I drew my line. *Keep it simple*, Alan used to say. And the simplest explanation seemed to be that my dead phone was a coincidence and there were no twins and this Chris was both my visitors and either mad or in meltdown because I wouldn't play or else desperate for the book for unknown reasons, or just bored and back to prank. And then I remembered something else from Alan: that every warrior needed six things and one of them was a frightener: something scary to throw the enemy, distract them, stop them dead in their tracks so you could trip them up while they were caught up in being scared or distracted. Like snake-haired Grag Medusa in Alan's stories: the ultimate frightener who turned you to stone when you looked at her like this stump-Chris's disgusting stump forcing open my door, that I couldn't stop looking at. That bobble.

I stopped looking at it. I couldn't close the door but I didn't have to. I stepped back, didn't say anything, left him yabbering over the chain, turned round and walked away from him down the hall, back up the stairs. He babbled things after me, names from Scritch, Alan's secret agent game we used to play as kids, desperate measures: 'How's Corpse Dog?' Then he was shouting after me, begging me, telling me I had no clue and was I Nim or something else, was I Nim but part of it?

Then another voice came from behind me.

'I'm recording this,' it said.

5

I turned round to see trembling Glen brandishing his phone like a cross to ward off Draculas. 'The police have been called. They are on their way. This footage is evidence,' swinging his phone between me on the stairs and Chris behind the chain.

With something—his hands? a tool?—Chris bashed the chain from the door frame and pushed into the hall and snatched Glen's recording phone from his tiny fingers and smashed it onto the floor and stamped on it many times with the new rotten trainers.

We all looked at Glen's broken phone on the mat.

I started to say things, Chris started to say things. I shouted at Chris to stop it, apologised to Glen, explained that Chris was crazy and I was glad the police were coming, shouted at Chris to leave. I came down the stairs. Glen, who'd been silent, just staring at his broken phone, scuttled back behind his door and slammed it shut.

I knocked on Glen's shut door. I wanted to apologise, get behind his door with him because Chris had grabbed my arm. I tried to shake Chris off, I tried to pull away, go back upstairs. I banged on Glen's door again, shouted for him to let me in, screamed for help. But Chris had me and was dragging me away. He was much bigger and stronger than me, he always was. That's how it works. I tried to kick but it meant nothing. He was pulling me back out of the hall, out of the open front door, saying he was so sorry but just couldn't be recorded, hadn't meant to frighten me or anyone, didn't mean to be frightening me now and sorry if he was hurting me but we had to leave: Glen had recorded him, called the police, Sean had been here, everything was tainted, the police weren't the police, everything was dangerous, I couldn't understand, time was nearly over, he'd take me away from tainted here to someplace we could talk.

One hand round me pulling me out of the building in my grey fluffy slippers. The other, the stump hand, jammed into my mouth, stopping me from talking or screaming as he forced me outside down the steps into the misty night.

Gone beyond, him caved-in. Little orange leaves glittering on the pavement ahead. Lights off, people asleep, empty roads, his jammed hand in my mouth. He nestled me into his chest, bustled us off towards the railway bridge, yanking my wrist back so it hurt, forcing me on. I bit hard on his hand, the stump, broke skin, tasted blood. But he pushed back, made me gag so I had to stop or suffocate or get my teeth knocked out. I bent my knees, went limp. He lifted me into his rank self and dragged me on, me kicking uselessly. At the bridge he forced me through the railings up the embankment into the trees and darkness beyond.

Up there was the Parkland Walk, a nature trail built over a disused railway track. He forced me along the path in the dark for perhaps ten seconds then pushed me down into a bush so I lay face-down on dead leaves, clay and flint, my face scratched by blackberry thorns. He lay on top of me, his bitten fist tanging my mouth with his blood and dirt. He got my hair and twisted my head and stuffed my mouth with rough cloth, tied some other rag over it and behind my head so I was gagged tight and could bite on that instead of his fist, did this expertly so I couldn't speak or scream, part of his planned kit, what more did he have?

We lay in the bush on the ground in the damp night staring out through the halo of fog smearing the orange street lamps down below. Above us fine droplets pattered on trees, reaching the ground as mist. He lay breathing on top of me, his mouth on my ear: 'I'm sorry.' Sirens, new smeary lights: we watched two police cars speed down my road below, saw the beam of their headlights in the wet air. They parked, house lights went on, neighbours in nightwear came out into the street, talked in clumps to each other and to the police. I tried to move but was pinioned by him: arms over my arms, legs over my legs, his heart thudding at my back, his mouth at my ear panting how sorry he was, telling me to look at all the police and was that really warranted for some noise complaint and how it wasn't Glen who'd called them and this proved it.

Proved what?

Below the police knocked at my front door. They must have come to help me, Glen hearing me scream having called them a second time. The door opened, probably Glen. Some chatting, they went in, modern uniforms, 'do you see?' Riot-wear, with visors and weapons, 'for some noise complaint? And there?' jerking his stubble at my cheek up to the misty sky, to the helicopter whirring above.

These days helicopters came sometimes at night, woke me with their noise. Modern policing, it wasn't that weird.

'For a noise complaint?'

For a kidnapping. Or for some unrelated but nearby crime. Or for you, I thought, squashed under him in the bush. He was mad and someone important, on the loose, like this for how long? What else had he done? They were after him, would have turned up anyway even if Glen hadn't called. Now I was his hostage. I went limp.

It fitted some pattern: him cornered, desperate, exposed, come to me as a place of last resort, his childhood sweetheart.

With the control to appear so fake debonair up in my flat the first time with his cheeses and bags of gags and disguises, wanting the book?

What was the deal with that book? Gold leaf, done by a famous artist? Like the beads: it wouldn't be the first time some Alan crud turned out to be worth loads and that always mattered to Chris.

But now Chris was a zillionaire, or had been last I'd checked. On the run, needing cash.

The misty night, the orange, the wet gag in my mouth, my torn lips and scratched face and juddering heart, the weight of him on me, the dead leaves, the patter in the trees.

It didn't have to make sense if he was mad. He'd gone so far, who knew what he'd been up to these past years, all that power and money, on a different scale to anyone, who knew what that did to you, enough to drive you mad even if you weren't crippled from the start.

'This is the worst,' he said, mouth on my ear. 'And it's the best, cos I never thought I'd be with you again. And it's the worst, cos now you're dead too but there's no going back and I wouldn't be here if it wasn't the end. We got to move now, they'll find us, they're coming for us now, they'll do anything, you don't know. You'll get up and come with me now, no fight, you just have to. For old times' sake, despite all this. For much more than you and me. You got to hear me out: not here, somewhere they can't hear us, where we can talk, it's not far. Listen to what I have to say. And if you don't like it, if I sound crazy, then you're free to go. I won't touch you, you can set them on me. OK?'

I nodded underneath him in the mud.

'Get up, come with me now, hold my hand. I'm about five minutes away. Just hear me out. For old times' sake.'

I nodded. We lay there. In the street below police torch beams shone into us in the trees then moved away.

He brushed his mouth to my temple then yanked me up, held me by the wrist, started running me through the bushes in the dark away from my road, up through the wooded sub-path that lay alongside what had been the railway track.

He stumbled on something. I elbowed him and kneed him in the balls.

He yelped and doubled over. An owl hooted. I yanked my hand from his and pulsed forward, felt for the gag knot behind my head.

He came at me from behind, grabbed my hand and hair, pulled me on and down back into thorns and thickets so I was face-down in dead leaves again, lay on me again, his breath at my neck. He kneed me in the back and tore my jumper and top off, pulled off my necklace, rings, earrings, belt, stuffed his hands in all my jean pockets, threw away keys, coins, fluff, everything. Searched again for my phone but didn't find it since it was dead in my flat, searched again. He pulled me up by my hair, yanked me on through brambles in my bra and jeans. He pushed me face-down again, lay back on top of me, put his mouth at my ear:

'You'll hear me out. It's crazy but. Haven't you noticed, for a while now? That something's off? Everything's changed? It looks the same but it's different, right? Over the past few years, when you stopped reading books? The future's happened but they didn't ask you. Nothing's real. Thought machines stealing your thoughts. What went on before seems…quaint. It's about the machines but it's not just about the machines. Perfect takeover: soft, no armies, no tanks in the streets. Geeks bearing gifts, buy your own fetters, spin you crud to lap up, everyone clicking away, all so fun and free and simple. The pup you've been sold, the world-wide lie, the dot con, getting formatted, get the kids formatted, turn the tap on, take the cookies. And me right at the heart of it. The plans they have for you.'

I squirmed under him, he pressed down on my bare back, crushed me against sharp ground. Above us the helicopter whirred. Columns of light beamed through the trees. He crawled me under him on my scratched belly under the bushes, waited for the beams to pass, crawled us on more. My only hope was the police, the helicopter above. But he was twisting us under bushes in the dark, they couldn't see us. The bridge, I thought. We were moving that way, no bushes on the bridge. But when we got there, the high bridge over Stanhope Road, he turned and forced us down the steep embankment instead, still all mixed up in the bushes, down what wasn't a path, grabbing on to twine and roots, tearing us, tumbling us onto the street.

Orange misty lights, silence, emptiness, parked cars. He pulled me upright by my neck. With his other hand he got my wrists and twisted them round behind my back and slipped something round them, a noose he tightened till it cut into me and then pressed me against the metal of the cold dirty white car parked next to us. My mouth gagged, my hands tied, my bare belly on the cold wet car, his hand still round my neck, squeezing hard when I tried to kick him. With his other hand he reached into his pocket, got out keys, slipped them into the lock and opened the car door, the passenger side, bundled me in there, into the foot well, a stew of damp newspapers and old food. He pushed on through into the driver's seat, reached back across to slam the door, pressed down the lock saying he was sorry, we had to go right now, they were here. Anywhere, just to get away, to some place where we could talk.

'Brechfa's where? In Britain? A real place? Some Scritch I forgot? That's what you said right: the Brechfa Forest, the sheep, the book? Nod if that's right. Is that where Sean's gone? Why? What book did Sean want?'

I wiggled up to nut him, thrashing my legs. He reached forwards and used the force of my movement to twist me up onto the passenger seat next to him, then put his hand back round my neck and pulled me up higher so I would have blacked out if it hadn't been for the painful thing he did with my bound arms. Which was: slacken their binds, yank them out from my back so he nearly broke them, crick round my body to force my arms over and down round the back of the seat so I ended up sitting on the seat with my hands tied behind it, lodged there. He retightened the knot. With another rope he bound my bare ankles above my ruined slippers, then brought that rope under my seat and up to where my hands were behind the seat and knotted it to them really tight. So I was tied round the seat with a gag in my mouth and another bit of rope now getting knotted round my already scratched-up waist, naked except for my bra and jeans. Nice rope moves Chris, where d'you learn all that? No way for me to twist free. He'd been practising. What else you

24

got up your sleeve? Pretty obvious I was sat there by force to anyone who saw us but there was no one at that time of night. And then he got something else from the back seat: a big black bit of nylon which he eased over my gagged head and over my whole seat so it covered my head and gag and ropes and backrest, and buckled the seatbelt too over me, so I looked like a big fat covered hunchback big-jawed Moslem woman strapped in there next to him with only my eyes on show.

I scrunched them shut. Jesus fucking Christ.

'Really sorry,' he said. 'Burkas. Very useful, I wear them too sometimes. Moslems, they know what they're up against.'

The crunch of the ignition, the car spluttering, failing to start, starting.

He drove me off into the night.

6

That he might kill me. Tied there in the blackness it was like he might, like he might do anything. That it might happen now with that void Chris who I'd let in. Everything I'd tried to be. How I'd wasted my life.

His fake self gone, this *other thing* driving me, unmasked bad innards spilling out of control. Some massive crisis at work, techno paranoia, now *their* victim—always playing the victim. Bad twins, his death trip, me trussed alongside.

No techniques to manage this, him operating out of nothing I could connect with. Trying to scream, the wet knot and gag I couldn't budge jamming my mouth open, stopping sound, suffocating me, dry heaves, retching, beating heart.

Grag Medusa. Old words woke me like they sometimes did: thanks Alan. *Stop. Breathe. Control your mind. Don't tell yourself stories. Park the big stuff. Go small. Focus on the practical. Where are you?*

Tied and gagged, in a burka, in some car, with some loon. Fraying skin on the sides of my mouth and the pain in my arms, from getting cricked, ropes cutting into me.

Focus on the ropes.

Tied so tight. I tried, from inside the itchy black nylon, to brew up a force to slack them one inch, burst my bonds. But he had the skills: nothing budged and I felt blood and worse pain in my muscles and cheeks and the vile cold dribble of saliva I couldn't wipe off, chafing and rash, sweat, panic, thudding heart.

Breathe.

Breathe through your nose. Blanche the terrain. Observe. The eye.

I breathed through black nylon and opened my eyes, saw from out my slit him speeding us up towards Shepherd's Hill, turning left towards the Archway Road. Gaunt, dirty, mad.

A swift blow between the top two vertebrae of the spine. If I could get my hands free.

Twist those ropes. Bide your time.

The car was old and filthy, a white Nissan Sunny.

'My dumb car.' He followed my gaze. 'Safe, to talk here. "Safe", cos I've scraped it myself,' all proud. 'Nothing digital. You have to go pre-'83, or thereabouts, all this has been going on much longer than you know, there's signs to watch out for.'

He told me these signs: no child locks, no central locking, no automatic anything. Analogue dials and dashboard, radio torn out, wires exposed.

'A physical engine powered by gas—petrol. I can fix every last bit myself. They hack cars, you know that, right? Get them to go anywhere, do anything: turn, accelerate, smash into tunnel pillars. Pull smartplanes right out of the sky. Every last cog with its own IP address and middle manager these days. The internet of things, the mark of the beast.'

Pure Tal conspiracy—or its impersonation. The lost self in crisis.

Unless it's all his ploy.

His ploy for what?

Go small. For now: we were driving, he was driving. I was safe, for now. He needed me, for now, for whatever reason. I had to remember that. *Use the time wisely.*

I breathed and worked the ropes.

He drove and talked on, about bank notes that spied on you, snitching metal and credit cards, remote control, objects brought to life and in the thrall of distant masters, lethal connection, modern animism. Just what you want to hear from the guy who's kidnapped you, bound and gagged you, is driving you where? He wasn't just dirty, he was also thinner than he'd looked the first time up in my flat, if I remembered right, and how would you fake that? Unless the first time he'd worn fillers or something, puffed up by water, technically possible, a professional job, for what reason? A waiting team, with needles and brushes to drain and paint him—didn't seem likely but the alternative was two of them and was that more likely?

And if there *were* two of them, why assume this one was my Chris?

Breathe.

He took a right at Muswell Hill Road and then right again down that side road by Queen's Woods with the old big posh houses, drove down past them to the bit where there's woods on each side and paused there with the motor running, rolled down his windows, craned up to the sky.

Silence. No sign of copters. Me tied there with him at night, dark woods on each side.

A cunning spot. He knew his way round, must have skulked about earlier doing a recce, all too calculated to be mad or on drugs, except ultra-calculation *is* madness and this whole thing screamed maximum fruitcake. He rolled the window back up and turned to me with his hungry searching jittery eyes.

'We shook them. For now. Stop writhing, you'll only make the knots tighter, you'll hurt yourself, I'm not going to hurt you, there's no way you'll loose them, believe me, I'll set you free in a bit. For now: the Brechfa Forest. Is where Sean's heading, right? A real place, not Scritch? That's what you said, right: the Brechfa Forest, books and sheep?'

Talking to me, talking to himself, not for the first time, one suspected. I writhed next to him, tasting my foul gag, hurting my wrists, my whole tied body in pain. He turned on the light and fished some mouldy UK road atlas out of the footwell, flicked through the index, trawled through the 'B's with his bitten stump till he found Brechfa, turned to that page, turned his mad scratched thin dirty face to me.

'Real. South Wales. Lots of sheep. The actual forest or the village?' map down, light off, stump to steering wheel, foot back down on the accelerator, turning the car too fast, screeching back the way we'd come. 'Why Brechfa? Who's there? Is it..?' and he came close, pulled the burka down a bit, watched my eyes, his heat and bad smell very near. Then he relaxed, eyes back to the empty roads.

'You told Sean you'd get a book from there tomorrow for him? You wouldn't give him the address. Good. A book of yours? Nod or shake your head.'

I sat there.

He nodded. 'You won't help. Not yet. But you will. I hope it won't be too late. You're scared, I scared you, I had to, I didn't want to. We're going to sit here together and I'm going to tell you and you're going to listen and we're going to head west to Wales and Brechfa by whatever knowledge I can glean by your eyes and pure nous till you get convinced.'

He turned right, went north up the Archway Road past sparse cars and unreachable people, drove in silence for a bit.

'Flora.' He whipped round at me, made the car jolt, made my ropes dig worse. 'It's Flora. That's where she lives. Brechfa, in her junk house. Scritchwood-upon-South-Wales, knitting her moonshine. I'm right, aren't I?' searching my eyes again. 'Flora's got some book he wants. I'm right.'

He *was* right, because I'd told him all that myself twice before: once up in my flat and once again in the hallway when he'd turned up the second time with his stump and costume change and gag and make-up and crazy twin tale.

Except I hadn't mentioned Flora the second time in my hallway, I was pretty certain. Oh for that lifelog. No, thinking back I hadn't mentioned Flora at all that second time. I didn't think.

And if I hadn't mentioned Flora in my hall then he knew the book was with her because he *had* been up in my flat that first time. So his twin talk *was* bogus. I could lay that to rest. His new look was special effects.

Psychopath, up to something. I felt full fear then: the lying twisted depths of him. And he saw it.

'I know Flora's in Brechfa cos I know everything about you, you should know that upfront,' he said. 'Or I *knew* everything about you, till six months ago, when I clocked out. Before then I had total access. Don't think I didn't abuse it. I've been listening in, to your whole life: all the pictures and emails and searches and much worse. Your therapist's notes. The texts your boyfriends send other women. You can't lie to me, tucked up in your cloud. I know more about you than you do, believe it. The whole world's been mine to peep. Don't think there's one thing about you I don't know.'

I sat pinioned in nylon on the dark empty North Circular speeding west out of London and he told me everything he shouldn't know about me, every iota of the past eleven years. My fears and interests, my every relationship, how much money I had, health issues, porn preferences, favourite ready meals, my every dirty secret, any contact with barcodes. Courses and jobs, cases and clients. What I bought, what I nearly bought, my music, my mortgage, where I went, the toxic-ex forums I visited, how I still read his horoscope, how often I searched for him.

'My way of staying close to you. I'm sorry, I missed you. Stalking you for years. Like you've been stalking me. But with better access. There's a shipping container, right? In the field next to Flora? Lots of old caravans round the back she covers in fairy lights at Christmas? Big summer solstice crustie parties you go to, I've seen all the pictures. And if I've seen them Sean's seen them too by now, bet your bottom dollar. He doesn't need you to give him her address, he's got it. You're a person of interest now, they're combing you right now, refining the profile, sieving the data. Sean's there right now, heading there for Flora, you betcha, hope she's OK. To get his hands on some book she has—is it your book? Nod or shake your head.'

I sat there, clobbered from the inside. Utterly seen. The *squirm* of him knowing all my searches, up in my flat, Mr Finger-Perfect, so debonair, chatting over cheeses.

Except fuck that. It didn't matter what he thought he knew, whatever he'd seen. He was a crazy violent desperate freak, so what if he'd seen some pics and text messages? My searches weren't everything, he didn't really know what was going on inside me, Flora's actual address, any of the rest of it. Digital me only went so far, he still needed real me, that's why I was tied up there with him. The only thing that mattered was me not forgetting that.

If you don't know what to do then do nothing. Yes, that one was useful. I sat there making my wrists bleed.

'You don't understand the danger you've put Flora in. We got to get to her before he does. He wants something, he'll do anything to get it, you got no idea,' jerking his eyes round at cars beside us, foot down, speeding ahead.

Dark rain, bridges, warehouses, superstores, the lit-up curve of Wembley Stadium, empty roads, gyratories, cold air. I prayed for copters and sank into my burka against him and the weather, only my bra on under the nylon, my scratched tummy, the heater blasting foul air but cracks letting cold in, nothing shutting properly in that junkyard on wheels.

'OK,' he said. 'Here's my deal. There's lots to say and it's pointless, you won't believe me, not yet, but I'll say it anyway. Let's start with New York. My bike crash. Remember? The warehouse in Bushwick, the police bringing me back all stitched up? My first time in hospital, no hospitals or doctors for us in Scritchwood, right? And then one week after the head-hunter called?'

I stared ahead, twisting my ropes. Let the bullshit reign.

'That head-hunter. Out of the blue. A new kind of job, right? Nothing to do with programming. From nowhere. A "vision piece", a "client recommendation", "confidential". So random, right?'

His take at the time: he'd impressed someone without realising it, maybe one stray comment, not so surprising since he was so brilliant. And a tech revolution was happening then: young guns knowing what old farts didn't, high ascents possible if you had a knack for it, which he did. Him and his machines. And he and I growing up shut off from everything in Scritchwood. So we came to things fresh, he'd explained to me then. *He* came to things fresh. He was on fire, pure instinct, could shape new landscapes, vision the future. He'd told me. Him pacing our room in Bushwick while I sat there nodding away on the sofa. The things you have to learn.

'You remember, how much they loved me? From the start? "International strategic consultancy". My own team, assistants, expense accounts, cell phones on four continents? Crazy money? Crazy, eh?'

I recalled it. I spent time with friends. I read. I was studying everything then, going to college, getting educated, for both of us, while he jetted. We bought an apartment. There were social events, I came to a few, felt out of place. We were soulmates, he said. I used to be someone special, what was happening to me? he said. Was I developing a bald patch? He started spending two weeks a month on the West Coast.

They were building tomorrow out there, he wanted to be part of it, who could blame him. On the fast track: new positions mooted with parent companies, venture capitalists. 'The money's the real creativity,' he told me then. By then he'd met Don Thabbet, 'You remember Don Thabbet?' Big old reclusive venture capitalist, his big boss.

It wasn't just funding. Don and co had their own agenda, their own vision, were asking the big questions, commissioning the constellation of services to take mankind to the next level. Who wouldn't want to be part of that? Astronauts of the mind. And they saw a place for him at the top table, good luck to them, good luck to him. I sold the bead and ran away.

'You never met Don. You remember me telling you about him, though? Thabbet the Rabbit. My dad. Oh yeah,' enjoying my stare. 'Don's my real dad, Alan wasn't my dad, I was right the whole time, I was stolen, they totally lied to us. 'Cept Don's not quite my daddy either. Turns out he's my, our, original. He...me and Sean? He made us. And the rest of us. Farmed us in tubes. Chips off the old block. We're Don's cuttings. We're Don's clones.'

He let this ricochet a bit, for what it was worth, driving me on down slippery roads in the rain. Because it was about 2 am and relatively empty there were strange things: cones and signs, massive lorries, closed lanes, spotlights, road-fixing machines painting lines, moon buggy-like rovers on repair trucks, high-vis men at work with their hoods up. I'd never met Don Thabbet but remembered photos from the internet a long time ago: a big fat ancient thing in huge Yoko sunglasses and a white sailing cap on a yacht, skin cracked like a mosaic. Hard to remember those images, to say if Chris was his younger replica under the shades and blubber. Unlikely. I itched to search but was tied up and had no devices. I itched to search lots of things. The sessions I'd have later.

'Yeah, chew on that. Cloning's relatively trivial, in the Valley. Not just Don, they're all at it, have been for ages, asexual reproduction, poking at the stuff of life. Wise up to what goes on in the world. That's how they spend it: ultimate vanity projects: hacking death. Forget silicon—it's carbon and protein now. Plenty of bio stuff you'll have heard nothing of. The mystery lives of the nought point percenters. Welcome to my world. Getting you to post us your DNA.'

Maybe it's true, I thought then. Maybe there *were* lots of him. He could be mad and a clone, why not? It kind of made sense: them up to all sorts in their campuses, knowing everything about us, cloaking themselves, hatching a future we had no say in. Cloning themselves was no great stretch—they did it with sheep, right, had been doing so for years? He could be the clone of an old man and the clone of someone his age, he could have a double, a triple, why not? Certainly explained why they'd been so keen to hire him, his crazy rise. Were they all as bad as he was? No wonder he'd gone mad.

Stay small.

But it was so creepy, thinking about two Chrises: Mr Finger-Perfect prancing about in my flat being someone else, up to stuff, knowing my data, having his fun with me.

Or maybe this stump Chris was the one having fun with me. Maybe they both had that eye scar, oh for that lifelog. Scars were easy: etch them on with lasers and stencils, no problem for robot-makers like them.

And who was this *them* going to all that trouble, for what? Don Thabbet and his crack venture capitalist special-effects clone squad? Watch out, I told myself: big schemes, going Tal-like. *Keep it simple.*

And the simple version was: I didn't need to know anything, I already knew everything I needed to know about Chris, had sucked it up years ago, let him tell his fucking stories. Chris was a cock, always would be. Only Chris mattered and Chris would do or say anything to help Chris, no matter how many of him there were, if there was only one.

'One day,' my driver said, about a year after I slunk off, a year of riotous living at the cutting edge of pleasure, he got an invite, a one-to-one with the old man himself, Don Thabbet, at home. A white villa in the hills outside San Francisco. Butlers, ancient art, gracious living. There in a library of Italian trick wood panels, Don told Chris what Chris really was.

'I look into his eyes, Nim. I can see it. He's old and fat and bald but he's me. I'm him. We're the same. He's been searching for me for years, found me by my blood after the crash, by his blood which is my blood, has had a watch out on our sequence forever, has been reeling me in slowly, watching from a distance. He shows me photos of when he was young. I want to puke. Do you know how it feels to see you in front of you, just a lot older

and fatter? Your exact DNA sequence? To know it made you?'
He ran his stump finger down his nose.
'My clone daddy, his clone baby. He grew me, he lost me,
he found me again. He showed me his hands, the whorls in his
fingertips, just like my fingertips. Our palm lines are different
though, slightly: we've been living different lives. But all that's
going to change now we're together again. He talks haplogroups,
other words I don't know but will now: chronic disease we're
susceptible to, the pros and cons of our sequence, best strategies
for optimum self-management. He strokes my face though he
knows I won't like it. Because he knows me, better than I know
me. Because he *is* me but's been at it longer with all the data.
He feels my muscles, shows me our freckles, his age spots, tells
me we're in it together, knowledge-transfer, an adventurer who
doesn't want it to end. He's got universities set up just to study
our sequence, our own hospital. He manufactured me. Know
how that feels? Growing up, feeling you're so unique?'
    It was great, his daddy said, to have his stolen self back, to
see what the genes did without informed guidance. Don's other
instances had been reared from birth in controlled environments.
Don himself had enjoyed a very particular upbringing. But
class will show itself, Daddy was proud of him, of what Chris
had made of himself from the humblest of upbringings in
Scritchwood, without Don's husbandry. Blood will out.
    'I felt like a fool. The whole thing? My rise? Nepotism, not
genius. I crashed at first: the shock, the craziness. I nearly ran
back to you.'
    Nearly but not quite.
    'Then I started to think different, under Don's mentorship.
Don's a genius, right? Don knows everything, I am Don, I *am* a
genius. But with things to learn. The feeling was: Crown Prince.
So he starts to train me. To do it right you need to start from
birth. But he's fascinated by what I know instead: my 'smarts',
what that brought to the sequence. Plus growing up with you,

of course.'

He patted my bound knee.

Shadows and lights passed over his mad face. 'We're bonding. He's telling me our mission, our fate and destiny, parts of the mission. I'm seeing the world through his eyes, you can't imagine what he knows. For the first time I understand, at last: the con, the mystery. Me and Daddy love each other. No love like self-love. But then he introduces me to Sean.'

Full-fingered Sean, my first visitor, according to this stump Chris.

'Sean. My bad, my weird.'

Bad Sean, from the same batch as Chris, but who hadn't got stolen by Alan, hadn't grown up with me in Scritchwood. Bad Sean who'd stayed in Don's labs, my driver said.

'Think it's freaky to meet your eighty-year-old self? Imagine what it's like to meet yourself now.'

Not that freaky. Like meeting a long-lost twin, I imagined.

'A you who hates you. A you brought up so weirdly you can't imagine. Optimised from birth to exploit mutual core talents, reared mathematically, ergonomically, to become the ultimate Don Thabbet. Tweaked. A mistake in retrospect, Don says: the sequence needs more freedom or it curdles. You but totally fucked up. Imagine meeting that. We sit there, over the supper table in the white villa. We eat a meal. Like looking into a mirror and watching it hate you. Don sits there with us. Don watches. It's intense, Don tells me later, the competitiveness you feel with a fellow instance. How well you've played the same dealt hand. And it's much worse with a same-age instance, Don says, completely identical. Though nurture counts for so much.'

A crazed laugh.

'So now Don's got two princelings: micromanaged Sean who's turned out wrong, and stolen *me*, grown up in the bus with you away from hospitals beyond Don's control, who Don now prefers, who Don feels like is most like him after all, the irony. Prodigal son. An heir and a spare. I'm the new toy. Sean's the broken one, then. I win, for now. Sean vanishes, I don't ask where. It's time for me to enter the very inner circle. Have Don tell me the real stuff. We're all feeling sorry for Sean, thwarted birthright. But that's life.'

He shook his head.

'The things I find out then...Things I can't take, Nim. Bad knowledge. Things that turn me away from Don. I wake up. And Don knows it. And then Sean's back in the picture, the golden boy again since I'm on the downer. Reformed Sean, back on track, ready to do whatever Don tells him. If it means Sean can destroy me. And so I duck out and come to you, with this stuff I've got to tell the world. With your help. If it isn't too late. If we can get to Flora before Sean does, find that book before he does, find out why he wants it.'

Ah yes, the book, that biz. *End bit needs more work, Chris. Rings a bit hollow.* And was that relief on his face, to have finished his cockamamie tale?

By now we were on the A40, passing bus garages, a big storage facility crowned by a sleigh-borne Santa, the Hoover building lit up green, a shiny American-style diner.

'I need a coffee,' he said.

He veered fast across lanes into the car park of a small service station to our left, parked up by the air machines where there were no cars. He sat there shivering next to me for a moment, scouting for danger, stretching and rubbing his bitten hand.

'Want a coffee?'

I nodded. He'd have to take the gag out. I could do things with coffee: spit it into his mad lying face. He pulled his hoodie down low over his forehead, reached behind him to the back seat for this big black weird walking stick, unscrewed the base, plopped some pound coins into his palm, threw the stick into the back where it thwacked against unknown other equipment. I shuddered. He opened the door, got out of the car, slammed the door and went into the building, left me free of him for the first time but unable to move or do anything, tied to the seat, my whole face and body in pain. There were a few cars and people but no way to shout at them. I writhed in my burka, tried my utmost to loosen the ropes, bounce my body against the seat but no one noticed. A fat hunchbacked Moslem woman at eccentric prayer.

He was gone a while, came back with two coffees. He looked worse, tight and pale.

'Black. That's how you take it, right, these days? If I take the gag out will you behave?'

I nodded.

'But will you? No shouting, attracting attention. No point and you mustn't. You don't know. I'm not about hurting you but I will hurt you if I have to. If you knew you'd understand. OK?'

I nodded. He balanced the coffees by the gearbox, reached down to my feet and put his hands up the burka, brushing my jeans and scratched skin, watching my eyes. I flinched. He reached up higher, undid the knot behind my hair wedging the gag in, pulled the eye-slit of the burka down, fished the sodden gag and knot out of my mouth, let me breath.

The joy. Moving my jaw and shredded lips and rough swollen tongue. Moving my face, my sore torn mouth back, my whole scratched tied body, my sore ankles and wrists, trying to wipe my wet face against the nylon burka, breathing through my mouth again.

'Untie me Chris,' I managed to say.

'Not yet. When I'm finished, I'm not finished, you'll try something.'

He pulled the burka down under my chin so my whole lower face was exposed, bent my face back and tipped gulps of hot coffee gently into me. I braced for it to scald but the temperature was perfect, very drinkable. Or my mouth was numb by now. Bits dribbled down my face. It was sweet, I didn't take sugar.

So he didn't know everything about me. But sugar was good, I needed sugar. I needed to drink, my mouth was raw.

I closed my eyes and let the coffee flood me. I didn't spit or shout or talk or say anything. He'd just regag me or worse and there was no one around. He'd do anything, whatever he was, that was clear. I had to wait for some flaw or chance, play along, bide for the right time, listen to the bullshit, hold my nerve. Chris or a clone, mad or plotting, it didn't matter. Whoever he was he was acting mad and out in the world and either was or looked just like Chris, a person with a public profile, a person of some importance, who couldn't be out in the world like this, who already had copters after him: bad for the stock price to have him rampant. There'd be doctors or security, already were by the looks of things. Build those bonds, work those ropes, till the doctors emerge. Positivity, planning and good sense had helped me many times, would help me now. He didn't want to hurt me, he wanted my help. He said.

He dabbed my mouth with the burka, wiped up the dribble.

Afterwards it seemed to me the coffee tasted strange.

7

We drove in silence for a while, me enjoying my mouth back, twisting my body to lessen the pain, working out how to play it, what to say. Car spray smeared soft light, rain pattered on the roof, the wipers squeaked, our breath steamed up the windscreen so he opened his window a sliver—no fancy demisting in this car. We passed a Victorian water tower, four artificial hills, the low lights of an airfield, then pure countryside: lorries and their spray, cats' eyes, the empty road. I felt better, calmer, buoyed by coffee, a warm glow. Tied and gagged under my burka but I'd find a way to handle this asswipe. He frowned at me. He seemed different and not in a good way: perked by caffeine but colder, tighter, a mode I recognised. Unsteadying mood swings, a cheap way to control me. *You let him.* Like normal, proof he was real Chris.

But nothing was normal.

Glower, you freak. Drum that stump all you like.

'Sounds like you've been through a lot,' I managed eventually. 'I want you to know: whatever you've been through, Chris, I'm here for you. We'll sort this together, Chris, like old times. Why are they after you? What have you done?'

'What have I *done*? I told you: learnt stuff, not liked it, escaped to tell the realm about it.'

'The realm?'

'What we call…your world. People who don't know…what's up. The dumdums with their phones.'

We turned on to the M25.

'What you got to tell us?'

'Their plans. What the tech's for.'

'And what *is* the tech for?'

'World control. All those maverick drop-outs busy in garages, trips to India? All planned from way back, seeds planted in greedy heads, tech shown. A front, the latest in a long line of fronts. Long-term mission: crunchable world. Birth-to-death peeping, total access, exposed souls, deep orders, much worse planned. Everything searchable, recordable, trackable. Everything with its own barcode, smart code, like in the Bible. It's not that they're smart. It's that your dumb.'

'Big whoop,' I said, riding a new tide of warmth and energy. 'We know all that already: whistle-blowers. And even before that we all sort of knew anyway.'

'Whistle-blowers are nothing,' he said, 'the ones you see on your social feed. They print rebels too. They *want* you to know, breaking it to you gently, your new reality, so you'll self-edit like they want you to, now you know you're always recorded. But, in the end, like anyone cares. Like with money. A key side project. They're phasing it out, can't you tell? No one asked you but they're getting rid of money, over the next few years everything's going to be cards and chips, then body chips. Your last cent trackable, your last twitch trackable, them knowing your cancers before you do, them placing your cancers, you completely known and slaved. Oh there'll be some paper left, for the holdouts, the reenactors. Till they die out. The dumdums'll give it up happily, like they gave up everything else. Jab you with anything, just so long as you can post those cat vids.'

I wanted to laugh, I nearly did. I felt good, too good. Relaxed, even, tied there.

'You drugged me.'

'I didn't drug you,' staring ahead, stump to nose.

Something subtle, feelgood, more than coffee or endorphins. Liquid cosh, new ways to control me if old ways wouldn't. I wanted to shit myself.

'What was in the coffee?'

'Calm down Nim.'

'What have you done to me?' I said, twisting my ropes, out of control, suspicious of everything I was feeling and also floating free above it all, wanting to laugh more: me in my burka. 'You fuck.'

He nodded. 'Calm down. I didn't drug you. Don't lose it. You need to hold it together.'

'Don't tell me how to feel.'

He nodded again. 'They've been good for you, for us both, your forums. I even pitched in sometimes, different usernames, sorry, keeping in touch. Insider tips, for the community, the very least I could do. Learnt lots about myself. Some things can't change but some things can, especially when you've seen and done what I have, bottomed out. I'm sorry, Nim. I'm not who I was.'

This utter shit. 'Untie me Chris.'

'Not now. Not yet. I'm sorry.'

Silence for a bit on the empty road. A line of tall lights cast veils in the mist. Imprisoned by him, controlled by him, possibly drugged.

Take control. Build those bonds.

Me at my ropes double-time with my new buzz, riding the wrong warm bubble inside me, using his drugs against him.

'So, Chris. Tell me about clones. What *are* they? Robots?'

'No. People, like anyone, real bodies, grown embryos, cultured in labs to be someone's copy.'

'How many of you are there?'

He shrugged. 'It changes. Accidents, experiments, botches, corporate terrorism, upgrades, clean slates. I don't know. We're not a family, as such. We don't all hang out, count each other. Hospitals of spare parts, I know that much. There were lots of us, once. There's a selection process. Sean and me were the first good batch.'

I twisted and bled and rubbed knotted wrists against the back of my chair under the burka, pictured tiny fibres fraying one by one with my new energy.

'Any younger ones?'

'Lots of babies. We're the oldest surviving, me and Sean. No other adults. That I know. Us and the babies and Don, nothing in between. Except the organs. That I know about. Ever met a baby-you? Ever met your liver? Pretty freaky. A batch of teens got destroyed, I know that much. In what you call the Iraq War.'

'What do *you* call it?'

'Something else.'

'How come Don lost you? How come you ended up with Alan in Scritchwood?'

He nodded, stump to nose. 'Alan stole me in my test tube then hid me out somewhere Don wouldn't find me. Deep cover in crank camp with the ex-airmen and crusties. No schools, no doctors, no hospitals, no blood. Alan used to work for Don once. Chew on that. I was so right. Nothing's what it seems.'

I pictured old Alan warming his hands at his brazier outside the battered green bus. Sticks at his side, foul dressings sellotaped together under long socks, old rum empties stacked in wobbling pyramids. Mahogany Alan of the long-curved fingers and nails and matted white beard and afro, in his rag nappies, his junkyard, muttering his songs. Unlikely ex-henchman of California techno kings.

'What did Alan do for Don?'

'Stuff.'

'Why did he steal you?'

He shrugged. 'Found out what Don was up to, turned against him, joined his enemies, wanted me for leverage. I dunno. There's lots I don't know.'

Ah yes, the holes in the story. I could definitely move my hands more freely now in my blood-slickened ropes. I twisted more to make more blood. In front of us: the turning for the M4 and signs: 'The West', a picture of a stag, a warning: 'Adverse Camber'. We turned.

'And what's the deal with the book?'

'I don't know. You tell me. What *is* the book?' he said.

I looked at him. '*The* book.' But he still looked blank. 'Come off it Chris.'

'I swear I don't know what you're talking about. It wasn't me up there with you in your apartment, flat. I don't know what he said, what book he wanted, he's not me. I swear on my life.'

Yes but. Because *my* Chris, my real Chris, the one I'd grown up with, would have known what I meant when I said *the* book. Because only one book was *the* book when we were growing up. Because of Scritch, which we played with Alan and Flora and Tal and other kids—the book was how we coded up secret messages, 'Scritch notes', for Alan's secret agent world, clues and mission hide-and-seek laid out by Alan in the Fall and down by the water. And the book was at the core of it.

He saw me looking at him, whoever he was with his stump. He saw my eyes.

'What's the book?'

'Shh. Hold on. Do you hear sirens?'

I couldn't hear anything. I could only sit there trying to see him behind his Chris mask. What if there *were* two of them and I was strapped in here with the other one? 'Grag Medusa,' I said. And he looked blank at that too. Pure ice chill cutting through my buzz, bringing me to. I couldn't move. He was a void, like Chris but other. With his stump, up to what? Looking at me, doing the maths, purest coldness, some robot? And the first one in my flat: him too or Chris or something else?

My dead phone.

Then I did hear sirens: an ambulance, coming fast towards us the wrong way up the hard shoulder.

'OK, the book, since you're testing me.' And he pressed his foot down and speeded up and overtook and put space between us and sirens and ambulances and told me all about the book: correct info, what it was, how we used it, stuff any Covert kid would know, stuff only he and I would know. Private games, between him and me, triple meanings, when we were trying to outfox Alan who never wanted us together, ways we used the book to give each other secret messages: when and where to meet up in the broken house, stuff I'd forgotten, lovers' codes. Nothing ever recorded or written down, nothing the internet could have told him. I felt.

'Don't test me,' he said. 'I'm me. Feel it. You know me. You really think I'm that cold fuck up in your flat before? What did he know? Not much. Primed, sure, piped info, chitter-chatter. But no real details, not what I know, you and me deep. There's only so much you can fake. Feel it, if you can, if you can feel anything. I'm me. Cut me some slack if I forget things, if I'm confused. They did things to my head, so much's happened, I forget things, you help me remember. And I'm always half listening to you and not listening to you, listening for them. The motherfucking book. Of course.'

The sirens were gone. I stared at him addled from my burka. Gaunt scratched face, bits of bush in his hair, cockamamie tales, him knowing all the deets just not straight away, the same but different to the first debonair Mr Finger-Perfect up in my flat the first time. Pale, thin, ill, smell, clothes, stump, stubble, aura, desperation. If he'd said 'the book' to me I'd have known which book right away.

But all that meant more to me than it had to him. He never loved Scritch like I did and had grown to hate it, because it was Alan's game and he'd grown to hate Alan and any restriction. Plus he'd been busy since then, formatting our new world. Scritch would be some blip on his landscape, there'd been plenty of games for him since then. And maybe they had done things to his head, would make sense.

And that moment before of pure coldness: of him being other, doing his maths: wasn't that just him, hadn't I had the exact same feeling during our last days? In the forest in Oregon, our last trip, among the redwoods, when I looked into him and saw only nothing, sensed he might kill me to blot me out, so he could start fresh without bother. And he'd definitely been Chris then, a long slow few years of whittling down to his core. His face that day among the huge trees, watching me search for him from up on a boulder above me, gripping a rock in his unstumped hand. A mask with utter chill behind it, me feeling I knew nothing about him at all despite growing up with him, always loving him, what I'd thought was him, the void he'd become. And still was. Doing all this now, pretending to be mad, tech conspiracy, saying anything, to get his hands on the book again for some reason. Insane power greed. Insane ambition. Typical Chris.

'Why the fucking book? Are you OK?' because he was driving with one hand on the steering wheel and the other clutched to his left temple like he was in pain and he was sweating.

'Yeah. They...did stuff to me. It comes on sometimes. It'll pass in a minute.' Then he lunged across me, still driving but reaching for something in my footwell: a plastic bag.

We swerved.

'For fuck's sake.'

Lucky it was late and the roads so empty.

'Sorry.'

He grabbed a handful of whatever was in the bag—brown dried twigs, plant stuff, bad-smelling, Chinese medicine perhaps—and shoved it into his mouth.

'Pull over. Let me drive.' A surge of excitement: my big chance.

'I'll be OK. This...helps.'

'What is it? It smells disgusting.'

'It *is* disgusting. But it works. "Herbal medicine". My last bag. It's been six months: rationing this, hiding out in woods, eating plants, stealing cars, scraping cars, running from people you can't run from. I'm sorry I've messed you in this. It's fatal.'

Six months during which he'd still been posting on social media, being charitable, doing press releases, I'd been following.

Assistants. Schedulers. Bots. Any old way.

'Pull over,' I said sweetly when he'd calmed down, stopped sweating. 'Untie me. I'll drive. You're sick. I'll drive us to Flora.'

'You won't. I'm fine. I'm doing this. I'm sorry.' He put his head in his hand again, we swerved again.

'For fuck's sake.'

He sat back up. 'I'm OK.'

Him so out of control, driving me, killing us by accident Or just dodging the awkward questions?

I breathed and watched him till he got steady.

'Why does Sean want the book?'

'OK,' stump to nose. 'It's pointless but. This is how I think it goes. I wanted to leave them, needed help to make my plan. Where could I turn? Not you, you're the last person I wanted caught up in this. Only one person, who stole me in the first place, set us up with all the games.'

My stomach opened. 'Alan's dead.'

'Bollocks. Alan's not dead and you know it. So-called Alan. Not my dad. Your dad. Like I think you know.'

'Fuck you Chris.' Grenading me with any-old to keep me off-kilter.

'I saw you in the town halls. I went to Maldon in your phone.'

The peeping Tom, scrying in at me just back from New York with my new name on my search for some kind of love and family, any trace of Alan or my parents. Trying to find Ann Wynn, my uncle's widow, who they'd left me with. Lurking with me outside the newbuild in Maldon as I talked to her niece, finding out Ann Wynn was dead.

A growth, the niece said. Eaten from the inside, her black bitterness. And the niece the same, leaning in the doorway: 'I got nothing for you. And there's nothing left from the old man if that's why you're here. Oh yes, he paid her.'

Alan paid Ann Wynn to bring me up. The niece saying she didn't know anything more and me not finding out anything more since.

And this shit listening in.

'You should know the truth about our past.'

Alan's your dad. The niece hadn't said that, it was Chris now saying it, to play me for traction.

Alan dark Indian or something, me pale northern, keep it simple.

But Alan had said he was Chris's dad and Chris was pretty pale and hadn't I felt something down the years? Alan had been *like* a dad, the closest thing I'd had growing up. Until he vanished and I went along with what Chris wanted instead of what Alan had told us to do if he ever vanished: sold the bead, swanned off to New York.

Alan and his games.

Park it for now.

The shape of Alan's legs, the three moles on his dark left calf arranged in exactly the same pattern as the three moles on my light left calf.

Coincidence, wish-fulfilment.

You wanted a Daddy and he knows it. Don't let him whet you with false papas.

'Alan's not my dad and he's dead,' I said on the big empty road. Fuck compassion, playing along. 'Don't try it, Chris. They found the body,' when we were in New York, Flora told us. Face-down, bloated in a ditch, five months dead. His last bender.

'Decomposed. He didn't have a face. They ID-ed him by his buttons. Scritchwood, Alan, Scritch games—what d'you think all that was really? Parked you with Ann Wynn to have you close but apart, for your safety. Seeded all those games into us. You ever found any trace of your parents?'

'It was him.'

'It wasn't. Some corpse dug up and left in his place. Alan's not dead, or least he wasn't last I checked, maybe he is now, your daddy. After tonight and Sean. I found out things, when I had access.'

'You are such a fuck,' the rough ropes sawing my flesh.
'I have to find Alan and so do you, he's the only way out of
this. And they mustn't find him, though they now will thanks to
you when he's dodged them all these years. Letting him down
again. And now Flora's in big danger.'
This *fuck.* 'You'll say and do anything.'
'It's the truth. You can't get your head round it, course you
can't. It's too big. It's taken me years. We need petrol.'
In front of us: the turn-off for Reading Services.
'We don't need petrol.' The dial said we had half a tank left.
'The dial's stuck. You have to work it out with the mileage.'
'Bollocks.'
But he swerved and turned us off the motorway through trees
to the pumps. He didn't look at me, just pulled his hood down
low, got out and filled the tank while I sat tied there in my burka
riding my panic and drugged buzz. Then he opened the back
door and poured a stream of coins out of one of his ridiculous
heavy sticks into a plastic bag, pulled his hoodie tight, told me
not to scream or he'd gag me again, that he'd be back in five.
'I need a wee,' I said.
'Do it in your pants. It's dangerous, they'll have cameras. And
you'll try something.'
'I won't.'
But when he took the stick and the bag and slammed the door
and locked it and his door with the key and pocketed the key
and left me tied there to go and pay, walking with the stick,
swinging his plastic bag, when he vanished from sight inside
the neon shop in front of me to go pee himself, perhaps, I started
to shout, with my ungagged mouth, I writhed around tearing
myself, trying to loosen my ropes. I screamed and shouted—and
his window was open, a sliver.
But it was so late and there was no one else there at the
pumps, except the guy in the shop and the shop wasn't close and
had thick glass windows and in my black burka in the car in the

darkness no one could see me writhing there, screaming, trying my utmost with the ropes.

Then I saw something—a fox? Some kind of animal flitting across the forecourt.

Then I saw something else: a white shape. Someone coming towards me, an old woman nodding at me, in a light grey coat with a handbag, coming for me.

I screamed for help.

She came close. I nodded at his window, open a sliver. I shouted I was tied up, being held prisoner, that I was locked in but maybe she could force the window down.

She came past the pumps and looked at me through the window. I looked at her: old dreamy, lost, thin, fragile. Not the sort to push things down.

'Get the man in the shop,' I said, breathing hard.

But she slipped her thin fingers in the space between the pane and the frame and forced down and the window shuddered down a bit. Her face was silver, her white hair was short, her lipstick was on wrong, she was covered in powder, she had an owl brooch in her lapel and the window shuddered down enough for her to lean into the car and with her long arm to reach me leaning towards her, to stroke my cheek in the burka, to shh me, to jab her long pink nail hard into my cheek.

I screamed.

Chris was behind her, pulling her off, prodding her with his stick: 'What the fuck do you think you're doing?'

She had plastic bags, her coat was filthy, she was some kind of bag lady, a tramp. She started laughing, she was drunk: 'Sorry, sorry.'

He pushed her towards the pumps. She sank slowly down into a giggling heap.

He unlocked his side, bundled in with his stick, breathing hard.

'You OK? Did she draw blood? Let me see,' coming in close

A little blood. My cheek throbbed. How strange.

'Are you OK? My darling. Let's get out of here,' he said.

8

I freaked out for a bit then. The broken window let in damp air, he blathered on: was I OK? Was the woman part of it or some random freak, he wasn't sure. 'Hope for the best, plan for the worst,' which was from Alan.

'The blood's not good, I should have checked under her nails, I should have checked her. But we had to get out.' He reached over, touched my cheek: 'Does it hurt?'

I flinched. My cheek stung and felt dirty: pierced by a freak. I wanted to touch and clean it. I had to get out. I was breaking down.

'Untie me.'

He shook his head.

'I won't do anything. I'll help you.'

'You won't.'

'What the fuck is going on?'

Here after Reading the land was different, less flat. Cats' eyes gleamed, lighted cones shed misty halos, red and white rivers of cars glittered up and down the hill before us. In the clearing sky you could see the nearly-full moon and stars—or were they satellites, capturing everything, brimful of data?

'Let's take the old road,' he said.

Closed, shut off in his own thoughts, not looking at me, staring ahead. We swerved fast and exited, took roundabouts, got onto smaller roads: single lane, fringed with fields and trees, the smell of wet earth wafting through the broken window, dark and empty, cats' eyes glinting the path for us. Just us: no other cars, no copters, nothing and no one except me and him.

'Seems clear. For now. Though you can never tell.'

I watched him as if for the first time, all past baggage junked. Something Chris-shaped, I couldn't tell. We drove too fast over a bridge, through a Christmas-decorated empty town, festive menus, through countryside beyond in silence, me oiling blood on the ropes, trying to breath and find morsels of buzz, trying to forget my opened cheek. A thin, dark, open country road, no signs, him driving, staring straight ahead, white fingers and stump gripping the steering wheel, not reaching for the atlas. In the grip of something, me needing to take charge if I could pull it together, me having to pull it together, there being no choice, my life depending on it.

'Where are going? Where are we, Chris?'

'The old Bath Road. The road west to Wales from London before they built the M4. A Roman road cut on purpose through the landscape to desecrate it. We're driving into charged land.'

'Really,' I said.

'Sure. This bumpy landscape? The little hills? If it was day you'd see them. Take my word: the landscape here's small hills. Slice the tops off and you'll find dead kings and queens inside, or their looted traces, curled up on their sides like babies in wombs, waiting for rebirth, aligned to the sun or moon or some personal star. Though the stars are in different places now to how they'd be back then, long slow rotations. This is ancient altered land we're driving through, a valley of kings as built as Giza or any modern city, coded with secrets for those who can read them.'

'We can sort this.'

'Where d'you think we are?'

'The A4?' because of a stone marker.

'We're on the White Road, heading for the fire. We're in Hyperborea,' he said.

The White Road was from Alan, part of the Chinese map we played with in Scritch, a map of Britain thousands of years ago when the Chinese ruled it which Alan had up in the bus. Which Chris had never had much time for. But now things had changed, it seemed.

We were driving, he said, towards the meeting point of three natural chalk ridges packed with flint. 'The one we're on starts in

Norfolk, one comes east from Dover, one comes up south from Weymouth and the Isle of Wight.'

'There's just one White Road, straight north-south,' I said, to be chatty. The White Road was Dorset up to John O'Groats, not three roads sideways.

'This is the real one. A Stone Age motorway, for Romans and Vikings, for much earlier people. The ways into Britain, a way into Britain, to the bits that matter, the matter of Britain. White from the bones of tiny dead sea creatures, from when this whole landscape was underwater whatever millions of years ago. And what d'you think's at the point where the seams meet?'

'No idea,' hard at it with the ropes.

'The ritual lands,' staring ahead in his dark dream or its impersonation. 'Avebury. Stonehenge.'

Ever since ever I hated this type of guff and he ought to have known it. The Merrie Folk section of the Covert, trees decked with ribbons by bearded druidessess — desperate naffery.

'Silbury Hill. You been there? You should. No one does, a pyramid in Wiltshire, older than the Great Pyramid in Egypt. White once, now overgrown. A built thing, like everything round here, made by people who made this landscape: stripped the trees, brought the sheep, shaped the hills. One huge earthwork, this part of Britain is. Neolithic Disneyland up ahead. Silbury Hill, the great white lie in its moat, the moon in its reflection. A white island, a spiral castle — you know spiral castles? Where you die and get reborn? Take the dumdums to the underworld, sell them the moon you made with your mirrors, stun them with fake magic, so they'll do what you tell them, high on your potions.'

'What are you now,' a friendly chide: 'crank Wikipedia?'

'What do you think Wikipedia is? Who d'you think wrote it?'

'Let me guess.'

'Independent, free, massive, global. An inclusive force for good. Anything like that's bound to have Don and chums behind it.'

'Why?'

'To be the word. To control knowledge, present their fake version. There's only one place people look for anything these days. Your one-stop-shop. Who reads books anymore? Not that they didn't write the books too, back in the day.'

'Why control knowledge?'

'Don't be dumb. They've always been in control, from way back, of everything, your mind, what goes into it. All post-truth, always has been. Fuddling you with their big news, outrageous presidents, viruses. Wikipedia, phones: just their latest thing. At it forever, thousands of years. Spinning you crud while they're up to their stuff: duping delight, global theatre. That's what I found out, that's what I got to tell, that's what this is.'

'Come off it,' I said gently after a while. Secret techno elites I could just about take but thousands of years? 'Ancient too? That's what this is? I'm sure you've got good reason but I feel sorry for you, if you really believe this kind of crap now, if this isn't some joke.'

'Joke's on you.'

Which it was, me in my burka. 'But,' I said, and told him what I always thought when I heard people spout this type of conspiracy thinking: that they were sweet innocents who wanted to feel there was some kind of order out there in our crazy pointless incompetent world where's there's nothing but everything falling apart.

'That's what they want you to think,' he said. 'Not believing in the world is the greatest taboo, right? It's about class and taste. Things are arranged so you get marked out as lower if you look at things this way, refuse what's on offer. It's only small secrets that need keeping. Big secrets keep themselves, by public incredulity. But let me tell you some things you won't find on your Wikipedia. What d'you know about electromagnetics? Bioelectricity?'

Not much, shitting Nora. Soon he'd have to sleep, we both

would, it was so late, there'd be some chance. Until then: step back, nod, smile, compassion, build those bonds, work the ropes, don't fight back, don't get caught up, one swift blow, let him do his haunted jumble.

'Electrical paths criss-cross the Earth,' he said, speeding us down the dark glitter. It was to do with Earth's magnetism and the reactions of everything to each other: the electric pop as cells grow, the sizzling contact of protons and metals. 'All official unarguable dumdum "scientific facts". But if you're sensitive—and many animals are,' he said: pigeons or those talented cats and dogs who, when lost, find their way back to homes and owners across continents, or sharks who sense their prey by the merest electric charge, one careless fish wink—then electromagnetic paths also became a guide.

'One thing about chalk: it's the great insulator. Walk the chalk even in blackness and feel yourself swaddled from the crackle in a great safe tunnel. If you're attuned to these things—and some people are and were—you close your eyes and use your nose, as they used to say, and flow through the chalk and know at once if other creatures are near or if you've strayed off-path. Feel the land inside you. Helped by smell, that other great lost sense, also located in the nose.'

'Are you attuned?' I said. 'Did Don attune you?'

'Sure,' he said and smiled. 'Don and others. Look,' he said closing his eyes: 'I can drive with my eyes closed.'

'Don't,' I screamed. 'Jesus,' I shouted when he opened his eyes after ten pure terror seconds of him fast faultless driving with his eyes scrunched tight shut—he was laughing.

'Sorry,' squeezing my bound knee. 'I won't hurt you,' stump to nose.

Jesus fucking Christ, gimped there next to that loon. The road was straight, it wasn't so hard, I supposed—once I could breathe—to drive with your eyes shut for a bit on a straight Roman road, and he was pretty good at driving, always had been, if totally reckless.

Or schooling you to fear him so you do what he says.

Grag Medusa.

'Come on, Chris,' I said, mustering a lighter tone. 'I thought we didn't have time for this. Flora's in danger. Right? Let's stop messing around. Let's get to her. Let's do this.'

'Humouring me.' He shook his head, the words coming out in chokes. 'So bad, being with him, but so good, the privilege of finding out. Thinking of you the whole time, what you'd do, telling you one day. Never thinking it would happen. And here we are and it's so fucked up and you're so closed and smart and sly.'

He was crying, I'd never seen him cry, the whole time I'd been with him.

'Miss-Clicky-Normal, picking up your pay cheque, suckered like the rest of them,' tears running down his cheeks. 'You're prepared to accept electricity and magnetism in their light bulbs and machines, inanimate things—you have to accept it: you see it and use it every day. You can probably even accept some animals and plants are tuned into it, to sense prey or navigate, their sixth sense. But start talking about it naturally streaming over the planet and *us* being able to sense and harness it and navigate by it? Watch them laugh, watch the dumdums scarper. Unplug yourself, understand the lie. Why are we so exempt? We're animals too. Once the greatest animals, kings of the senses. That's how we got to now: where we rule and can tap away on phones and don't need senses at all. Except sight, that's how they've got you.'

'Chris...'

'All those dumdum scientists denying there's anything magical going on—apart from that one moment once in the barren universe when life started. They're forced to admit one single magical thing happened once. Right?'

I didn't know. I didn't have a fucking clue. 'I guess.'

'But what if it always happens? What if everything, every single rock is alive and fizzing on an endless pulsing mesh that people before knew and used, that Don knows and uses, that Don and the Dons have cut you off from, kept for themselves?' We were on a tree-lined stretch just before Marlborough, according to the signs. 'Steady,' I said, us weaving all over the road.

'I might need a break,' he said, holding his head.

You might indeed, mateykins. He lurched left, we swerved off-road, ploughed down some track into woods. The car jolted, we nearly hit a tree, came to a halt nose-deep in branches, yellow berries, vines. Then he cut the engine so we sat there in the dark. I screamed. He moved towards me, down to my footwell, to his bag of brown stuff, grabbed some, stuffed it into his mouth.

'Mushrooms.'

'Not what you think. Not magic mushrooms.' He put his head in his hands.

'Chris...'

'Shut up. Shut up. Do not speak.' He stuffed his mouth, sat there chewing and rocking, the tears gone, a low voice now. 'I'm a shit. I lied to you tonight and you know it. You've seen through me, you always did. I'm a fucking sham.'

9

I breathed and watched his profile from my burka in the car among the old bare trees.

'I told you I didn't know about the book. I lied to you. I knew about it. I wanted it myself. I've got a message I need to decode. I need the book to decode it, I knew you had it. That's why I came to you. To use you. Again. But I didn't want to admit that. I set them on you, they must have been following me, I didn't know that, that's why they set Sean on you. They must have the message too and now they're heading to Flora so they can decode it. I led them to both of you. I'm sorry. I'll never lie to you again.'

We sat among the moonlit trees.

'It's a message from Alan. There are old networks and resistance. He taught us how to contact them, how to contact dead people. Do you remember?'

And he told me about what I'd forgotten: the Cuckfield Board, a place in Scritch with crooked trees and globe-shaped hedges where you went to talk to the dead.

'It's a real place,' he said: a church in a village in Sussex called Cuckfield. 'Easy to figure out Scritch once you know it's for real. Very old, the trees in the graveyard. Inside the church: thirteen arches, a carved skull, a visitors' book on a black wooden board,' like in Scritch. 'I knew I had to get out, I knew only Alan could help me. I sensed he was alive. I remembered Cuckfield. I escaped there, opened the visitors' book, wrote some comment, signed it Boyd Parsons like he taught us. I went away, waited three days. I come back: there's a message for me there, from "Leslie Snags",' one of Alan's Scritch names. 'A message written in Scritch, for me, from Alan, telling me what to do now, I need the book to decode it. I tore it out, but *Don* must have been there before me, waiting for me, recording it, following me to you so they'd know how to decode it, knowing enough to know the book will crack it, so they can track Alan down and get what they want.'

Mad bollocks. 'Why lie? You swore on your life.'

'I had to. My life's finished. This is the last thing I'll do. I got the message in Cuckfield, couldn't understand it, knew it was in Scritch, knew I needed the book, knew it was with you. Didn't want to bring you into this, knew the risks, that bringing you into it was killing you. But. Can you imagine how much I'm looking forwards to turning up at yours and asking you for it? And then—I don't have to, cos *he's* been before me and you're already talking about the book and I can...use that.'

'Use that?' Icy feelings, established techniques. A liar who'd lied to me before. Shifting stories, like the old days, exploitation, hard cold cunning, nothing crazed about it. What the fuck was he up to?

'I know. It's bad. I'm sorry. But. Plus: I wasn't really sure about you, if you *were* you, who you were by now. Perhaps they'd got to you. But. I know now, who you are, that you're you and I can trust you.'

'How do you know I'm me and you can trust me?'

'I just do. Cos I've been with you. Again. Cos I can feel you, the real you. Cos I can still feel. Can you? That's all we got in the end.'

Silver words.

'You lied to me. So you could just pretend—what?—that you were back cos you were sorry, desperate? Not just cos you wanted something from me. And introduce the book stuff bit by bit? And so what?'

'Not much. Except that I am also sorry and desperate. But that doesn't matter.'

Oh yeah, I knew by now: the stakes were much higher than piddling old scores between him and me. Vast ancient conspiracies we were talking here.

'But what about "Sean"?' I said. My supposed first visitor, full-fingered 'Sean' whom this lying stump Chris swore was a whole separate other person, his long-lost clone if you please, someone cleaner and healthier and fatter, stuff you couldn't fake except maybe you could. 'Sean', who'd swaggered in and straight-out asked for the book—so he could track down and wipe out Alan and some kind of resistance to the world's secret rulers? 'So how come "Sean" knew about the book?'

'Cos they'll've got Tal somehow, Tal told them. Or I did—they've had me in comas, harvested me over and over. Every bit of my mind and memory is mirrored in some satellite or data hub in Antarctica, you betcha. Plus their other ways. They always know everything, almost everything. Except what the message means, how to find Alan. Hidden by old ways. Which they probably know by now, he'll think it was a trap, that I tricked him.' He clutched his head. 'We got to get to Flora before they do.'

Flora, whom he was so concerned about. Asleep in bed in Wales now, I hoped. Or with Sean, was it even possible? And us driving to her, maybe even getting there, then what? I sat there among the trees. Him versus Flora and Rhodri, her boyfriend. Him with his sticks and lord knew what else.

'Bollocks. You pretend. You kidnap me and tie me up and lie to me and hurt me. Fuck off, fuck off, whoever you are.'

He turned his white hollow face to me. 'Cut me some slack. You don't know what I've seen, I've seen everything. I've peeped into everyone, every last text. The mystery's gone for me. I've seen what people are, endless duplicity, even from you. I can't trust anyone now, even you. I hate myself, I hate everyone. I've told you everything now. I wish it had never happened. But it's the truth.'

I looked away down the avenue of trees.

'Put yourself in my place,' I said. 'We grow up together, we run away, you lie to me endlessly, you belittle and betray me, make me feel bad about myself, string me along, you fuck me over, you treat me with contempt, you slink off without saying, I never see you again. Then you turn up out of the blue and do all this to me and tell me this beyond bullshit story about the book and clones and tech and electricity and Alan and secret world rulers. And then you tell me it's not exactly the way you said it because you can't trust anyone cos you've read all our texts. Face it: you came cos you want the book, for whatever reason. You came to use me again.'

'I came cos I had to. No choice. This is worse than me lying to you. This is me drawing you in. I've sacrificed you, you have to know that. And you're the only thing I care about.'

'Don't even.'

'For real. It doesn't matter now but you're the only one and I'm so selfishly glad to be here with you to say all this to you after all this time. For real, no cams, no screens. I'll say it, you can't stop me, nothing to lose. You and me. Fuck everything else. The only true thing: growing up with you, the feeling between us. That I betrayed. Watching you for years, through your cams. Your every move but not able to talk to you. Haunting your screens. Getting to know you so well, better than I knew you before, better than anyone knows you, better than you know you. Yeah, super creepy. The old bad dream of being with you again. And you feel it too, you can't lie to me: searching for me through the screens. Talking into the ether and I heard you, did you think I might?'

So twisted. *Don't fall for it.* A deep dark creep of the internet, unhinged by the tech he'd got mangled in. Or a networked prince, knowing just what to say.

'Yup, I'm a creep, but who loves like that anymore? Now he's plugged you all into your mirrors? Glutted you with porn? Did you sense me, did you hope? In bars and movie theatres. In the background. In your dreams—I know how you dreamed of me, like I dreamed of you. In the flesh—the only thing that matters. Fuck tech, fuck dreams. The risks I took. Once in that Uber? That was too much—I thought you recognised me, did you recognise me? So intense. Sourcing and fucking women who looked like you or seemed like you or were nothing like you, faces, behaviours. My whole-world catalogue. You don't know, where I've been, what I've done, the power I've had, looking up every dirty thought of everyone, rifling through kinks, source whatever itch. Hook up by seeming chance with anyone anywhere, knowing all about them up front, engineering the meet. Scanning for faces that look like you, don't look like you. And not one of them meaning anything. And no going back to you, I knew that. But here I am back and it's the last thing I want and I don't care anymore, if you believe me, if you don't. And you don't, you can't, it's too big. And it still hurts, it clouds you, what I did to you not just in the end but always: lied, not loved you like I should have loved you, like I learnt to love you when I lost you. Cold little empty boy drunk on ambition, craving the world to fill my nothing. That's all gone now. But for you the dent's still there, you can't open your eyes, even to this. You've shut yourself up, you're warped, you can't chuck it off and see this clear, you never will. And his tech hooking you, blurring you, you aren't even you any more, no one is. But it doesn't matter, it doesn't stop me loving you, even if you don't exist, I should never have brought you into this. I'll manage alone somehow. I'll set you free. You can go.'

We sat there among the dark trees.

'Nice touches, the Uber,' I said after a while. 'And clever, psychologically. And probably right. You hollow fuck. You're a user,' I said, ice-clear. 'You are and were, of me and everyone, anyone useful. Here and now, back in the day. You've got all the words, and now the tech to spy into everyone's weaknesses, twist for your reasons. And you had me once,' for a long time. How useful I'd been to him, once: a pal, a warm body, a family, a source of support and knowledge, a worshipping base from which to venture out into the big bad world and make it his own. And how young and dumb I'd been, once, how in need of love and family myself, willing to make do with any crumb of affection, at the mercy of hormones—I cut myself every last bit of slack. It had worked, once, his game on me. For him, once, I'd gone against all sense, betrayed Alan again and again. I'd done everything, once: gone along with his recklessness, skipped out on Alan, sold the bead, financed his dreams of New York, got myself educated for us both, loved him. And once his plans came true he was off, in the coldest way, as he would be again once he had that book.

'Isn't it more like: you've got what you wanted out of me, where the book is, you can cut me loose.'

'And that's really what you think?'

I hadn't thought it until I said it but what sudden terrible sense. Here now, in the middle of the woods at night alone with him, whoever he was: turning to me, reaching down between his legs, the glint of something in the moonlight at his feet: his knife. Lifting it up while I watched dry-mouthed, watched him lift up my burka, reach for my belly, cut the ropes there, do the same to my bound wrists behind me and my bound feet in the footwell.

'It's OK, I'm not going to kill you, is that what you think, that I'm going to kill you? I'm setting you free,' pulling off the ropes.

My aching arms and shoulders. My damaged wrists and the blood. Set free in a forest. What was worse: alone in the trees in the dark here or with him in his car?

With him for sure.

But.

'I'll drive you somewhere, anywhere. Someplace you can get a bus.'

I undid the seatbelt and scrunched my shivering body up in the seat under the burka, my throbbing wrists under my arms.

'And then what you going to do?'

His eyes flicked over me. 'I'll drop you off.'

'And then? Drive on to Flora?'

'And then drive to Flora.'

Off-grid Flora, whom I couldn't contact till morning at least, unless I tramped through the forest, got the police, and what would they make of this? Flora and Poppy, her seven-year-old daughter, and the new baby I hadn't met yet: let this Chris loose on them before I could get to the police, persuade them, wait till they heard this story.

'Without me you don't know where she is.'

'I know enough. Somewhere in the Brechfa Forest.'

'Cos you still have access to the machines.'

He looked at me. 'Is that what you think?' He shook his head. 'I had them once, that's enough. The shipping container in the field, that's enough. I'll drive down every road till I see it. I'll ask people. I'll find her.'

'Then?'

'Deal with whatever's up. See if Sean's got there first. Make sure she's OK.'

'Then?'

'Try and find the book. If they haven't found it. Try and fuck with them if they have. Get her to come with, decode the message, bring her with me to wherever. Look after her. She has a daughter, right?'

And a little baby boy. And Rhodri, her boyfriend, who built things, who had muscles. 'You're saying all this so I'll come with.'

'I don't want you to come now, it's over, I should never have come to you. I'll look after them, I won't hurt them, I swear.'

'On your life?' He opened his mouth but had nothing to say. 'Look. If there's one iota of truth in anything you've said: leave her alone, forget the book. Tell me the message you found in Cuckfield. We don't need the book — I knew it off by heart once, maybe I still do.'

He shook his head. 'We...can't. It doesn't matter what I feel about you. Some things go beyond people and what they feel about each other. Even if you know it by heart. I need the book.'

'Why?'

'I need to see…what he sees. You can't understand. I won't hurt them. And I won't hurt you by telling you things they might pull out of you later.'

We sat there. 'I need to wee,' I said. I scabbled round, tried to pull the burka up off the back of the seat. He reached into the back seat and dragged out some dirty dark hoodie I pulled on over the burka. It stank of him, authentic old Chris B.O. if I recalled it right, for what that was worth.

I opened the door, stepped out free into the trees, watched him put his key back in the ignition, switch on the headlights.

I stood with the burka over my jeans in my ruined slippers in damp cold among gnarled trees lit by car and moon. My sore, swollen, bruised body: I could barely stand, I was filthy in the hoodie, the nick in my cheek, my swollen wrists and ankles and aching shoulders and dirty scratched body.

I walked away from the car, turned and watched him let me, free of him at last.

I went behind trees and wee-ed, listened to hoots and rustles.

I stood there among bare old trees at night in the wind.

What was he up to? Him and his stump.

I could hitch.

There are no cars.

I could walk, even in the forest, even in the dark. Anything except get back in that car with him.

He's calm now, he's OK, he's done his bit, he's pathetic, he's crazy, he's used himself up, he'll drop you off some place, you'll find the police. Or else he'll just drive off now, get to Flora way before you find anyone, leave you here in the trees.

I went back to him in the car.

He was staring out of his windscreen, a path lit before us by his headlights. 'Britain, land of yews. "Loegar", the lost land, they call it in Welsh. "Savernake Forest", this place is called. Seven oaks, sacred grove. A biofactory grown on purpose from wayback to make timber for ships, kept on as a hunting ground for those old kings whose pleasure was hunting, who came here to ride off the cares of the world by murdering prey. Who came here to compete and cast off rank and roles and fuck whores in hunting lodges in the middle of the forests. Who lived by the good creed: honour, valour, wit, seduction. Blazing out, like the sun. And who cares about that anymore?'

We sat there.

'You're certainly pulling out all the stops,' I said. 'But I've got a life, things to do in about four hours. I've got a job, meetings, responsibilities, all that dull stuff. I've even got a boyfriend, of sorts, for fuck's sake. As you'll know. I'm sorry you're caught up in all this, whatever this is. It sounds bad. I'd like to help. I'm really sorry.'

'Yeah me too.' He looked at me. 'It's the good choice. It's good, what you've become, grown up. Nim Burdock. Put the past behind you. Sensible. I'm glad you're fine, normal. I'm glad you chose well. Thank you. Sorry about everything, the craziness. Don't worry about Flora, she'll be fine. I'll make sure. I give you my word. You've given me so much but this is my battle. There's things you deserve to know. I'll make sure you do, one day. I hope. But now go back to your life. I'll drive you to Marlborough or Swindon, I'll drive safely, with my eyes open, I'm sorry. You can get a bus. Go to the police if you want, it's OK, it won't make any difference, say what you want. There'll be some weird stuff, for a bit, but you'll be OK, they'll know you don't know anything. Back to your old life. Thanks for everything. It's meant everything. You can't know,' the silver glint of the key sparking the ignition.

'I thought you stole this car?'

'I did.'

'So how come you have the key?'

'Stole that too, from the guy's pocket.'

'Did you?' I said, suddenly feeling so sleepy, so dreamy.

'Sure I did,' he said, starting to back the car out.

10

He wafted a coffee under my nose, prodding me from thick sleep: 'I need your help.'

Semi-dark, me tucked up under a rank sleeping bag seeing my breath. Us parked in fir trees off a thin country road next to a sign:

Grid gwartheg
Cattle grid
Anifeiliad
Animals

Wales, in the damp winter dawn. Me still with him in that fucking car. I felt sore and groggy and sick to my pits.

Suckered again.

'We're near Brechfa. Not far now. You've been asleep a while. It's about 7 am, I reckon. Deep sleep, out for the count. Tried to wake you in Swindon, in the bus station, do you remember? All those weird people, no buses till 6 am, didn't want you there left all alone conked out like that. Tried again at Pont Abraham, when we came off the M4. Abraham, Brahma: has it ever struck you?'

It had never struck me.

Reeled in, walking back to his car of my own free will to the sweet tune of his repentance.

Plus the liquid cosh.

This scum.

'Drink,' handing me the coffee, then shoving that atlas at me. 'Where to from here?'

I clutched the tepid cup. I was frozen. I wasn't tied up. No central locking in that dumb car. I could run.

'Sorry,' he said, not sorry at all. 'But we'll be with her soon, it's faster if you're with. We're here, just beyond Brechfa village,' showing me where on the page with his bitten stump while I gripped warm coffee to tamp the panic. 'But she's not in the village, right? She's in the forest, somewhere, off-grid, up some road near here, right? Which road?'

Who knew but not far now from that book he had to get his hands on at all costs.

I sat there, staring at the map, clogged by sleep and terror, and maybe drugs, and fury at myself for not running when I could.

You can still run.

He'll get there before you can tell anyone.

You set him on her.

He drugged you.

Think.

Flora's place was really remote. That's why she'd chosen it, her and Rhodri: off-grid freaks wanting out of the world. Up in the forest outskirts, industrial nature, open hillsides of neat firs grown for flatpacks. That's why it was off-grid: any prettier and the internet would come, phones, power lines, estate agents. Her and Rhodri and Poppy and the baby in their place, another couple and their twelve kids a bit further up. Other friends in a sort of encampment perhaps five miles away, networks of hippies in the wider area. And in the field next to her: the shipping container and the wrecked farmhouse it belonged to and the men who lived there. Who might or might not be drug dealers: hydroponics or meths in their container, people said. Different people lived off-grid for different reasons. The men were OK, a bit silent, I'd met them two summers before, the last time I'd been up, a big summer party. Three burly young men from Liverpool, big muscles in their wrecked farm with their shipping container in the field.

Them versus this gaunt stump Chris with his sticks and knives and ropes and gags and tall tales and bogus history and mock craziness and what else? Guns? Drugged coffee? Plenty more up his sleeves, I was sure. The book at all costs.

I held the coffee and studied the map. A paper map: prehistoric. When I'd visited before I'd taken the train to Carmarthen, Flora had picked me up in the yellow campervan and driven me where? Up into twisty hills, tiny fast streams. White space on the map: winding roads, everything looking the same. Gwernogle: a village name on the map I remembered. Then up from that, maybe half-way towards Rhydcymerau, which felt familiar, seeing that on signposts. Maybe. And then, yes, marked between them: Llamian Blau, that was her village, the one nearest to her. The one with the farm shop a couple of miles down the hill from her where you could buy eggs and phone and leave messages. I was pretty sure.

'Well?'

'I don't know. I can't tell from this. Need a more detailed map.'

'We don't have one.'

'From some shop in Brechfa?' There'd be people in Brechfa, call the police if I wanted, run out screaming right now.

'Nothing opens till nine, I tried before. When you were asleep.'

Oh really. 'So where's the coffee from?'

He pointed out his window at a small camping stove on the grass beside the car.

'Mushroom coffee? Did you drug me before?'

'Nescafe, I swear. You should drink it. You should eat something. Biscuits? An apple? One of these?' offering a tiny green chilli from a chilli plant in a plastic bag in his footwell which I declined. 'Appetite suppressant, perks you up.'

He opened his door, got out, did stretches, tai chi or something, big lunges. He packed up his stove, put it into an army-looking duffle bag, bundled that into the boot.

If he had a stove why buy coffee from service stations before?

Especially since money must be scarce, his ridiculous coin sticks. And how come he had a stove, money, coin sticks if you couldn't trust metal? How come he had car keys, for a stolen car? How come he had a car at all?

I undid the seat belt, threw off the sleeping bag, wedged up the peg of the manual door lock, opened my door, stepped outside into cold damp Wales with his hoodie on over the burka over my jeans, my freezing feet. He watched me from the boot, didn't say anything. Bringing him here with me, close to her, like a virus. I shivered, poured the coffee away, crumpled the foam cup. I stamped my feet and stretched a bit myself, to warm up and get good air into me, still in that big hoodie that smelt of him. I was so sore, my muscles and bloodied swollen wrists and ankles. I went behind a tree for a wee and a think. I was starving. I ought to be at work in a few hours, they'd try to call me, straight to voicemail or was my dead phone now working? Where were the bloody police? Why weren't they after us, since the Glen stuff in my flat? And what would I say to the police?

Gimme some tips, Alan.

Fuck Alan. This one's on you.

I could scream, run into the road, head for Brechfa, wherever that was, if we were even near Brechfa. Run away, find some house or car, get mown down by him, maimed in the legs, bundled back into the car. I could dodge him, run, flag something down, call the police. Call the farm shop, leave a message warning her? Get the farm guy to go up and check on her right now, then call me back. Could work, might not: if someone said all that to me I'd think they were crazy.

Speed off fast, get to Flora now in his car.

And that remote chance that he was right, that Flora was right now with someone who looked like Chris but wasn't, his twin.

Or was it me here now with the one who looked like Chris?

The big looming trees.

Breathe.

He was sorting stuff out in the boot, one eye on me.

I went over to the driver's side.

'You'll want this,' he called from beyond the open boot, holding up the keys to me through the front mirror.

The empty useless ignition.

'Should have learnt to hotwire,' he said, like Young Pete had taught him with coat hangers in Scritchwood.

Should have done. Then I could be driving off right now, reversing back over him, if I had a wire or coat hanger to hand.

We looked at each other in the mirror.

'I'll find her. Even if you're not with me,' his gaunt face pale in the grey dawn, his glittering eyes. 'Go up and down every road, ask around till I find that shipping container. Find out if he's got to her. Quicker if you come too of course. Get there faster. Safer for her. And her family.'

The three container muscle men.

'I'll drive,' I said.

'No.'

'That's the only way I'm coming. If we need to get to her faster.'

'Do you know the way? Do you remember?'

'I will if I drive. Or else leave me here. I want to get to her. As much as you want to get to her. More.'

So I drove, screeching him down narrow empty hedge-lined roads, out up into higher land, right next to streams, down wrong turns, reversing back. Him strapped into the passenger seat trying to instruct me, following my eyes, trying to get me to say where we were going, me with the atlas page spread in my lap. After about maybe forty minutes of this we came to a sign: Llamian Blau 5m. But a mile or so on up a hill there were cones and cordons and the road ahead just stopped. It had cracked and crumbled away.

I got out to look, clutching the car key. The weirdest thing: the tarmac just gone, the ground beyond looking just the same as the side of the hill we were driving up: mud and scree, torn trees and branches. A wrong dead end, the road eaten by nature.

'A landslide,' he said, squatting down next to me to touch crack and gravel.

No way on. The road had crumbled down the hill.

He started to shake.

'There's other roads, other ways round,' I said.

He shook his head: '*They've* been here, can't you smell it?'

'Just a landslide. Pull yourself together.' That kind of thing happened out there, I knew it did.

We got back into the car. He wanted to drive but I insisted, said I'd chuck the keys down the hill and jump down behind them if he tried anything more. So I drove, reversed back down that steep narrow hill path with no metal barrier, checked the map and drove back and up and round and down the detour to get to Flora's from the north-west side, drove in silence for maybe ten minutes, him pale and shaking. Till the road widened into familiar land, modern nature: a nowheresville plateau of ordered firs, sheep, fields, windfarms in the distance, patches of reddish earth, burnt stumps. Then suddenly, out of my window: the field and the dumped container, 'Londis' on its side.

He saw it too.

'There,' I said, pointing to a junky cottage to my right.

He squinted. 'You're sure?'

I nodded but it wasn't Flora's cottage I was pointing to. This one belonged to the container guys, hers was further on. This was my plan: I couldn't take him to her, I needed allies, I needed him overpowered by the container guys. Then we'd see.

He frowned at me. How close had he studied my holiday shots, could he really remember what Flora's cottage looked like?

I stopped the car on the other side of the road, put the key in my pocket while he watched me.

'OK so,' he said, very serious. 'From now: special measures.

Trust where I lead. Do what I say. Or else. Assume the worst, that they're in there, that they've got them, that they're lying in wait for us, will use them to prise info out of us, anything—I'd go in alone 'cept I know you won't let that. Where's the book? In her house. Where d'you put it?'

'I don't know.'

'What d'you mean, you don't know?'

Like I said, mate. I hadn't put the book anywhere, *Flora* had put it somewhere. My first days back from New York, me sad, she'd driven all the way down to London to cheer me up and take all traces of him and Scritchwood back with her. To store them for me, so I could make my clean start, lock it all away. Because I couldn't quite face burning them.

'But it's still in her house somewhere. You're sure? She won't have put it somewhere else, got rid? Do you trust her?'

I looked at him. He knew, he ought to know, that I trusted Flora with my life.

But did I trust her now, he wanted to know. 'When d'you last see her, speak to her? What's she like these days, how nutty, how loyal? Strong? Addicted to anything? Money trouble? She's got kids, a kid, that's a terrible weakness, for them to have over her. She could be up to anything, they can make her up to anything.'

'I trust her.' She was Flora.

'You don't know. If I say "coffee", leave straight away, out the door, however you can, get back here to the car if you can. OK?'

I nodded.

'If I...don't make it, and you do,' and he swallowed and bogused about how he'd made a copy of the supposed Cuckfield message—the one he couldn't understand, needed the book for, wouldn't tell me—into the visitors' book of some church in Rochester, as insurance. He told me the name of the church and which date to look under, in case something happened to him, so there was some record, some way for me to carry this on and read Alan's message and act on it if he, stump Chris, ended up dead.

Yeah right. Wouldn't they have followed you there too? According to your bollocks. Why weren't they following us here?

We sat there. Stump to nose, his pale profile in the grey, what I hoped were our last moments together. My torn face in the mirror, my bloody wrists, the bruise marks from his fingers round my neck.

'What time do they usually get up?'

I shrugged. 'Early.'

We sat there. 'Look at it. Feel it, if you can. Anything different? Anything off?'

I looked across at the ratty cottage. Between the drive and the neighbouring field was a sea of junk: two ex-cars, broken breeze blocks. a sink, a toilet, several broken toilet seats. Blue plastic sheets, branches, unused fencing, boxes and an upturned shopping trolley, other junk piled up behind like a drained polluted river. A truck parked outside, smoke coming out the chimney — looked like the container guys were in.

'Looks fine to me.'

He scabbled round in the back seat and fished out a rank anorak for me to put on over the hoodie and burka. He got some huge dirty socks and made me put them on under my ruined slippers. He pulled my hoodie down low. Then we got out, crossed the empty road in the drizzle, went over to the grey pebble-dashed house with its weeds and closed grubby curtains.

I'd be quick and direct: just explain I needed help, that he'd kidnapped me, show them my wrists and neck. Step aside from him, act fast, rely on them to intervene if he grabbed me, did anything, hope for luck. I couldn't see any other way.

So nervous, hiding in my anorak so he wouldn't see it. I knocked on their peeling door.

No reply. It was early. Smoke coming out of the chimney.

I knocked again. He twitched next to me.

'You sure this is the place?'

I was about to knock again when the door opened to show a large red-headed young woman in a dirty white t-shirt with LOL written across the front, frowning at us, one front tooth missing, a big ugly rose tattooed on her arm.

'Yes? What you want? Oh hello,' she said to me, her face changing, a big smile, a Welsh lilt. 'I know you, don't I? *Flora's* friend, right? Nim, is it? Last summer was it? What can I do for you? Looking for Flora?'

I was about one hundred per cent sure I'd never seen her before.

11

'Where's Flora?' Chris said.

'Who's this?' to me, 'your fella?' She reached her hand out to shake his, fixing him with a stare. 'I'm Margi. And you are?' Back to me: 'They've cleared Flora out. You couldn't find her, back at her place?'

Cleared Flora out. I didn't like that.

'This isn't Flora's place?' Chris whipped his head round at me, grabbed my cut wrist tight.

Her eyes watched this but she didn't do anything, just carried on talking: 'Flora's further up, you forgot? You won't find her, though, she'd been cleared out, you didn't know? Chemical spill, they say, couple of days ago. Big lorries round here, these tiny bendy roads. Forestry Commission, you know. Police came up, cleared us all out, the fumes. All these crashes, the things they carry, you think they'd take more care. Or is it all an excuse, to clear us all out, see what we're up to?' She laughed.

And all the while her small darting eyes looking at me in my hoodie and burka and jeans, looking at Chris in his hoodie, my messed-up slippers, me trying to wriggle my wrist from him, my cut wrists that she was looking at but not saying anything about. There'd never been a woman here before with them, I was pretty sure.

'When did this happen?' Chris said.

'Oh two days ago now. Nenog way, they say it's still not safe, everyone taken down in the church hall in Gwernogle, though I think Flora and Rhodri and the kids went to Rhodri's mam in Llandeilo, I think that's what they said, till we get the all-clear. Very bad luck, you popping up in the middle of this. Surprise visit, was it? Or is she expecting you? The roads still blocked, I thought, didn't think you could get up yet, thought there were signs, did you not see signs? Where did you come from, how did you get up? You OK?'

'How come *you're* still here?' he said.

'Ah well me. Decided to risk it, hid upstairs,' giving us a little smile. 'One of us had to stay. Someone has to take care of things, feed the cats. Well done you, making it up anyway. Get you anything, a cuppa? Where d'you come from, London is it? Pop in, what a shame, coming up all this way.'

His fingers tightened round my wrist.

'Where are the others?' I tried to pull away.

'Which others?'

'The ones who live here? Who lived here before? The Liverpool guys?'

'Oh the boys, you're missing the boys. Down in Gwernogle. We're expecting to hear the all-clear today, they'll be back, if you can wait, perhaps Flora too. Or tomorrow, it can take a while, these clear-ups. Come in, you're welcome to stay, I'm sure the fumes have passed, Health and Safety madness. Come on in, it's freezing. Tea or coffee?'

'A tea would be great,' Chris said.

'I'd love a coffee,' I said, staring at Chris. I had a bad feeling about this LOL-woman and her jolly tone and useful info and staring eyes. We'd never met, I was sure. I had a bad feeling about Flora, wanted to get on, get to her real cottage.

But Chris was stuck in there, asking if LOL-woman knew Rhodri's mum's address in Llandeilo.

I reached over, put my free hand in his free hand so it looked like we were holding both hands, super lovers. I kissed his cheek, to make it look real. I started stroking his free palm. I stroked it with my thumb. I pinched *SOS* out into his palm using Alan's pinch-hand alphabet.

But this stump Chris I was with just turned to me, like he didn't know what I was doing, like he thought I was out of nowhere getting flirty, choosing a weird time for it.

For a moment. The he took *my* hand and pinched out *OK*.

'You know what,' he said to me, relaxing his other hand's grip round my wrist, 'we still got all that coffee in the car. In the thermos. Thanks so much, we don't want to trouble you,' to the woman.

'No trouble. Could do with the company. Here on my lonesome nearly three days now, does your head in. And so lovely to see you again,' nodding at me. 'Two years ago, was it? That solstice party. All got a bit fruity as I recall.' She laughed and shook her head. 'Come on it. I'll brew something up, let me take a look, think I've got it written down somewhere, Rhodri's mam's address.'

'No it's fine,' Chris said. 'We'd best be off, not safe here by the sounds of things. And *you* know Rhodri's mum's address, right?' nodding at me.

I said I did. We told her thanks and set off to cross the road for the car.

'Don't go.' She'd come outside now, was padding after us onto the road with grey bare feet as we got into the car and I revved up, drove us off. Standing there on the road looking after us, still calling out to us, hands on hips, LOL t-shirt and leggings and bare feet in the cold morning.

'What the fuck are you playing at?' Chris said furious as we sped away. 'That's not Flora's place, where's Flora's place? Who was she, what is this?'

'What you think I was going to do? Take *you* to her, to her kids? I know the men who live there, who usually live there. I needed some back-up.'

'Fucking fool. Who's that woman? You know her?'

'Never saw her in my life.' We drove on, my stomach cramping. 'You think it's true, the chemical spill?'

'No. Who the fuck knows. Where's the real house then? Where you leading me now?'

'It's here, it should be here, a bit further up.' But by now we were beginning to head down the hill and Flora lived just before the crest and in fact now that I looked back I could see in the field behind us the fence and the trees and the swing and slide and some of Rhodri's caravans, old wrecks he bought and did up for fun, and Poppy's red bike on its side and the shed where Flora dyed fleeces and dried the roving. Just not their house, the red cottage at the crest of the hill. It just wasn't there. Every last trace of that cottage had gone.

12

'It's vanished.' I stopped the car, sat there feeling mad. Everything else was the same but it was like the house had been cut from the scene. And now only these new views of the hills rising behind the caravans at the back and where the house should have been just grass, fresh green grass, not even debris, like nothing had ever been there and the only habitation ever in that plot the breezeblock shed and those big dead caravans.

'Fucking hell, Chris.'

Flora and Rhodri might have torn it down. Something might have happened or changed, without me knowing.

Everything perfect, smooth, normal, except for the gone house. Their bikes and washing line.

I sat there gobswanged, wondering if I was on drugs.

He tugged his hoodie down low and tugged mine down low and sank low and craned round at where Flora's house should have been. Then he pushed my head down below the steering wheel and squashed on top of me, crouching us both down as low as we could, which hurt and made it hard to breathe. He pushed my feet aside to get at the pedals and turned the ignition and drove a bit like that, crouched on top of me, down the hill, further on, taking a turn to the right. He swerved and we stopped and I pushed him off.

Back in woods, of regular Christmas trees.

'I remember the shed from your photos,' he said, crouched low in his seat and panting, pulling me down again low with him. 'And the swings. I'm sorry. They do things like this. Yank up buildings, foundations and all, crane them away in huge trucks, normalise the aftermath. Replace it all later if they need to, seamless, back to normal, like nothing happened. When they really need to find things, check things, fine-tooth-comb, analyse from all sides. Load them into monster machines, probe in surround, three-sixty sniffers, heat sensors, infra-red. Crunch and model, interrogate the house. Nothing escapes them, dismantle everything, put it back together.'

I couldn't believe it.

'Whole houses? Whole houses don't fit in trucks.'

'You'd be surprised. Chop them up, slot it all back together, the machines plan it, the machines do it. Seamless, trivial, they got the bots, mega and nano. Have you been listening to anything I've been telling you?'

His whole crap turning out real.

'Where's Flora?'

'Probably fine. They probably...bundled her off before they got down to it.'

'Bundled her off? To Gwernogle? You think she might be there?' Them saying a chemical spill, getting Flora out the way to Gwernogle first then...taking the house? Whoever *they* were. I couldn't believe what I was thinking, saying.

He looked at me sadly. 'Maybe.'

'And that woman?' Margi. 'She said there were lorries.'

'She's part of it.'

A cast. Which sounded crazy.

Two Chrises.

Grag Medusa.

I could not believe it. I had to go back and check.

I watched the Christmas trees in neat grids in front of us.

What if it was real and they'd taken Flora and Rhodri and the kids? What if his whole crazy story was true and me blind to it because he was a twisted asshole I had to believe?

Breathe.

'They must have seen us,' I said. 'If they did this. They'd still be there. They'll know we're here. They're here,' staring round at the trees and sky and him.

His blank face. Not up to it. Like in Scritch, before, me more aware, better at it, picking up the clues.

'Let's go. I'll drive,' he said.

'Where?'

'Anywhere.'

'What about Flora?' No matter what, Flora was missing. If that house was really gone.

He shook his head. 'We got to go.'

'No.' I had to go back up there. I had to see it again.

'You'll get sucked up.'

I didn't say anything, just opened the door, stepped out of the car, slippers into mud. I had to go and find out what had happened to Flora and see it again, check if it was real with my own eyes. It was the maddest thing I'd ever seen if it *was* real.

He shunted over into the driving seat.

'Get in,' he said, motioning the passenger seat, his stump hand over the keys in the ignition. 'We're going now. Pull your hood down.'

'What about the book?' I said.

'They got it. They got the house, they got the book, they got the info, they got Alan. I fucked up, again. Let him down again. We've got to run. We'll work out where later.'

'But the book's not in the house,' I said, the car door open, him in the driver's seat.

He sprang out and grabbed me, 'Tell me now. Where's the fucking book?' the car keys in his hand.

I pushed him off

'Is this real?' I said.

'It's real. Where's the book?'

'Why do you want the book?'

'To decode Alan's Cuckfield message. Where is it?'

'At hers,' I said, the words just coming out. 'Or it was. Just not in the house.'

'Where?' grabbing my shoulders. 'You said you didn't know where she put it.'

'The bunker,' pushing him off hard. 'Jesus, Chris. I don't

know exactly. She said she put it in deep storage, that usually means the bunker, I wasn't going to tell you all that. But they probably took the bunker too, right? I don't know if the caravan was still there,' trying to picture the scene again, see if I could remember seeing the caravan at the back that the bunker was built under. Like there was any sense, that fucking house gone.

'What bunker?'

'Underground. That Rhodri built. For nuclear war, whatever. At the back.' Didn't seem so mad now, Rhodri's deal, why they were living out there like that in the first place, survivalists. More fool me for laughing at them. 'Under one of the caravans. She stores stuff down there, he doesn't want her to. They could be in there too, right?' I meant Flora and Rhodri and Poppy and the baby, suddenly seeing them huddled down there. 'Maybe that's where they went. When they heard weird stuff—this is exactly the kind of crazy shit Rhodri built it for, this is what he thinks the world's like, Jesus fucking Christ. But they'll have found it too, right? Your...guys? With their...probes, whatever.' Heat sensors, infra-red. 'Can they lift up things from underground? They might be down there, Flora. I'm going back.'

'We can't. You said. They'll be there.'

'I'm going.'

'I'll drive you.'

'I'm going to walk,' I said. 'They'll see cars. Crawl. Go low.' Scritch-style, prowling through woods. I didn't care if he came or not. Cut the lumber loose. He was nothing now, gone like water, other worries. I turned my back on him and set off, walking fast, alert, trying to stay low, keep to trees, stay practical up the hill on my pilgrimage through the gridded forest till I got to hers, where hers should be, trying to remember why Rhodri was so suspicious of the world, remembering Tal and his spiders.

He lolloped after me: 'What's this? More shit? You got people waiting for me up there?'

'I got to see if they're there. And maybe the book's down

there.'

'Or you're just saying. Who are you, what is this? You said you didn't know where she put the book.'

'Course I said that. I wasn't going to tell you.'

'You're telling me now.'

'Course I'm telling you now. Someone's nicked her fucking house.'

13

It took maybe ten minutes through the neat forest, who could tell, ragged breath, blurred green and mud, the pump of my blood. At the end was a wooden fence broken in places and a field beyond, their hedge ahead, impossible to see yet if there was a house. Beyond that was another hedge enclosing Margi's house, if that was still there. We crawled through into the field, edging round to the back of their land, away from the road, where the caravan should be, keeping down, slithering on our bellies on wet red earth, through rough cropped stalks, getting covered in mud, scattering jackdaws.

We stopped at the hedge and pushed our faces through.

Green grass, no red cottage, no trace. Where it should have been: lush regular lovely grass, too lush.

The wonder.

'Thick turf carpet,' he whispered next to me, 'laid over mess, you could lift it up, if you went close.'

I was almost glad, to see it again, that it was real.

Grag Medusa. Get a fucking grip.

But no matter what, this wasn't how the world worked, how I'd thought it worked. Disappearing homes, like magic. His mad chat spooling out true in front of me.

Two of them. Mr Debonair Finger-Perfect up in my flat.

'I'm sorry Chris,' I said, my side vision going black, my stomach cramping.

The caravan was still there, that the bunker had been under, not far from where we were: a cream and white run-down caravan you'd attach to a car. Rhodri liked fixing them up, guests stayed in them. But not this one, his secret hatch door, set out by itself towards the back away from the trees and their roots, facing away from where the house had been. In case of emergencies.

I edged forwards into the hedge, he pulled me back, listening for something, looking round, white and panicked.

'I'm going,' I said. To the caravan, to see if the bunker was still down there, if Flora and Rhodri and the kids were down there. To get closer, see what the fuck had happened, bow down to it, bear witness. I just had to.

'You don't know the risk.'

I didn't know anything, in this new world. But he was scratching himself through the hedge alongside me, wanting to come too, for the book. Of course he was. And maybe that was right, maybe there *was* a message from Alan reaching out to us to help, to make sense of this.

We burrowed towards the caravan on our bellies. The grass back here felt old, mucky, not newly-laid, solid in the earth when you tugged at it. Nothing seemingly around, nothing up in the sky. The caravan looked normal: no wheels, dumped on the ground, dirty shut curtains at the window. An old TV aerial on the roof next to a tall brown metal pipe poking up: secret ventilation for what lay beneath.

We lay on the old grass next to it. I looked at its base: metal stuck in earth, moss and grass overgrown round it, deep embedded, not recently cut-and-pasted. It seemed. He was fiddling about with the bottom of the door, trying to jimmy it open from the base. Then he leapt up quick and kicked the door down in one neat move, pulled me in with him, made us stay low, shut the door behind us, peered round quick through dirty windows and then inside at everything.

Brown, seventies, thick mildew air, stains and patterns sporing up your nose, down your throat every breath you took. Damp mouldy fug that felt undisturbed for ages, but what did I know, maybe they had sprays.

'What feels off?' he said.

So much in general but nothing I could see here. Everything like the one time I'd been there before, Rhodri showing it off.

A cramped run-down old caravan: bedroom and kitchen, old brown-stained mattresses, musty old bedding, damp. The hum though—the electrics still worked, was the giveaway: connected by underground wires by Rhodri to their generator that must still be working.

'Was anyone here?' I said.

He shrugged, went for the fridge, opened the door, stuck his head inside: 'I dunno. Nothing in here. That I can see.'

Except there was plenty inside that fridge with its light on: medicine bottles all neatly lined up, antibiotics and whatever post-apocalyptic essentials recommended to Rhodri by the internet.

'I mean: no messages. That's what they do: leave messages in fridges, if they've been, if they need to, for each other.'

'For who? What messages?'

'Them. Don. Messages to each other. It's their way. Every place has a fridge, or a cold box or a cold place where you keep food. Head to the coldest place, see if anyone's left you anything. Fridge-postboxes. It's a good system. Their version of Scritch.'

He touched his temples. He crouched down, wrapped his arms round his head, doubled up in pain.

'Chris?'

He crouched there rocking himself. 'It'll be OK. Give me a minute.'

The mushrooms, whatever, were back in the car in the trees at the bottom of the hill. I touched his shoulder but he shook me off. He rocked himself.

He took deep breaths and stood up slowly, his face red and sweaty. 'I'm OK.' He stood there breathing, getting normal.

Caught up in this with this malco.

I needed this over. I hooked the hinged beds up against the wall, he helped me. I rolled up the dirty old carpet and showed him the metal hatch door beneath, padlocked shut with a massive iron lock.

'It means they're not inside,' I said, a bad lump inside me. 'If they're inside they take the padlock in with them, bolt it from the inside. Unless someone's locked them in.'

We stared at the lock, me wondering how you could tell if it had been recently opened.

'Knock,' he said, calm now.

'You knock,' I said.

He looked at me, knelt down and knocked, the five and the six. No reply. He knocked it again. 'You know where they keep the key?'

Somewhere in the gone house. Or on the big jangling ring attached to Rhodri's belt. Wherever Rhodri was.

He got something out his pocket, a blackened metal wire he fiddled into the lock.

'What's that whirr?'

He pulled out the wire and held it to me. A normal wire. The end felt hot.

He shifted the lock out, yanked open the hatch. New smells of deep cool rot rose from the darkness. I knelt next to him, called down to them, felt the boom.

Nothing. Maybe the whole underneath was gone.

I called again down into that black well in the middle of the caravan floor. He pushed me aside, got a matchbox out of his pocket, struck and lit a match, threw it down the hole where it flamed the metal steps down before snuffing out.

'Were they there before?' meaning the steps. I nodded. 'You know where it is down there? If everything's still down there?'

He meant the book. That's what he cared about. Fuck Flora.

I shook my head.

'Tell me where she put it,' he whispered. 'I'll go check. See if they're there. You stay here, keep watch. Shout if you need.'

'I don't know where she put it. I don't even know it was here, for sure. Stay, I'll go down,' though I didn't want to. 'Give me the matches.'

'Who knows what's down there,' moving into the hole, shifting round, getting his feet on the slats, going down.

14

I went down after him. He stopped and reached up past me to lower the hatch above us and then latch it shut with the sliding bolt built into the door from inside. *Well noticed.*

Me and him on the ladder in the pitch dark.

He lit another match, whispered, 'Any other way in or out?'

'Not that I know,' reaching behind him to flick the switch Rhodri had built on the wall. It still worked. The bare bulb above flooded the place with light to show everything as it should be, not craned away. Like before: a big storehouse, the door to the other room, a sealed underground concrete box set into earth, enough stuff to support a family of four for six months or was it the other way round?

Them maybe above us now, ready to claw us out or seal us in. *Park it, for now. Focus on what's real.*

We moved down the ladder, him first. No sign of Flora or Rhodri. No sign of disturbance, but what could I tell: disappearing homes. Tins and rotting root veg in crates lined up against the wall. No apples—they gave bad gas, according to Rhodri. Supposedly you could keep root veg for years.

I was starving, not quite yet ready for raw swedes but getting there. No tin openers that I could see, they'd be somewhere. Chocolate and crackers and energy biscuits in sealed containers somewhere, I remembered that. Powdered noodles. Vats of water.

'What's behind the door?'

A second room, the kind of bedroom, also security: you could lock it from the inside. He opened the door, no one in there, but mattresses in plastic rolled up against the wall and Flora's big plastic storage tubs stacked on top of each other.

'Here?'

He meant the book.

'Maybe.' I flicked on the light.

He pulled down crates, rifled through fabrics, tools, yarns, weather proof clothes, tins, equipment, books, candles and matches wrapped in plastic, old baby clothes, old photos, dolls and crochet made by Jassy, Flora's mum. A torch. And the big green welly box I'd put my stuff in.

I lifted up the lid. Letters from him, old words in his scrawl. Bits from Scritchwood: some pics and Polaroids, a leather pouch made by Alan, my half of a broken horseshoe pendant. The big iron ring, small other bits I took after the fire. An old card pricked out in Alan's Braille that I could still read: *Happy Birthday Nimmywim.*

And the book, old, red, gilded.

He came behind me, snatched it from me, flicked through. 'The real one? Nothing torn out? Nothing different?'

Old book smell, rich pictures, creatures of our childhood: the well-dressed ape, the goose in her crinoline. The dedication to me, his biro scrawl, his eternal love. The stiff gilded cover, the marbled insides.

Birds, Beasts and Fishes
An Alphabet for Boys and Girls
Sixpence, or with the Plates Coloured, One Shilling

'It's ours. I think.' The same tears and yellowed tape, nothing fiddled with, what did I know? *Chris's* book first, belonged to his mum, according to Alan. And then *mine*, cos Chris gave it to me, with his eternal love.

I reached for it but he kept hold.

'Let's go,' I said. 'Take it all with. Look at it later. Take food. They're not here, we got to find them.'

He stood there with the book and the box. 'Let's do it now. In case we can't do it later.'

Waiting for me to do his work for him.

'You do it,' decode his Cuckfield message himself using the book. We'd both grown up with the book, right? We both knew how to work it. If he wanted to decode his message now here he could. 'You don't need me.'

'You know I do.'

His tired scratched face.

'Show me the message,' I said. Something from Alan, maybe. I'd be the judge.

'Didn't write it down. Lodged it,' tapping his temple with his stump, meaning he'd stored it somewhere in his mind bus, the mental image of the inside of Alan's bus that Alan had taught us to picture and make stories from, so we could store info there for Scritch, for other things. Very useful, later got me a law degree. Stories are stores, Alan said.

He closed his eyes and spoke from that place, recited what he said was the Cuckfield message, left by Alan's Scritch alias Leslie Snags in the visitors' book in the church in Cuckfield:

A sly bird, a sloven, two sweet singers, and a golden leaf. My second visit with Zita.

'Zita?' I said.

'Who's Zita?' shining the torch at me. 'Oh yes. Zita.'

But he never knew about Zita, that was between Alan and me. Later, when everyone else was too old for Scritch and Alan and Chris had fallen out. Zita stories Alan used to tell only me, about a girl rescuing her magician dad from imprisonment in the Fortress of Zoll. I'd never mentioned them to him, I was certain.

'Do it. They'll be coming,' he said, whoever he was, me locked down there with him underground behind the disappeared house, his gaunt face and its angles.

'It's easy,' I said. 'You do it.'

He slumped, so tired, poor him. He picked up the book, shaking his head. His hands trembled. 'You don't understand.'

14

He flicked through all the pages. He smiled. 'The first one's J. The sly bird's the Jackdaw, I'm right, aren't I?' pointing to the picture of the jackdaw in schoolboy cap and spotted neckerchief.

He was right:

J is the JACKDAW who looks very sly
When I trust him I hope there'll be somebody nigh

The sloven was the stained Elephant with pipe and books:

E is the ELEPHANT, and very few
Are so learned, so big, and so slovenly too

The sweet singers were two Nightingales in crinolines crooning at a piano:

N is the NIGHTINGALE singing a song,
I'm sure I could listen for ever so long.

And the gold leaf was the Yellowhammer beating metal bars at his three-legged stool:

Y is for YELLOWHAMMER, a goldbeater's name.
He hammered the gold leaf that gilds papa's frame.

'J.E.N.Y?' he said.

'J.E.N.N.Y. Two singers.'

'Jenny. Right. And "my second visit with Zita?"'

'Jenny 2.'

'Jenny 2?'

I looked at that blank, whoever he was, locked with me underground. 'You know.' He should know. If he was *my* Chris he'd know all about Jenny 2.

'Stop looking at me.' The rage in his white face under the

neon. '"Should", riddles. They fucked with me. I'm not who I was.' Then his face changed. 'OK. I know. I remember. From the map. Of course.'

'What's the map?'

'Still testing me,' shaking his head. 'Come on, let's go. Alan's map, from the bus, that we did Scritch off. Alan's Chinese map of the inner body.'

'Alan's Chinese map of Britain,' not the inner body, which this stump Chris ought to have known. Alan's treasure map of when China ruled Britain thousands of years ago, that he taught us the geography of Britain off, that he told us stories from and that we used to map on the land when we played Scritch outside in the Fall and other tangles of woodland down by the water. Where the White Road came from, for fuck's sake.

'It's a map of Britain but it's also a map of the inner body,' he said, closing the book, putting it back into my green box with the other stuff, putting the lid back on, putting it under his arm, moving back into the big room. 'I'll show you. It's in the car.'

'Bollocks,' I said, standing there. Nothing was real. No way he had that map in the car. That map got burnt with most of the rest of Alan's things the day Alan vanished, when Young Pete set the bus on fire.

'I got a copy, in a book, in the boot. It wasn't just Alan's map. It's a thing. A Chinese chart of the inner body, called the Neijing Tu. A Daoist chart, Chinese religion, you know, like the Tao and I Ching? Daoists don't think it's a map of Britain, they think it's a map of…energy flow inside the body.'

'It's a map of Britain.' It looked just like Britain, who was he? I had to get out of there, I couldn't be down there with him.

Poke his eye. Kick him in the balls. One swift blow.

'It's a map of Britain too but dumdums don't know that,' he said. 'Even Daoist dumdums. Come on, we'll work it out in the car.'

But we didn't need to work anything out. We already knew — I already knew—what Jenny 2 was.

'It's a place, right, Jenny 2,' he said, watching me close. 'Of course,' he said, as if things were clicking. 'Kraton's barn, where Kraton was born, the Ickthwaite Barns, where the Lost Royals go if Kraton disappears, where the Lurkers leave messages, where the troll is, that Enbarr the horse guards. Ickthwaite, which turned out to be a real place, which was where, in the Lake District? Which Tal found out. Where we were supposed to go, where we nearly went, when Alan went AWOL. We had this message before, didn't we? Alan left it in the shed when he vanished. Right?'

Right. That bad day looking for the old man, going down to the shed, knocking the five and the six with no reply, smashing down the door, finding nothing inside except a message on red paper: this same message, 'Jenny 2' without the Zita bit, just that, waiting for us there. Left by Alan we supposed. Us so confused, Chris saying 'but we're already in Jenny 2', cos when we played Scritch we pretended Alan's shed was the Ickthwaite Barn, your place of last resort, where you went if things turned bad. And Tal saying 'well maybe it's a real place too, in the Lakes', cos that's where Jenny 2 was located on the Chinese map, and us looking it up on Ann Wynn's Atlas of Britain and finding there *was* a real Ickthwaite, on Lake Coniston. And me and Chris going to New York instead.

I'd even been there, after New York, which he probably knew, useless looking for traces of Alan. A pretty old stone village on the banks of Lake Coniston. A red post box in front of a done-up jumble of barns like in Scritch, a big house where the troll lived in Scritch, a big locked gate I couldn't open. An old woman in the cottage next door telling me the family were away.

But that wasn't the only Jenny 2, right Chris? There'd been another one too, that only he and I knew about, that he and I'd made up, back when we were first at it and needed some place private, our own world away from everyone, the broken house he'd found. The actual smashed-up shell of an old workman's cottage by the water almost at the start of the town, kind of on its own island, with a staircase you couldn't go up, the broken house of rubble we cleared and started calling Jenny 2 to fob off others. *Later in J2.* The mattress on the ground. Which this stump thing with me ought to know.

'Come on,' he said, the scar under his eye ever so slightly different in the harsh light it seemed or did it? reaching over to pat my neck so my hairs stood on end.

'How come you got a copy of the map in the car?' in my new high voice.

Get out. Hand in the pocket for the car key, up the stairs, run.

'Just a hunch. I knew I might need all Alan's things to... decode any messages he might leave me. I've come to know the map's part of it.'

So why not know the Jenny 2 right off? 'And now you got the Alphabet too.'

'*We* got it.'

'And you got me to decode things.' I had to get away from him and his grip. 'If you've got the map with, if you knew you might need it, why didn't you know what I was talking about when I said "Jenny 2"?'

'I forgot. They fucked with my head, I'm not who I was. Understand,' taking my hand, making me touch the top of his head, feel the big dip in his skull under the hair, under the skin. 'They took stuff out. A while ago.'

Me frozen there, fingering the hole in his head, him holding my green boot box under his arm. Him with bits missing, and me locked down there with him, something wonky from their underground labs?

The hole was a perfect circle, machine-tooled, cut out of his skull under the skin.

I tried to pull my hand away.

'You got to believe me,' grabbing my wrist, pulling me close.

'Else they've got us, don't fall for it. It's you and me trusting each other or they win. Fuck knows it's freaky, you're freaked out, course you are. We'll talk but not now, we've got to get out of here right now, see if we can't find some trace of Flora.'

'Grag Medusa.'

He looked at me. 'No frighteners, I swear. For real. Come on.'

'What are the rest?'

'Of?'

'What heroes need.'

He sighed and shook his head, looked deep into me. 'A Grag Medusa: a frightener, to distract. A flying horse to make you fast. A cloak of invisibility. A knife to kill. A mirror to trick. And the eye, so you can see into people and can't be tricked. Look at me. Stop testing me. I'm old bad me. Under a shitload of extras.'

Something massive crashed down above us. We froze, he let go of my wrist, put his finger to his lips. He switched off the new torch then killed the overhead bulb from a wall switch and crept into the big room and switched off the light there. I followed him.

Absolute blackness, something above us, mushroom air. He reached for my hand. We stood there frozen, straining for the slightest sound for a long while. Then he began to edge forwards, inched us blind to the bottom of the cold steel steps. We stood, listening to our fast breath. Otherwise absolute silence, nothing more from above, him next to me, them ready to what? Gouge us out?

He pulled his hand free, I grabbed for him. He pulled free again, pressed my shoulder down as if to tell me to wait there, put his foot on the first step, waited to see if his weight would make it creak.

He inched up, going where, with my box and the book, to join them? I stood there holding the bottom of the steps, feeling the shake as he climbed up away from me with the green box under his arm and his solved message to do what? Leave me down there? I'd be able to breathe, there was air, the caravan pipe ventilation. There was food for a year if it was just me, I'd go mad or get hoisted away, carted off in a lorry, snatched in the claws of some huge machine. I started to climb up too behind him. Then a new noise: him sliding the bolt, trying to raise the hatch door.

'It won't open,' he whispered.

I joined him with dry mouth, short breaths, pushed up at the hatch with him. The bolt was open, it was the door that wouldn't budge, something huge and heavy blocking it.

Trapped down there with him and his missing bits in our new home.

Bad panic in my stomach, I was sweating. 'Is it...them?' I whispered

'Dunno. Push.'

Push and find what up there? But we couldn't stay trapped, had to see. We pushed hard together from the top of the steps, then pushed again, there was the slightest movement. We strained, he pushed his shoulder against it and together we inched it open, felt the weight of whatever was blocking us shift and slip slightly. A pale slit of light lit up his eyes. He held up his stump, made me stop, together we listened. No sound of anything or anyone except us.

'Hello,' he said, eventually.

Nothing.

He forced the door up a little wider. New cold mildew air, more light, whatever was blocking us being pushed up by our force.

'The bed,' he whispered, putting his head through the gap, forcing the hatch up more. 'One of the beds fell down.'

I could let go, let the hatch snap down on his neck.

But I didn't and he pushed up more, waist-high, showing how one of the beds I'd folded up against the wall, hooked securely in place with the fitment, had slipped down. He was looking round the caravan from our gap in the floor sniffing the air.

'The door's open.'

A scuttle.

'It's a cat.'

Tigs, their orange cat, scampering off through the open caravan door the moment she saw us emerging.

I pushed past him, squeezed through the gap into the mouldy humming empty caravan. No one else there. That I could see. Maybe they were outside. I wanted to go outside, find Tigs, hug Tigs, could Tigs have pushed the bed down? What was physics, what was possible? I didn't know anything anymore.

He came up behind me, folded the fallen bed back up against the wall, refastened the hook, whispered: 'Are you sure you did it properly before?'

Pretty sure.

'Look.'

I crawled to where he was, looking out the open door to where he was pointing: something stuck to the hedge at the back that we'd crawled through, a white bit of material the size of a pillowcase with a red diagonal line drawn down it.

'Fuck,' he said.

Red on white: the red warn, the sign of danger in Scritch. You made it with whatever you could, with your own blood if you had to, drew your finger down something pale. You saw that sign in Scritch it meant one thing: get out now.

'Was it here before? Is it new?' he said.

'Don't know.' Too much information, my poor brain. The hedge was behind us when we'd crawled into the field. I hadn't looked back, I didn't think, no reason to look back.

A coincidence, could it be? Some daub by Poppy.

'Let's go,' he said.

The red line diagonal, pointing down.

Sometimes you drew them so they pointed down at buried stuff.

I set out, he tried to hold me back but I crawled out of the door and back down into the outside and the grass, away from that caravan, crawled up to where the pillowcase was on the fence and started scabbling in the freshly-dug ground there, digging a hole in the place in the earth where the red diagonal pointed, a place that someone else had recently dug. Let them find me, I didn't care. I wanted to see them.

My fingers hit something hard. A red plastic pencil case decorated with white kittens. A box,casket or other object hidden in the earth, like we did in Scritch, that we called 'terma'. Secret messages Alan hid round the place that could tell you massive information, words that were clues, sometimes coded up using the Alphabet. Or pictures. Or another object that meant something. Or who the fuck knew.

He was next to me. 'What is it?'

With dirty muddy trembling hands I yanked it open, the zip getting stuck on something: a folded up bit of paper I pulled out, him right next to me, peering over. Inside: a note, lined paper, torn from a notebook, ragged edges, Flora's handwriting, if they could disappear homes they could fake handwriting, would be watching us right now:

Gone to stay with Jenny for two weeks.

15

I crouched there holding the note in my dirty hands. The same instruction, the world talking to me. Really playing Scritch for real. In which case: what should I do next?

Blow this unholy place.

Get out now, away from red warns, find a safe space to think in, get my bearings, with this note, that Flora might have left me. A trail laid by Alan—or someone who knew Alan's games.

Where is safe?

The big question, there by the hedge in the middle of nowhere with stump Chris, the bunker and gone house behind us, the note in my hand.

Find some clump of trees, go back to the car? The car they must have seen. The Dons watching us right now, me with him, the forgetful glitcher with the head hole clutching my green box who'd read all my emails, looking just like the Chris I'd grown up with and crouched next to digging up clues when we were kids, knowing just a little bit less than he ought to. Jackdaws, the grey sky. I crouched by the pillowcase with the note. No map, no sense of where we were. Flora nowhere. All the old rules gone.

Talk to me Alan.

'Back to the car,' he said.

Get out while you can.

It started to rain, fat splodges. I mangled the splattered note back into the pencil case, did one last look back at the blank and went back through the hedge, him with his holes alongside. *Park him for now.* Down on my belly, snout to earth, feeling like the trees and hedges could scoop me up any moment, casting my mind wide. Cased back through the years to try to find stories to help me, my brain calling out into big emptiness, everything I'd tried to park back with a vengeance and me not remembering enough. *SOS.*

Move.

We slithered on the wet red earth through the cut crops, getting scratched, the rain getting heavier, bare minimum cover, heading for the trees as soon as we could: more cover and shelter, those regular evergreen firs. Running down through Christmas trees drenched by plump splats, the world tilting, rain sliding down my face, blinding me.

Towards the car, which had maps and food and clothes and shelter. If it was still there, full of them. Leap in, close the doors, the window that wouldn't close, speed away, winnow out the ten thousand thoughts later. Or else what? Crouch here drenched in this new world I didn't know, head for the hippies, no idea where we were, ripe for plucking?

Flora.

Jenny 2. Scritch. Training. Telling us sideways. The Corpse Dog Clan. Zita, that I'd never mentioned. Nodding along in the evenings, keep the old man company, Ann Wynn and Clarice, thinking about Chris. A weird childhood in a weird place— teaching us ways and codes now of use versus secret world rulers? *Tell me Alan.* Alan maybe out there, drawing me in? *Don't let him down this time.* My whole ridiculous life having some purpose and meaning after all. If only I'd listened properly.

What was this? What was my life? What was the world?

I stood frozen by trees in the fat rain, it was like being on drugs.

Mushrooms.

So cold and wet and scared and tired and jittery.

He was with me, wiping rain from his gaunt face with his stump hand: 'You OK?'

'What have you done to me?'

He shook his hooded head.

'Did you drug me?'

'No. Come on.' His eyes, scar, desperation. He pulled me close to him so I felt his warmth and smell and fast-beating heart keep pace with mine for a moment. 'I'm me.'

He grabbed my wrist and yanked me down on behind him through the rain. We saw the flash of white that was the car. We stopped. Something known, away from the rain. Escape. But.

'Are they here?' I said, great splashes drumming through my thin anorak, my mud-drenched socks and slippers, the tang of earth and pines rising up, him holding the green box under his anorak. 'Have they been here? Why haven't they found us?'

'Maybe they have. Maybe they're watching us.'

To see where we went next, what we'd do. Blurred fear, so creepy: hidden audiences, solving clues for them.

He pinched into my wet hand: *NEED NEW CAR.*

Get out. Any direction. See what happens. Work it out later.

'Drive,' he said, handing me the key.

Slamming the doors, closing off the outside and the rain. Anorak and sodden slippers off, wet socks, pushing my wet hair out of my face, backing away, driving us off in any direction, speeding up hills, squeaky windscreen wipers pushing off torrents, him pulling off his wet hoodie and t-shirt to fug the car with heavy B.O. His pink stump on the atlas planning backwater routes, craning up at the sky, telling me not to drive madly, trying to give me directions.

'To where?'

'North, to Ickthwaite, you know we are.'

I didn't know anything.

'How do we know the note's really from her? Why would she go there?'

He shrugged. 'They sent her a message too. Or she sensed something wrong. The "chemical spill". Or Sean turned up pretending to be me, she didn't like it, cleared off up there.'

'To play Scritch for real?' After all this time. 'She didn't take the book.'

'She didn't need it.'

'Who are you?'

'I'm Chris,' looking at me square, stump to nose. 'Please believe me. What can I say? What do you feel?'

Skidding there in the rain on those windy roads I tried to feel him, see inside. It felt wrong. But everything felt wrong. And it always felt wrong with Chris.

The big wet empty land, only black jackdaws watching us. That I could see. Rain beating down and into the car with us, empty Welsh countryside, no way of knowing anything. Me sounding mad the moment I tried to tell anyone any of this.

'Tell it to me,' I said in my wet clothes. 'The whole thing. From the start.' Then I'd make up my mind. 'Tell me the truth. If you lie I can't help you. What is this?'

'You know what this is. You always knew it. Nothing's real. The world's a lie. Don's in charge.'

'And you're Don's clone and Sean's your clone and Alan stole you and might be alive. What's Don up to? What does he want?'

'I don't want to tell you things they could cut out of you.'

'You'll tell me everything, Chris, if you want my help.'

He put on dry clothes from his back seat store, told me I should take off my wet clothes, put dry stuff on or I'd get ill.

'I want to go to the police,' I said.

'The police aren't the police, don't you get it? Even if they were, what we gonna say? "They stole her house"? Flora's told us where to go, we're going there, to Alan. We only trust us now. Fuck the police.'

'We don't know it was her who wrote it.'

'The same message. We're going.'

'What about Tal?'

'What *about* Tal? I told you: they'll have him by now, he'll be strapped down somewhere pumped with blab juice telling them everything.'

Telling them Scritches and red warns and terma.

I wanted to stop and call Tal's hospital, check. But there was no way, he said: 'no phones, not even phone boxes, specially calls to Tal'. And anyway there *were* no phones, there was nothing except rain and trees and hedges and fields and streams and stone walls and hills and jackdaws. And then a sudden new bad feeling out there in the nowhere.

'Is this real? Is this drugs? Or are we...is this...some' — what? Cooked-up Silicon Valley nightmare, us in headsets in some California lab, cut-and-pasted houses, tall tales, new product beta testers, can you ploy the person who least trusts you? 'Better not be.'

'This is real. You can feel it. You can always tell.'

It felt real and wrong. But what did I know: disappearing homes. What Alan used to say: if you have to ask if it's a dream then it's always a dream. This wasn't a dream, I knew it wasn't. But I was still asking.

'What's all this about?'

'It's about the old knowledge.' Stump to nose. 'What people used to know. The fragments from...before.'

'Fuck off Chris.' I reached across, tried to open his car door and push him out onto the road. We swerved into a bush, he pushed me back and grabbed the wheel. I pushed him off.

'I'm telling you,' he said when we calmed. 'It's about things from the deep past. That you don't know, that dumdums don't, that Don wants. Secret knowledge, about the world. For Don to feed his machines. That Alan used to forage for. For Don. Go left,' because we were at a junction. 'Look,' pointing ahead. 'What do you see?'

Some tiny country back road, single lane in green nothing. Hedges, trees, fields, dead periwinkles in dry stone walls. A stone ruin atop some hill in the distance.

'Yeah what's that?' he said. 'Ruined castle. Pretty. Bet it's got a nice tea room. Who built that castle?'

'Don? Fuck off Chris.'

'Not Don. The English? The Welsh? And who *are* the Welsh,

exactly? All those "warlike tribes"? So many old castles and forts in Wales. Can't go five minutes without banging into one: Norman, Roman, Iron Age, Bronze Age, older, all over Wales and west Britain at the mouths of rivers, high up, controlling the land. Crumbled now but still there in plain view. Dumb land, overgrown secrets. Guarding what? What's here?'

'Fuck off Chris.'

'I'm telling you. What's Britain really? What's Wales? There's clues. What's the symbol of Wales? What d'you see everywhere, signs, flags, pubs? Dragons. And what are dragons, really, in Wales, in China, everywhere, George and the dragon?'

'You saying dragons exist?'

'I'm saying dragons are code for something they don't tell you about what this land is, marking the land if you can read it. Guarding treasure. Fire coiling up through their bodies, blazing out of their mouths. Dragons are volcanoes. And all these hills?' nodding out the window at a line of hills next to us, the ruin now behind us. 'That you think are hills? They're volcanoes. Or they were once. Now they're extinct, chuffed out. Everything here? That you can see? The whole west coast of Britain? From Cornwall to Shetland? The husks and plugs of a line of dormant volcanoes, cooled goo from inside Earth. Full of metal. Very useful. Top secret. That's what Britain is: the fire line. Beyond the wind, off-limits. Hyperborea, they called it, in those myths you think are Greek. Treasure island, secret land of the dead, where heroes slay dragons, where Oillipheist the dragon lives, where Jason stole the Golden Fleece from a sleeping dragon, where monsters get turned to stone.'

'Steady,' I said, looking for the mushrooms.

'Britain,' he said, 'west Britain and Scotland? Stashed up to the gills. They tell you about water rivers, horizontal, but there are vertical rivers too, some even have names, on maps that aren't for you. Fire rivers bursting up from the sludge they say we float on. One long seam from when the land got stretched and cracked. When it pulled apart to make the Atlantic. That's always pulling apart and pushing together, making different oceans and mountains again and again, very slowly. Like Earth is breathing.'

'Don't get lofty.'

'When all this was underwater, millions of years ago. Britain's rare. It's not like that in other places, France. France is limestone, dead sea creatures. Can't make swords and cell phones out of that. Except the very west of France, Brittany. And west Spain and all down the Atlantic coast, where the volcanoes were, before the crack shifted. Celtic places, Phoenicians or Venetians. Iberia, Hibernia, the Hebrides, Hesperides, Hyperborea, the Hebrews. Where the stone circles are, all the way down into West Africa, from those so-called cavemen of so much earlier who hoisted their massive immovable stone circle maps into the earth from Nigeria to Iceland, to show the next guys where the treasures were. Signposts tattooed into the land for privileged eyes. Laid by metal-mongers, from way back, with deep connection to the land, sifting it for ingredients. People from before, with deep animal knowledge of the world, who got wiped out, almost wiped out, left their traces if you can read them. And whoever told you any of that?'

'So what?' Tech, secret internet: fair enough. But this pseudo-ancient—what?—geology?

'You're dumb. That's how he likes it. Understand: west Britain's got the shit to rule the world. What Gold and Bronze and Iron and Silicon and Bio Ages are built from. Packed into these hills here: portals to the inside. Imagine what it was like here once: heavy nuggets lying around, before they got snuffled up. Your matter of Britain right there. Inner goo. Imagine when people handled the gold, picked it up, turned it into coins and jewellery, felt the weight of it. Before the Dons locked it up, palmed you off with plastic. Golden apples—gold has properties you know nothing about. Not on the syllabus, not for you to know. It's for you to dig. Still is. His slaves. Why's everyone in Britain called "Smith"? The stuff they still dig up here, bleach the land dry for, things you don't know, not in your periodic table, so much you take on trust. How many elements are there really, what are their powers, have you tested it? Wi-Fi, TV, radios, electricity: how does that really work? Do you know? Do you care? Can you build a computer? Can any dumdum? What goes on down the Works-Only access roads? What's in all those lorry canisters, oil drums? What's really going on with the wires, windfarms, pylons, cooling towers, power stations sucking up what from the gash? Look there.'

16

He was pointing to something out of his window: an isolated farm, a house and some barns, rusty machines at one side. And a dirty old blue Ford Fiesta parked next to them.

'Perfect,' he said and made me brake. And then jumped out of the car and, keeping to the edge of the fresh green field, crouched low and made his way to the blue Fiesta and stole it, with his useful wire I guessed: opened the door, started it up, drove it slowly through the field towards me in the car, drew up alongside, engine humming.

'Drive behind me. Quick.'

The new car he wanted, to cover our tracks, in case they were on to us. If they ruled the world then they'd be onto us. But I did what he said, followed him in the white Nissan for maybe twenty minutes down the single-lane empty road, turning off into something more foresty by a lake.

It had stopped raining. Nothing but nature, no signs of other machines or humans, not even a track. We halted the two cars among trees and piled all his stuff out of the Nissan and into the new filthy dumb car which smelt of manure. Flora's note and pencil case, rank clothes and burkas, the green box, the duffle bag, plastic bags and sleeping bags, crusty rugs, bits of tarpaulin, damp maps, the atlas, books, his mushrooms, big plastic water bottles, his big heavy sticks, apples, chilli plant, plastic cups, packs of mouldy white sliced bread, the rest of his worldly goods. And four or five licence plates: he unscrewed the Fiesta's with his wire and replaced it with one from his stash, put the old plate into the Nissan's boot. Then we managed the Nissan through thick trees to the steep bank and heaved it into the water, watched it splash and sink.

'They mustn't find a trace.'

I lay on the bank knackered, feeling bad and starving, aching all over. I was filthy and damp. I went behind a tree, wiped my hands with leaves. He gave me dry clothes to dry myself with and a pair of his jeans that were shiny with ingrained filth and much too big for me. I put them on, rolled up the legs, pulled a long rag through the waistband as a belt, bunched up the waist and folded it over.

I tried to squeeze water out of my slippers, it was useless. He gave me more socks and I layered them up. He gave me plastic bags and told me to tie them over my socks as makeshift shoes which would make it hard to drive, slippy on the brakes. But maybe it was his turn now to do some driving, in the keyless new car only he could ignite with his hot wire, my brain gone.

I sat on the ground trying to get red earth out from under my nails and cuticles with bits of twig. He tossed me something out of one of his plastic bags: an oldish Chinese paperback, poor quality, flimsy cover, but inside good coloured plates. He made me flick through them till I came to the one that was a reproduction of Alan's Chinese map.

'They call it the Neijing Tu. It means Map of the Inner Flow. A body and Britain.'

I stared at the familiar picture, smaller than Alan's, the details hard to see but I knew them in my mind. A Chinese painting of Britain with the west exaggerated, Cornwall, Wales and Scotland the main zones of interest, Chinese people busy at work all over the land, ploughing and spinning, downwards Chinese writing at the side. Jenny was a person, Queen of where Wales was, a Chinese lady with the hair and silk dress, sat at her wheel spinning red yarn which spooled up from Wales over and underground to northern Scotland where it wrapped round behind a mountain to emerge as a rainbow enveloping Bill and Ben, Alan's names for the wise old men playing ball on either side of Loch Ness. But before Jenny's red yarn reached Scotland it flew over the two main bulges of the north-western English coastline. The first bulge was kind of where Liverpool and Blackpool are—we called that first bulge 'Fylde'. The second bulge was the next bit north: the Lake District, known in Scritch as 'Furness'. That's where Kraton the centaur was born, in a place called the Ickthwaite Barn, which turned out to be real. Jenny's second bulge, Jenny 2.

He gave me apples and bits of stale bread, water from a big plastic bottle, chillies, a pack of mints from the new car. Then he scabbled about by trees and dug up tree roots, shaved them with his knife, brought them to me, told me to suck them, packed with nutrients, something else they didn't tell us, better for me than my ready meals, even the posh ones. Telling me this was how he'd lived for months after his great botched escape.

Tough bitter roots, they weren't doing much for me. He brewed Nescafe on his stove, sparked the flame with flint, metal and dry grass in a tinderbox like Alan's, poured in sugar from a plastic bag. I drank it from a foam cup, Flora's note in the folded pencil case jammed into my new jeans pocket, watching him and his survival skills.

'So who's my mum?'

He shrugged.

'Why do they clone themselves?'

He shrugged. 'To pass it on. To live forever through us. To set it up for the future, bypass nature, maximise us, long term. They're always at it, cloning, their way, before the tech. Pharaohs marrying their sisters, ruling classes marrying each other, keeping the bloodline. Don's just perfected it—or his grandpa before him. Don's a clone too you know. The tech trickles down to dumdums in the end.'

We got into the new old farm-smelling blue Fiesta, he drove us away over dragons. I sat there in the passenger seat with the Chinese map nestled open inside the atlas on my lap, the green welly box at my feet, my dirty grey face in the mirror.

Two Chrises, gone houses, books, games, red warns, codes, boxes full of messages in tree hollows, Scritches where we had to spy on Covert newcomers, report back to Alan, the cogs of the past meshing together. The old man sitting atop his treehouse, watching out for what, or wrapped in sleeping bags on the torn Chesterfield outside the bus, warming his hands at the brazier crammed with his lit scribblings, making me remember his bus off by heart. The Corpse Dog Clan: relentless enemies bent on total destruction, seeking to find all the terma then torch Britain. Ann Wynn hanging the washing in the backyard facing the Fall. Rain beading down the windows of *Merriweather* on a grey winter's afternoon, some pale stew on the hob, me staring out beyond the fence to the bus, Chris and Alan inside. 'I got nothing for you.' Tracing my finger up Jenny's red yarn instead of the atlas, spooling north to merge with the White Road past Bill and Ben up to the mountains of north Scotland and the big crystal on the map there. Which was what, according to him, if it was also a map of the human body? Was Scotland the brain? The old man reeling me in.

When I woke up we were back in the world on a busy motorway. The M6, the signs said. He was nudging me.

'We need petrol. We need to eat. I need a break.'

I stretched: stiff and sore. A double-sided service station ahead of us, an old one, built on both sides of the motorway, linked by an overhead bridge. We took the turning into the car park, drove round slowly, parked towards the back by the berm. I unbuckled my seatbelt, put my left hand on the door handle, to exit. But he took my right hand and held it and pinched: *SOS*.

17

We sat there.

THEY HERE, his left hand pinched into my right hand while the rest of him did other things: looked at me, smiled, told me he was sorry how crazy all this was and we'd be with Flora soon, he could just feel it, I shouldn't worry.

NOD, his hand pinched while his mouth said he needed food, petrol, a wee.

I looked round to try to see who or what he could be talking about.

STOP, he pinched, meaning I should stop looking round, and jolted his right arm just a fraction so I could see his right hand in his right jeans pocket bunched up and moving as if it were writing something inside the pocket.

STOP, he pinched, meaning I should stop looking at his hand writing inside his pocket, and he carried on writing or doing whatever while his mouth told me he was so glad to be with me after all this time.

I sat there, holding his hand, doing nothing, us having our moment to all intents and purposes, to anyone watching from cars or via CCTV or a drone or things hidden in trees. A large Asian family got out of their hatchback, lots of children. He was still writing or doing whatever in his pocket, this Chris-not-Chris with the hole in his head.

'I'm starving,' he said. 'Service station burger, you want one?' giving me a big smile. 'Food of the realm, I can stretch to it, this once, fortify us,' his ridiculous coin sticks. 'Put the burka on, cover your face, hide from the cameras, no bolting. You promise, if you go to the loo?'

Going to the loo without him. Out of the car, back with other people, built places, back in the world. A burger I could certainly deal with. A burger and a realm service station and a read of whatever he was writing, if he was writing something. A warm full belly and the eye on whatever new spin this was. Then we'd see. People all around.

'Be natural,' he said, looking at me, meaning all sorts of things.

I pulled on the burka over my hoodie and big jeans and plastic bag shoes and got out the car, watching for watchers. Innocents in bright clothes bumbled about in cars, chatted on phones, headed inside for burgers. *What I've seen*, I wanted to tell them, my realm fellows. *Scritch was real. Disappearing homes.*

He pulled his hood down and got coins out of one of his sticks, then locked the car doors. We walked together in our odd outfits, joined the throng. He reached for my left hand with his right stump hand as if we walked hand-in-hand now, as if things had changed between us, a tight high feeling in my throat, the fear and special knowledge. He passed something into my left hand: a wad of paper from his pocket, spooned my fingers tight round it as if to say *don't read yet*.

'Desperate for a wee,' he said.

Into the mill of other people and shops, gaudy plastic, screaming children, magazines, fast food, wires, cameras, infra-red, the people on their phones. I clutched his wad in my hand. Neon, cashpoints, massage chairs, the hum of machines, blank kids hollowed by games. Me not running to them, feeling estranged and in his separate story, secret danger. A number well done on me? *Read the note, let's see.* Twelve bad hours, maybe, since he'd come for me in my flat, it felt so much longer. We glided for the loos, he gave my hand a last squeeze, turned left for the Men's, set me free for the Ladies', his note in my hand.

Bright white walls, warnings of a male attendant, women coming in and out of cubicles washing their hands, doing their make-up, tending to children, chatting on phones. *Guess what about dragons*, I wanted to tell them, the slit of my eyes in the mirror, cameras above the tampon machines.

Inside the cubicle I opened his note. Bad pencil scrawl on two cramped pages of torn lined paper, words written on top of each other cos he'd written it blind in his pocket in the car.

They R on to us. Being followed. Pinch not speak. Bugging me or car.

A white van, did U C it? Since B4 Chester, you asleep. Saw inside, know the guy, one of Don's.

We R fucked. They R seeing & hearing us.

Can't let on that we know.

May have bugged my eyes or skin. Tech U don't know about. Trust me please. Don't write or speak 2 me, real things. Pinch or nothing. I'm contaminated. They may C & hear through me. Don't speak real.

We drive on like we haven't twigged. Stop pre Ickthwaite. I write U new note then, say what next.

I have plan.

They need us, what U know, how 2 find Alan.

Never speak it or write it to me. Pinch only. Like I'm them. Don't let on. I'll just speak ancient history to U, nothing of interest 2 them. Do what I say, 4 Flora & Alan. Please.

Now tear this up, flush down loo.

We just parked & van parked next to us. So I'm sure now. Check it out when U come back if U don't believe me, bet it starts up when we do, follows us all the way.

So, reading this, sitting there on the loo.

At least there was some external truth validation possible: the white van, checking it out when I came back.

If I came back. *Do a runner.*

To where? Up to Ickthwaite to find Flora and maybe Alan? Find some way to do that before he did, get some car, get clawed up by some machine?

The maybe, just maybe, that he was telling the truth.

Letting Alan down, before, disobeying messages. Being closed and smart and glib, being dented and cloudy, at the end of my tether, exhausted.

Keep it simple. Look for the white van, wait and see it with your own eyes, see if you think anything's following you. Then decide.

I tore up the note, flushed it down the loo.

He was waiting for me outside the Ladies: 'You didn't run?' Grinning but extra desperate behind his face now, scouring my face to see if I was swayed. He took my hand: *FLUSHED?*

YES, I pinched back.

'OK?'

I nodded. He stuffed a fast food bag at me, took my hand, pulled me on through plastic and neon to the outside. 'Eat up,' he said in the car park, giving me his new secret look: eat up, we need strength for what may come, this might be our last chance, our last meal.

'OK,' I said about the food—at least he hadn't prepared it, 'at least it's not mushrooms.'

'You wish,' he said. 'This muck?' holding the bag. 'Don's population control.'

I tugged down my veil and shovelled the slop down right there, wolfed the steaming grease and chemicals, stuffed my face with tumours as we walked back to the car. Parked right next to us: a dirty white van. And dirty, it seemed to me, in a way I'd seen before, the streaked lines. But I couldn't trust my memory, I couldn't trust anything.

NO LOOK.

But I couldn't help it, and then had to grab his hand hard because a figure in a black anorak came from behind past us, went over to the van, unlocked it via a remote key, opened the door and climbed in, shut itself off behind tinted windows. Someone not recognisably tall or short, thick or thin, male or female, whose face I hadn't been able to see hidden in their hood.

The Chris yanked me towards him, made me walk with

him away from the van and car so we sat on the berm for a bit finishing the mulch together while the van sat there. As if we were having another new special moment together, instead of it being because he didn't want me staring at the van with the black figure inside.

We sat there for a bit eating, not looking at the van.

The van didn't move.

NO LOOK.

FLORA IN VAN?

DON'T KNOW.

We finished, got up, threw the wrappings away, went back to the car. He was talking stuff about Don and burgers and ready meals and dementia and rats' arses and phone radiation and sperm rates. Whatever came out of his mouth didn't matter. What mattered now was pinching and eyes.

He could be working with the van.

He unlocked the door and we got into the car and he started up the engine and we drove out of the car park and on to where the petrol was. And he got out and got coins out of his sticks, the whole rigmarole, and the dirty white van sidled up and parked near us to one side, not by the pumps, as I seemed to remember a white van had done the last time we filled up, near Reading, when the old woman scratched me. And he went and paid and the van sat there and I tried not to look at it, and he came back out and started us back up and the van started up too and drove out onto the motorway behind us and kept itself alongside us and drove close by us with dark tinted windows as we drove on north in fretting silence to Jenny 2 up the crack.

18

At Preston we turned off the motorway and took small roads following signs to Coniston and then Ickthwaite into the hills, slate, walls of the Lake District, the white van in the rear-view mirror all the while. He took my hand: *IS OK.*

My time before, my useless post-New York Alan guilt-tour, I'd taken the train to Ulverston and then a couple of buses and some walking among sheep in the sunshine. Now he drove me up the road I'd walked on a different day. Grey skies, fields, drizzle, drenched earth, stone, lakes beyond reeds, steep hills, small crooked trees crippled by wind and weather, purplish slate on the ground and roofs. The built things here were made of the land, no plastic, only washed-out colours and birds and sheep. Stone walls locked together without cement: 'mini-Stonehenges' he said, 'last traces of the megalith builders'. The lake to our left, the hills to our right.

'Volcanoes?' I said, to swab the fear.

He nodded. 'Undersea volcanoes, the ash got forced down under big pressure here to make slate. That's why the Japanese love it round here so much,' nodding at Asian tourists milling round a parked bus, 'even if they don't realise it: Japan's the Lake District in a few million years' time, all those earthquakes, built on the live crack that surrounds the Pacific. Here's a taste of things to come, for the Japanese, once their hot dragons die.'

'Look,' I said, feeling worse, because the tourists were taking pictures of something on our left: a huge metal sculpture of a horse in the field next to me, facing the lake. Which hadn't been there when I'd visited before, I was totally certain, unless I'd walked a different way. And this was a horse from Scritch: Enbarr, the biggest horse in the world, protector of the Ickthwaite Barns, who crushed intruders under his hoof.

Again the cold rising feeling, tanged with old Scritch flashes and the aftermath of burgers.

'Is this real?'

'It's bronze,' he said, stopping the car in a lay-by to look, letting the white van drive past and off into the village ahead of us, telling me the horse was a piece of art, a modern sculpture.

I looked at him.

'Enbarr,' he said. 'I know.' It wasn't warm but he was sweating.

'Give him the sign,' I said. You made a circle with your finger and thumb to show Enbarr you were friends, so you wouldn't get crushed.

'Don't test me,' he said and reached for my hand and pinched MAKE FUSS so I did: asked him for Ickthwaite details from Scritch, made him do the sign and tell me about Enbarr and Bugg the giant troll who owned the barn in Alan's stories, the huge milk churns you could hide in, the red post box that marked the Lurkers' secret entrance from their underground world. What was he saying, I said: 'The Lurkers are real, midget messengers really do live in mazes of ancient tunnels under Britain?'

Britain was honeycombed with secret tunnels, he said: 'better believe it'.

And while this was going on with our mouths I could see his right hand bunched up in his jeans pocket writing me another note.

He took my hand. GET OUT he pinched so I did: opened the car door, said I'd had enough of him and needed a wee, marched into the field to look at the horse and crouch in reeds in my billowing burka and unfurl, discreetly, the note he'd palmed me. And from out there I could see the white van, parked in the next lay-by, waiting for us.

Nim, his scrawl said,

We're looking for Flora but if we find something else they'll B watching and I can't B let near it or they'll see it too. I'm tainted,

100% sure. So U do this alone.

I'll distract them. Don't worry about me, been waiting 4 this a long time. End of my road & I'm fine w/ it. U + Alan & F is all that matters now. Finding A or what he left, making U all safe.

When U come back to car, this is what U do. Tell me U don't trust me, U don't want me anywhere near U. That whatever's here, U R going 2 do it alone, find Flora, some message, whatever. I want U to say U've had enuf of me, U don't trust me, that's it, your only interest is finding Flora, U R doing this alone or not at all.

I'll play along, try persuade U, make U take me w/U. Fight me, don't let me, it won't B hard 4U! Let me come with but don't let me see anything, stand me well back. & don't write anything down. If U find smthing memorise it then tell me U want a coffee. Then we work out what 2 do next. We R only of value 2 them if we know things they don't. That's how it works 4 them. I'll write & pinch & talk ancient stuff. Distract them. Don't worry about me. I'm fine w/ whatever happens 2 me. I deserve it. U + F + her fam + A are all that matters.

Tear this into tiny pieces & bury in ground.

Which I did, crouched among tall reeds in the field.

I went back to the lay-by, him leaning by the car, munching his nasty mushrooms, looking grim, sweating though it was cold.

'OK?'

'I don't care about any of your crap,' I told him. 'It's only about Flora for me.'

He gave me the tiniest nod.

I did what he said: told him I didn't trust him, that whatever was coming up I wanted to do alone. I'd carry on but only to find her, I didn't want him near me. It came pretty easy. He did his bit, tried to 'persuade' me. He lied and acted well, I noted. We got back in the car, drove on a bit, came to signs for Ickthwaite. No signs of Flora or the yellow campervan. We passed the red post box, the Lurkers' entrance in Scritch and then on the other side of the road, where I'd been before: a metal plaque fixed to a dry stone wall: *The Barns.*

A farm once, these would have been the outhouses, now done up. Where I'd been seven years before, where we were supposed to come twelve years before, me and Tal and Flora and a Chris who was maybe him.

We parked, I got out, shooed him away, as per his script. I told him to wait for me, that I was going looking for Flora and didn't believe his Alan-alive crap, that whatever else he was interested in was of zero concern.

I crossed the road and stood shivering in front of the big iron gate in my burka. Last time this was as far as I'd come: pushing the locked gate, failing to open it, the old lady in the house next door. This time I pushed the gate and it opened. I stepped onto shingle made of purple slate.

I was in a courtyard of several converted barns with a set of small workers' cottages to my right. No sign of Flora or anyone else. I knew this place. Not because I'd made it through here before but because it matched the Jenny 2 shed layout Alan had built at the bottom of the Fall.

I looked back. Him leaning against the car on the other side of the road, hoodie low over his face, his arms folded, looking at me, looking skanky.

I closed the gate and turned back to the barns.

The two biggest were straight in front of me, joined together, painted black, fully-renovated: someone's house, corresponding to the biggest pile of logs in Alan's Fall version. In Scritch: the home of Bugg the giant child-eating troll who slept all day and roamed at night.

All the layers of this.

Trying to remember.

It was about 3pm I guessed, the light already low on the horizon. Coming up to the shortest days now and we were quite far north. Probably about an hour left before Bugg woke and went roaming, according to Scritch, who or whatever Bugg was in real life, if Bugg existed in real life.

I didn't want to find out.

Old fears of being shit at puzzles, of not being able to solve things, standing cold outside, the fading day.

Flora.

To my far left was a run-down barn with a huge rotting door chained with a padlock, Bugg's storeroom in Scritch. Between it and the troll's house was an open roofed area of chopped logs and jumble, the milking shed in Scritch, corresponding to where Alan's actual real shed had been when we'd played, the only real shed, the one he'd lock himself into, that you could only get him to open if you knocked that five and six. Alan's shed had four walls and a door but this one was open, no knocking necessary. In Scritch: the place where Kraton the centaur was born and where Bugg milked female centaurs and laced their milk with potions he got drunk on at night and slept off during the day. This was also where the Lurkers hid their messages in a three-chambered casket buried deep in the straw, using Bugg's presence as deep cover for their activities. If there was a message here—from Alan, from Flora—this was where it would be hidden.

Are you talking to me, old man? You or someone else?

In Scritch we used Alan's strongbox as the casket, stuffed under his messy desk. A metal strongbox with the three compartments.

I went over and had a rummage. Old furniture, bad art made from Coca-Cola cans and rams' skulls, a huge gilded mirror reflecting black-robed me ferreting around. Rotting armchairs, a rusty pram filled with pine cones, bundles of twigs and brooms, a plastic clothes line and pegs, an old fridge, various chairs, an old white dressing table with three drawers. No sign of Flora or Alan or anyone. No strongbox or casket.

But an old white dressing table with three drawers.

I stood before the junk, a priestess at the altar of a religion I didn't know.

Letting who act through me?

The slate crunched behind me: him come through the gate from the car, leaving the gate open which was silly surely.

I didn't say anything. I didn't answer any of his questions. I told him to get lost. I meant it. He fiddled round with things in the shed, opened the empty fridge, poked around in it, for traces of *them*, must be. Watching me but leaving me alone.

I went over to the white dressing table. I opened the drawers.

In Scritch all three compartments would contain messages but two of the messages would be bogus: decoys to fuddle the enemy. You'd know which of the three messages was the real one by a sign that would leap out at you when you saw it, if you'd been following Alan / Kraton's previous game clues correctly.

Each dressing table drawer was crammed with junk but each contained an identical postcard of Manhattan, stamped and addressed but not sent, from someone called Judy, telling three different people about the fun she was having in the Big Apple despite the rain. Three different people, three different addresses, waiting there for who knew how long, for twelve years perhaps or recently planted, by who? For who? For me?

Barry Clyde
120 St Sepulchre Street
Scarborough

Marsha Devens
217 John Kennedy Street
King's Lynn

Betty Fields
226 Vengeance Street
Barrow-in-Furness

I ran my fingers over their surfaces. No pricked out Braille, which Scritch clues were sometimes written in. The New York skyline of these postcards was recent, no Twin Towers. Instead: the new replacement building. Which was finished when? Five years ago, perhaps.

'Want a coffee?'

'Maybe,' I said.

In each of the drawers were other things: coins, trinkets, pins. And then I saw what stopped me.

In the Vengeance Street drawer was a child's pink bead Hello Kitty purse, identical to the one given to me by Tal perhaps two years earlier, which Tal had found in his hospital, he said, with a note inside telling him to come and visit me and give it to me.

And where was Tal now?

I picked up the purse. I opened the zip. Inside, heavily tarnished, was Alan's half of the broken mini horseshoe pendant, what looked like Alan's half.

Hello.

The question was: if Chris saw that broken horseshoe would he know what it was too? Probably, but just a little bit delayed, was the pattern. Because they'd fucked with his mind, cut his head open. He said.

But if he wasn't Chris, if he was something else, a twin or clone who'd never played Scritch or grown up with me in the Covert, someone relying—somehow—on second-hand info leeched from Tal or humming in from Antarctic servers, then wasn't his whole 'they're-following-us/I'm-tainted/You-do-it-alone' a brilliant ruse to get me to do what he needed, snuffle out his info for him without me testing how well he could read these clues himself?

But the van. Parked where now, turned back, heading for us?

But he could be working with it.

Whichever which way: so much planning, so many people involved, had to be.

Unless he'd run up here before coming for me in London, seeded the country with nonsense for me, for no clear reason.

Disappeared homes all alone?

Fed me drugs.

Cooked me up in some underground lab.

I held the half-horseshoe in my hand.

He was looking at me and the purse, the purse he wouldn't know because it had been Tal's, or one just like it.

Where was Flora?

The eye.

226 Vengeance Street. I lodged it mechanically in my mind bus. Twos were the white china swans on Alan's cardboard mantelpiece, sixes were the battered golf clubs he kept with umbrellas in a carved wooden elephant's foot by the side of his front door. The club smashed the swan, it lay on the blue patterned floor wanting vengeance: simple.

'I can't find anything,' I said, holding the purse. 'Just junk. I'm tired, Chris. I need a coffee. Where's Flora?'

'I don't believe you,' he said, a flash of private double meaning in his eyes. 'You've found something, haven't you?' ever so slightly wooden, coming for me, taking my hand, gripping my wrist with his stump hand so I couldn't move, pinching my palm so lightly, snatching the purse, finding the broken horseshoe, looking sharp up at me, putting his stump on my pulse, looking into my eyes, looking into the drawers, his fingers still clutched tight. 'Yes you have. What is this, what does it mean?'

A woman's voice behind us: 'Hello?'

I turned. An old woman, crunching down the slate towards us, from out of Bugg's house—the door was open. An old woman with a cane, poshly dressed.

'Are you the police? Is it about the accident?' she said in sharp London tones, staring at me, her cane decorated with painted flowers and topped by a brass knob.

Central casting.

'What accident?' I said. The Chris was pulling at me.

'Who are you? What are you doing here?' the woman said, but it wasn't threatening.

'What accident?' I said, feeling that's what I was supposed to say. The scene had changed into something heavy, I could feel it from both of them, 'Chris' and the woman, playing off each other. *Not good enough actors.*

'The family in the van,' the woman said, coming closer. The Chris was pulling hard at me, trying to get me to move with him towards the gate, pulling his hood down. I pulled back.

'Come on,' he was hissing. 'Don't,' his white face and dark eyes trying to say something. 'It'll be their trick.'

'What family?' I said, playing my part. Let him run for the gates.

'There's been a tragic incident, I'm sorry to say. A man... gassed himself and his family in a campervan overnight just down the road from here. A woman and a little girl and a baby, truly dreadful. Estranged husband, they're saying. What makes them do it, I don't know,' shaking her head.

Oh really? Where was I, what was happening? *Too much info.* It felt completely wrong.

Sirens, two police cars screeching up from opposite directions to stop at the gate.

'I'm sorry,' the Chris said, 'but we have to go now,' pulling me while the woman watched.

The police, in their black, getting out of their cars, coming through the gate, walking in unison, coming for us, talking to the woman: 'We'll take it from here.' The Chris ran off, left me there. The 'police' grabbed me, dragged me out through the open gate towards their waiting cars. 'No,' I said, because from out there in the road I could see what hadn't been there before: barricades closing off the road ahead, police lines and cordons around a yellow camper van parked a hundred metres down from the Fiesta by the field side, their rainbow stickers in the back window, four sheeted shapes laid out on the road in front of me, two big, one small and one tiny, Poppy's blue bunny at the window closest to me.

Was it what it was supposed to be? The 'police' pulled me towards a car.

A shriek and then Chris sprang at them from low in the bushes next to us, whacked them in the knees with a coin stick wielded from above his head, whacked one of them on the head. I saw blood, a crumpled face. That was real. They buckled, let me out of their grip a fraction. Chris seized me, pulled me, tore me back through his bush into the field beyond twisting us up, clutching his head. He pulled me on through bushes and mud while I screamed, pulling me on and through and past bog and reeds beyond the sirens towards the lake and the setting sun.

19

At the water's edge was a green boathouse with a wooden boat and dark water for a floor. Inside he slapped me till I stopped shouting or doing anything. Nothing seemed real but something terrible was happening. Noise and glint of police with torches and dogs.

He forced me into the freezing water and under the boat. I thought I'd die. He yanked me up, the noises were gone, he put his mouth to my freezing ear.

'Can you remember what you found? Don't say, keep it in your head.'

He bundled me into the boat in my wet clothes, pushed us out of the boathouse into the lake, hoodie right down over his face. He rowed and kicked me quiet. The oars, the wind in the reeds, screeching things. It getting darker and colder, the helicopter overhead. Everything was really happening, his screwed-up terrible face forcing us faster over black water in the fading light.

We hit something.

'Now,' grabbing my hand, pulling me out and under, tipping the boat so it was over us and we were treading water with only our heads above water under the boat and I could only see his outline in glittered flashes, clutching his head. He grabbed me and moved us nearer the bank so we stood on plants with the upturned boat over us, chest deep in water, going numb, swallowing water, dragged by my hair, slapped over and over to make me shut up. His fingers jammed into his temples, jabbing at his ears with something, a knife, till they bled. Him whispering it was OK, we were escaping for real this time, he was sorry, this was what it took to escape them, me just beyond. Twisting himself, the glint of his knife, scraping his knife all over his face so it bled, a blunt shave, no more top layer. He held my hair and with his other hand sliced his clothes off with the knife like cutting skin, peeling a banana: his hoodie and t-shirt and pants, pulled off his socks and shoes, came with the knife for me and did the same to me and all my clothes, the layers, my hoodie under the burka, my jeans, my bra and pants, skinned off fast by the knife, cutting me while I gagged on lake and ex-clothes sunk in freezing water mixed with our legs.

'We have to,' doing something over and over to his leg underwater in the dark next to me that made his body shudder. 'Shut up,' holding the knife to my neck, sticky with his blood.

He jerked the knife over his bloody face and body again. He hacked his hair off, lifting up tufts, binding my legs to his under the water. Then he did the same to half-drowned me: sheared me bald with his legs knotted round me, ran the blade over and over my head to scythe the last bits off, cut my head, cut my eyebrows and eyelashes, gouged me, scraped me all over, inside my ears, whispering how sorry he was while I bled and snorted water, told me he was wiping *them* off, then cut me deep on the thigh with the knife in a 'V', a bad down-and-up.

He let go of the knife and it glittered down.

We were naked in the freezing water under the upturned boat, missing skin layers, covered in blood and hair and ribbons of clothes, going numb. I could hardly see him, he was panting, it was freezing, every so often patches of light dappled bad sights through the water, pure fear, no control. He ducked us underwater beyond the boat, into the open lake, his hand round the back of my neck.

He forced something vile into my mouth: a cut piece of rubber tube, thick and sandy. He pulled me down, forced me to stay underwater as he dragged us forwards through the lake away from the boat, forcing the tubing back in my mouth when it came out, forcing me to learn to use the tube as a snorkel, the only bit of us to poke through the water surface. I swallowed lake, choked, blacked out, half drowned, was numb so couldn't feel my hands and feet getting torn on rocks and plants at the lake shallows he was forcing us through. Underwater, bleeding, shorn, naked, cut, breathing water in through the tube, spluttering half-dead, pulled down and on by him, doing this for numb time till he yanked me out.

20

I came to sneezing naked in the dark on my belly face-down in a deep bed of reeds and mud under trees somewhere on the lake bank, his weight on top of me, shushing into my neck, noise from machines and the ground juddering from things flying overhead. The long thin lake—I knew its shape from the mouldy atlas worlds away. We were slathered in mud, he'd caked it on, covered my whole skinned face and body while I'd conked out. I tried to shift, he pressed down.

The shudder of machines passed. If they didn't come soon with their dogs it was bad, he whispered after a long while—it meant they'd found us already and were biding their time, waiting to see what we did. But we couldn't risk being clever, we had to move on now in the dark up the stream, cake more mud on as ours got washed off, paltry defence.

He whispered how us being cold made it harder for heat-sensing tech to track us and that the mud and water would mask us from their dogs a smidge—there was still no tech to beat dogs in the matter of really tracking people, he said, not yet.

He stuck his fingers down my throat and made me puke. 'In case there's things inside.' Then he slithered us up the rocky creek on our skinned bellies very slowly, cocking his ears at wild noises, sniffing close to my ear, grabbing the back of my neck, stuck to me with puke and mud.

A terrible bleat and something ghastly turned its grey face to us: a woken sheep.

I came to face-down shivering in a bush, covered in new mud and leaves, away from the lake, in a moonlit forest. He was near, in the ground, doing something. He heard me stir, came over, shoved sharp dry berries and what he said was tree fungus into my mouth: good for me, he said, vile jelly. I couldn't stop shivering. He forced me up, whispered I had to help with what he was up to which was digging a hole in the ground for us to hide in. I stank, so did he, we were naked and caked in new mud which smelt of shit, which *was* shit, he said, in part: precious deer or fox shit he'd gathered and smeared us with to mask our scent from dogs till it wore off, by which time we'd be in our hole if I'd now help him dig faster.

I couldn't do anything: I was mad, skinned, half-dead, caked in shit. But he forced me to get up and dig, told me work would warm me and there was no choice, gave me a big stick to dig with, kicked me when I lay down or tried to get away, kicked me till I dug like he said, his calf trussed with vines to staunch the stabs he'd done to himself in the lake.

It was cold, bare, still, clear, a big moon and stars between the trees.

'Their setting,' he said. 'He controls the weather. Best conditions to find us, the slightest ripple. His liquid crystal ball.'

It was a hole in the ground about three feet deep, seven feet long, four feet wide, for us to lie in. Our grave, smeared with shit to guise us, covered by big branches he'd found, these covered in turn by the dug earth and that covered by moss and fallen leaves to look natural. Sturdy enough to be driven over, he said. He tied two logs together with vines and leaves to serve as our camouflaged door. We'd breath through vents he'd made round the edge.

He forced me down. We lay naked covered in filth next to each other on the leaf floor he'd mingled with shit to muddle the dogs. He replaced the door, we lay in damp earth together.

He'd gathered berries, mushrooms, fungus plus leaves and twigs and roots he said we could eat. Water was easy, would collect on bark he'd put under the vents. We'd be fine, he said. Wait it out here a while. He was used to all this. This was how he'd lived before, waiting it out in holes on the run till they caught him. You got used to it. People in Tibet sat in pitch-black caves for twenty-four years to gain enlightenment, he'd seen them. Tranced you out, took you to a higher state.

He was really sorry about all this: Flora, the baby, Poppy, Rhodri, me in here, the lake and escape, cutting off my clothes and hair, skinning me, coming for me in the first place, dobbing me in it. For now I should put all that out of my head. I was so right about him, he was a desperate fucking freak, selfish and bad from the get-go, born under a bad star, would be the death of me. He was so sorry I'd got mixed up with him now and in the past. He took my hand and pinched how sorry he was.

IS OK, I pinched. I was sure he had good cause.

I zonked out the first few days. I was basically very ill. He wrapped his mud poo body round me to warm even though it was warm and sticky and fetid in there and worse each day from what came out of us that he scooped up with leaves and buried on his side. I lay there with my thick head filled with stench. Things sometimes walked over us: animals, people, dogs. They didn't find us or perhaps they had found us and were tracking us. He could hear helicopters, drones, other machines I couldn't hear though sometimes I could and felt the earth shake with their whirr. He said Don had tiny drones the size of flies that whizzed through trees to spy and kill, that the new black ladybirds I'd surely seen everywhere the past couple of years were Don-made snitchers brewed in labs, that bats and birds got hacked and mated with tech in their eyes and brains to serve as Don's agents in wild places, that atom-sized armies combed Earth, ready to mince at Don's command.

He hadn't told me all this before because he hadn't realised the extent of the deployment, that it had happened already, the flicked switch. And he hadn't wanted to worry me, or seem mad. It sounded so sci-fi but was true: this was the world. I had to know everything now, understand why we were here, buried together, running for real. He wasn't mad. Wake up to life outside the realm. Things were not what they seemed. I had to open myself up to that, everyone did, or else risk massive regret at the point of death, when you realised you'd wasted your life living a fake life, your one chance. Wake up, this was real. And death was close to us. It was a human right: to know the lie of our lives.

We were lucky we could still escape, or still had the illusion of escape, he said. Soon even holes in the ground would be accessible to Don. Every square inch of the planet, above and below, that was the plan. It had already started: nanocams, mini camera-sensors smaller than salt speckled everywhere, tiny self-replicating biodegradable robot cameras laced into petrol and scattered out of planes, cars, drones, helicopters, the white lines in the sky salting the whole earth, making everything visible, fibre-optic yarn wound round the ocean floor, getting pulled tight. Don's trillion trillion eyes cooked into plastic, glass, gluten, nylon—Earth's new coating, Don alert to every vibration, everything come alive and pulsing back to Daddy through his techno veins.

That's why the burkas and hoodies and all that shearing and shaving and scraping us raw in the lake, paltry defence. That's why we were naked, under our shit, though probably still encrusted with the nanocams Don smeared everywhere, over people and hair and clothes and trees and animals and shit. Definitely in towns and cities, soon in forests and holes in the ground, borne down by soldier-ladybugs, worms, roots, grown into trees.

'Hope for the best, plan for the worst.' As Alan used to say.

Did I remember the message or whatever I'd found hidden in the drawers in the barn? I could talk freely now, he said and pinched: it was OK here, no nanocams down here in the dark yet, he hoped, they couldn't hear us anymore though maybe they could though he'd gouged out his tracker. He knew I'd found something in the barn, did I remember what? Had I stored it in my head, lodged it like Alan taught, my useful mind bus that had garnered me a law degree? Could I visualise what I'd found now? Would I tell him? Could I remember the Alphabet off by heart? How about the Chinese map? *YES OR NO?*

Bad about Flora. Who knew what had happened there. Might be real: was their set-up but could have real dead bodies in it too, to really freak me out. He was sorry.

They'd operated on him a while ago, some bollocks about a polyp in his calf they needed to cut out as cover for the insertion of the tracker he'd found and gouged out in the lake. Kind of them to even pretend: usually they zonked you out, did their deeds, woke you up none the wiser. Nanocams were random but trackers were for life, unless you dug them out, ball and chain. That's how they'd been on to us, he now saw, or else via a million other devious ways. But now the tracker blabbed from the bottom of the lake, our ritual offering. Now we were free. He hoped.

Except we weren't. They'd have things inside him still, probably. And him my only tainted last hope. They'd get us by his innards. And mine too by now: my inner roads patrolled by Don's tiny troops, the old woman's pink nail.

But they hadn't got us yet. Or at least weren't showing themselves. So we were going on, no matter what, against the odds, blazing out, like the sun, like they did in olden times. Burn your fuels in glory, no eking out. The big fuck-you, the freedom we all have inside us even if it kills us. Like rocks stars, that's why dumdums love them. Thumbing your nose. Honour, valour, wit, seduction: the old values. You do what you want till they drag you away. You don't do their work for them. Right?

Yes, they had the tech of trackers inside you using the fizz of human cells for their electrics so they never ran out of juice, unless the host died. So much tech I didn't know. Cross-breeds, trans machines: the realm would get it all in the end. Tech trickled down to the dumdums eventually, most tech. Mobile phones since World War One, that kind of thing. How did I think we'd won world wars or had empires or any of the rest of it?

Pure black tech magic veiled from dumdums, now focussed on me and him, the missing vectors. Something dark had glommed onto us then lost us. Now it wanted us back.

We were lucky: we could still hear them. They'd operate in total silence soon. We were at the cusp. All that magic in books, that Alan had ever told us, Scritch things? Objects appearing out of nowhere, cloaks of invisibility, wands, seven-league boots, like in olden times? It was starting to happen again, Don's way this time, Don's man-made way. Could I feel it doing its maths?

What had Alan mentioned about the old magic? What had he said about the good and bad, that people once knew, that Don was on the hunt for to crunch and render? Had Alan mentioned a jigsaw, the missing pieces? This poor Chris whispering into me in our grave couldn't remember too much of what Alan had said, what with his nasty times and missing head pieces, the poor brain-mangled thing and the dip in his skull which I touched as I lay next to him, smoothing his stubble, feeling the soft hollow, the perfect circle of bone cut from the top of his head with skin grown over like a drum, a soft spot I could jab open to rummage through wet and find out who or what he really was.

'They say it's good for you,' this hole. An ancient practice: 'trepanation'. 'It's different after. Old stuff means less, whatever dragged me down, took me out of the present. I never forgot you, though. I'm not the same person I was.'

I didn't believe all that crap about civilisation starting in Mesopotamia or India, did I? No dumdum did, in their bones. Knowledge kept from us: walls of mega stones slotting perfectly together in Peru. A different knowledge, that something happened to, or that did something to itself with its knowledge. It stripped and shaped hills and rivers, brought trees and livestock, sailed the world. What we knew when we were animals, a body of knowledge starting then: the sky and plants and stones and magnetic lines, global paths, that got wiped out, a line drawn under. But bits of it surviving in our version and in remote places, songs they chanted. Powerful knowledge about the world and what it did, that Don wanted to snuffle up at all costs.

Keys, fermentation, booze, bread, glass, trained dogs, metal, big stones, maps, world trade, world travel: the things that are always there. The oldest pyramids were perfectly aligned, the biggest and the best. Indonesian cloves found in six-thousand-year-old Sumerian graves in what was now Iraq alongside blue stones from Afghanistan and black obsidian from the South Pacific half a world away. Cocaine and nicotine from South America preserved inside Egyptian mummies. Underground cities deep below Turkey. South East Asian yam trees in West African forests. Indonesian megalith hills that are twenty thousand years old. The oldest part of Rome being the sewers, they sailed battleships down there thousands of years ago. Ancient tech we still couldn't replicate even with Don's machines: hydraulic power, massive pyramids built high on cliffs, lugging those huge stones up there. The knowledge of the before-world, everything better the further back you went, the brilliant solutions, mega engineering. The golden age, everything downhill. Everything the wrong way round.

Animal knowledge, physics as instinct, your soul hitched to universal waves. He'd seen it himself first hand, teen holidays in Polynesia, conquering the Pacific alongside master sailors with no tools except their bodies and senses, navigating via their inner computer: the wind, stars, smells, the colour and patterns of waves. Encoding that knowledge in stories and movement and chants and shanties, passing it on that way, though it was dying out, like everything else. People as living libraries. Monks chanting sutras for eternity up high mountains, forget the server farms. You lose it when you start to write it down.

Plant knowledge, from the reptile brain. Knowing the stars like migrating birds. Sniffing our way round. Our lost birthright.

Dragon-hunters, reading the lay of the land, barrelling down those White Roads, snouting out the pots of gold.

Logic was just one take, right?

The long journey out of Africa to Australia and the now-drowned continent that Indonesia and Malaysia are the tips of. The journey from supreme ape to cultured human. The skills you'd have to learn, and learn to encode so you could pass on, the user manual for the planet. Better make those stories memorable. Like Alan did. Was I starting to see?

Chickens are their supreme art. Stupid flightless egg-layers, bioengineered food machines, perfect portable protein factories got that way on purpose from regular birds who laid once a month and could fly away. 'Centaurs,' because that's what centaurs like Kraton in Scritch really are: half human half beast, people who've retained their animal knowledge. Magic people—because magic is just deep knowledge of nature. Dangerous knowledge: where to press. The properties of everything. And what are plants to dumdums now? A whole bank of knowledge cut out of you and bits sold back to you as products, medicine. The taboos put on individuals with too much knowledge of nature: witches. Cut it out of you. Don's cutting projects.

'Every dumdum knows magic once existed. They crave it: their books and movies. They knew they'd been duped, the de-enchanted world.'

Once: astral travel, energy paths, ley lines, Santa and his reindeer flying over the world on wind superhighways, riding the veins, nerves, chakras, inner body of the Chinese maps which weren't Chinese but were much older. Once: a nose for magnetism and direction, human homing pigeons, feeling. Now: any fool with a cell phone. Everyone telepathic with headphones. You engage with a computer, you're engaging with something man-made, that something like you built to trap you. But engage with nature and you mess with something built by something bigger than you, you can be deeply altered.

Don wanting all that for himself.

Don would say: that knowledge is dangerous, it destroyed things once, you can't risk it in the wrong hands. Maybe he's right. And maybe it's good, after disaster, for the survivors to say: let's reset from here, build it twice, forget the past.

But you can't build good on a lie.

Things always getting wiped out. The bad deal we're at the sharp end of. Meteorites smashing in, other natural forces banging bits of land together, causing mountains, forcing up gold, splitting to make oceans or craters, wiping out the weather, killing everything. Life on the planet was so fragile no matter what we liked thinking, whole cultures razed in one second, not one trace left. Who really needs that kind of knowledge? Don would say.

Near total obliteration, the slow picking-up-the-pieces, our wrong world built on top. Scattered fragments remaining, the survivors locking away their knowledge in islands or high up on mountains away from fault lines, doing their chanting.

Indian Ocean cowry shells in Yorkshire Stone Age graves. Babylonian star observation records going back three hundred thousand years. Orbs and sceptres: they always knew the earth was round and that you could strike it. The Great Pyramid in Giza, with a latitude in metres that's exactly the same as the speed of light in metres. Massive terma, secret messages from the past, cooked up by old sages to survive disaster, metres are an ancient measurement proportioned to Earth's dimensions, no matter what they tell you. See what they knew then: direct transmission blasting whatever current story, the lies.

No phones down there, that I could see, no way for me to check. I'd have to take on trust, this secret petrifying history of a world and its destruction that Don had told him, that Don had burnt into him, that he was burning into me in our rank hole, about the old knowledge and what it had done.

Had Alan ever said anything about a number, got me to store

it? What was all that about terma, buried messages from the past Alan taught us to locate? Had Alan mentioned apples? Any immortal apple orchards in Scritch? Apples in old stories were code, did I know? For terma, metal, other treasure. Him and me, caught in Don's terma quest, buried in the world.

Don chasing apples of knowledge to bite into as per the Garden of Eden and we all knew how well that had panned out. Britain was the land of apples, Hera's immortal apple orchard in Anglesey, once called Mona, after Manannan Mac Lir, the Celtic sea god, who also gave his name to the Isles of Manhattan and Man. Avalon: land of apples and Apollo, who ruled Britain once under many names, as Don did today. Apollo visited Avalon every nineteen years, which is the exact amount of time it takes for sun and moon rotations to match up, as he was sure I didn't know but that Don did and had taught him. That kind of knowledge, about rotations, had been cut off from dumdums by Don and the Dons. But rotation was important: governed plant growth, weather, Ice Ages, tides of water and melted rock seas, ran your inner ebb and flow.

He held his hands over me and told me some people and animals could feel for metal ore underground, sense vertical rivers, and those people were called dowsers and could find metal as well as water and dowsing worked and dowsers were employed right now by Don and every mining and oil company in the world. He told me you could dowse over a paper map as well as over land but not via computer screens with their other energies, and you could dowse over bodies and sense sickness and lies. He said dowsers were an ancient caste trained from birth to maximise their natural talents and that castes were a left-over from the deep past when people were bred like dogs and other animals, mated deliberately to enhance useful natural attributes by masters of nature with long-term plans.

He told me that pub names meant things: The King's Head, The Royal Oak, The Red Lion, that everything meant something, if you could read, even the placement and type of trees on the land, and from the way dumdums talked you'd have thought they knew everything but they knew nothing and it was petrifying knowing more, being on the other side.

Dogs on the scent, like the so-called Normans, Romans, Celts, Napoleon and Alexander in Egypt, the Chinese, the Mongols, the so-called Phoenicians, Rosetta Stones, crusading knights not after Jerusalem or Constantinople or Baghdad but after the knowledge stored there, scraps of ancient scattered power they found bits of, taught them how to build cathedrals, the maps lodged there, ways to America, Bolivian silver, ancient copper mines of Michigan, locations of Welsh dragons, goo knowledge, the treasure in the hills. The Arab library in Toledo that the popes got their hands on. Why did I think Iraq got invaded? The library of knowledge saved from the Mongols that Don rediscovered under the sand in Iraq, had to get his hands on. Don on the scent, snuffling it up.

Don's machines, crunching every library and codex, squeezing the juice, building the model. His Doomsday book, Project Knowledge, Project Jigsaw, knowing more than anyone in the past eight thousand years. There was an event once, they caused it. We live in its scattered embers. Him and me had to stop Don lighting the flames again. Would I help? *WHAT U FIND IN DRAWER?*

How ever long of me shitted up next to him listening to this? Or drifting off into the space of my childhood, back in time to Scritch and Alan and Zita and Corpse Dogs, the trees and grey skies and gone houses, low light in the Fall. He talked or we slept. He could sleep with his eyes open, he said, shorn and scabby. I was no better, what bits of me I could see from the vents when it was light. It started to rain, for days, making our hole vile and muddy. Don's weaponised weather, trying to flush us out, he said. We were safe, though, he said, giggling madly in our burrow, in our damp forest hunting lodge taking time out from the world.

We got ill and shat and ate berries, leaves, acorns, mushrooms, fungus. He dressed his wounds with leaves and talked. I did bad poos next to him and cried and tried to work out if Flora was dead. I screamed at him and tried to get out and he trapped me and shut me up in different ways and told me it would be OK and about Irish boats having the same sails as Egyptian dhows, and Phoenician monuments in Malaysia and Brazil.

WHAT U FIND IN DRAWER?

He ate soil and chewed tree roots and told me to eat soil and chew tree roots and leaves and sorts of things dumdums were told not to eat: flowers, weeds, plants, bugs, mould, if you knew the right sorts, blackberry bushes and nettles scattered everywhere on purpose in the old days as emergency food. Tree roots were good for me, contained all the minerals, were natural medicine that would make me better, replenish minerals lost by tears and tummy troubles. Tree roots were nature's metal detectors, they sucked up what was underground. If you cut tree roots open you could see what the land below contained and then dig if there was good stuff, that's how they used to do it. Trees were labs for converting minerals into leaves, nuts, fruit to feed and heal. Trees were our earliest friends, even before dogs, providers of food, wood, shelter, metal, lookouts. No wonder they worshipped trees, the bridge between earth and air. Don's vast blunting that meant we'd forgotten that: autocorrect, driverless cars.

Did I know why bunches of trees growing up from land humps were called 'copses'? Cos they grew out of corpses, once, he said. He said when people used to die they'd have trees planted over their graves, so the tree roots would feast on their rotting bodies, make fruits from their minerals to be eaten by family, would be their life after death. Now there were other ways for life after death: cryopalaces and worse. He shivered. If we died here maybe a tree would grow out of us both. He held my hand.

Our spiral castle, where Sleeping Beauty goes to wait for her prince to re-life her. Crystal castles, Snow White with her apple, where kings get buried and come alive again in the old stories. The islands of the dead: Skomer and the rest off the west coast. Caldey. Glastonbury, Silbury Hill, Burrow Mump, on the line? Spiral in and spiral out. Have you ever been to Spiral Castle? It means: have you died and been reborn?

'I'm not the same person you grew up with. So much has changed.'

Right.

So much talk but not about our past, Scritchwood, New York, the rest. No flagged words to help them find us. He said. 'And it's dead to me. I was a different person then.'

A different person with a stump and head hole. The old scar under his eye that was maybe the same but no joyride scar on his shoulder: I felt for it with my hand.

'That,' he said, without me saying anything. 'Grafts, plastic surgery. You have to be just like Don. Don wants his Donlings perfect.'

Except for his eye scar and stump. But the stump had come after, his punishment, when he'd turned against Don, his righteous rise-up once he'd clocked pyramid lies. He said.

He told me about the school in the desert where they sent him for training, the school for Dons. He told me about his top empty life as Don Junior going everywhere, having everything, peeping into everyone, always missing me, islands in the mid-Atlantic not marked on dumdum maps. He'd killed people, he told me, he didn't want to talk about it. Got blooded, you had to. Death was part of life, for most people. You couldn't rule if you didn't know.

He told me about running away and living wild in forests by himself for months at a time, all those useful teenage summers in wildernesses living off leaves, the yoga and breathing, shutting yourself down, passing days in suspended torpor. 'There's so much about bodies that dumdums don't know.'

He'd escaped and lived wild but how come he'd ducked Don's passport control and got to coated England?

How come teenage yoga summers in wildernesses when we'd grown up in Scritchwood together?

His accent was more American but he'd lived there for years now.

He had a hole in his head and no back scar and was circumcised now, I'd seen it.

He said Alan was out there, calling me from afar.

Four white sheets.

Were they dead?

He told me to be suspicious of potted plants which they could hook up to sensors and use to measure emotion: fear, trust, treachery and other hormones in nearby humans. Like the chilli plant in his car, how often he'd washed it down. He told me they were cutting out the knowledge of how your inner plants relate to outer plants—your inner plants being your organs, your lungs and heart etcetera. He said organs are individual plants inside our bodies, that lungs grew like creepers on walls, that cancer is mould on those vines, that you have to change the soil to get rid of the mould. But the soil now in dumdum bodies was trash from Don the realm gardener laying lines in our connected plastic bodies, children and the unborn rewired from scratch by the fake milk, fobbing us off, controlled.

He told me not to say the word 'Don', to use codewords, that Don was a black toad squatting over earth, the 'black turtle' and to listen out for those phrases from anyone else. He told me not to call Don 'black toad' or 'black turtle' but instead call him 'black T' or 'BLT' or 'bacon sarnie' or 'Sammy sandwich' or other silly names he made up so they were ours alone.

Flora, Poppy, the baby, Rhodri. 'Alan,' I said sometimes and he shushed me. No Alan, not even down here: a flagged word for hacked worms. Even though he'd said it and much more in our cars.

But he hadn't realised then that Don had already flicked the switch.

He said.

CAREFUL, he pinched into my hand.

We lay in silence and he pinched lots of things slowly, getting me better at it: favourite music and TV shows. Helicopters overhead, he said, endless rain. What I'd lodged in my memory, could I remember it? The Hello Kitty purse and the broken horseshoe. My phone going dead an age ago. His coffees. The old woman's pink nail.

All those eyes but they never seemed to find us, except maybe they *had* found us. 'Nanocams', but not everywhere. Yet. He said. Maybe it didn't matter, being watched. He'd done terrible things, to me, skinned me alive. He'd killed people, he said.

Who knew what pressure he'd been under if one inch of this was true?

All that wacky history, petering out. Sucking tree roots, getting changed by their minerals.

WHAT U FIND IN DRAWER?

He had a stump and a hole in his head and no scar or foreskin but he knew everything, most things, just not immediately.

He knew ancient wipe-outs, black obsidian but not that Jenny 2 was also the broken house.

Teenage summers in wilderness camps but maybe I'd misheard him. Teenage Pacific tours. My kidnapper and shaver but maybe he'd saved me. Four bodies. Tal's purse. Red warns.

I was dying in a hole in the ground under a forest next to him having to listen to this, maybe with the keys out of this.

Maybe with Alan waiting for me.

What do you feel?

'OK.'

21

I said Barrow-in-Furness, I didn't tell him the street name: 226 Vengeance Street.

He didn't like that it was Barrow and that I wouldn't say more. He looked deep into me in our dim hole, his hands cupping my face.

'The sarnie rules Barrow directly,' he said after a long while. 'He grows machines there. In plain view. Maybe that's why it's Barrow: their own turf, won't think to look there.'

Barrow wasn't far. He knew the way: about twenty miles south and west, on the west coast of Jenny 2, on the sea, a place of natural defences facing the ball of fire that was the Isle of Man on the Chinese Map he called the Neijing Tu and said was a map of the human body.

'Any Scritches about Barrow? That I've forgotten?'

None that I remembered.

Him and his head.

It wouldn't work but it would only work if we were together in full trust. No time for doubt. We'd have to be each other.

He did a test. When the sun set he crawled up and stood outside in the open for a long time while I stayed buried.

Nothing happened.

He came back in and woke me, it was still dark.

NO TALK.

NO PINCH.

TRUST.

I crawled out with him, naked, muddy, unsteady things newly hatched from the earth into the trees and big cold air. We stared at each other. I didn't care about being naked. We'd got past all that now. He stretched and looked at the black sky. I shivered. Naked, barefoot, freezing, ill, deranged in a dark forest. We looked for poos and mud and smeared them on. The walk would warm us. You could heat yourself from inside.

The forest rustled and hooted. He limped cos he'd gouged half his calf out in the lake and then put poo over it. I tottered about shivering.

He took my hand with his stump hand and we slipped low, naked and freezing through the black forest by night, our eyes already tuned to the dark. We cut and stubbed our bare feet, walking on wet leaves when we could, keeping close to evergreens and bare boughs cloaked with ivy, heading down next to a stream, nature's paths. Creatures made noises, things crackled, there were thorns and blackness, trees sucked up minerals from cooled goo, bare branches leant in to tell us things. We moved fast, to keep warm. After a while we hit the lake and squatted in tall reeds along the shore looking for something. Looking for a boat, he whispered, belonging to slack people, holiday people who left their boats out over winter, crossed their fingers. He loved slack people, he said.

I hated the idea of boats and the lake again. What did we know about boats?

At its south point the lake turned into a river which would take us out to sea and round the coast to Barrow, he said.

Did it? How did he know that? Trying to remember from the old mouldy atlas and the Chinese map. Water was best, he said. Or else walking miles through forests, stealing cars, public transport? Naked us, tired and weak. The water would take us, minimum effort, the tides in our favour, he'd make sure of that, work it out with sun and moon and stars like he'd been taught. He knew about water and boats now, he said. Wild dark water, you can't tag it, yet. We'd stick to the shore as much as we could, steal clothes from somewhere, knit them from reeds, whatever, travel in the dark flow. He had a good picture of the river and coastline in his mind, he knew this part of England pretty well anyway.

'How come?'

'Because.' This part of England seemed remote but was important to the sandwich, strategically.

'Why? Metal?'

'Lots of things.'

The water was cold. We found a wooden boat upside down in the reeds with a big hole in the bottom and then a bit further down a blue plastic canoe with no hole. No oar, though, so we went back to the wooden boat and hurt our hands prising off planks to use as oars till we found something better: 'there'll be useful crap in the banks, always is.'

We sailed down the dark glittering lake using planks and his hands, me in front, him behind. The rowing warmed me, stopped the shivering. My feet went numb. As the water narrowed we glimpsed a dark shape he said was a house. He lodged me and the boat in reeds and went off for quite a long time, came back jolly with two coats, scarves, wellies, woolly hats and a lifejacket from a slack boating shed he'd broken into. We dressed, wrapped scarves round our thighs, sailed on using our planks. The water became a thin river, we slipped down past reeds and thick whispering trees. We rowed and sometimes rested, let the black water carry us. I shivered in stolen clothes at the helm flowing through the world.

The water was high because of the rain, he said. After about an hour we came to a low bridge we had to duck under. Then the water fell fast away down a frothing weir. He laughed then skimmed us sideways easily down white rushing water in the dark while I clutched the sides.

After that the water moved fast. He'd stop and test plants, eat things snatched from the bank, make me eat leaves to give me energy, bundling wet plants and flotsam into the bottom of the boat, flashing big smiles at me when I looked round, enjoying freedom, speed and danger. After a couple of hours the trees stopped and we floated past open fields.

'Can you smell it?'

The tang of oncoming sea, the cool new air, my hands blistered from the plank. I turned to look at him: shivering, pleased, free on the water, sliding us into wide forces.

'One thing.' Perhaps he should have mentioned it before. This sea we were coming to? It wasn't sea proper. More like an estuary leading somewhere, Morecambe Bay? Had I heard of it?

Sure I'd heard of treacherous Morecambe Bay, dead cockle pickers caught in quick tides on sinking sands. I spun round.

'Yes,' he said: fast tides, quicksand, easy death. I wasn't to worry: only dangerous if you didn't know what you were up to or walked out when the tide was out. We'd be in our boat on water hugging the north coast, we'd wait for the right tide to sweep us out, we'd pay our respects, he knew all about it.

'Trust me.' We'd park somewhere, wait for the tide, he knew the signs. We were heading for Kraton and friends.

How could he know any of this: tides, where we were, how to get to Barrow via water from Lake Coniston, that Lake Coniston turned into a river, how to navigate Morecambe Bay? How could he picture the shoreline? We had no atlas, that I knew about: we had nothing except the stolen boat and clothes, nothing from before. Or at least I had nothing. And no chalk here: slate and mud, which carried no charge, he said.

'That Welsh dragon?' he said. The red one on the Welsh flag that meant mineral treasures to privileged eyes. 'Can you picture it? Forked tongue out? Paw raised?'

I tried.

'Not just a dragon,' he said. 'Also a map.' If you flipped the dragon the other way round, he said, so it faced east instead of west, you'd find the dragon's head and front body mapped pretty much exactly onto the shape of the Irish Sea, so the paw raised was Cardigan Bay, the back of the neck the east coast of Ireland. Yes, the Irish Sea was the shape of a dragon. 'Check it out next time you can.' A pretty goofy-looking dragon, a secret in plain view. The negative of the Chinese map. A useful way to come to know the coastline, what you got taught in desert schools. A vital coastline for sarnies now and in the past, metal empires. He'd had to study that dragon, commit its bends to memory, sing its inlet songs. We were currently moving towards the dragon's snout. He said.

No way to check on the boat in the dark. I had to laugh. His whole style this crazed journey: when in doubt, hit me with something truly insane.

'And where d'you think the dragon's eye is?' he said. 'Come on, you know, out there in the Irish Sea, cloaked by mist. Come on. What do you know about the Isle of Man?'

Not much. Like Jersey or Guernsey: part of Britain, kind of, but with its own laws, no tax, lots of banks, a good place to hide money, famous motorbike race. A ball of fire on the Chinese map.

Full of rare metals, he said. From the top of its highest mountain on a clear day you can see England, Ireland, Scotland and Wales. Ancient watchmaking centre. The fifth most likely nation to send someone into space. Was and is Britain's true capital, the eye from which all power radiates, the eye at the centre of ancient metal empires fringing the Irish Sea, once the most secret place on earth. The eye at the exact centre of the triangle which is Britain and Ireland when you look at them on a map, if you can trust the maps, the pyramid eye from US dollar bills from whence fires were lit to send and receive mainland signals, from when sarnies lurk and see and control the world even today.

'Yeah chew on that. Here's the real Mediterranean. The other's a decoy. Those warlike tribes. And Barrow's Man's hub. The nearest mainland port.' No wonder he didn't want to go there. The Furness peninsula, Jenny 2, chief receiver for the Dons, for thousands of years. The big cut-off landing point, protected by sea, mountains and quicksand, where parcels wrapped in straw got traded, where apples got smelted into machines. Where we were heading, past the forts, castles, priories, hidden abbeys, monasteries, watchtowers, lighthouses, spyholes, black friars of its shoreline. Cos what did I think monks were really? Man-agents, manual CCTV, apple-counters, chief scientists, root-inspectors, purveyors of mind-tools to trance the dumdums whose land they tickled, chanters of bogus books with triple meanings, seekers of the past.

So that was why and how he knew how to get to Barrow, sarnie-central. He said.

'What did Alan say about the fireball on the map?'

That it was like the sun, a place so hot no human could survive there. Not to go there, never to look at it directly.

'Can't remember,' I said. 'Can you?'

'Look,' he said.

We were sliding slowly past tethered boats into colder air and wind. There were lights to our right: something coming up. A big road bridge ahead over the river and beyond it something else: a wider blank, lights shimmering far away in true huge openness.

'OK,' he said. The tide was high, he could tell from the watermark on the bridge. Time to get out, find shelter, eat, wait for the tide to turn so we could ride it out to sea. A couple of hours by his estimate. He had to get out, take a closer look, to be more accurate.

We slipped under the bridge and saw beyond a much bigger bridge and something neon to our right. A service station, he said and shuddered, pulling his coat hood right down over his face, reaching over to do the same to me.

He moved the boat closer to the right-hand shore, made me get out and pull it with him through mud far up against the bank and hide it in reeds as best we could. Then we headed up in the dark into thick trees, found a bush for me to sit in while he headed out further to take a look at the water and tides, and to try to find food.

Leaving me there on my own. The first time since the burrow.

Me alone in the new world.

'If I'm not back by dawn then move on, wash the mud off your face and hands, pull your hood down, walk along the shore as long as you can till you end up in Barrow, you can't miss the docks. But no service stations, steer well clear.'

Then I should go wherever we were heading in Barrow, the precise address I wouldn't tell him, see if old Kraton wasn't there.

'Where is it? Tell me. Just in case. So we can meet up there. If it goes tits up.'

My last card. 'Vengeance Street,' I told him. I didn't tell him the number.

'Vengeance Street?'

Yup, weird, I knew. I nodded. No I didn't know where it was, had never heard of or been there before, no Scritches.

'We'll find a map or something once we get to Barrow. Ask someone, we'll sort it.' He shook his head, shivered, then smiled again. 'We're already dead. Is the best way to think about it.'

Comforting words. He stroked my face and left.

I wrapped myself in the coat and scarf and leaves and sat there shivering in the bush, feeling woozy. He came back and woke me. It was still dark. I was ill. He forced me to eat mushrooms and shrivelled berries and what he said was yarrow to perk me up. He'd poked through people's bins and brought back plastic bags, bits of old t-shirts. I wiped my runny shits with leaves and tied bits of t-shirts and plastic bags round my body and legs and numb feet, stuffed them back into the wellies like he told me.

The tide would soon turn, he said. We should head out now before it did. We'd have to go under the massive railway viaduct spanning the bay ahead and had to do it now, just before the change of tide, or the strength of surge could batter us up against the bridge columns. After that the turning tide would do the work for us, ride us out up the dragon's snout to the forehead that was Barrow, chamber of the red dragon's pineal eye.

21

We sat cross-legged by the tree and flooded ourselves with energy. You didn't need to sleep if you knew which body buttons to press, he said.

I sat there wobbling next to him, smelling him and his shit. I sat there and filled myself up with the dark.

Back in the gloom with the boat, shivering under the coat and scarves and plastic bags, facing the hazy world. We pushed it down into the river, got in, me back in front, sailed on under the road bridge into the vast freezing black estuary, under the massive railway viaduct, squeaking through its narrow columns, forcing ourselves through.

Morecambe Bay proper now in the turning tide: big choppy water, flat wide black dotted with white lights from the shore and red lights out to sea he said were turbines. Moon, stars and satellites above.

'Nothing fancy,' he shouted. We'd stick to this course, hug the shore, follow the lights. We'd get there eventually, we'd be safe.

No talking after that, you couldn't hear. Three or four hours of fast black sea, wind, freezing swells, bumpy water, spray, getting soaked, zonking out, clinging on, flowing down dragons, till the light started to change and the tide began to outrun us. We started getting stuck in raised mudbanks, having to push ourselves free with hands and sticks. Mud flats: the deeper water channels further out now, away from the shore, in real sea where we wouldn't go.

We sat there, stuck.

'Too dangerous now.'

We shouldn't force it. We had limits. We'd been doing this a long time now: rowing, coasting. It would be dawn soon: new light and bird noises. We shouldn't travel in the light. Soon the tide would be out completely and then it would change, come roaring back at us. We were pretty far along the snout. We'd done well.

We were tired and I was ill, we needed to rest, stop off

somewhere at the shore, sleep, prepare. Get out now, before the fishermen came, leave the boat right here where it was, stuck in mud, too stuck and heavy to drag to the shore. It had done its work, got us here. Thank you, boat. We'd move on by other means. We'd wrap things round our hands and wellies to make mud shoes, increase our surface area so we could slide well and not sink. Quicksand took you when all your weight stood on one or two points. We'd crawl on the mud to the shore with our new hand and leg wadding, spreading out the weight, moving slowly but safely on our stomachs to the shore, find some place to crash during the day, wait for night to move on to Barrow.

A place to crash. What would that look like? If the turtle owned here and had salted it and turned all surfaces into snitchers?

We wrapped our hands and shins with junk to bulk out our surfaces, got out of the boat and just left it there. We got down on hands and knees and crawled through sticky icy salt mud in the half-light towards light on the land, pushing through seaweed and silver pools, scattering little white birds, trying to make out what was on the shore directly in front of us: regular lights, green solar panels, small white and beige boxes facing the sea.

'Caravan park,' he said.

I lay half-dead in the mud. An empty caravan park in late November: bingo, surely? Climb the fence, force some door.

'No way. Cammed up to the gills. Places like this? On the coast here? Looking all remote?'

It was lighter. We pushed on, him yanking me on across freezing chocolate in search of shelter: fallen trees, sheep pens, things with half a roof.

Easier said than done. That coast was open and bare: sea walls, lone houses, open fields, no forests. We came to a red, yellow and brown brick obelisk sticking up out of the mud, a seagull peering at us from atop, Don's agent no doubt. Beyond it were boats and boat parts stuck in brown like dinosaur bones, then a road, houses, land, jumble.

'Here,' he said and stumbled me onto the shore.

Two muddy fools holding each other up, swaddled with trash, ridiculous-looking. Him stooped up supporting me, me barely walking, a drunk, the most suspicious duo, forget about nanocams: injured tramps walking off a wet bender in the muddy dawn.

In front of us was a small settlement, a pub, a few houses, then a locked gate and beyond that a lone stretch jutting further out into the sea: a pier and a mess of boats and houses with something else lit up on the horizon beyond it still: the hazy ruins of a castle out to sea, on an island. He nodded at some small upturned boats a bit further along the shore, and a large beached rusty trawler half on its side, stuck in the mud. He slumped me against a broken row boat, pulled the muddy coat hood low over my face and went to check the orange trawler out.

He popped up on the trawler's deck, thumbs up.

He came back down and hoisted me up and dragged me over and then up the trawler's ladder to its deck and then down another ladder into the dim hold.

Cans and bottles, plastic bags, mouldy sleeping bags, scrunched-up paper, bad smells: we weren't the first to think of finding shelter down there in our filthy clothes.

'International spy station?'

He laughed. 'You never know.'

So good to be inside. The low side of portholes faced out onto the sea and glistening mud. It was lighter now and we saw people out there doing things with boats: shrimp and cocklemen, he said. To the left, across the sea from us, was the glimmer of something huge across the big bay.

'Heysham,' he said. 'What they call "power stations". Don's big rooms up and down this coast.'

Direct in front of us were big things out to sea: gas drillers, he said and wind farms out beyond—so-called gas drillers and wind farms. And to our right was what he said was Roa Island, which wasn't an island at all but a bead at the end of the road. A bead split in two by the road: on the left side little houses, to the right the crammed-up boats, the weird castle out beyond in the water behind it. Everything was brown mud, sea, red lights, channels, mist, tiny brown and white birds.

In this foul tramps-nest we unwrapped our poor muddied knees and feet and tried to get warm using anything, pee-smelling sleeping bags with most of their stuffing gone. He cleared space, shook things, made a makeshift bed and pillows out of what rotten stuff he could, pulled them over sick sneezing filthy grey us, pulled his arm round me so tight so we warmed each other.

I slept.

22

Early afternoon. Leaves and seaweed, more runny shits in the corner. I was worse, lots of snot. He cleaned me with rags, wrapped grotty sleeping bags round me, told me it was good I was so ill and they hadn't pounced cos maybe that meant they weren't on to us after all. Since I was so important to them, they couldn't have harm come to me, would've stepped in if they'd seen me this bad, cos of who I was, what I knew, so precious. Not that he'd got me ill to test.

We looked out of a porthole and watched light fade over shimmering brown mud, little brown birds dancing and pecking in channels, street lamps switching on to reflect the red sky in pools across the chocolate trap. The big dun cube across the bay that was the so-called power station lit up again, the sky was huge with wispy dark grey clouds stretched out like words I couldn't read over the setting sun. He told me about the bay and Piel Castle on the island, an old Man receiver built by so-called monks on the ruins of much older spiral castles, Barrow tucked behind where we couldn't yet see. The so-called drillers and turbines in the sea lit up red. Just before the light went the bluest kingfisher hovered for a moment right beneath us. We watched, he held me tight, told me these were our halcyon days.

He talked magic and plastic and machines and who'd agreed to any of it, and undersea wars and minerals and weaponised quakes. He talked the Isle of Man and its flag of three legs that meant something, about the dragon sea that was this Irish Sea in front of us and other seas memorised in desert schools: the horse-shaped North Sea, the stag-shaped Baltic and its islands, how the Baltic island of Saaremaa is the stag's eye, its Man equivalent, how the island of Gotland is its dapple, how all seas have shapes and songs, how mainlands are always controlled by islands, how the dead are buried on islands, about Ibrasilia, the Celtic island of the dead in the west that was maybe Brazil, how islands are the tips of mountains: Madagascar, Sri Lanka, Hawaii, Java, Taiwan.

When I woke it was night. We had to wash, it would make me better, he said. It wasn't too cold outside, we had to risk it, outdoor air would do me good. He lugged me over his shoulder up and down and into mud in the mild dark outside lit by orange street lamps. He propped me up by the trawler and ferried sea water to me in empty booze bottles and washed me tenderly bit by bit, doused my scabby head in cold stinging sea water, dabbed me dry with some washed tramp rag, washed himself, lifted me home.

On the trawler's tipped deck he found a metal box and made a small fire from bits of bush and rubbish, sparked it with a found lighter, made me sit and warm myself. I watched the flames. He boiled sea water in tilted bottles, strained it through washed cloth to take the salt out, boiled it again, put seaweed in, made me drink some and stored the rest in bottles, called it champagne, toasted our grand dodge.

I had all the sleeping bags and felt better. 'Your headaches,' I said. He hadn't had a headache for a while, since Flora, which I didn't want to think about.

'Yeah weird,' he said. Perhaps he'd been allergic to something, in the white Nissan, or the tracker in his calf. Perhaps outdoor living suited him, doss wrecks. We laughed. He hugged me to keep me warm in the boat.

The next morning I woke late, feeling better.

He wasn't there.

I went to the porthole. The tide was in, the dun box facing me across bronze water. He was outside, hood down, collecting things. Up on the deck he built another fire and fried us seaweed and crunchy tiny fish on a stone. We lay side by side in the dirty boat waiting for the sun to set.

It got dark. About 5pm, he said. We drank our champagne

and put our coats on over plastic bags and rags. It was time. Only a couple of miles north to Barrow. Old muckers like us, we'd find the way, hug the shore. Blaze out. Could I walk? Maybe. We'd huddle together, hoods down, two old tramps hunting cockles for tea. We'd walk weird, to fox the gait-recognition tools they had, ID you by your slouch even with your face covered.

We looked out at our view for the last time, street lights shimmering in mud puddles, the lit-up power station, Roa Island's two sides, the red lights. He put a sprig of dry seaweed into an empty bottle of Blue Nun at the porthole, jammed it in place with a curled wad of paper.

'Our sign, to mark our stay,' he said. 'We'll come back, bring real champagne,' when all this was done and dusted, bring Alan too, the whole gang. Our haven, out of harm's way, our tramp honeymoon suite in the tramp trawler, keep the champagne in the broken cold box in the corner. Our rendezvous, if things went tits up, if we lost each other: come back here, OK? If we could. The fallback, like you always did in Scritch, could never be too careful. 'Tramp champagne' would be our codeword.

There were things he wanted to say but not now and not in words—which were also part of it, of course: alphabets, the deepest tools to control our minds, to prime us for their computers, get us before we were born.

He took the lighter, some rags, nails and a bit of rusty metal from the deck.

He helped me up and out, a bit steadier on my feet. We squelched across mud in the dark and then onto the orange-lit road in our coat-and-trash get-ups, hoods down, odd walks versus posture spies, poisoned tarmac, tampered animals, the whole shimmering coated watching world.

There'd be a path along the coast, he said, there always was. He shuffled me past cars and innocents on their phones. We came to houses and a pub and a sign for a nature trail: bingo. We followed the sign behind the pub and found another sign: three miles to Barrow.

I stood at the gate and he crouched and touched the trail. Probably a railway track once, he said, to shuttle apples. Other ways now: drones and tunnels—there were lots of tunnels, Britain was riddled with them, the world was riddled with them, cut into the limestone under us now even out to sea, if you knew which pub basement or Chinese restaurant backstairs to walk down.

He pulled our hoods right down.

'Don't be fooled,' he said. From here on in: say cheese for the cams, no talking, only pinching if I had to. 'Close your eyes, you can always sense everything, if you're being watched, if you're being filmed. If it twitches.'

I stood there holding his hand. The whole world twitched.

We went through the gate.

A country path, fringed with bushes and trees with last yellow leaves at tip branches. It was dark but not that dark even though there were clouds and not much moon. We walked, me with him in my sick trance. A few dog owners passed us and nodded and once a cyclist sped by, helmet and earphones on, a camera fixed to his forehead. Something strange started to happen: a white glow ahead and then orange flames jetting into the sky, and a bad smell and the sound of something.

'Gas works,' he said, and we came to them after a while where the trees went away and the path widened into a huge flat place. The lights of Barrow up ahead, mud sea to our left and to our right this bank of massive spaceship-looking metal monsters caged behind barbed wire, orange flames outside shooting up to the sky.

NOT GAS, he pinched. Something else, which he knew about and I didn't, which they were busy with up west Britain, gobbling away 24/7 sucking juice up from the crack.

'What's that?' I said, slow and stupid, cos there was something else: music, drifting slowly at us from Barrow lit up to our left across the water.

We stopped and listened to the slow haunted pop floating across the darkness of the bay under the massive sky.

'From a boat,' he said slowly. 'I think. From a cruise ship, some party.' He was shaking.

We limped on, towards the music. A flock of birds flew up at the water's edge. He dragged me on, not letting me rest, didn't speak or pinch now. We came to a blue pill box and a sign and a choice of path: carry on up the road to Barrow or turn left for the docks?

We stood there in light drizzle.

'Hold on,' he said.

He wanted to check something by the docks. He had a bad feeling, needed to check something, wouldn't say what. Him basically carrying me by then, pulling me down a slatted wooden path lit by orange lamps, the mud sea to our left, a wrecked car stuck in nose-down. To our right: a big calm field of water that was a dock, Barrow and the music twinkling ahead.

And then something massive in front of us lit up.

He gripped me to stop.

Right there in front of us ahead, alongside the path a little way up, bright white and wrong. Huge, in the blackness, right up against the side of the path perhaps five minutes ahead, on a different scale, shining, playing sad Asian pop.

'We're fucked,' he said.

23

Another secret gas works, I thought. But it was a ship, a lit-up massive ugly container ship, weirdly close to us given how huge it was, how deep a dock it would need. The path we stood on, I now saw, must actually be a super-high wall cloaked by water with this giant bit of lit-up industry at its side, ugly like a shark, wrung against the weeds of the path and the whole dark rotting muddy dockside.

'Fucked,' he said again. Then he dragged me back along the dizzy wall to the pill box and the signs and ran us up the other path towards the city. We stopped, doubled over, for a moment under the railway bridge.

'Don?' I said.

He nodded, shaking and sweating.

Don's ship. 'Don's here? After us? What do we do?'

'Run away.'

CARRY ON, he pinched.

WHAT DON WANT?

His white eyes through the hood: 'To gobble me up.'

We raced through Barrow in the rain, past people in cars and on the streets on their phones, past squat red-brick houses, cranes, eerie looming massive zigzag hangars on the water that were huge rooms, secret enclosed docks for Don's machines. Early evening in a city, maybe ten days since he'd come for me in London so long ago. Shops, the realm on their phones. They looked at us in our plastic bags with our hoods right down, filthy tramps in mad panic. He stopped people, asked where Vengeance Street was, they didn't know. A young woman got out her sparkly phone. We shrank back but it didn't matter now.

'It's on Walney,' she said, showing us her screen.

An island, at Barrow's far west, joined to the city by a bridge, she showed us. You followed the road round past the superstore then over the bridge. Twenty-one minutes by foot.

He studied her screen, turning the route into an animal shape or story in his head?

We ran on, him pulling me past street lights, brick walls, massive warehouses, fences, mess, shops, docks, machines. We saw the island across the narrow mud then crossed a bridge with black-wrought spiked iron and upright barriers, got to Walney on the other side.

Small boats, street lamps, small grim pebble-dash houses, empty roads. Him bearing me on round the encircling road and down residential streets with back alleys, turning to see what was following us but seeing nothing but the lit mess of Barrow proper behind us, the huge zigzag rooms where Don's monsters got grown.

We found Vengeance Street, saw the sign, followed it down. Blank small grey two-up two-downs, tiny windows, pointy black roofs, each one slightly different, ramshackle.

'What's the number?'

I stopped outside number 226. A yellow door, no lights, net-curtained windows.

HERE?

Eyes watched us from a neighbouring window: a cat. Warning stickers: 'My terrier lives here', 'Beware of the tortoise', which Alan used to hang on the front door of his bus. I saw the door knocker: a black metal head of a bulldog wearing a baseball cap, tongue out, neckerchief knotted round the neck. Alan's shed knocker, except this one looked proper, shop-bought, not carved out of wood and painted like Alan's one in Scritchwood.

He saw where my gaze was. 'What's that?'

He should know.

He went up to the front door and knocked the bulldog knocker, the five and the six, looking at me the whole time, showing me he knew the score.

No answer to his knock. I looked up, at the window of the

second floor. There, stuck to the glass in front of the closed net curtains and lit by a street lamp, was the sticker of a rainbow, just like the rainbow painted by Alan onto the window of the shed.

He looked at me looking at it.

'What is it? Hurry.'

He looked around and up at the sky, then knocked again, any old knock this time, frantic.

'Nim. Wake up.' He grabbed me, pulled me back up the street and round the corner to the back alley, counting down the back doors till we got to number 226.

Empty streets, street lights, lights on in houses but not that house.

A wooden fence, easily scalable. He hoisted himself up, I kept watch, he yanked me up.

Silence. Utterly empty streets.

A tiny back garden with dead plants in plant pots, a small shed painted the same pale blue as the chicken coop outside the bus. A small barred window with blinds down that wouldn't open.

He was fiddling round with the back door, trying to prise it open with his bit of rusty metal. At the window to the left dangled a big yellow wooden sun ornament like the sun ornament at the first window of the bus, carved by Alan, painted by me outside on the grass one sunny day with yellow acrylic got from Jassy, Flora's mum. Except this one was shop-bought.

The earth-ware plant pot to the left of the door was carved with two faces, one at each side. The Janus pot from outside Alan's bus, except ours had cruder sillier faces. I knelt down to touch it, the Chris next to me panicking, hacking at the door in a frenzy. I slipped my hand under the heavy pot. Like in Scritchwood there was a key.

He snatched it from me, didn't say anything, turned the lock, opened the back door.

We stepped inside.

24

Thick musty air, like Rhodri's caravan but drier, mould at work for years maybe. It was dark, he felt for the wall, switched on a bare overhead bulb.

We stood in the tiny kitchen of a two-up-two-down on Walney Island off Barrow.

We stood in the tiny kitchen of Alan's bus.

We stood in a cobwebbed place of half-versions. A real-looking elephant's foot full of umbrellas and golf clubs beside us. Plates with the same patterns except these were china and Alan's had been painted wood. The pan hooks that were the number five screwed into the ceiling. A Victorian picture of a steam train at a station on a sunny day and milling ladies and gentlemen with tails, bustles and parasols, though this picture was a faded detailed print with many extras, instead of Alan's crude Scritchwood painting, done from memory, perhaps, by Alan himself.

We were in a place I knew because I'd grown up with its version *and* because I'd been taught to visualise it, by Alan: my mind bus, that I could close my eyes and see in my head and use it to lodge other information, for Scritch etc. Torts I knew, stored in the glassware cupboard next to the sink, the blue-and-white patterned floor lino. So freaky, seeing it for real again, a version. This one was filthy with dust and spiders.

The lightbulb still worked, though. Something from Zita came back to me: her breaking into a seemingly abandoned house in search of her lost dad but the lights still working, someone still paying the bills, watching for those kinds of details.

You were prepping me.

Why not tell me?

Are you here?

'Hello,' I called. No one answered.

'Where are we? Quick, they'll be here.'

I glided into the next room, switched on the light, him behind panting. The big room in the bus, or a chintzier version: dark patterned wallpaper and carpet, tasselled lamp, sofa, chairs and table, bookshelves, mantelpiece crammed with better but familiar objects: curved sword Alan called the scimitar, the carriage clock, the three porcelain baby-faced Chinese wise men where we'd had three blue plastic Smurfs, a much scarier long-nosed black Venetian mask. The swan that was the number two, the snowmen that were the number eight, these were china, we'd made ours from white pompoms. An identical conch shell with its hole that was zero. A mantelpiece over a real fireplace made of real black stone instead of black-painted cardboard. The Chinese map framed behind glass on the wall. The crochet coverlet over the back of the sofa, the seeming same colour arrangement of the squares except our Covert one—made by Jassy, Flora's mum, to Alan's very exact instructions—had burnt in the fire that had destroyed the bus, I'd thrown away the charred remnant myself. Yet here it was again whole, or a version. Made before or after? Were these things the copies or the first ones?

'What's it saying? Which Scritch? They'll be here. What's this place, what's here? Think.'

He pushed past me, rushed upstairs, calling out to see if anyone answered. I just stood there in the gap between two places at once.

The bookshelves: lots of stories and law coded in there. Some things were familiar and some not: Rupert the Bear annuals resurrected from the fire. Similar but not the same guides to stones and minerals, the coastlines of Britain, football annuals, stream ecology, knotcraft, *A Little Key To Drawing*.

I reached for that book, pulled it off the shelf.

The same blue leather binding, the identical gold lettering. But this one was different, this one was real. In Scritchwood this book had been a dummy: when you opened it up there was no book, just a wooden box that would often contain the first coded clue to a Scritch game. But this was a real book, very old, printed on gossamer paper with dark print that was hard to read and full of symbols, nothing to do with how to draw, it seemed, but about the properties of stone and water. It fell open at page fifty-six.

It fell open because of a newspaper cutting left in there, from the New York Times, dated three weeks earlier, an article about a royal pregnancy printed on one side, part of a car ad printed on the other, slashed with a red line. Slashed with a red warn.

I picked it up, felt bobbles. The cutting had been pricked with Braille that I ran my fingers over, Alan's Braille that was a message to me:

Darling Nim
If you're reading this you're in terrible danger, especially if you're
with someone who says he's Chris Kipp...

'What's that?' He was back down the stairs next to me, snatching the paper from me, skimming the article, not noticing the Braille, seeing the red warn. He snatched the book, flicked through the weird pages, took the article again and ran his fingers over it, noticing the bumps now, not knowing what they were, though, not being able to read it, holding it up to the light. Not knowing anything about Scritch Braille, not knowing anything about Scritch at all.

'What is this? Some kind of message? From who? Alan? What does it say? Tell me now,' jabbing his piece of rusty metal at my throat.

Noise outside, then the doorbell rang: one long ring.

We froze.

It rang again, then the knocking and a man's voice: 'Police. Open up.'

We stood there, the sharp metal at my throat. He held up the article. 'Please. What does it say?'

I moved slightly. The metal nicked me. The bell rang again.

'We know you're there. Open the door or we're breaking it down.'

Silence, then the big thuds of them battering down the door.

He came so close, his lips and mad wide eyes, grabbing my hand with his hand that held the piece of newspaper.

'What's the number? Say it. It's all a trap, it's a fake, Alan's not your dad, he's not here, that's what they told me to say to get you. They control everything except what you know, that Alan buried into you, that he left here for you. What's coded up inside you that they'll do anything for. Tell me before it ends.'

His grip round my wrist, his white face. Splinters at the edge of the door. His fast mouth so close to me.

'OK you're right. I'm not him. I'm not your Chris. I didn't grow up with you. I'm the other one, I'm Sean, the freak from the desert. I brought you here for them. It doesn't make me the bad guy. I went along and then I rescued us, tried to get us away for real. You know I did. Your one's pure evil, Don's sap. Beware. They know you from before. Tell me what this says.'

I watched him, not Chris but the same apart from the stump and accent and head hole and the no foreskin or shoulder scar. A grown thing, a creature from the mirror rabbitting on about numbers and Don and Chris and Alan and the end of the world.

The door caved in. He let me go, grabbed the scrap of newspaper, ran his fingers over it one last time then stuffed it in his mouth and scuttled into the cupboard under the stairs, pulled the door closed. Covered people in yellow plastic swarmed in wearing gloves and boots, their faces covered with plastic and goggles, hazard suits against contamination, holding guns and truncheons.

I stood there.

'Where is he?'

I pointed to the cupboard under the stairs.

They went over, yanked it open. He was inside, whatever he was, hacking himself with his metal, hacking his body, hacking his eyes out, blood everywhere. They dragged him out, hands in his mouth, pulling out pulped newspaper and teeth while his cut red blank eyes bled and his body went limp. He moved his head wildly, calling out words for me, pulp on his tongue, filthy nails, his blood on their yellow plastic.

'The boat. Sad nothing weed. Nim.'

Calling out my name though we didn't know each other, though I'd never met him or loved him, Chris's shadow, something from the lab. A bloody pulped mess reaching out madly for me, no eyes now, blood running down its face like tears.

'I'm sorry. The boat. Don't fall for it.'

I was screaming, they belted him in the face, scooped the pulp into bags. They yanked him up, pulled his wrists behind him, pulled his head back, did something to him. He flopped back, stump Chris, the no-eyed fake, cuddled into their arms, getting bundled out of the door.

They cradled me in their yellow arms, told me it was OK, that they were with me now and I was safe and it was fine. Pricking my neck with the syringe.

25

I woke to terrible screams.

I was propped up on a white metal bed in a small space hung with blue plastic curtains. I wore blue robes and a brace round my chest. A helmet attached to the bed locked me in place so I couldn't move my shoulders or my head. Tubes jammed into my arms joined me to plastic bags on wheeled hooks by my side. My arms and legs were untied but I couldn't move them either, they just lay there. Above me: bright lights, a filthy ceiling. Around me: wires, sockets, baskets of sickly-smelling creamy white flowers. The hum and vibration of machines, a bad lurching in my stomach. 'Change me,' a woman was yelling from beyond the curtain.

I screamed: for help, for Chris, for stump Chris who was Sean. The woman screamed again.

Silence, then the curtain parted. A fat woman in blue scrubs peered in at me then whooshed the curtain shut. Moments later it reopened: a thin man in green scrubs holding a bag of clear liquid. I screamed again but could do nothing. He hooked up the bag and attached it to one of my tubes.

I woke up again in a small grey room, the helmet still on my head, more flowers. Black-and-white people in hospital scrubs peered down, told me not to try to move, that everything was OK. I was in a private room in Barrow General Hospital, they said. Could I confirm my name, date of birth, address? There three weeks with serious injuries, induced coma. Trauma to the head with blunt instrument followed by a nasty fall leading to concussion, aggravated by exposure, pneumonia, dehydration, exhaustion, malnutrition, infected cuts, suspected poisoning. They'd had to amputate the tip of my right little toe. I'd been living rough, eating plants it wasn't good to eat, plus traces of sedatives and sleeping pills in my blood. All worsened by the psychological trauma: kidnapped by a maniac posing as my ex, forced to see the murdered bodies of my friends. I'd been in an induced coma for several weeks, temporary paralysis for my own good, was now in recovery. Prognosis was good but I had to lie still, take things very easy. I'd been victim of and witness to serious crimes, was now safe and on the road to full health. The police and lawyers would explain the rest of it, they'd be here soon, with my friends and colleagues. The next few days were vital for my recovery, the most important thing right now was complete rest and no moving my head while they assessed me. Thus the helmet and temporary paralysis. Cranio-spinal issues, tiny nerves. The slightest wrong move and I'd be mangled for life.

My head ached, I felt sick and dizzy under the helmet. My arms and legs lay unmoving under the sheet, I wanted to see my docked toe. My tongue felt thick, coated.

Flora, Poppy, Rhodri, the baby, I asked. They shook their heads. The police would explain, police matters. Yes, very sorry and terrible, all dead. Nothing more they could say, were authorised to say. I'd been drugged, confused. The police would explain. I had to now focus on getting better.

And no, they couldn't say where stump Chris was now, where the Chrises were, what had happened. The police would explain in due course. They were medical professionals, it wasn't their business. Did I have friends and family they could be in touch with, who was my next of kin, anyone who could be here with me during my recovery once I was removed from isolation? There were cards from work and friends, people had been worried.

No, I couldn't go back to Vengeance Street and have another little look. I couldn't go anywhere. I couldn't read my medical records, I couldn't read, not yet. People could read to me: the police, hospital volunteers, Victim Support, my lawyers in due course, they'd all be round later. I couldn't do anything myself. I couldn't get up, hold things, look at anything. Nothing that required brain focus. No moving at all, they couldn't stress that enough. No internet or speaking to anyone on the phone, or seeing anyone, for the time being. No phones. No stress. The only thing I could do was lie there and watch TV, very quietly.

The TV was up in the corner of the room. They switched it on.

I watched TV. Perhaps it watched me. Either way I didn't like it.

26

The story was I'd been kidnapped by a maniac posing as my ex and forced as his drugged hostage on a crazed spree up the west coast of Britain culminating in the murder of my friends and the Vengeance Street break-in. There, after ransacking the place for no reason and resisting arrest, he'd held me hostage and hit me on the head with something blunt and heavy — a poker? — causing me to fall backwards hitting the fireplace. Thus this extended hospital stay. He'd shaved my head and whole body but there was no evidence of sexual assault — they'd checked. Real Chris had ID-ed me remotely from California, a coma livestream. Friends and colleagues had been informed. The family were handling things, it was a sensitive case. I could look in the mirror in due course, I might be shocked by what I saw, they lifted up my leg to show me my smooth docked toe, the tip gone due to infection, barely noticeable, I could still move it. I was making great headway.

Good story, I told my visitors: the police, medics, shrinks, Victim Support. But what about police needles in the neck? I wanted to speak to and see my friends. I wanted to get out. I wanted a lawyer. I *was* a lawyer, I knew my rights.

All in due course, they said. My health first. I was in a serious condition and wasn't to be stressed, was currently a patient under strict doctor care, was in no state for lawyers. My medical insurance had insisted on this. That's why I was in this private room receiving specialised care: my top notch medical insurance, part of my work package, supplemented by Chris who had insisted on top London specialists. Chris was deeply involved in my care, felt so responsible, wanted to talk, all in due course. For now I needed to lie perfectly straight and heal.

Poor old clunked and drugged me, bound to remember things skewiff, disappearing homes. And, they said gently, Stockholm

Syndrome, had I heard of it? Thralled by the kidnapper, it could happen. And was worse in this case: me thinking he was the real returned lost love I'd never got over.

'I got over him,' I said.

He was fake and called Sean, the police said, was real Chris's sick twin. Twin not clone. No secret world kings. No one related to Don Thabbet. Don Thabbet was real Chris's boss, nothing more. I'd been fooled, Sean had made up a real tall story, I'd fallen for it—understandable given the circumstances. I shouldn't blame myself or feel ashamed, these things happened. Rest would cure me. Lie down and look out of the windows at the red roofs of Barrow. Sean was ill, a lifetime condition, crazy from birth, multiple incidents. He'd confessed all, was now back in secure professional hands, would face the law in due course.

Yes, real Chris had a dodgy twin, which real Chris had never known until his reunion with his birth mother's family some years before after tracking them down, expensive Californian investigations he probably now wished he'd never bothered with. Real Chris and his statement to the police. No, it wasn't possible to give me info about why the mother had let one twin go off and live with Alan and kept the mad one, private family info I wasn't privy to. Real Chris yearned to be with me now here in Barrow in person, and would be—if it wasn't for that pesky Icelandic volcano, had I seen the news? Yes, it was at it again, sharding the air, all transatlantic plane traffic quite impossible. For the moment, how inconvenient. Real Chris would be over on the next possible flight, fingers crossed.

Meanwhile: white flowers. His people sent fresh baskets every day.

The smell of the flowers made me want to vomit. I felt them sensing my hormones, snitching my moods to secret elites peering at me through smeared cameras baked into every surface. I felt mad and woozy and conned. I looked at the roofs of Barrow, I watched TV, I thought about Scritch, I couldn't think about Flora, who was dead with her family, they said. No, they couldn't say if Sean had been involved. I made them take the flowers away. The helmet, its hum, other clanking and machines, vibrations, a metallic tang in my mouth, screams from the corridor, the bags and the catheter. They gave me bed baths, creamed my sores.

I lay pinned to the bed by the hot buzzing helmet gaining back movement in my arms and legs. I watched the weather forecast and saw the Irish Sea dragon and the eye of Man winking away. Victim Support showed me my cards from friends and colleagues, the ones from real Chris, it looked like his handwriting. They put me on loudspeaker to hear my friend Lara send her love and commiserations for one minute. She'd be up in due course.

Victim Support read me a printed email from real Chris. How he wished he could be physically present with me in Barrow during this shocking time. The unfortunate volcano. So very sorry, so devastated about Flora and her family, so very worried, so very grateful I was in good hands, etc. How awful that it had to be this incident that brought us together after all these years. He'd never stopped thinking about me, loving me deeply, trying desperately to find me but failing, what with my name change, me being Nim Burdock now and not Nim Wynn. Always hoping things had turned out well, always honouring me and our time together. So much to say, so longing to say it in person. Drat that volcano. He couldn't wait to see me after all this time. The shame of what he'd put me through back there in New York and Silicon Valley. He hoped I had it in my heart to forgive him. He'd been going through a lot in those days.

The unique sound of this creep. How could I have for one moment fallen for Sean the fake? And yet this real Chris seemed to be suggesting it wasn't him up there in my flat the first time.

'He's desperate to talk to you,' the Victim Support lady said. 'The doctors will make an exception in this case.'

So we video-talked briefly, me and real Chris, him jerky from America, Victim Support holding a tablet screen up above me in my helmet, a specially modified device—she said—that wouldn't interfere with my medical machines.

'Nim,' he said, freezing and pixellating but exactly as he had been in my flat, plump and whole, American lilt, running unstumped finger down his nose.

'You were there,' I said. 'In my flat. You were the first one.'

'I can't imagine what you've been through. So very devastated about Flora and your loss.'

'Such a tragedy', he said, in a follow-up email read to me by Victim Support after she ended the video call due to me getting stressed and upset. Sean was a genius in some ways, photographic memory. Pathologically jealous of Chris since their first meeting, the shock of that meeting for someone already so fragile. How finding he had a twin had sent Sean over the edge: meeting Chris who wasn't damaged. From that moment on: an urge to warp everything Chris touched. An urge to pass himself off as Chris, how dreadful I'd been exposed to that pathological hatred. Flora and her family, words couldn't express.

They put things in my bag to calm me.

I lay there in my helmet which was doing what?

The four white sheets.

What's coded up inside you that they'll do anything for.

It was him the first time.

I had to get out, I screamed. I needed to see to friends, colleagues, a lawyer, to talk to my own doctor, to Jassy, Flora's mum. I was a lawyer, I knew what was due to me. I demanded my rights.

More things in my bags.

'Where are we?' I whispered to African cleaners at night.

'Barrow General,' they said.

I wanted to speak to Jassy. I wanted to speak to Tal. I wanted to speak to Sean, fake Chris, stump Chris, the plant-eater, the jealous loon. How was he? Where were they keeping him, could we speak? When I was better? Could I write? I knew it wasn't standard but I had a few questions, might help me in my recovery.

'Unlikely,' the lawyer said, squirming in embarrassment for poor thralled me. The family were powerful, US-based. As the lawyer understood it, Sean was back in their care.

The lawyer was young and from Barrow, arranged by my firm in London who felt it was good for me to have someone local, the lawyer explained. He got them to let me talk to friends and colleagues, phones on speaker, many commiserations, what crazed circumstances. I could have actual visitors in a while. Flora's mum Jassy didn't want to talk to me, was in a bad place, needed space, hoped I could respect that. I shouldn't talk too much anyway, give away too many details to friends, the lawyer said. The story, currently, was being kept from the press.

'Brace yourself,' the lawyer said: when the story came out things would get juicy. Important people, multiple homicides. He wanted to know if I thought it remotely possible that Sean had killed Flora and her family, gassed them in the camper van while I wasn't looking?

I slept a lot.

The things in the bag.

The helmet on my head.

They told me it was Christmas, festooned a wall with one strand of tinsel, showed me cards and gifts from friends and colleagues and real Chris, opened them for me: books and toiletries, for when I was better, cams for me to slather on. They worried about my mental state. I watched Christmas programmes on my TV.

The police came and talked me through the whole caboodle: Scritchwood, Alan, Chris, Sean, disappearing homes, my dead phone. The family had had an inkling Sean might come for me, the police said: computer forensics had uncovered his long-term obsession with me, the chucked first love of his sworn enemy, a fellow victim he was determined to track down and pass himself off to. I shouldn't be ashamed, he'd passed himself off to others many times before, had been researching me for years, remote stalking, building up info, deranged.

'But he knew everything.' Not just my online traces. 'Sean' had known everything real Chris had known, almost everything, intimate details. Real Chris must have briefed him, I said.

Sean was a skilled hacker, had infected my machines and listened in to conversations from my cameras and microphones and speakers, knew every keystroke, the police said. I mustn't blame myself for being fooled.

'But he knew about our relationship, childhood.' Things that predated any phone or computer. He'd known how to pinch, for fuck's sake.

But perhaps I'd been recorded talking about it, to friends? Therapist's notes? Nothing written on anyone's machine or spoken near a device was safe from Sean's arts, they said. Connected boilers, digital watches. Even when things seemed switched off, for someone with those skills.

Or perhaps real Chris had told Sean big details when in California at their first meetings, before knowing how crazy Sean was, when he first found Sean and tried to bond? Or perhaps Sean had hacked real Chris's machines? Perhaps real Chris had written it all down somewhere, our history, and Sean had broken in? And Sean could of course hack all Chris's face ID, fingerprint recognition. Apart from that stump. But maybe he'd done it before the stump occurred. And maybe pinching wasn't dreamed up by Alan, was some Daoist thing like the Chinese map.

Or perhaps it was Tal. He knew most of those details, right?

How *was* Tal? I had questions for Tal. I demanded to speak to him.

Tal was fine, the police said. Safely sectioned, normal prattling. I could visit him when I got better. His hospital had confirmed that someone signing themselves as Chris Kopp had indeed visited Tal on the evening of my kidnap, I might be interested to learn. And it could be confirmed that Alan was dead.

And not my dad.

But why had real Chris come to see me first that night in my flat, wanting the book?

Real Chris hadn't, the police said. It had been Sean twice, stuck-on fingers and make-up. Sean had confessed.

No, I couldn't read Sean's confession, yet. In due course. And no, nothing was anything to do with the secret powers behind the internet. When I mentioned that kind of thing people looked down.

Who did I think *were* the secret powers behind the internet? Why did I think they'd be interested in me? Sean had built me a cathedral of doubt and I'd stepped right into it. Was I lonely? the therapist said. Who did I see in person, regularly, apart from work colleagues? Who were my actual friends, boyfriends? I'd had a strange childhood and history, by all accounts. Was that why I hadn't gone to the police when I could after Sean kidnapped me? Cos it had actually been nice, to be with someone? Cos I was still in love with real Chris and obsessed, to the exclusion of normal relationships? Could we explore that? I'd brooded over real Chris a lot over the years, hadn't I? Lots of online forums? Had I ever thought of digital detoxes, taking a break somewhere, working less hard, taking up a new hobby, stepping back from the virtual and commercial world? Crafts could be good for you. Yoga and mindfulness. There were people she could recommend. Perhaps it was worth examining why I'd been so susceptible, why I wanted to think important people were interested in me, that my childhood contained important secrets, that I was special in some way? Conspiracy thinking felt good, she understood that: made powerless people feel connected, discovering their own world instead of what was handed to you. But that feeling could be exploited by the unscrupulous, she explained. Lots of fake news these days, you had to check your sources. And it denied people agency, to think there were vast conspiracies. Had I been in therapy before? How had that worked out for me? Current events entitled me to four free follow-up sessions once I was released and back in London, she felt I might benefit from more. Sometimes events like this could have positive outcomes, remote as that might seem now, serve as 'wake-up' calls. Did I ever think of writing it all down? Sometimes that could help, when I was ready, when the helmet came off.

Which would be?

Soon.

On the TV news: yet another terrible quake in the South Pacific. The goofy dragon on the weather. The eye of Man, sending people to space.

Friends and colleagues called and heard me out on loudspeaker. My friend Lara drove up from London and they let me see her for twenty minutes, sworn not to excite me.

'He told me things,' I said.

'I'm sure he said plenty,' she said. 'But what's the alternative? Ancient conspiracy, massive police collusion with secret techno elites. Controlling the weather? No wonder you want the internet.'

I wanted it but no one would let me have it. 'No mobiles or computers,' staff said with real compassion: it interfered with my helmet and other specialist equipment. Apart from that exception in real Chris's case. Plus I needed to give myself space to heal and rest, tone down my enthusiasms. The helmet would be off soon enough, I could gorge then.

A nurse took pity on me one night, looked things up for me on her phone, read out slow-loading pages in monotone. No mention of Flora and her family being dead. No mention of my kidnapping, of me here. Nanocams: did not seem to exist. The Isle of Man *did* have a thriving tech and space industry, *was* the fifth most likely nation on earth to launch a spaceship. The Great Pyramid in Giza *did* have the same latitude in metres as the speed of light. Real Chris: the standard bio, no mention he was Don's son. His various concerns and philanthropies, his still-churning social media. Yes to the Icelandic volcano.

No mention of mad twin Sean that the nurse could find, we didn't know his last name: Sean Thabbet? Sean Kipp?

A rare business mag profile of Don Thabbet, that well-known venture capitalist and philanthropist. A far-sighted titan who had shaped our age. Current age: ninety three. The youngest scion of a Midwestern steel and banking dynasty. Early fascination with technology. Relocation to the west coast, immersion in the early personal computing revolution. A recluse. A quiet, commanding, behind-the-scenes visionary even at his advanced age. A gimlet eye for opportunity and talent. Intensely private, rarely mentioned, wholly necessary, vast wealth, commanding vision, gentle guiding hand, ruthless business instinct. The man behind the men—no women here. A passion for fine food, opera and sailing. Had found happiness with his third wife, a Norwegian model. A son who'd died in a boating accident years ago. One photo, the one I'd remembered: fat ancient Don in big sunnies and white cap on a yacht, cracked skin, perhaps looking like an old fat wrinkled Chris. Hard to say.

I begged but that was it. And she wouldn't do it again and neither would anyone else, even my friends on loud speaker. No one wanted to encourage my 'research'. Calm and rest, everyone said, so I could get out quick. Then I could search all I liked.

No way I could go back to Vengeance Street, sorry. Me and fake Chris had broken into private property, me under duress but still. No info on the owner of the house could be provided to me at this time, suffice to say it wasn't Alan's. Sorry, the Victim Support lady said, even if closure on Barrow and its contents was the only way I could begin to recover or believe their story. Vanished houses, poor thralled me. First-love vulnerability, being extra-susceptible because I had no real family, a heady brew, the ache of old wounds. All to be unpicked by proper

183

professional counselling which wasn't to be confused with Victim Support which was a quite different thing. A crazed imposter had dreamed up a pack of nonsense, I shouldn't blame myself. Some huge paranoid opera I'd got suckered into. Perfectly normal given the circumstances. Now rest and letting go, walks in nature, the therapist said.

The helmet and tubes came off. They put me in pyjamas, wheeled me to a private room full of plants and flowers for the last few days before my release, made me practise walking. Still no internet, the servers were down. I did physio, ate brown food, looked at my pale thin face and shorn hair in the mirror, clutched at the sink. I felt bad: dizzy and groggy. I puked and puked.

The labyrinth in my inner ear, my bone labyrinth and vestibule, did I know about them? the doctor asked. The ear did hearing, it also did balance, she explained. The bone labyrinth and vestibule of my left inner ear had been damaged due to the Vengeance Street fall or the blow to my head. Not permanently, they hoped, but for now I had labyrinthitis, a condition which could cause loss of balance, a sense of vertigo, nausea, permanent dizziness and queasiness, a ringing in the ears, the feeling that the room was spinning. I might find my sense of time was affected. That's why when I looked into the mirror my reflection seemed to lag and even smile at me. It would pass eventually, they hoped: it could be two weeks, it could be more, it was very unlikely to be permanent. Treatment meant a combination of medicine and physio. In a sense I had to retrain my whole body to walk and move about, much of it was about eye coordination. She showed me eye exercises: blinking and jerking I had to do while walking up and down in straight lines. A relatively minor ailment with relatively major symptoms. Studies had shown that recovery was very much linked to positive attitudes and psychotherapy. The condition could be caused by traumatic events. I needed calm and rest.

My door opened onto the ward corridor, the nurse's station

directly opposite, nurses eager to help whenever I stepped out. The other patients were very old, shuffling up and down in dreamworlds, no one I could connect with. The doors at the end of the corridor were opened by staff passes I didn't have. There were no windows in the corridor or in my room. I yearned for natural light. I was unsteady on my feet, needed help at all times. I lay in bed and looked at the peeling grey walls. I did my exercises but felt worse. The me in the mirror lagged and once winked at me, I was sure. They gave me pills. Release and friends' visits were delayed. I couldn't leave or see people. No devices till I was better. To get better I had to get fit. I walked long straight lines with African nurses up and down the corridor, jerked my eyes round like they showed me.

My new room had a new TV, fixed up in the corner in the same place. I found, by fiddling with the interactive button of its new remote, that this TV had a crude internet browser for clunky surfing as one of its features. Laborious text input via the remote, a small price to pay. At last: my solo spree. Flora and her family's death: still no mention, my kidnap: ditto. No missing houses in the Brechfa Forest area, some landslides due to larch-blight. Chris, Don, Sean: no new info. I needed Sean's last name which no one would supply. My current location: Barrow General Hospital, on the outskirts of Barrow-in-Furness, rated Satisfactory . My ten thousand unread emails, the concerns of friends and colleagues. Social media chugging on. Normans, chalk, electromagnetism, west Britain, the isles of Man and Manhattan, Britain's metal. The goofy dragon, the horse of the North Sea, the Baltic stag: all kind of, if you squinted. 9/11, moon landings, lizard kings, Illuminatis, the sacred geometry of Washington DC. I searched at night, mentioned my secret access to no one.

I found a page listing every ship that ever docked in Barrow. I guessed dates, went methodically through each ship looking up images and info, expecting nothing.

There it was.

An unforgettable image: grey hulking lines, so ugly it was stylish. The container ship from the docks. The *Skidblad*, it was called, built in South Korea, registered in Cape Verde. One of the largest container ships in the world.

The lawyer brought news of 'approaches'. The family were hoping there might be a way for things to be kept under the radar. Admission of guilt, a settlement, with me and Flora and Rhodri's families. Sean was already locked away, serving time for previous incidents in a secure environment, was too ill currently to face trial. If things could be kept private it might be more healing for all concerned. No need to drag things out in front of a court.

Who was making these approaches? What 'family?' I said. Real Chris? And murder, kidnap, were criminal offences, no way this could be kept out of court.

'Yes and no,' the lawyer said. Sean wasn't really fit to stand trial. And there was an argument—looking somewhere beyond me—that I'd consented, been party, gone along with Sean of my own free accord. Or at least that argument could be made: me the duped co-adventurer on a deranged quest, swept away into madness by the apparent return of my lost love.

'Fuck off,' I said.

And then there were Rhodri's drug connections. Yes, things were murky on the Rhodri front. Gangland slayings, a bad temper, might be quite unconnected, what had gone on with poor Flora and the kids. Might be nothing to do with Sean after all. In which case the only real crimes apart from my 'kidnap' had been the stealing and breaking into Vengeance Street, minor offences. Charges could be dropped, things smoothed out, in the circumstances. If I'd work with them.

'Think about it,' the lawyer said. As he understood it the family were prepared to offer quite a bit of compensation. Computer people, California-based, venture capitalists, very private, didn't want this getting out. Plus other considerations: I'd been party to stealing, breaking and entering, CCTV footage existed showing me very much going along. I may have been drugged and duped but it didn't look like I'd been acting under duress. Not good for my lawyering career. Plus, as he understood it, there was a suggestion that the name I called myself, my entire identity, wasn't exactly the name and identity I'd been born with. It seemed some people were suggesting I'd grown up with real Chris in Scritchwood Covert Motorhome Park under a different name.

'That's not a crime.'

It might well be, he said, as I should know as a fellow lawyer, if I hadn't gone about my name-changing via legal routes. If, for example, I'd purchased new passports, IDs, for substantial sums in dodgy places, had been purporting myself about the world on bought papers, received qualifications under fake names. I'd be struck off and worse: major implications for my future life, potentially. Plus the suggestion of nuttiness: disappearing homes, secret kings.

And were 'they' threatening all this would get out?

The lawyer shrugged and shook his head. 'Take it,' he said. They were generous people, what was the point? They'd already been so generous: my private room, my private treatment, my new clothes, soft towels. Who did I think was paying for all that?

Until then I hadn't thought about it but now I did it was clear that my room and whole hospital set-up weren't standard NHS. Private room, ensuite bathroom, long chats with doctors, therapists. My new soft pyjamas. Quinoa salads, posh bread. All the books and magazines, my new pants and toiletries.

I got up, opened the drawers of my small room, saw clothes, cashmere, cotton I'd never seen before, that hadn't been in the drawers the last time I opened them. A black wool coat with fancy silver lining hung from a peg on the door. The fluffy dressing gown I was wearing.

All from real Chris, the family, where did I think they came from? the lawyer asked.

Snitching clothes, stitched with what art? And where was the lawyer from? Who was paying his bills?

I screamed, tore my clothes off, tried to run out of the door. Nurses and the doctor came, new injections.

'It's OK,' the therapist said when I woke.

I wanted to get out right now, I said in a quiet voice. No more lawyers, no more *her*, paid minions. I wanted the police, right now. I wanted my real friends. I couldn't stay here any more. What date was it, were they drugging me? Was that why I was so woozy? I wouldn't eat or drink anything they gave me, no more medicines, fuck labyrinthitis, I'd rip out all the tubes. I wanted to see the sky, go outside. It was my right.

My stomach heaved, I felt the room lurch.

I got up, went to the bathroom, puked again, cleaned myself with snitching towels. They'd dressed me again: clothes I'd never seen before, soft comfy sweat pants, jersey top. Who'd dressed me, seen me naked and conked out?

The me in the mirror winked at me again.

The therapist came into the bathroom to comfort me. It had been a major trauma. There was lots to process. Everything was going to be OK.

'I'm going now,' I told her. I wanted to see the sky, go outside, get some fresh air.

I was lost inside my head, she said next to me at the mirror. This was a dangerous time for me, my recovery depended on not succumbing to whirlwind thoughts, I had to keep things clear. She'd walk with me, down long hospital corridors. I needed to walk in straight lines. I'd soon feel better, get rid of those crazy Scritch riddles clogging my head.

'I'm in this with you,' she said. 'I'll help you, every step of the way. You tell me everything, we'll work it all out together. I'll take the leap and believe you, how about that? You tell me about

Scritch, every last word, I'll write it all down for you, we'll go through it together: all the games. You know what? I'll even go along with you and believe the missing house.'

'Who pays your salary?' I said. 'Real Chris, right?' I was leaving this so-called hospital right now, I told her. I was fine. Let them send the police to arrest me with their syringes. Call the lawyer.

I went out of the bathroom, put on the coat. Who cared if they were all science clothes? I couldn't leave naked, all I cared about was getting out. I'd reshave myself later, steal new clothes, tie on the plastic bags, suck roots.

She came out after me, we stood in my room. The room lurched again. I stumbled, she stumbled too. Books on the shelves fell on their sides. Not just in my head: the whole room was moving.

I pushed past her, opened the door, stepped out into the corridor. She followed. Just us, no other patients and the nurse's door was closed. The ground swayed, we stumbled. I ran, she came after me. I got to the end of the corridor, pushed against the ward doors which opened. I ran down a new empty grey corridor, found spiral metal stairs, started to climb.

Up and up, round and round, the chime of the metal, holding the banister, looking for an exit, a window. After three or four floors I found one: a round window, a set of round windows.

I ran and looked out.

No Barrow, no hospital, no shops, no land, nothing. Just sea, grey wrinkled sea under grey clouds, white churn. I was on a ship, I knew its name. Sad Asian pop played.

27

The therapist, who'd told me her name was Ramona, manhandled me back down the stairs with help from three burly men dressed as hospital porters.

'Are you going to inject me?'

'If we need to.' I'd had a troubling day, she said, who knew what I might need. Lots of old fears and repressed memories bubbling to the surface. The very best thing for me was going to be trusting her, telling her everything, all those old stories of Alan's rattling around inside my head, that seemed to be mixing me up, delaying my recovery so. And after that sleep, which my body and mind so needed to heal, after all I'd been through.

They mangled me down the humming corridor.

Back to the ward, my old room—what seemed to be my ward and old room or cabin? But what did I know: grey empty identical floors, corridors of closed doors.

The room seemed the same: books and toiletries strewn in the exact mess I'd left them and even, from the bathroom, the same linger of vomit. But it seemed brighter, no peeled paint, and there were new elements: a large print of Alan's Chinese map up on the far wall and below that the old white Ickthwaite chest of drawers. On an easel: Alan's pinch chart: a drawing of a human palm with letters and numbers at each point and knuckle line. On the table: a thin silver laptop, a thin silver phone, two books and what looked like the green welly box. The books seemed to be the Alphabet, last seen in the blue Ford Fiesta in Ickthwaite, and *A Little Key To Drawing*, last seen in Vengeance Street with brailed newspaper tucked inside. And next to the shelves: a new white door, seemingly to the next cabin, with a small black panel where the handle should be.

'Let's pick up from where we were,' Ramona said. 'Your books. That you've been making such a fuss over?' Good news:

real Chris had wangled them from police evidence lock-ups, for me to work through with her, tell her everything Alan had ever said about them, every last Scritch.

Whoa, I said. Real Chris, that fine fellow, so very cold he'd really let them do this to me to squeeze out Scritch stuff? Really and truly? I knew Chris had morphed into something awful, I hadn't realised it was this awful. My old chum, selling me down the river so they could find out what? Ancient mysteries Alan had buried in us? That meant so much they'd go to all this trouble? Bunch of freaks. Why not—I didn't know—hypnotise real Chris, inject *him* with their nanocams to film his memories— real Chris already knew all the Scritch stories, had grown up with them too, if he really was real Chris. Or was he Don or some other clone or triplet gone bad? Could Ramona be sure? Could she be sure of me? Maybe I wasn't me. Perhaps I was duping her, perhaps we all were. And where was this so-called real Chris? Aboard? Was Don here too, peeping in? Any other Chrises? How about a Sean? Did they all ever appear together, a high-kicking Chris chorus, Don in the middle leading the tango? How about the babies and toddlers, a Chris crèche? A virus of Chrises, dragons preserve us, each as displeasing and dishonest as the next. Could I talk to them all? I'd tell them everything. No need for me to transact with the likes of her, whoever she was, who was she? Young, black, beautiful, stylish, cropped hair, silver hoops, slight West Indian lilt.

'Chris is on annual silent retreat, you don't remember?' He'd explained in Barrow, just before I came onboard, during my breakdown when he visited, Ramona said. Didn't I remember my breakdown, the visit of real Chris? Worse than she'd feared, they'd have to up my meds, reconsider electroshock. Chris had sat by my bed, held my hand—she said—explained it all: how he had to go off with his guru to the snowy forests of north Norway, he went each winter, a business-critical head-clearing. I didn't remember? What a state I'd been in. How worried everyone had been for me. How lucky I was to have friends like real Chris with the means and connections to get me aboard the *Skidblad*, the very best place on earth for long-term trauma recovery, healing at sea. Compassionate real Chris, who'd be coptered here post retreat with his clear head to sort me, who'd got her onboard too, for continuity of care. Whatever it took, for as long as it took: that was real Chris's pledge to me. How *was* I feeling?

Better, I said, with the passing of the labyrinthitis, just sea-sickness and their ploys to deal with.

She nodded. 'You'll soon find your sea legs.'

'And you,' I said: where did they find the likes of her? Stooging on the high seas for the world's secret rulers: was she hired or one of them, born to it? What did they look for in recruits, what was their approach? And that army of extras: the grannies and lawyers and doctors and nurses? Part-time actors paid in bitcoins or some other currency I had no ken of? Did they tell their secrets all at once or did you worm your way up, earn their trust? I was flattered, I told her, that they'd gone to all this trouble for me, got in such a quality interrogator. I spat at her, she slapped me lightly, men dressed as porters strapped me to the bed, she warned the helmet could return at any time. From a new fridge under the bedside table she cracked open a Coke can containing green juice she tried to force me to drink, foul stuff I spat back at her till they forced my teeth apart with an orange plastic funnel and poured the juice down me dregs and all.

After that I was in a much better mood.

No more need for porters or restraints. I relaxed on my bed, blabbed anything she fancied. What a splurge of relief to chat it all out. My ridiculous life. Stupid old Alan, crank camp, Ann Wynn and grim Clarice, her girlfriend, though I didn't realise that at the time. Bringing me up coldly, for money, Scritch games: fancy all that connected to secret world rulers! Fancy me now tucked up aboard their *Skidblad* with Ramona! How we laughed. Now with her help I could sift it finally, make some fucking sense of my weird history. I told her all: strange childhood, shambolic schooling, unregistered, no doctors, ex-airforce people, the crusties, the drug addicts, the dullness, Chris and Alan the golden beacons out of it, Chris and his machines. What it was like to fall for Chris, my escape from the nothing, how I'd always loved him, his dark recklessness and black moods, how attractive all that was when you're young and dumb and estranged from yourself and feel love can cure all and you can give solace with your heart and body and that will make you mean something. Nice old me, tending to Alan, peace-making between him and Chris, listening to those Zita stories. Grim Ann Wynn. Odd Clarice. My parents dying young, in a car crash, supposedly. Hanging out with Flora and her family, how they were my real family, crying when I talked about Flora.

'Poor old you,' Ramona said.

She drew on thin clear latex gloves, made me do the same, took me over to the Ickthwaite drawers. She yanked each open in turn, tweezered every last object, each nail and bit of fluff, quizzed me for any meaning, talked our results out to the walls. The walls were modern and recording us, she explained.

'Anything missing?'

Flora's note. The Hello Kitty beaded purse with Alan's half-horseshoe inside, what had seemed to be Alan's half-horseshoe. Somewhere at the bottom of the lake.

Back on the bed she got out the Alphabet. Did I really know it all off by heart? She opened it, tested me:

A *is the APE, who is dressed very well*
Though he is none too wise, as most people can tell

B *is the BULL, very stubborn is he,*
Although he's enjoying himself as you see

C *is the CAT, looking round very sly*

At a journeyman Dog, who is passing hard by

So I didn't need the Alphabet physically? I could remember every word?

I remembered every word, I told her, but words weren't everything, it depended how messages were coded. Sometimes you needed the pictures too: messages could refer to tiny details in the illustrations rather than the text itself. I knew the text but didn't have a photographic memory of the images so the physical book was still necessary. It had been Flora who could remember details of the pictures, Flora who was good at pictures and making things, from Jassy her mum who was good at all that.

Ramona passed me hankies, let me cry. 'Scritchwood,' she said after a decent while.

I told her again. The rain, the cranks, the mud, the mobile homes, the static homes, the caravans, the hippies, the druids, the nodding skag-heads, the grey rainy sky. Alan and Chris outside the fencing at the start of the Fall in their green bus. Tal and the gang. Me with Ann Wynn. The deserted airfield across the road.

'Is Alan my dad?'

'We're not sure.'

Alan, basically a tramp, of seeming Indian heritage, who said he was Chris's father though Chris came to dispute that. Alan was dark and Chris was white.

'Some story,' she said. 'Didn't it feel weird, like something was up?'

What did I know? I said: we were born into it, knew no better or different. It was definitely weird. Check out my therapy transcripts, I told her.

She nodded at the flatscreen TV so it came on. Something weird on the screen: strange blocky fragments in crude colours, jumpy angles, high and low, close and far, snatches of

Scritchwood Covert Motorhome Park in the rain: the gate, the path, the green, the new modern static houses at the bottom by the fence where we'd grown up, *Merriweather* replaced by some flash new bungalow, no trace of Alan's bus, BMWs now in the drives.

Crude empty silent images, no people, unfinished from a computer, sometimes the whole screen, sometimes a patch of screen, a meld of close and far angles patchworked from one zillion tiny cameras.

'Nanocams?' I said. 'From when I went back after New York?' That cold day in the half-snow, prowling the Covert for any trace of anything, going down by the water: had they been with me then?

'Live,' she said as the footage went high: bird's eye views of the Covert, the empty airfield, a new set of modern office buildings, the creeping suburbs, the railway line, the water, the big new road. Then swooping down by the water, juddering shots of the broken house worse smashed, diggers and big building works nearby. Inside: graffiti, needles, cans, rubbish patched together from all angles. Our mattress and cleared space long-gone, someone else's paradise now.

She gestured with her hands and the image froze and zoomed onto the new graffiti: people's names, crude words. She wanted to know if it meant things to me, which it didn't. She switched the telly off with a flick of her hand.

'So. How did Alan say he ended up there?'

He didn't say much. A past selling trinkets on the hippy trail from Greece and Israel to Goa and elsewhere, depending on the season. Meeting Chris's mum on that circuit. Her running off and him ending up in a disused bus parked outside the fence of the Covert just at the top of the Fall.

'Nice story,' she said.

Nothing special, I explained. Things were different now like they were everywhere, BMWs in the drives. But those days were the very tail ends of a separate way of living: old people from the old airfield, when it had been an RAF base during the war, who'd enjoyed the chaos of the war and didn't want regular life. Joined by younger people, different drop-outs. No digital tech then, you could be really cut off.

'Or think you were. So how come he paid Ann Wynn to take you in? That's what you found out? From her niece, right? So who are you?'

'I don't know,' I said, suddenly sad.

She passed me hankies. 'These trinkets,' she said, when I was ready, 'of Alan's? From the hippy trail. That he sold, collected. Things like this?' flicking her hand so that an image of the bead came up on the flatscreen, 3D but nicely rendered this time, full-screen, moving round.

A Jewel of Thram. One of two nearly identical beads we used as treasures in Scritch, that Alan buried in places for us to find according to his clues. White and brown smooth hollow oval stone beads speckled with red that Alan kept on a red cord and told us were lucky charms. Beads we used as toys that turned out to have high value.

'Which Young Pete told you.'

Which Young Pete told us after Alan vanished and we were going through his things, before Young Pete torched the bus.

'And Young Pete was..?'

Our Covert ne'er-do-well, odd-job man, scrap dealer, sometimes drug dealer, Chris's pal and bad influence.

'Who knew the bead was valuable how?'

'I don't know!' The whole cast of them. 'They were all part of it?'

'Maybe. This bead...'

'The dzi,' I said helpfully, because that's what the beads were called, I'd looked them up later. 'Dzi', pronounced 'zee'. Very old stone beads from Tibet, different coloured stone melded together through unknown processes. Some sold for millions.

'How much did you sell them for?'

Seven thousand pounds and two passports for the first one, from an old Chinese man in a smoky room at the back of the Elephant and Castle shopping centre, which got us to New York. Five thousand dollars and one passport for the second one, from a young woman at the back of a Vietnamese restaurant in Queens. Which got me back to London with a new name.

'You were robbed.'

'Is that what this is?' Trying to get your hands on lost beads of great value?

She laughed. 'Let's see. What did Alan tell you about terma?' flicking her hands to change the flatscreen so it became a browser, a Wikipedia page about terma, pictures of Tibetan boxes and writing and statues. 'Terma is real,' she said, reading from the screen: "Hidden treasure from the past".' A so-called Tibetan tradition, she said, of hiding precious information from the deep past in caskets in trees or rocks or in the ground or in lakes or the sky or in people's minds, so it could be found on purpose or by accident centuries later, direct ancient knowledge to blow away current perceptions, or to store secret information. The informations were sometimes written in a magical script that disappeared as you read it, she said, as the onscreen text began to fade. People who found terma were called "tertöns" she showed me, pointing out the umlaut on the 'o', the last thing to remain before the screen went blank.

'We think you might be a tertön,' she said. 'Or a terma. With knowledge hidden inside you, by Alan. Maybe I'm the tertön, discovering you. How exciting,' picking up something from the green welly box.

The iron ring. A huge dark heavy ring, for a big man's finger, the kind of thing a Viking chieftain might wear, the setting shaped like a miniature castle, with hinges you could open to reveal a dark cube with two hollow cylinders entwined with etched floral swirls.

'The Ring of Seeds,' I explained. In Scritch: a sign that the wearer was evil.

'Really. What did Alan keep in there?'

'Nothing.'

'What did he say it was for?'

'Playing with.' So much junk.

'And this?' Unfolding from a plastic bag the crochet coverlet, the one—it seemed—from Vengeance Street, not made by Jassy. Maybe one hundred multicoloured squares of bright acrylic stitched together in apparent random pattern.

'The same colours? As your one in the bus? What did Alan say about colours? Did he link them to numbers? What did Alan say about numbers, the personality of numbers? Did Alan make you remember any numbers, did he code them into the blanket?'

Not that I recalled. The swans, though, the snowmen, I told her.

'Any specific stories? We'll work on that,' she said, 'later. Mix you up some new juice, see if that jogs things along. And we'll pinch,' pointing to the hand chart, 'you'll show me how, we'll have fun with it, OK?' pulling the gloves back on, making me put on mine which I couldn't remember taking off. 'This,' she said, leafing through *A Little Key to Drawing*, handing it to me. 'A pacey read.'

I wouldn't know, I said. I'd never read it. The Vengeance Street version I was apparently flicking through—gossamer pages, old words, black ink, splotched symbols—wasn't our one from Scritchwood. Our one had been a dummy: a wooden box when you opened it up.

Page fifty-six, I thought it had been. *Darling Nim.*

'What's wrong?'

'The note, from Alan. It's gone. He tore it up, Sean. He chewed it. I only read the first bit.'

'The Braille? What did it say?'

'That he wasn't Chris. That I should beware. Was it from

Alan? Is Alan alive? Is he sending me messages?'

The green juice wearing off. Me crying again.

'It's getting late,' Ramona said. A good session, we'd do more tomorrow, discuss Alan, go through the rest of those things in that welly box, do some pinching, some Braille, go deep into Scritch. All the stories, I should get ready, the Zita stuff too, plus we'd talk Tal and more terma. And if I did as well tomorrow as I'd done today she'd tell me a bit more about Sean, AKA fake Chris. Just one last thing and she'd leave me.

Another nod and flick at the TV. More 3D fragments, mini camera surround footage, of Vengeance Street this time, with sound. Wobbly me, crazed fake Chris getting dragged out of his under-stair cupboard from different angles by covered people in yellow plastic hazard suits. His eyes gouged out, swallowing pulp, blood pouring down his eyeless face, them trying to restrain him, stop his hacking. Dreadful: me screaming, him screaming, shrieking nonsense at me from the weird screen:

The boat. Sad nothing weed.

'Yes that.' Ramona froze it, played it back slo-mo a few times, stretching the words. 'Scritch? Done with the Alphabet? What does it mean?'

Not the foggiest, I said. Not Scritch as far as I could remember, and in any case Sean didn't know Scritch, was fake, right? Except he *had* known so much Scritch, how had he known it? A warning, to me, about this boat, the *Skidblad*, maybe?

'Perhaps it'll come to you,' tomorrow, whenever. If it did I should speak it to the walls. Or call her on the phone if something strong came on—she showed me the phone: standard apps, her the only contact, US prefix. And now she'd be off and I should eat, wash, sleep, fortify myself for another very strong session tomorrow, OK? I'd done well.

'And if you do as well tomorrow I'll let you have this,' pulling the tip of a red envelope out of her jacket pocket. 'To you. From Sean.'

She left, old nurses in new uniforms wheeled in sushi.

I wasn't hungry.

I sat alone on the bed feeling the juice wear off, watching the sushi, watching it wriggle. Real Chris: so cold that he'd agree to this harvesting of me, for what info? Me being fooled by Sean, fake Chris, who was so different from ice-cold real Chris, how could I have fallen for it for one instant? Me selling out Sean, pointing the way to him in his under-stair cupboard, what he'd tried to tell me, what I hadn't believed.

They'd have found him anyway.

All that blabbing to Ramona, what had I told her?

Help me Alan.

The hacked-out eye.

I tried both doors—the main door to the corridor and the new side door, leading where? Both locked, no handles, only black panels, for pass keys, fingerprints, retinas I didn't have.

I screamed and screamed, banged my head against doors and walls till there was blood. I opened the laptop, felt its light warm me, felt them watch me from the other side. Anonymous make, standard operating system, a picture of the *Skidblad* as the desktop, 8.16pm on January 16, apparently. The browser had my bookmarks. For laughs I looked up the *Skidblad*, now seemingly registered in Norway to a company registered to a company owned by a company owned by a company owned by a company called *Thabbet Investments*, the browser said. No mere container ship but the ultimate in discrete luxury, an exclusive set of zillionaire condos-at-sea.

A place to stash ultrarich but forgetful grannies while you got your hands on their assets, a message-board comment said. Lock up your black sheep: heroin teens and inconvenient wives. A floating gold outhouse for the embarrassing and incontinent. Max security ahoy.

An occult ship, another message said. Filipina prostitutes found cut in its wake.

I looked up Flora, who was now alive and on-grid, had set up a website for her new yarn business. Rhodri had a new site too: caravans glamping in Wales, images of their tarted-up caravan collection, him and Flora and the kids with big smiles among sheep welcoming holiday-makers with slices of sponge cake and steaming mugs of tea, their returned cottage in the artful blurred background, the baby now alive and a toddler, golden curls, links to their new social media. Flora and I were now social media friends: I clicked on my feed: joyous new photos of me on a Scottish New Year's walking holiday, with friends in London over Christmas, outside a new flat I was moving into with some hunky new unknown man I had my arms round, the tip of my index finger missing.

I accessed the same page via the browser on my new phone: sadly my social media had become a shrine. I'd died in November, friends and colleagues left emotional posts of fond memories, would hold me in their hearts forever. I looked myself up: *Troubled Lawyer Found Dead.* After disappearing from my flat in London, after many years of anguish and a disturbed cult childhood, I'd overdosed in the hotel of a motorway service station outside Slough. On the phone I looked up Flora too: very sadly she was also dead and her whole family, after a dreadful fire tragedy when a Forestry Commission lorry laden with chemicals skidded on wet bendy roads and smashed into their remote home.

I accessed the same page on the new improved TV browser after trying and failing to switch TV on by flicking my hand like Ramona, having to resort to the old remote. The TV was now different: no more bog-standard Barrow General Freeview, dull UK channels, North West Tonight local news. Now it was passing itself off as the *Skidblad*'s personalised onboard menu:

Welcome Nim Burdock!
Information | Entertainment | Journey Planner

According to the browser, I'd actually hanged myself in Barrow General Hospital after a mini crime spree, had left various notes.

I clicked the TV's Journey Planner, found it was 10.09 am on February 4 and we were in the South Pacific, heading from Australia to Fiji. I checked the phone: it was 4.34pm on April 31 and we were rounding the tip of South Africa, according to the location app. *Antarctic Mobile* listed as the carrier, but all calling was disabled, I tried to call Flora on her new mobile listed on her new website available on the laptop. I tried to call Ramona, the only contact in my phone address book. I tried to call the police. I tried to call my own number, my dead phone.

Cheap laughs. I sat on the bed, felt everything watch me, comb me for Alan's ancient secrets. *What were you up to, old man? Using me too the whole time?* The room heaved. I got up, puked green juice down the loo's new steel innards. I sat back on the bed, watched the things hum.

The plants were the worst: ferns and Easter lilies bending in to report my hormones. I got up, yanked them out of their pots, pushed some into the bathroom bin while mirror-me watched, squashed the rest into my drawers of posh clothes: soil, roots, leaves, cashmere: a bad mess. I mixed the sushi in there too, hoped I was entertaining the walls. New moods burrowed into me, my lungs full of Don-made digi-spores, swallowed cams trawling my veins. Porous me, infected by surfaces. Why bother with green juice when they patrolled me, could alter my moods with much less drama? But they'd have some reason, hypermaths plotting my personality versus their wanted outcomes.

'You fuckers,' I said to the walls.

I was lying down, I got up, tried to find things to prise doors open with, could find nothing that wasn't blunt or screwed to the floor or walls. The Ickthwaite drawers full of crap were gone, the Chinese map, welly box, Alphabet and *Little Key* with them. I went into the bathroom, looked at the lying mirror, my eyes, a big yellow bruise on my forehead. My hair seemed longer. The same clothes. Had I slept? Had time passed? How long?

Could I trust the mirror? I prowled for other reflective surfaces, pulled my sweatpants down and saw the 'V' cut into my upper thigh by Sean in the lake. Healed now, part of my body, a clock of sorts though with skin grafts, they could fake it, what couldn't they fake? I opened drawers, found the soil and mess. Withered plants, stinky sushi, pink fish hard and curled at the edges. I closed the drawer and opened it again: green plants, fresh flesh. A shrimp tail curled.

The room lurched, soil and sushi fell all over me, I went to the bathroom to wash it off. The me in the mirror sneered.

I checked pipes for ways out, checked the new toilet, crawled the soft carpet, opened every drawer and cupboard, found a life jacket and evacuation instructions under the bed. I opened the fridge, found no messages I could see, just the 'Coke' cans. I read every last label, every last e number, cracked the cans open, poured the juice down the loo.

I sat on the bed. The room lights began to dim, I yawned, felt sleepy. I fought against this, pinched myself, fought against everything I felt, microtroops on parade.

I screamed and screamed. I got up, tried to turn the lights up, found there were now no light switches. I ran full tilt at the cabin door, hurt my shoulder, nothing budged. I did the same against the new door as the lights dimmed right down, ran at it again and again with head and fists, made everything bleed, ran at that door till it opened.

28

Black in there and the light in my windowless cabin almost gone. A lurch, a chemical new smell, of paint perhaps.

I stood in the doorway, called out 'hello', waited for porters.

A thudded reverb to my voice: I was calling into something padded.

I felt my way back to my bed.

I got the phone and, using it as a torch and sensing them with me, went back to the doorway, knew they'd planned this, let it happen, were watching, could feel them watching, their reality TV.

I shone the phone into the new room.

The feeble beam lit a cabin like mine but not like mine. A stuffed cabin that was—what?

I froze.

A cabin that was the front room from Vengeance Street, as if entering from the kitchen: burgundy velvet, sofa, mantelpiece, objects, bookshelves, flocked wallpaper, chintz, doilies, pictures, crochet coverlet. I stepped back, not trusting what I saw, not trusting my brain. But there it was: the original from Vengeance Street, that Alan had fashioned his bus into a copy of, that Alan had taught me to visualise inside my head as my mind bus, my memory palace where I learnt to store Scritch and law and other info, the room I knew by heart.

Except this wasn't quite the original. They hadn't cut out the actual front room from Barrow and hoisted it onboard. Things looked the same but were…smaller, kind of three-quarter-sized and made of…all one thing. I stepped inside, felt the walls, the objects lit by my beam. Everything looked kind of right but was… fake and melded together: the Chinese map on the wall, the books on the shelves, the Toby jug, the scimitar on the mantelpiece that I tried to pick up, the three wise old Chinese babies, the swan, the snowmen, the conch shell. Even the peacock feathers weren't soft, were joined to their vase and that joined in turn to the side table. The whole room and its objects had been — what? — carved and painted from one muchness, 3D-printed, layer by layer? Made from plastic, resin, foam that set. Discount magic, one big organism.

My chore for tomorrow, begun early: decode this room for them.

Or was I performing on schedule: supposed to think I'd broken in illegally and had one over on them so they could track my eyeballs, see where I looked when I thought they weren't watching so they could crack my secrets.

I looked down, at the blue carpet swirls.

How far did it go? I had to know, before I performed the magic I was planning. I bolstered myself and went in further, towards the stairs: had they built an upstairs, could I go up there? The white net curtains, the windows — but they weren't real windows, were screens behind glass displaying streetlights of Walney Island in the rain.

The stairs led up to a blank wall. But the low under-stair cupboard was there, where Sean had tried to hide, where Sean had cut his eyes out, so weird to me then, so understandable now. I tried the low door but it was fake and didn't open.

Why not print that too? How did they know Alan's secrets weren't buried in there or up the stairs?

And what *were* Alan's secrets and were they buried in here or in me?

Cloak it. Micro-spies taking notes up in my brain room. *Don't be in here thinking any of that. Block off your thoughts.*

I went back to my own cabin, put down the phone and picked up the laptop, the only thing of any heft that wasn't screwed down. I opened it up so it gave light, then took that back through the door to fake Vengeance Street, swung that laptop round.

The hardened foam or whatever the place was cobbled

together from wasn't too firm: the laptop did damage, let me wreak havoc: mash the place, reveal the white polystyrene innards, mince fake Toby jugs, mantelpieces, bookshelves.

Lights on back in my cabin: Ramona and co.

'Tsk tsk,' she said when I was back strapped on my bed, funnel in mouth, absorbing the green juice.

'It's important,' she said, standing next to me in the doorway, soft lamps now lit in Vengeance Street before us. Hard to say how much time had passed. Time enough for them to mend the smashed room, heal it, regrow it, print it again. Which might take no time: the press of a button, rotate the walls, Vengeance Street on-demand.

'Some things mean a lot,' Ramona said. 'It's more than you and me. It matters. For the world. The numbers Alan stole.'

I was juiced up to the eyeballs, she was my friend. 'I'm really trying,' I said. I cried. I shook my head. I could tell her statutes, stories, Scritches I associated with the objects but not what she wanted, not numbers, I couldn't remember any specific number stories though swans were twos and hooks were fives and the snowmen were eights.

'You need your right mind. Sleep will help, remember your dreams, in sleep we solve things, let's try again tomorrow,' leading me back to cabin and bed.

When I woke the juice had passed. The lights were on in my room and Vengeance Street, the connecting door open. My hair seemed the same length. My bruises and scars looked the same. The door onto the corridor was still locked.

They'd left me a new laptop to replace the smashed one. I took it into Vengeance Street and smashed it up again. I smashed up my cabin too. I smashed the mirror and the TV and the drawers, I smashed everything, turned on the taps.

'Seven years bad luck,' Ramona said while the porters dragged me out into the corridor and downstairs to distant floors. Far down into the empty humming bowels of the ship—if it was a ship, if we weren't lurching on vast hydraulics, a massive set.

A tiny cell, no lights, no furniture, nothing.

'Think about it,' as they slammed the door.

29

Echoing reverb, locked in black solitary inside cold metal, bobbing on sea or hydraulics, me and the hum.

At least it was honest: no weird doors to plastic rooms.

I lay freaking out in the black cell for a long time.

But losing it was too easy. I had to show a little bit of fight: how they'd played me, what they'd done to my friends.

And it was something to do: try to focus my mind.

And now I remembered that in Zita the dad sat in a black cell for twenty years and trained his mind to make its own movies and project them on the wall. And when Zita was captured she was put in another black cell and the dad communicated with her, through his mind movies. 'Rainbow Theatre,' Alan called it.

Zita, buried in the ninth layer of the underground maze—the layers had names: Ice Cold Hell, Slash and Murder Hell, the Hell of Acquired Goods, others I'd forgotten.

'Fear is only a distraction,' Alan said. 'A possibility you can give into, but only a possibility. There's always other possibilities. That's what makes everything bearable.'

Alan was in the corner in white holy man robes with a staff, looking a bit older, talking a little stiffly. His hair was pure white and plaited into two pigtails. He had a neat centre parting. He held out a bronze begging bowl.

'I'll tell you anything,' I screamed to the reverb. 'I don't know what you want. I'll calm down, I won't smash things.'

Them enjoying this: hacked night-vision microbes watching me lose it, micro-paparazzi waiting for peak meltdown. Roll up, roll up, watch the lady shit herself.

'Come on,' Alan said. He was either there with me or my rainbow theatre. Or their actor or projection. Now he was dressed in a bright orange prison jumpsuit.

He made me get up and start pacing the cell with him.

Physical action to get me out of my mind and start making a system, like Zita did. Drinking her urine, licking pipes and walls for condensation, pacing the cell and counting, doing exercises and meditation to see if she couldn't exit her own body and float free through steel walls as pure spirit, find her dad that way.

I got up, licked walls, started pacing, making my system, perking up and feeling better.

The meditation was called Zoo Wang, Alan returned to remind me. Now he was tatty trampy Scritchwood Alan. You sat cross-legged and let the world melt away. A place you could always access, once you'd learnt how to access it. A good place to go to when you found yourself in terror in hollow trees. If you could do it.

You felt a warm bubbling in your back and saw a semi-transparent white mist.

I'd never done it.

Supposedly kids couldn't do it, it would come later.

But later I'd put all that away.

I sat cross-legged in the black cell and tried to remember how you were supposed to do it.

Zita hadn't managed it either, then. Instead she'd gone practical: felt round and found on the wall one pipe that was big enough to climb.

I felt round and found a pipe. It had rings which gave you a foothold. I put a foot up on the first one, hoisted myself up. It was pretty easy, inching myself up that pipe till I reached the ceiling, it wasn't far. And then I found—just like in Zita's cell—that if I stretched my arm I could feel in the middle of the ceiling a small hole that was a bulb-less light socket I could put my hand through to lift up and shunt aside the surrounding circular panel and make a hole in the ceiling big enough to hoist myself up into.

In Zita, what was up there was the Cwyd, a large ticking thousand-eyed worm burrowing labyrinths of passages through the bronze walls of Zoll by means of her soft puckered mouth and twenty-thousand steel teeth. Passages you could get lost in or find your way through—if you knew the way, if you could avoid or murder the Cwyd before she gobbled you.

Giddy with my escape plan, for a moment.

Except Zita wasn't caked in snitching disco flakes.

I slid back down to the floor.

They wanted me to go up there, that was pretty certain. They knew Zoll and Zita. And Cwyds.

Nevertheless.

I got up, climbed the pipe, craned over to feel for and find the hole in the ceiling, lifted up and shunted the panel aside and hoisted myself up into the lair of the Cwyd.

30

I lay squeezed inside a dark warm plastic-smelling flat-bottomed tube packed with pipes, cables and insulation foam above. A utility space, it pretended. There was room enough only for me to crawl forwards on my belly one way—I was at the end of the tunnel. Even then there was only just room for me.

No hum. No tick of the Cwyd.

In Zita she crawled round the maze till her mind received rainbow instructions beamed from her father, and she made her way to him and they burrowed out together, narrowly escaping the Cwyd.

I replaced the panel and slithered in the pitch black, hoisting myself along on my elbows, roiling with waves or fake waves as they hit, a nanocam myself crawling down the veins of some vast beast. The metal beneath me felt warm and smooth apart from the ridges of doughnut-shaped panels I encountered every so often, doughnut-shaped panels like the one set into the ceiling of my own cell. These panels, like my own, had small holes at their centres—where lightbulbs should have been? The *Skidblad*, if I were still aboard, was a container ship: I guessed each room or cell or cabin was a whole or partial container with these panels set into their ceilings. The holes were big enough to stick my arm through, into blackness below.

Where lay what? Other prisoners? The cast of nurses and grannies? Alan himself? A projection?

I heard no sound. I thought about whispering down but couldn't risk drawing attention to myself from any sensor.

Except all sensors had already clocked me in this live video game for my remote controllers. Ship or set, it didn't matter: trapped inside their arena, waiting for the thumbs down. How many of us, I wondered: crawling round this machine for our various reasons, blueprinted by Alans or similar, waiting to bump into each other or Cwyds round the next corner?

Whatever the Cwyd was.

I wouldn't think about the Cwyd.

I found, with a bit of fiddling, that I could shunt these panels aside too, and therefore enter, if I wanted, the black containers or whatever nasty twist lurked underneath. But I didn't want to enter anything, even if the containers were empty, even if their doors might open—into what? Some corridor? For now I'd crawl my tunnel, find where it led, where they wanted to lead me. Later I might enter the containers, to dodge Cwyds, maybe. It was good to have options.

In Zita, the other cells in the Fortress of Zoll were occupied by the Empire's most savage villains and freaks.

After a long while of crawling perhaps the entire length of the ship I banged up against a dead end. I felt for the pipes and cables above me, found they coiled up into empty space above my head just big enough for me to stand and follow. I forced myself up the now vertical cables, used their regular ties as footholds, moved under as they coiled round again to run overhead in a new tight tunnel—laid out above the ceiling of the ship's next-up layer of containers, I assumed—or they wanted me to think.

This new tunnel was different: dotted with pinpricks of brightness, a runway of dim lights stretching out before me, the light they gave enough for me to see—for the first time in ages—the outlines of things: cables, my own hands. The light came from lit containers below me, I discovered, rooms I could peer into via the pinpricks, which were tiny magnifying peepholes set between the doughnut panels which continued on this floor. But here the panels were different: the outer doughnut surrounding a filled-in circle of metal at each centre—from which hung light fittings in the rooms below? And with their centres filled, these panels were unbudgeable: no way to get your hand in and lift up the panel, no escape into the rooms below.

In Zita, she knew when the Cwyd was approaching when the hands on her dad's quartz watch, which she wore on her wrist always, started moving round too fast. But I had no watch.

The rooms, as seen through the domed peepholes, were large comfortably-furnished cabins like my old cabin—not cells— some with pianos and art. All empty, bed sheet corners folded back identically, no sense of current occupation. A deserted five-star hotel.

Then I came to a room that was different: done-up Renaissance with draped purple velvet, gilt and mahogany, silver mirrors, old-looking tools and instruments on the walls. A five-pointed star on the black-and-white chequered floor. A wooden desk with a wooden globe and next to it a metal object I wanted to say was an astrolabe. A wall stacked with shelves of glass containers. A table with an hourglass, a huge egg in a wooden holder, a silver bowl full of water, a candelabra of lit candles, metal scales, pens and ink, a pile of old books, a pair of white gloves.

Ramping up the heebie jeebies. *Flattered, my good sirs. No expense spared.*

Except it was all probably cheap as chips, 3D plastic printed from the internet, cut-price devilry done on the fly.

The next room was the printed Vengeance Street front room, course it was. Or *a* printed Vengeance Street front room: undamaged, pristine, ready for me to enter and solve or mince if I felt like it which I didn't. If there was a way to open the closed doughnut panel and drop in, which there didn't seem to be.

Was that why they'd lured me up here?

I lay there for a while, one eye at the magnifying peephole, looking down at the Vengeance Street, taking care to look at no one spot in particular in case of eyeball tracking. Not that I knew where I ought to be looking, but nevertheless. Had people lain up here watching from peepholes when I'd been down there smashing the place up? *If* this was the one I'd smashed up. I remembered them dragging me down many more than one floor when bundling me down to dark solitary.

The next two peepholes showed my old suite: cabin and freaky bathroom with the freaky mirror, or what looked like my old cabin and bathroom, except fixed and tidied: uncracked mirror, new TV, new laptop. And one obvious new thing: a red envelope on the bed.

The red envelope, clearly, that Ramona had shown me the tip of in her pocket, supposedly containing a letter from Sean, fake Chris. My reward, if I blabbed correctly. Was this why they'd led me up here? Was I supposed to be so dumb that the sight of this red envelope would lure me into the room? How? To do what? To read it, some made-up thing? To believe it really *was* from Sean, lying there unattended?

Or *was* it really from Sean? And what would happen if I made it in there, read it?

And how was I supposed to get in?

I wiggled back round to the room's closed doughnut panel. No way to budge it.

Except, when I fumbled round in the gloom I sensed what I hadn't sensed in panels before: a kind of long metal strap or clasp like the embedded arm of an old record player reaching from the panel's centre to its edge where it was tethered to something—something that felt like a combination lock set into the tunnel's floor. I fiddled with this lock: six moveable cogs engraved with letters or numbers, letters or numbers it was still too dark for me to see.

But they were big enough for me to feel them. Numbers: zero to nine, that could be moved round, to do what?

Release the clasp of course. If you knew the combination. And if the clasp could be released then the panel could be opened, was the suggestion.

I felt them watching. I even felt—shamefully—the old Scritch desire to please by solving, to boost my score.

But if I *did* do what they wanted—what I felt they wanted:

open the lock, move the panel—how was I supposed to know what the combination was?

Their challenge, not that I was interested in them or their challenges.

The numbers Alan stole.

The numbers I had no inkling of. But if they'd coded the combination with Alan's numbers it would mean they already knew Alan's numbers, in which case they wouldn't need me to enter them. Right?

Fuck knew.

Idly I spun the cogs, felt the numbers. Then I arranged them: all ones, all zeros. In order: one two three four five. Reversed: five four three two one. The five and the six: five six five six five six.

A click and I felt the clasp rise and release. High fives all round for Chris and Don the wrinkled world king or what I was beginning to feel must be *the committee*, the team of humans, computers, robots, 3D printers watching me, real-time plotting this game for me.

Whoa, Chris. You'd really let them do this to me?

The void.

The eye.

I lifted the clasp, now free from its tethering at the doughnut's edge but still connected to the central inner circle. I found the clasp now functioned as a kind of winch to unscrew this inner circle. I unscrewed, the circle came loose, I pulled it up, found a hot bulb attached beneath, clattered it down next to me on the tunnel floor. The bulb continued to shine—battery operated? I saw myself and my tunnel's surrounds properly for the first time: tubes and wires and dust, the foam, my dirty hands and clothes.

I put my hand down into the empty centre of the doughnut, gripped and shunted aside the panel next to me in the tunnel, as I'd been taught. The hole beneath me was now big enough for me to enter the room below—by jumping down, I guessed, hoping for a soft landing, or by dangling from the ceiling which wasn't that high, letting myself drop down. Then I could read my letter.

I had no intention of doing any of this. I was just exploring my options, the illusion of options.

I replaced everything, relocked the combination lock, crawled backwards down the tunnel to the Satanic room and further, retracing my steps, squinting and feeling to see if combination locks tethered other doughnut panels. I found they did, and that the same simple code unlocked each one I tried.

I crawled back to my so-called room and peeped down at the red envelope, now positioned on the bed a little differently, I felt. Not that I cared. No way I was going down to investigate any portion of their set-up.

I toyed with unscrewing the light again, to have a torch for my onwards journey. But that was too risky: I could be sensed from below, other variables. Plus now I knew: I could get a light any time I wanted, if all locks and panels operated similarly.

If they did.

I left 'my' room behind me, crawled on above new empty rooms till I came to a place where the tunnel split. The runways of pinpricks running at right angles, *a fork in the path*, as happened to Zita. You bore to the left each time, that's how you found your way out, I remembered.

Your way out where? Into the sea?

Into the vast empty plains of the Steppe, in Zita: the borderland between the land of men and the land of beasts, where Zita's father had friends who were lions.

Deal with that when it happens.

But what if I didn't take left forks, disobeyed all scripts: theirs, Alan's?

Desperate, tired, starving, angry: it made sense to me then to go random. Fuck the pre-plan, trying to listen for rainbow directions. Instead go wherever, try my luck, take my chances.

Feel the twitch and flow.

I went right, crawled on, found new forks leading left, leading right, leading up. I took them or not, as I fancied. No one came for me, nothing stopped me, no Cwyd, no click, no hum, no sense of instructions getting beamed in from anywhere. I climbed up, squeezed through, followed pinprick runways, felt locks and panels, peeped into peepholes or not, saw endless empty hotel cabins, cabins with nothing at all in them, cabins half done-up. I brushed past thick cobwebs, as if no one had been through in ages, in contrast to the clean tunnels I'd come from down below. I was lost in a maze defying orders and it felt good. *Head up, wait for natural light.* That was my only plan. At one point I came upon three fresh Vengeance Street / cabin-bathroom combos. One of the Vengeance Streets was pristine but the other two were mashed-up in different ways that looked like my prior handiwork. The cabin-bathrooms seemed strewn with my stuff, as I'd left them. In one the mirror, TV and laptop were smashed just as I'd smashed them.

As if I really was on a backstage tour, behind the magic, had wound up in places I wasn't supposed to be, as if what was happening beneath me wasn't the seamless shunting of containers so that exactly what they wanted me to see next was delivered on-demand to my next peephole as I meandered, me versus their machine.

My body hurt by now, especially my arms and shoulders. My knees and elbows were rubbed raw. I decided moving up was the priority, taking any pathway that opened above my head. Even if it cost me my last strength to hoist myself up I had to do it. How many levels down could a ship's hold be?

If this was a ship.

It still swayed.

I made my way up, glutting myself with their cyberdust, stopping to rest when I had to, eventually coming to a new sort of level where the rooms were done up differently, as posh hospital rooms, medical paraphernalia. Not exactly 'Barrow General' but something similar. Perhaps I'd find a nurse or pensioner to help me. But there were no people in these rooms.

Or none at any rate till I came to one that did have someone in it, someone attached by tubes and bags etcetera to the bed, their eyes bandaged, lying on their back there naked facing up at me.

Someone who was Chris.

31

Or someone who was Sean, or supposed to be Sean, fake Chris. Because the thing down there right below me tangled in a sheet and lit bright for me to see more easily had a stump. And the thick beige bandage wrapped round the eyes. And the dip in the head—the head and face were shaved. A healing big scar on the calf. Other healing wounds, where he'd slashed himself, on his face and arms. Even, I could see via the magnified peephole—as though it had been set up for me to see it—the faintest outline of my own teeth marks on his left hand where I'd drawn blood when he'd kidnapped me from my flat so many moons ago.

It seemed.

I lay with my eye to the peephole, felt my heart thud, watched him from above. The fake, splayed for inspection. The real fake? The real stump Chris who'd come for me, dragged me into this, pretending? Who'd cut me in the lake, lain next to me in the burrow, told me about the world, shown me dragons, cared for me on our boat? The Sean I'd shopped? Was the thing on the bed under me Sean or was it another of them or something else cut to look like Sean? Was it Chris cut to look like Sean? Or a robot or a print-out, a bit of hardened foam with Vengeance Street wounds?

It slept. Its chest rose. It sniffed. It moved, the sheet moved. I saw the meaty circumcised cock.

I lay there. Big laughs in the control room, the pleasure of their cunning. Stepping it up, me trapped in big plots.

Grag Medusa. The eye.

I'd come here at random, what if I'd really outfoxed them, found what I oughtn't to: real Sean in his prison? The glimmer of possibility, had to be, right? Couldn't be one hundred per cent impossible.

Certainly could, real Sean would have said. The only other

person I see in this whole set-up and it's him? Laid out like that for me to inspect, on a platter? *Say cheese for the cams. Don't fall for it.*

Why? What could they want from this?

To get me to open the panel, get in there.

To do what? Rustle him out, blind Sean?

Why?

I moved backwards away from the peephole, back to the panel. I felt for the lock. But this lock was different from all the others: a long thin heavy metal cylinder not embedded in the floor but lying loose next to me, a small metal 'U' at its end attaching it to the panel's clasp. This cylinder felt old, heavy, made of something not steel, notched with age and events—or made to feel notched—warm and buttery. I wanted to say it was made of silver, old silver, that was the feeling, composed of many moveable wheels of numbers: smooth-moving, newly-oiled. The whole thing, when you felt it, was moveable, like a well-used Rubik's Cube. Many more than five wheels on here. I tried my old five/six code, nothing happened. I tried it six five— still no joy. Idly, I spun the numbers, they moved smoothly, were designed to line up to a groove at the top.

What was it?

What did they want me to think it was?

An old lock, I wasn't educated enough to know how old: Babylonian? Medieval? Hand-crafted, made to feel hand-crafted.

Printed yesterday.

I crawled back to the peephole. Their game of the panels, to train me up, for this next level. If I wanted Sean I'd have to crack this code.

The numbers.

If I wanted Sean.

If that was Sean.

Why was he sleeping with bright lights on?

Was he sleeping? Was he waiting?

And who *was* Sean, after all?

I didn't know Sean, I only knew Chris and Sean-pretending-to-be-Chris. The only thing I knew for sure about Sean, real Sean, eyeless real Sean, was that he was a fake, a liar.

Who maybe had good cause.

I wanted to laugh

I knocked on the tunnel floor: the five and the six.

Below me he twitched, jerked up, put his hands to his head.

He moved like a human, not like a robot.

Their robots would move like humans.

Neither of us moved for a moment. He sat upright on his bed. I lay above him at my peephole. I knocked it again.

He put his bandaged face up towards me at the ceiling. He mouthed 'no', perhaps he said it out loud, I couldn't hear him. He lay back on his bed, curled up into a ball, pulled the sheet over him.

Ignore. Crawl on. Find natural light.

In any case I couldn't open the panel to his cell, not with the fancy padlock and the ten bands of numbers I didn't know. I could break it perhaps, the small metal 'U' at the end, if I had a tool. I crawled away from the peephole, back to the cylinder and this 'U', peered at it in the gloom. It was thin, I could perhaps prise it open, with some sharp instrument, from the heebie jeebie room? If that wasn't foam-printed, if the instruments in there were hard and real. Maybe that was the purpose of that room: not to scare me but to arm me. If I could find my way back down to that room so many floors below — in this live computer game I was trapped in — then perhaps I'd find something helpful.

If I could find my way.

Or something here among the wires?

Real Sean would have found some tool, he was resourceful, as well as a liar.

His whirring rod.

My brain hurt.

Idly I spun the cylinder wheels again. Like some toy, oddly satisfying.

Something clicked.

One side of the 'U'-shaped hook opened up, letting me pull the cylinder from the clasp, untether the clasp from the floor of the tunnel so I could pull the strap up and see it worked like all other panels: you wound it round to open the central hole.

These things worked smoothly, made no noise.

I stopped unscrewing the hole in the middle of the doughnut panel. I lay there with my head in my hands. I didn't want the cylinder to have opened. I didn't want to open up the central hole, I didn't want to shunt the panel aside. I didn't want to get to 'Sean', I didn't want anything to happen, I just wanted to get out of there.

To where?

Into the sea to drown?

I crawled forwards back to the peephole, gazed down again at him balled up in the bed under the sheet.

I crawled back to the panel, looked at the cylinder, the opened hook, the random sequence of symbols I'd spun that had opened the hook so coincidentally, had seemed to open the hook. And then I screamed cos the central doughnut hole was rising up, unscrewing of its own accord, light from below entering my tunnel, the clasp spinning, getting pushed up into the tunnel with me, by a hand now gripping the inner hole of the remaining doughnut panel: a hand with a stumped index finger, a hand now grabbing my wrist.

32

I lay there in the tunnel in the ceiling, my wrist gripped by the hand with the stump, the lightbulb from its room pushed up into the tunnel next to me, lighting my dust and cables, my faded teeth marks on the flesh. I looked down. There, next to the hand under the hole, glaring up at me, the bandage now pushed up over its forehead, was an eye. Greeny-brown, gold-flecked: Chris's eye, Sean's eye as was, that Sean had gouged out in the cupboard. An instance of their clone eye and a mouth, Sean / Chris's mouth, which opened to hiss in an American accent:

'Who are you?'

Who was *I*? I wanted to laugh. Instead I screamed.

'Stop screaming. Who are you?' pushing its eye up closer, letting go of my wrist and grabbing my ear, pulling me down to its hole by my ear so our eyes were this close with only the hole between us.

'I'm Nim,' I said, my mouth twisted and pushed against the tunnel floor, my ear pinched, half-ripped off. 'Who are you?'

'Fuck you,' it said, moving its face back, spitting up at my cheek, still gripping my ear. 'Fuck you. It won't work.'

'Chris? Sean?' I said very softly, my face covered with his spit, my yanked ear in unbelievable pain. Was this them catching me, punishing me? 'Sean?' I said, because he seemed to be being Sean except with healed eyes. Sean the resourceful violent liar. 'It's me. Nim. I promise. Stop. You're hurting me.' Playing to the script, for now.

The mouth laughed. The eye stared at me, the eye I'd seen him pulp. The accent was American now, he'd only been talking British before to fool me, pass himself off as Chris. And sometimes that accent had slipped.

But he couldn't be Sean. He was cut to look like Sean, had to be, with those perfect eyes. A third instance, pretending to be

Sean?

A third instance pulling my ear off who could be anything.

Cos whoever he was, he wasn't Chris, so I didn't know him.

Except maybe he *was* Chris, masquerading as Sean, for some reason, how creepy. Chris, slashed and stumped, pulling my ear, gone real violent, nothing to do with the Chris I'd grown up with.

And wouldn't they be the same after all, the same relentless DNA?

'What are you doing up there?' he hissed.

'I escaped,' I said, almost passed out from pain.

'You escaped?' He laughed again, yanked hard. 'You escaped them? So how come they're not here, how come they haven't stopped you? No one escapes them. Screaming your head off escaped on their ship?'

'Maybe they can't hear me, see me up here? Stop it. I don't know. Maybe you're them?'

'I'm them? They can't see you?' He laughed again. 'Fuck you,' spitting at me once more. 'Well they can sure see me. Hello,' still yanking my ear but spinning round wildly to talk to his room, standing on a chair, I could now see, in order to reach the hole and me in the ceiling. 'Fuck you.' Then back to me: 'Have you come to kill me?'

He lifted his legs off the chair and hung from me, swinging from the ceiling by my tearing ear.

'You're tearing my ear off.'

'Good. What are you, what have they done to you? This won't work,' he said wildly to the room.

'I'm me,' I whispered, crying from pain. 'I'm me.' Why fix his eyes? If they wanted me thinking for sure that this was Sean then he should be blind.

'How come you're here? Why aren't they here? You can't escape them'

'Alan showed me,' I said. 'Maybe they *are* here. Maybe they're coming.'

He pulled harder, clawing his stump into my ear hole for better purchase, to stop slipping, then put his legs back on the chair in thankful release when it felt he might slip off.

Less weight but still gripped to me, moving closer, putting his eye and hissing mouth right up next to me at the hole, bits of blood from my hot ringing torn ear staining him, staring right into my eye, looking inside me, to see if I *was* me. It seemed.

'How did you open the ceiling?'

'There's a lock, I opened it.'

'A lock?'

'A combination lock. You put in numbers.'

He froze for a moment. 'What numbers?' yanking my poor ear again.

'For fuck's sake! I don't know! Random numbers, yours was different to the other ones.'

'Different to what? What numbers?'

'I don't know! I can't remember, it was random, any old numbers.'

'What old numbers?'

'I don't know what fucking numbers, I don't know the numbers, how many fucking times do I have to tell you all?'

'You entered a number and a lock opened? What have you done? Show me the lock. Don't show me anything. You're a trap. How have you been programmed?'

'Why do you have eyes?'

'To see through your shit with.' He started pressing my eye and with it the doughnut-shaped panel around the hole. The panel moved up a bit, he pulled back.

'It moves?' He let go of my ear and punched the panel up, moved it and me with it, shunted it and me aside, put both his hands up into my tunnel, yanked himself up from the chair and slithered through so he was squashed up in my tunnel with me and the light. Naked, grabbing me hard:

'Show me the lock, the numbers you put in.'

The two of us, jammed together.

I showed him the silver lock with its ten panels, shined the unscrewed lightbulb onto the lock so he could see the random numbers that had opened it, apparently opened.

'What's the number? Where did you get it from? What does it mean?'

'No idea,' I said. It had a lot of nines in it. I showed him the whole mechanism: how to replace the panel, how the lightbulb and fitting got screwed into the centre of the panel by the winch that became the strap and clasp that hooked the lock to the tunnel floor. Nothing they hadn't seen me do before if they were watching. But when I hooked the lock to the clasp the lock clicked shut, even though I didn't move a single number, a single panel. It clicked shut and wouldn't open, so we were locked into the ceiling together, me and naked him in the new gloom, whatever he was.

'Open the lock,' he said.

I tried. 'I can't,' I said.

'You moved it,' going for my ear again.

'I didn't touch it. You moved it.'

'I didn't touch it. You know the number, put it in again.'

'This is the number, I didn't touch it, it just went shut,' trying and fiddling.

'Fuck you. You changed it. Put it in again. How did you know it in the first place?'

'I just spun it! It was random, it just opened.'

'Fuck random. Do it, do it,' while I tried to spin the well-oiled panels like I'd spun them before.

Nothing opened.

'Fuck you, fuck you.' He smashed the lock against the tunnel floor. 'What kind of fucking lock is this? What is it? What are you, what do you want from me?'

'Why do you have eyes?'

'Do you know what you've done? You fucking fool. All for me. All for him, cos I look like him. Your bait. Damaged goods.'

'What *is* the number?' I lay there on my belly. 'And anyway,' when he didn't speak: 'if they used the lock to lock the panel then they knew the combination already. If I unlocked it somehow then I can't have given them anything they didn't already know.'

'Unless the thing was ancient and they could never unlock it and they built the hook and panel and whole fucking set-up round it, built this whole boat round it in readiness for you to crawl up here and open it for them with whatever your Alan coded into you.'

Which I hadn't considered. A bad feeling. I lay there. 'I didn't enter any number. It was random.'

He did his hollow laugh. 'Nice work,' not to me. 'They've captured the data already, you betcha. You know they have. They've got what they need from us, well done. And all cos they know your hook: how much you still love your Chrissikins. Nothing more for us to do. Except kill each other before they kill us, don't give them the satisfaction. The only good choice now.'

And then from not far behind us: a tick and hum.

33

In Zita first her watch went backwards, then the sounds. Then sixty-six seconds to jump back before you saw it: wet puckered flesh over steel mouth, diamond-tipped maw ready and open.

'We got to go.'

'What is it?' he said but I was already on the move.

'We need something long and sharp,' to pierce the red spot, the Cwyd's only weak point: the red spot under its mouth, how Zita killed it, with a metal rod found in her tunnel, jutted it up there.

But we had no rod, nothing sharp and no time.

'What is it?'

'The Cwyd. It'll kill us,' moving off.

'Cos you gave them what they need. You're trash now, like me. Served our purpose. Two-for-one deal. Let them kill us.'

'No way.' I let go of him, crawled off alone till I got to the next panel above the next room, fingers crossed it had a normal lock that I could undo with the 565656, nothing Babylonian. Don't do their work for them, right? No way I was getting chomped up there if I could help it. Fuck him, whoever he was, their dismal agent. I'd open the panel, enter the new room, hope the ceiling hole was too small for the Cwyd to follow.

And what would I find in the new room? Another Sean? Chris? Don himself, the grand high poobah?

The new lock felt normal, I prayed it opened with the 565656 combo.

Praying to whom, you fucking fool?

The hum grew. With jittering fingers I tried the numbers. The lock opened. The strap and the winch, unlocking the central hole, as per normal—my new normal, speed it up. Down there was black, no way to see what was in the cabin. I shunted the doughnut panel aside.

He'd come to see, was close to me now. 'What the fuck are you doing? What numbers did you put in? This is what they want us to do.'

It was the normal 565656, I explained, not like his room, his room had been different. 'I thought what they wanted was us to be killed.'

The roaring hum, a blinding light. I turned for a nanosecond to see the tunnel behind us fill with steel whiteness barrelling towards us, a train with circular jaws globbuling in and out like a puckered mechanical arsehole, red in the middle, the wind of its suction.

Ten metres away. No way I was hanging around for that encounter. I jumped down the hole into blackness, he fell down after me, hard onto wooden floor, the Cwyd whooshed over the hole above our head.

We lay winded on the floor in the dark, me moving my limbs, checking I still worked.

'The cleaning bot,' he said. 'Cleaning the vents. What did you call it?'

'It would have killed us.' I laughed, big joy. 'We escaped.'

'You dumb fuck. No one escapes. The whole world's smeared. No one gets to escape, have adventures, any more, don't you get it? Only Don has adventures. The rest is airtight. We're here cos they want us here, cos their machines planned it. They know all your stories, don't think you can twist them. And where are we now? Into the fire. With them watching. Don't say you weren't warned.'

He got up, started pacing the black of wherever we were. There was echo and more sway, in this room, and the clink of something and the sound of—what?—lapping? Waves? The sound of water.

Light flicked on: he'd found a switch at the wall. We were in a large pale wooden space like a ballet studio, much bigger than all the other rooms / containers I'd crawled over, peered down into. A strange space because in the middle, surrounded by a glass barrier, was a supersleek, hypermodern speedboat. Everything else was bare.

He slid down the white wall, naked, sat folded up on the floor, put his head in his hands. He looked up at me, with his eyes: 'What are you?'

'Where are we? Why do you have eyes?'

He got up, naked, came for me, yanked down my sweatpants, felt for my upper thigh, the v-shaped scar he'd carved into me in the lake, my branding. Not that they couldn't have copied my scars too, if I wasn't me, if I were some clone or machine sent to snare him. He got up, held my face tight, smearing blood down my cheek, the blood from my torn ear.

He bored into me with his eyes, the perfect eyes that shouldn't be there if he was Sean. But if they were trying to trick me why not rustle up a gouged, blinded, scarred instance? If their aim was to make me think this one was Sean, my Sean?

What did I know about their aims?

What were they doing, why weren't they coming for us? Could there be bits of their ship they didn't track or notice?

No.

He bored into me with the eyes, I did the same to him. Clutching on, searching blindly, both of us, to see into the truth of each other.

'I'm me,' I said.

'You don't even know what that means.'

I prised his hand off my cheek and pinched into it: WHY EYES?

He looked at me. 'I have eyes,' he said, 'because they fixed me. Because that's what pleases Don. Cos I *am* Don, or his thereabouts. I belong to him. He wants me with eyes, he has hospitals full of eyes, eyes are trivial.'

'And Chris?'

He laughed. 'Ah yes. Your Chris.'

'What is this? Why aren't they here? Are you Sean?'

'I'm Sean,' he said, standing naked in front of me. 'This is my garage. Was my garage. When I was Don's. Before I turned. Where I docked my boat,' nodding at the speedboat. 'My toy room. The fuckers.'

The speedboat sat in water, partitioned off from us by the low glass barrier. Some kind of internal dock for the speedboat within the vastness of the container ship.

'That's your boat?'

'Unless it's a replica. Clone garage, clone speedboat, more games. The fuckers.'

The speedboat was smooth, dark fibre-glassed wood outside, high luxe inside: white cream leather, two seats, chrome, dials, screens. Across its bow was its name in florid script: *The Chimera*. Beyond it was a metal wall different from the white walls of the rest of the room. I looked at this metal wall.

'A door? To the outside? To the sea? D'you know how to open it? We're at sea level? You know how to get out of here?'

The glint of this possibility. The elation. Escape from the fun house.

Trying to weigh if it was possible we could get out like this, without them noticing. That he had to be part of it if they weren't coming for us, that even if he *was* fixed Sean, he could still be part of it, their agent working with them always. Just cos he'd been nice in the tramp wreck, cooking me seaweed.

Or we could both be caught here.

Or else what? Go back up into the ceiling? Do what?

My head hurt. I had to get off this crazy ship.

'Why aren't they coming for us?'

'They are.' He stepped over to me, took my hand again, pinched into it: *LETTING US* while his mouth said: 'We got to go before they get here.'

He went over to the glass barrier and pressed one partition. It slid back, he went through, stepped into the boat. He ran his hands over the controls and steering wheel, pressed his finger to a glass button. The deck lit up, a warm low light gleaming from the displays onto the polished wood. He sighed, put his head in his hands, sank into the cream leather.

'Full tank. No dust.'

He sat up, stared straight ahead, closed his eyes, did deep breaths.

He stood up and went down the steps deeper into the boat, to where? Some berth?

I went over to the glass gate, called for him. He came back up wearing jeans, pulling on a white shirt, carrying a leather bag.

'They packed for us.'

Drenched in cams. I didn't give a shit. Outside there was hope, no matter who he was. If we could get outside, into what they hadn't built. If it wasn't some new room or wider set. 'Can you sail it? Will it still work? Did you start it up? Can you open the door?'

Fuck the hell out of dodge by any means necessary.

He looked at me. 'Why do you even trust me? Who I say I am?'

'I don't. But I've had enough of here. We can deal with each other later.'

'Can we?'

'Why did you cut your eyes out?'

'To damage myself. To spite Don. He's vain.'

'Why did you lie to me before? Pretending to be Chris?'

'I had to. It doesn't make me the bad guy.'

'Can you sail this boat? Can you open the door? Is it sea outside?'

'I dunno.' He stepped out of the boat, came over to me behind the partition, took my hand, opened the glass, led me through into the boat.

We sat in the two seats hand-in-hand. Slowly he pinched: *I'M YR DRIVER. THEY FIXED MY EYES 2 DRIVE U. THEY WANT*

US 2 DO THIS. CAMS EVERYWHERE. NO SPEAK. JUST PINCH.

We sat there holding hands.

He reached into the leather bag, drew out two thick waterproof jackets, put one on, made me put on the other. He ran his hands over the steering wheel, then punched numbers into a keypad. The engine purred.

'My old code.'

His numbers. He punched in more, there was a clank from behind. The metal doors shuddering open, letting in dark night and wind, seeming actual cold salt air, the unbuilt outside. I hoped. The doors opened more, sliding back to show us the huge black night sky and ocean behind us. Or dock or set or whatever they were letting us out into.

'Strap yourself in,' he said, beginning to back us out. 'Hold tight.'

34

Fresh salty mild air, black sea, him churning round, speeding us out into the night over dark water away from the *Skidblad*, floodlights on, into the huge outside. Too fast: hitting waves in the open boat, me crushed against the side. 'Hold on,' while I screamed, holding my hand to hold my hand, not to pinch, clutching on, both of us braced for death, capture, something to stop the elation of us escaping faster and faster, his face lit up in the spray.

He hunched over dials and shouted: 'Behind?'

I tried to see. 'Nothing.' The final white lights of the Skidblad, specks in the distance.

'Sure? Above?'

I looked up: clouds, stars, satellites, a big moon. 'Nothing.'

'Copter?'

I shook my head.

'We did it. We're free,' grabbing my hand again. *WLD SEND THINGS. THEY LET US.* 'Maybe the sub's below.'

Subs, copters, dials, screens, levers, whipping through water, putting big space between us and their crazed containers on some sea or vast set somewhere in the world. Him at it, big thrills. In the Lakes I'd been shocked about how well he knew boats but then he'd been pretending to be Chris. Now he was Sean Thabbet, reared different in his desert to maximise the sequence, taught boats by Pacific sailors, animal instinct, no longer having to pretend. Unleashed by Don to drive me somewhere. The Chris-shaped blank page speeding me away.

Not quite blank: I knew *some* things about him, if he *was* Sean, the body I'd been with in Nissans and Fiestas, who'd kidnapped me and skinned me in lakes and nursed me, who'd lied to me all the way. But there'd been something in Sean: a desperation, a vulnerability, a knowledge of pain and the care for others that knowledge gives. Feelings unknown in cruel, cold, closed Chris, something I'd responded to. Something that couldn't be faked.

You hope.

Clones. They'll all be the same.

We sped like that for some time on the dark sea, me savouring freedom, him chatting merrily about how we were free, how brave and brilliant I was, how clever Alan had been to teach me Zita, show me the way out for us both. How sorry he was for tricking me before. How, without me, he'd have been trapped on the Skidblad for all the rest of his natural born days. He reached for my hand. *BABBLE.*

'Where are we?' I said, figuring it was OK to speak normal questions that had nothing to do with knowing they were on to us, as long as it sounded like I thought we'd really escaped.

'Somewhere in the East Atlantic, according to this,' nodding at the dashboard screens, pinching: *NO IDEA.*

'Where are we going?'

'To Barrow. Get what they want, whatever's hidden there they want so badly. Leverage. Then we'll see.'

NO BARROW, he pinched. *OTHER PLANS.*

WHAT?

But he shook me off, put both hands on the steering wheel, big man in charge. I kept my face neutral for the cams but didn't like the sound of these *other plans.* Either he was their agent, in which case absolutely no thanks, or else he was straight up what he was purporting: Sean, someone who was against them. Someone I'd been with against them before, who'd cobbled botched plans that hadn't ended well, for either of us, for Flora and her family, despite the gouging, the shaving, the boats and the holes. His smiling face at the controls, lit up in the spray: full of plans: an eager reckless amateur. Chris and Don's crap clone I'd got mangled with, who thought he knew, who didn't know, who knew less than Chris had.

I was the one with the stories after all.

A pang of regret but I couldn't have stayed on that ship. Better here on the waves with him than trapped in their containers with Ramona and co. Better odds. Here at least, zooming through water, you felt the illusion of escape, to buoy you up and maybe give you that extra inch of vim to burst you through into real escape, when the chance came. Then we'd see. And the chance would always come: there was always a chance, a crack, when you were out in the world they hadn't built and couldn't fully factor, even with their machines, when you weren't sealed up in their floating lab.

Which they must have factored-in when working out the ' odds before letting us out.

Maybe we'd escaped after all. Me getting us out, Zita paying off, him not wanting to acknowledge I'd saved us. Like when we played as kids: having to be Mr he-man, though I was the one who usually solved things.

Except this one had never played Scritch.

Or at least not with me.

The blood running down his face from his old gouged eyes.

When the light started to change he cut the engine and we bobbed for a bit with no power on. Just us looking at each other in some grey sea under clouds, trying to see into each other. A whole black world beneath us, fathoms deep.

He lay back on his seat facing the sky, then reached for me and held me to him, cupped my face. FOR THE CAMS. 'You can't know what this means.'

He got up, cased the small boat, checking things in the new light and by the gleam of the dials. Sean himself, no longer being Chris, prowling round in a new way that gave clues about who he actually was. He went down the stairs to the berth and came back up with a metal bucket, leant over the side of the boat and drew up water, tasting it. Then he lifted the full bucket high and swung and smashed it down onto the control panels, fracturing displays and surfaces over and over.

I was horrified and tried to stop him.

'We don't need their lies,' he said.

'We don't know where we are.'

'I do,' looking up at the sky.

This crap clone. Broken dashboards meant nothing in this cammed world. 'It's not going to work like this. You got to tell me. Before you do stuff like this. We're in this together or we're not together.'

'Look,' he said, nodding at black clouds at the horizon, smiling. 'They're pissed. You don't need subs if you control the weather. We'll use it against them.' He pressed his finger to the smashed control pad, to start up the engine again? But nothing happened.

The reckless dick.

'It's fine,' he said, getting up, going back down the stairs into the berth again, coming back up with a key: 'Analogue back-up.'

He put this key into a slot, the engine revved, all panels blank. *His keys.* He pressed levers by the steering wheel, we set off, towards the dark clouds this time, into rain.

I pulled my hood up. 'Where are we going? Are there covers? Can we put up covers?'

He didn't answer, just sailed us faster. It started to pour, a real storm at sea: choppy water, thunder, boats smashing against waves. I looked for covers. I was scared.

'Stop.'

But he sailed on and on, right up into high waves and wind, drenching us.

'Stop!'

He cut the engine again, let go of all controls, reached over and grabbed me tight round the neck, suffocating me, making me thrash, his terrible Chris-face dipping and rising, lit by lightening: 'Their cams won't work in this storm. Now tell me who the fuck you are.'

35

His crazed white face on top of me, previous calm wiped, true aim revealed: 'Are you Nim? Or what thing?' Water everywhere, nature in charge. 'Scream all you want, they can't hear you. Let's see what they send in to save you.'

'I'm me,' I babbled under him, gulping salt waves. Trying to show him the scar on my thigh, the—I didn't know—cut on my hand from when I was nine that he wouldn't know because he wasn't Chris.

'Yeah all that. Even if: what are you up to? Why did Chris come for you that night in your flat?'

'No clue.' Didn't matter what he did to me, I was the dumdum, Scritchwood Nim, the Alphabet monkey, trained up to be full of what I didn't know, to be used by them all. 'Stop it, get off, control the boat, we're going to die. *You're* the one who knows. What's *your* real story?' Not Chris but he could pinch and knew everything? 'You're so full of lies you think I'm the same.'

'Don's fault,' he screamed in my ear. 'Don's genes, nature and nurture. Pure con: growing up with that, having that turn on you. You wouldn't trust anything and you'd be right.'

'Maybe. But that's not me. And you know it, that's why you're talking to me like this. Feel the twitch, right? What does it say about me? Be honest, if you can.'

We slid together on high waves, him trying to X-ray me with his fixed eyes, bruising each other as the boat tumbled down steep walls of water.

'OK,' he said. 'But.'

But what? His hands still squeezed my neck.

Squeeze harder. Kill me in this nowhere. Except you won't will you? There's still stuff you need me to decode for you, right?

'But,' he said, still squeezing. 'Maybe you *are* you,' the same body he'd taken from Archway under false pretences. 'But what

have they done to you? On their boat? Do you even know?
Programmed to kill by one word, the trigger of a gesture? What
did they whisper to you in your sleep? You're a timebomb,
detonate when I most need you, like in Vengeance Street,
betraying me.'

'You know what?' I said, mangled with him, rising and falling
in the water. 'Maybe you're right. How would I know? How does
anyone know anything about anyone in the end? Cross your
fingers, watch for triggers, take the risk. Or just kill me now.
And what have they programmed *you* to do? Drive me where
with your shiny new eyes? Fuck you,' I said and headbutted
him: someone had to control this boat, sailing it couldn't be that
hard.

He rolled off me and lay next to me panting, laughing,
rubbing his head, putting his arm out to stop me getting up.

'One thing's for sure. You definitely *do* have a trigger,' he
said, lying there in thunder. 'Real Chris. That's why you went
along with me in Britain in the first place.'

Excuse me: I hadn't gone along with him, he'd taken me: here,
everywhere. I was here, about to die, because of him. Real Chris
was the warm-up act.

'Easy meat,' he said. 'Led through the nose. Willing to go
along with any old bullshit if it meant I was your Chrissikins
come back to you *so sorry*.'

'Fuck you,' I said. The pair of them.

'Major weakness. We're up against the darkest forces
including your Chris. But one look from him—or someone who
seems to be him—and you're floored, I know it. They don't need
to do anything to you.'

'I listened to you cos you said you were with Alan. Where's
Alan?'

'Fuck knows. You can't shit me. I know more about you than
you do. I've crunched you. I smell you. Why did you even rescue
me now?'

'I didn't.' The lock had just opened. *He'd* come up there with me. 'Look,' I hissed. 'Even if I *was* still in love with real Chris, at least I've got a good reason to be here with you wanting to believe you. But as for you: who are you?' New eyes, a rebel versus Don, here to save the world: I only had his word for it. 'Everything up to this point between you and me: total lies. The only truth is you're their clone, you're the same as them, you *are* them: will do or say anything to get what you want, right? And what *do* you want? You don't say.'

He rolled back on top of me, eye to eye. We rose and fell in the waves.

'I can't tell you till it's safe,' he said after a while. 'Not even here. Not till I am sure of you. How much did you tell them?' moving off me, crawling for the controls, revving the engine. 'About Scritch? About Vengeance Street? In their boat.'

'Pretty much everything,' I said, gulping, panting, feeling— what?—relieved? that he was starting the engine back up, that some part of this seemed to be over? That he wasn't strangling me anymore? 'They drugged me,' I said and told him about Ramona, the Alphabet etcetera, the fake Vengeance Streets. 'What else could I have done?'

'Killed yourself.'

'With what?'

'Anything. We both should have. In the ceiling, let it run us over, crush what we know. So he can't get his hands on it. They wouldn't have let us.'

'What do we know?'

Terma, tertöns. Secret knowledge buried round the world by old sages. If all that was true.

He shook his head. 'You didn't tell them everything,' he said, the engine on but us not going anywhere, still smashing from side to side. 'Or else we wouldn't be here, carrying on their job for them.'

'I told them every single thing I could think of.'

'There are ways of burying things in people.'

'Is Alan alive?'

'I don't know.'

'What about the code?' The one in his ceiling, the buttery lock that maybe the whole ship was built round. 'Didn't I already give it to them?' That's what he'd said back in the ship.

'Their set-up. That code's for shit. Sinister prop. To get me to come up there with you, take a look at what you'd done, get trapped up there, end up on this boat with you. Otherwise, they know me. Nothing personal, but I'd have resisted you. The only thing that could have lured me up there, that number.'

'What number?'

'Later. When we get to where we're going.'

'Which is where? We do this together, Sean.'

He pulled me close, spat into my ear over the waves. 'Here's the deal. We're fucked. You fucked us, you might have fucked everything. It's on you. You got us in, I'm getting us out, my way. I'm in control. I'm taking us where we can talk. Back to Vengeance Street but via a detour. Use their plans against them. But first we'll go somewhere, have a conversation, get back-up. There are still some places in the world Don doesn't own. But before we get there you'll nod and do what I say and say nothing and ask no questions and not pinch. I know the deal, you don't. Even if what I do or say seems bad or freaky. You shut up and trust me.'

'Or else?'

'We cut the engine and die.'

Some choice.

Nod away, get to dry land then ditch him. There'd be some way. Sunny Nim. My glass-half-full nature.

But. Clutched onto the sides I looked into his new eyes, the flecks of gold.

'They won't let you take this "detour". If what you say is true, if they control the weather. They'll kill us in storms first.

They'll capture us.'

'They won't kill us. They need us. They need you, what you know. They'll let us go, they have to. They couldn't get it out of you when they captured you, they need you to think you're free, solving of your own free will. And they need me, to drive you. They know where we'll end up. They'll bide their time.'

'No more violence, I've had enough violence.'

'Sometimes there's no choice. But I hear you,' beginning to move us off. 'It's a long way. We'll have to use the wind, ration fuel. Go down and switch everything off,' nodding at the stairs leading down into the berth.

Ordered about, I didn't like any of it. Space away from him to think. I went down the stairs, into a luxe white leather cabin with bathroom and kitchen, closed the door behind me. Dry, muffled, away from him, out of the storm. I huddled on the rolling floor. After a while I took off the soaked coat, fiddled about looking for knives or weapons, found towels, switched things off: music player, coffee machine, oven, fridge containing chocolate, caviar, champagne, shrink-wrapped steak, pomegranates. Their food, which I'd been eating for lord knew how long on their ship, had already swallowed all the microphones.

. I was starving. A bit more wouldn't hurt, unless it would: mesh my unconscious with deeper triggers.

I didn't eat. I found a dry waterproof and went back up and sat with him, watching for dry land. Their storm was behind us, he'd got up a sail, was trying to find the wind, he said: the right one would whizz us where we needed without fuel or navigation instruments. Wormholes, zephyrs, he said. He knew that kind of thing.

Bully for him.

'What's your Atlantic map,' I said, 'the shape of Mickey Mouse?'

He laughed and started telling me about the Atlantic, that had once been a river, and the Iapetus Ocean before that, an old sea with its different names that kept closing and opening over its fault line, banging things into each other, and how many times had that happened? How north Scotland was made of America, the bit above Loch Ness. About how Loch Ness *was* full of monsters, prehistoric sea creatures, the last trace of the Iapetus. And Don's islands in the mid-Atlantic that you don't find on dumdum maps. Where he'd grown up, in part, this Sean I was beginning to have the pleasure of knowing for real. Don's desert islands, where he'd got trained, where the *Skidblad* docked, where the Company had homes and hospitals, from whence the world was ruled, the new isles of Man. The flowers and herbs and ancient caves and temples of those islands, Phoenician and older, from the first guys, before the wipe-out. The old ways to America—they'd always known about America and its properties.

I reached for his hand, even though we weren't supposed to pinch: *ATLANTIS?*

NO.

TRUE?

SOME.

REST?

BABBLE.

And so we zipped over water somewhere carried by wind towards the golden dawn.

36

When I woke it was hot, sweaty late morning under grey clouds on the swell. I got up, went down to the berth for water and towels, came back up, took my waterproof off. He sat at the controls in his white shirt and some hat munching their coffee beans. He hadn't slept but was OK, he said, knew which pressure points to press to stop tiredness.

Lucky old you.

I joined him, sore and bruised, drank their water and watched him: fixed eyes, hands at the controls, the hands from round my neck.

He seemed calm, whoever he was.

'Sean Thabbet. That's your name?'

'What Don calls me.'

'What should I call you?'

'Fuck knows.'

I sat with him in blank sea, watching for dry land, the immense freakery we were caught up in making it hard to breathe. I felt almost shy, sitting there, next to the non-Chris I didn't know, the water-boarder who'd made tramp champagne for me.

'How much of what you said in Britain was a lie?'

'Lots. Not all.'

'Why did you lie?' No answer. 'Is Alan alive?'

Reaching for my hand: SHUT UP.

'Where are we?' No reply. '*Is* this your old boat? Or a clone boat?'

'Clone I think. Accurate though. Pixel-perfect, down to the scratches.'

'How can you tell it's not the real one?'

'Cos of how it drives. Tiny things. You can replicate objects down to the nano-level but you can't control how energy flows through them. Yet. Some clones are better than their originals.'

He smiled at me. 'Sometimes. Look.' He pointed at birds in the sky, a few at first, then flocks, dark vectors. 'Know what that means?'

'Don?'

He shook his head. 'Land. See how many there are?'

'Where are we?'

'Coast of West Africa. Western Sahara? Mauritania? What you call Mauritania?'

'How do you know?' I'd vaguely heard of Mauritania, had no idea where it was.

'Because of the birds. Going south for winter? You must have heard, in your dumdum education, with Alan, in New York, wherever? About the birds?'

I knew birds flew south for winter, unimaginable distances, from Britain, from the Arctic. I didn't know this was where they ended up.

'One big party. Largest bird sanctuary in the world.' Sandy islands and shore all the way from south Morocco to what was known as Senegal, Gambia. 'A haven for birds, for other things.'

Whatever. Dry land coming up, that's all I cared about. Dry land in West Africa, maybe.

'What do you know about West Africa?'

Not much. Ebola. Terrorism?

He snorted. 'Diseases he made. People he's trained you to think of as terrorists.'

'Where are we going?'

He shook his head.

Watching birds in the hot air, watching him. Looking for a life vest, something inflatable, so I could jump off. Picturing him bear down on me with the boat. Trying to comb through any useful Scritch.

I saw flashes of land, small islands at first. 'So-called nature reserves,' he said. Spits of land covered with birds, where they bred, swarming there now because it was the end of March and the hot season was coming. Time to go back north. He said.

The end of March. Three months their prisoner aboard the *Skidblad*. If I could believe him.

Sandy islands thick with birds. We got closer. He pointed out things: breeds, middens—which were man-made mounds and even islands made of old shells poking out of the sea from thousands of years of people eating shellfish here, throwing the shells away.

'That's why the birds come. Rich pickings.' Because of the fish, who came for the shellfish, who came for the plankton who came because the water was warm and rich with minerals leaking up from the crack beneath, the same crack as Britain.

'We feel it like they do, when there's metal. We're attracted to it, we connect to it in the land. Our bodies know what we need, to get us to the next level.'

Whatever.

We saw boats, small coloured wooden ones at first, with sails. The people nodded at us in our ultra-modern speedboat, dark fishermen in rags who watched us.

'Do we have weapons? Knives?' I said because the men scared me. 'Did you have them before on your real boat?'

'Look,' he said.

Ahead, shimmering in the heat: a weird modern city, a jumble of spiky orange metal on the shoreline.

He smiled, really pleased. 'Ship graveyard,' he said.

We sailed closer. It looked like a city but was a junkyard of massive old boats on their sides, broken and rusty.

'Scrap metal,' he said. So-called rogue states let lazy owners junk their old ships here, just roll up and beach them, for a fee. 'Yup, an eyesore, but quite good for the birds and ecology in the end. Ironically.' Shellfish ate the metal from the boats, fish ate the shellfish, birds ate the fish and did their droppings, the seas got richer. 'Maybe that's what'll happen to the whole world after Don's new apocalypse': shellfish getting fat on the steel of sunken cities, earth bouncing back and adapting like it always did, nothing wrong with a bit of climate change.

I'd heard climate change was dangerous, I said.

'Course you have. More con. Like we mere blips have control over climate, vast forces, always changing. The arrogance. Something for rich dumdums to protest, let them think they're good people. Divert attention from the real issue which is unequal wealth distribution, elites living well off millennia of exploiting other people's resources. Protest marches are easy. Sharing your actual money is what's hard. Especially now we can all see into everyone's lives via Don's magic mirrors. There has to be a rebalance, the poor world won't stand for it, that's why Don's so scared of the realm, wants the control. That's what the fight against Don's all about.'

And then pulling me close so I could feel his heat and salty Chris smell, he whispered something else: that there were people in the rusty boats, that we were sailing towards a secret border, that beyond was a different world with different people I'd been conditioned to fear, people I'd been taught were terrorists, drug dealers, smugglers, warlords, pirates, traffickers. So-called 'bad guys' who were watching us right now, Don's enemies, who could help us.

I didn't like that. 'Are Don's enemies necessarily our friends?' I whispered back. 'Do Don's cams still work here, can't he still hear us?'

'He can't act here. Repercussions. He doesn't control everywhere. Yet.' Then taking my hand: *I HAVE INS.*

What 'ins'? Sailing closer to the rusting wrecks.

'What about you?' I whispered into his ear, specks of his salt on my tongue. If they were Don's enemies they'd know his face the moment they clapped eyes on him: Don's clone. Thinking ahead for this amateur.

'What's the choice?' he whispered. 'Given what you've half-told them. Trust me, shut up. You got us in, I'm getting us out.

Like I said.'

Ah yes, the mysterious *thing* I didn't know I half-knew, that he'd tell at some point when we could talk and were safe, you betcha.

If you're reading this you're in terrible danger, especially if you're with someone who says he's Chris Kipp...

'Do we have a knife?' I asked, because a small wooden boat was coming for us, four dark men on board pointing long guns at us.

'It's OK. Don't worry. I know them. Kind of.'

37

We put up our hands, they drew alongside, pulled the boats together, boarded ours. High-cheek-boned men in rags, dark hard-to-place faces, waving guns, shouting instructions I couldn't understand. Sean, whoever, seemed calm, relaxed. He let them rummage and spoke to them in what seemed to be their language—Arabic? 'Ahmed,' he kept on saying to them. *AOK* to me in my hand. *PALS*. Then he was putting something secretly into my hand: a ring.

'Put it on. So they think we're married. Safer for you.' Speaking out loud, in English—which the men couldn't understand?

Safer for me to wear a ring because we were in some place where Western women with men and no wedding ring weren't respected?

'From where?' I said, about the ring.

'Tool box,' smiling, deft, pleased with himself.

And where was the tool box? Down in the berth? Got while I was asleep?

So he'd planned for this moment. What else had he planned for?

'What's going to happen?'

'Trust me. It'll be fine. Put on the ring. We're already dead. Anything else is a bonus.'

Great. I felt the ring in my hands, put my fist round it, put my fist in the pocket of my sweatpants, put the ring on, took my hand out to look. It fitted. A dull grey metal hoop. Did toolboxes contain rings?

Guns in my face.

Our shotgun marriage, my fake husband. He smiled and nodded at me, we sat there, they rummaged, collected up things, went down into the hold, brought up champagne, steak, the whole tainted feast. Then they made me sit on deck with two of them and their guns, and the rest took Sean off into their boat, towards and into one of the huge rusty ships nearby, hoisted him up into it, gun at his back.

He turned and smiled at me, told me with his eyes it was OK.

The duff clone, bundled into their rusty office, customs point, beheading / ransom zone. My last sight of him, this instance? It was bad with him, it was worse without him, sitting there on the boat with my gunmen wearing my ring so they'd respect me. Dark skin, fine features, torn white t-shirts, cloth round their heads, unreadable faces. I could duck and dive, go for the eyes. Seize the controls, jump overboard, beg for help, tell them I was as scared of Sean as I was of them, had nothing to do with him, wasn't married to him.

I couldn't speak their language.

I could mime it. They might understand.

I did nothing. Mime what? Swim where? They'd just shoot me. The key wasn't in the ignition, he must have taken it.

Useless, hopeless, sweating with heat and fear under the white hot sky, almost wishing for the *Skidblad*. At least there was order there, solid planning. At least they needed me, cherished my special knowledge.

Gunmen brought Sean back out of the big ship, put him on a small boat, rowed it over to me on the speedboat, forced me on too. He was smiling at me, thumbs up, glittering with excitement, the doofus, who I'd have to think for, grabbing my hand:

AOK.

The men were on our speedboat, shouting in their language, putting the key in the ignition, revving the engine, speeding away.

'You gave them the boat?'

'Small price.'

'For?'

'Our ticket. To where Don can't hear.'

Energised, powerful, proud of his cunning, getting us out of what I'd got us into, my fake husband, driving us blind into the fire. One of the men bowed to him. Then they handcuffed my right wrist to his left hand and rowed us to the shore.

38

A white tent facing sea and clouds on white sand in the heat. We sat together sweating, cuffed and bruised, arms touching, watching birds. Around the tent, men with black cloth wrapped over their heads and faces squatted with guns. Our armed guards, our new owners.

'We're guests,' according to him. 'Waiting. They're sending a message—they don't use phones. Someone has to go there in person, tell him our offer.'

Tell some guy who was their leader, who was far away. 'Ahmed', except we couldn't say his name either.

'Call him "A".'

'What offer?'

LATER.

This dumbfuck. The cuffs were tight and heavy. I hated them. I hated everything. I wanted to run, was tied to this deadweight. Wrapped men in rags brought us black coffee and croissants.

'We can eat them.' He ate them. 'French food,' he said. French because Mauritania had been a French colony, didn't I know? Not that we were in Mauritania, though we were close. This was still Western Sahara, he reckoned, which had been Spanish. Now it was nothing, claimed by Morocco. Lots of international interest because of the oil and other things recently found here, crack-fruit.

So what.

I couldn't eat and couldn't remember the last time I'd eaten, was shivering though it was so hot. He sat closer to me which made me feel worse, made me drink water. They laid out new white clothes for us: loose shirts and trousers, tan canvas shoes. Then they uncuffed us and turned their backs to us and he turned away from me and told me to take off everything I was wearing, my tainted Skidblad gear, put on this new stuff instead, like he was doing. I did it, saw my bruised body from him in the storm. They turned back round, recuffed us, took our old clothes and underwear, 'to burn', he said. To burn away Don's snitchers, except didn't Don sprinkle everywhere, wasn't here tainted too, wherever *here* was, West Sahara, Mauritania?

'What about the ring?' From Don's toolbox, the dull metal band.

He pulled it off me, called to them, handed it over, calm and lordly.

'What about our skin and hair?' remembering him basically scalping me in the lake, that horror, what you had to do if you really wanted to scrub Don off.

'Later,' he said. 'They'll have ways. Before we meet "A".'

We sat recuffed under the awning in our new loose white clothes. He scratched himself with sand to scrape off Don, told me to do the same. He stretched, cuffed to me, told me to stretch too, for my health. He scratched me, my visible flesh, scraped away cams as best he could while I sat there trying to think for both of us.

TERRORISTS, I pinched.

'What does that even mean? All your ideas about the world? Made for you by Dons. Lecturing values to lands they've sucked dry, trying to plug us all into their rigged set-up built by slaves from plundered goo. We're safe here, among friends. They've helped me before. You don't know these people, what they live by, how they live. Honour, valour, word as bond. Can you even imagine what that's like?'

He shifted into the sun. I stayed in shade. He lay on his back in sand and basked for a long time, soaking up sun.

'Try it,' he said. 'Gives you energy. Recharge your batteries.'

Elite super-knowledge, sun-soaking lizards. World-ruling yoga masters. I hated him, I hated my powerless self cuffed to him, my bad choices, *dry land*, thinking for one second he might be a good bet. Just like real Chris—and where *was* real Chris?

Out in the world, plotting against me?

Unless—and this was super-creepy—that thing cuffed next to me on the sand *was* real Chris after all, up to something truly freaky, pretending for whatever reasons to be someone else, a dark hollow creature exploring his worst nature, triple-double crossing me?

Get me out of this Alan.

We lay on rugs in the tent and slept.

When I woke it was later afternoon and cooler and he was whispering next to me:

'Tell them anything they want to know.'

There were new men in the tent talking. I smelt food cooking outside, it smelt good. I felt hungry and better though my wrists were sore. They took us outside, we ate fresh fish and bread cooked on a fire. We drank sweet tea, still cuffed. He watched me with his mended eyes.

'I want us to mark ourselves,' he whispered. 'So we'll know each other. Just in case,' stabbing a white hot fish skewer from the fire into my cuffed wrist to make it char with pain.

I screamed and tried to yank away, smelt burnt flesh, saw him do the same to his cuffed wrist so our burnt flesh bubbled and bled together.

'You fucking freak,' I screamed at him, trying to get up. His marks on me, his violence. 'You got no control.'

He yanked me down, men came over, he shooed them away in their language. I called after them, begged for help in English, they must have understood what I was saying. But they ignored it. Because this was how they treated women in the new world I'd entered? *Take me back to Don.*

He tore strips from his shirt and bound them round our wrists to soak up blood and wad against the cuffs. I let him, blotted everything out, focussed on the pain.

They came to us with black cloths, wrapped them round our heads and faces.

'Protects against sand and wind,' he said from behind his. 'And it'll hide us. Men's clothes. Men wear the burkas here. Wards off evil spirits, lets you go anywhere undetected. Invisibility cloaks, free from Don's made magic.'

New armed men arrived and forced us into a jeep.

39

A low-tech army-looking jeep, plastic bottles and bundles lashed to the roof, windows down. No radio, minimal dials. A driver, someone else in the front passenger seat, both bandaged in the black so you could only see the eyes. Us cuffed together in the back, cuffed again on either side to two tall armed men in the bandages, men whose eyes were hidden by mirrored shades reflecting back my covered face.

'It's OK. We can trust them.'

Oh yeah.

He didn't say anything more, didn't spell. Powerless, I sunk into my cloth and the burn pain in my wrist. We drove away from sea on rocky sand, no roads. Through the left-hand windows the sun was setting, we were heading north, I could read things, plan-free, the sick lurch in my tummy, the wide blank useless dry land.

We drove for about an hour through flat bare shingle, minimal plants and trees. Then on the horizon a set of squares became concrete bunkers, some kind of small modern village part-covered in sand. We drove in, down what might have been the main road, past empty ugly squat concrete buildings full of sand, sand up to their sides. Smashed windows, metal grilles, Arabic graffiti, no sign of people. Some abandoned fortification. We came to a grey building surrounded by barbed wire with bandaged men and guns at the gates. The jeep stopped outside.

They uncuffed us from each other, kept us cuffed to our guards. They yanked us out, pushed us inside.

His eyes smiled at me. 'Cleaning time.'

Inside: a semi-medical hive. Low ceilings, dirty walls, covered people in robes, machines, wires, syringes, tubes. Sean got bundled into one room, me into another. They uncuffed me from my guard, cuffed me instead to a chair. A woman wrapped in white cloth talked to me in some language, unwrapped my black cloth, took blood from my arm with what seemed fresh needles from a new packet, checked my eyes, tongue, ears. She uncuffed me, took the dirty cloth off my burn and put something on it that stung, made me take off all my clothes and strip-searched me, put her gloved hand inside me, swabbed around in there with a nice bright smile and apology cluck. Three white-robed women shaved my head then ripped every other hair out of me with wax except for my lashes and eyebrows which they cleaned one hair at a time.

They put a bucket next to me and gave me a drink which made me vomit. They did this a few times, then took the vomit away. They made me drink lots of water, then took me into a small hot sauna, made me sit there sipping water for ages, to sweat the Skidblad out of me? Afterwards they scraped me with brushes and some kind of stinging scrub, then oiled and massaged me and put ointment on my bruises. They deep-cleaned my mouth and teeth with a tiny dental polishing machine, scraped my tongue with wood, gave me a new white-trousers-and-shirt set, brown canvas shoes, put gauze and plasters over the burn.

I sat gleaming next to an electric fan in another room. A black-wrapped man questioned me in bad English. I told him everything he wanted to know, the whole crazy story. I was quite used to rattling it off by now, with the Skidblad escape as a new bonus extra. I asked him for help, to get away from Sean, he nodded and wrote things down. They brought Sean in and sat him next to me, pinkly clean too now. The man questioned him. They took him away and told me I was Sean's prisoner and they'd rescued me and was safe with them and could tell them everything now. I told them I'd said everything before.

They put wires and patches on my body and bald head, held my pulse. I told it all again and again, no change in my story. This went on for ages. They pushed me into a room with a white mattress on the floor. I slept and slept.

I washed in cold water, put on fresh white clothes, ate hot bread and drank sweet black tea the women brought me. They wrapped me in the black cloth and pushed me outside into sharp blue heat. Sean stood wrapped in black, cuffed to his mirrored guard leaning against the side of the jeep. He smiled at me. His left eyebrow was cut. He saw me looking at it.

'I'm fine,' he said. 'You OK?'

They cuffed me to my guard, pushed me back into the back of the jeep with Sean and his guard, cuffed me and Sean back together. Us four joined in our line, the wrapped driver and smaller man in the front seats, if they were the same people under the black cloth and shades. Impossible to say.

The engine went on, we set off, my burn hurting under the plaster. I touched Sean's hand. *U FUCK*, I pinched, extra-hard. A hot blue morning somewhere on shimmering gravel, me and him cuffed to armed guards driving off where, on no roads, in whose power? Him bumping along smiling, all jaunty and clean, thrilled with himself, touching my hand: *IT'S FINE.*

Oh yeah, tickety-boo. Cuffed westerners in deserts with robed gunmen, no bad bode, right? Specially with him being Don's clone and all. If that were true. But he was quite keen on death, seemed to be, this Chris version, if that's what he was. *Burning out*, was this one's motto.

I shook him away.

He reached for me again, force-pinched: *AT LEAST I KNOW. U REAL. PASSED THEIR LIE TEST. DEAD OTHERWISE.*

I balled my hand into a fist he tried to stroke but I pushed off. Rising heat, crammed between salty men, digging metal on the burn. More heat coming through the rolled-down windows, sand and grit everywhere. No roads, no buildings, gravel bumps and hills, a few pathetic trees. I closed my eyes, pretended I was back in North London surfing the web, tried to find a Scritch to match this, anything from Alan. 'Sean' started talking to the men in their language. Monosyllables from them at first, then a few words. Building bonds.

Good luck with that you turd.

'Familiar land,' he said to me, nodding at the nothing outside. Because of those Atlantic island deserts he'd grown up in as Don Junior, the training and languages they'd slotted into him there like the Arabic he spoke, though our guards' version was a dialect.

Lovely jubbly champagne bubbly. Like Jassy used to say.

He told me about going wild in those Atlantic deserts in four-wheel drives, teenage machine tournaments with other scions and instances. 'Lethal fairs,' he called them. 'Where you learn. Get hardened by brute experience. Theory means nothing. You got to have blood.'

I turned my head away but he went on: Don's inner circle, company bigwigs and their offspring smashing into each other in armoured jeeps on no roads just for the hell of it, drawing blood, showing mettle, getting crowned, cracked bones and teeth, fame through peril. 'Blood will out.'

We drove into less trees, flatter land. The sun got high, our cuffed guards snoozed.

'Watch Gramps,' he said, nodding at the old small man in the front passenger seat with an old vertical scar cut down through his left eye. Our guide, Sean said, who knew the way through featureless desert even when sunlight masked the stars. Natural GPS, intact animal knowledge, that old gubbins: sun position, shingle patterns, faintest tracks, the smell of exposed minerals in the bare ground, flow hooked to Earth's magnetism.

'One-eyed. Sometimes they do it to themselves, to heighten their other senses. They say the best Saharan guides are blind.'

Did they?

He told me how the path we were on, and all paths across the Sahara and its network of wells, dated from earlier times, when the land was green, before the dry-out of the past eight thousand years. How you could find stuff from before the change: stone carvings, dwarf crocodiles in oasis pools, left-over Cyprus trees, arrowheads, terma, traces of paths tramped by humans and animals bringing cargo north-south along now-dwindled roads only sensed these days by trained heirs like Grandpa. A world-wide cargo network that was always there.

'Timbuktu, Chinuguetti, Tingus, Carthage, Cyrene, Alexandria, Yanbu, Socotra, Hormuz, Basra, Gujarat, Calicut, Quilon, Jaffna, Nagapattinam, Tamralipti, Pegu, Takuapa, Lankasuka, Sumatra, Java, Brunei, Banda, Raja Amput Fuzhou, Xiamen, Hanoi, Guangzhou, Ningpo, Quanzhou, Nagasaki, Osaka, Monks Mount pyramid south of Chicago, Corvo, the pyramids of Tenerife.'

Showing off his trained mind, information pegged to the stars and the whorls on his fingertips so he never forgot. He showed me the fingertips of his cuffed hand. 'Like your mind bus, just much better.'

'What did they cut off,' I asked, nodding at the stump of his index finger, 'how not to bullshit?'

He laughed. 'It talks.'

We drove for ages beside a long sandstone cliff, him telling me about the old cargo. Slaves, leather, fur and swords from the north, gold and medicine from the south, from the rich coast jungles of what I'd know as Nigeria and Benin where the Atlantic cracked first and metal bubbled up to make powerful plants. Down there were ruined overgrown jungle cities no one excavates, massive earthworks, Jewish Africans in Indonesian fabrics playing Malaysian xylophones, south-east Asian palms and yams, mountains of pure gold. He told me about kola nuts from down there brought north by donkeys and later camels to stimulate the brains of pharaohs and emperors, ground up and mixed with South American cocaine to make a royal potion which became the basis of Coca-Cola.

Cold bubbles I longed for in my throat.

The sun began to wane, the feeling around us in the nothing

changed. The blue went pale, the cliffs darkened, for the first time there were clouds, stretched out long at the horizon. The air became crisp. The men talked.

'We'll stop in a while,' he said. 'Something to eat.' Flocks of birds flew overhead. 'We won't camp, not tonight. They want to head on. Make it past the mountain by tomorrow morning.'

He whispered in my ear about the mountain: a huge solid block of iron in the gravel not far from here. A massive magnetic chunk whose force fritzed Don's signal, wiped nanocams, bankcards, computers, a place where even compasses didn't work. Natural defence and beyond it more defence: the big blank cam-free nothing of true desert where we could talk freely at last and he'd tell me everything, where people like Ahmed camped and shot down whatever came from land or sky.

'Plenty goes on that you know nothing about. Everything, in fact.'

We stopped at the end of the cliffs, got uncuffed from our guards, stayed cuffed together, got out of the jeep. I wrapped an invisible force round myself, separate from him. They made a fire in a sand hollow from a dry bush and snatches of yellow grass from the cliff side. The driver slept on cloth under the cliff shade, the old man got busy with pots and flour sacks. We pulled down our face cloths and drank water from a big plastic vat from the jeep roof.

The men smoked. They had long thin fluttering hands. We stood cuffed together as light wind swirled sand round our ankles and canvas shoes. The whole ground moved in the wind when you looked. Coarse grains, small rocks. Unstable. The men had guns, long old-looking rifles slung round their shoulders.

'Is this the Sahara? Who are these people?' I said. The sun went down in red hazy clouds. Everything was changing. 'Am I on drugs? Is this real? Where are we?'

'This is the Sahara. It's real. You can always tell,' he said. 'The tech will never match.'

But was that true? Things had moved on without me realising, without most people realising, even him perhaps, it seemed.

'Maybe we never escaped.' He'd bruised and burnt me and it had hurt, but maybe these days you could feel pain and still be inside one of their concoctions. Maybe we were both still Don's prisoners in headsets wounding each other in some bare cell.

'Why did you pretend to be Chris? What do you want? How come you knew everything about Chris and me and Scritch? If nanocams then how come we could go anywhere in Britain and they didn't find us till Barrow? Where's Alan?'

'Not here. Not yet. Get beyond your sulk. Have some faith.'

I laughed and turned away.

I built my wall higher and wouldn't look at him. It got dark. They draped an itchy brown blanket round us and we sat cuffed by the fire under the massive black starry sky. We ate flatbread and dry salty cheese and drank very sweet black coffee poured into glass tumblers from a silver pot. My burn hurt. The moon was nearly full. The men muttered beside the flames and smoked. Birds flew overhead, outlined in the Milky Way.

It got cold. We went back into the jeep with the blanket, still cuffed, me still not looking at him but using his heat. They didn't bother cuffing us back to our guards. Jolting along in the empty desert at night: where were we going to run, where was I going to run with him chained to me? I fed the blanket between my cuff and the burn gauze. I slept a bit, we stopped a few times to wee and for the men to smoke. The sun rose through the windscreen: we were heading east. He traced the patterns on the blanket, told me the patterns meant things, were maps and coded info, like bibles, tarot cards, stone circles, cables knitted into fishermen's jumpers: all transmitting bits of the knowledge.

The blank grey desert was full of things, if you knew where to dig. Stone goddesses with multiple tits, guns, drugs, ancient books and maps preserved in the dryness. Gold panther harnesses, gold Bantama fetishes from the Ashanti kings of

Ghana. Ghana, Guinea, New Guinea, Guyana: all the same word. It means 'gold'. Pure, beautiful, untarnished. Made by the sun, formed in supernovas, like we all are, folded into planets, seeping up from cracks. Immortality is gold, it's in the Hindu Vedas. And who wrote them and how old are they and where do they really come from? The old religion, Hinduism. Carved stories from before.

We stopped by a brick well and an old rusty bathtub he said was for goats and camels to drink from. The men knelt and prayed and made a fire, gave us coffee, salty cheese and a kind of porridge. We sat on carpet and huddled in our blanket. The men smoked. A tiny lizard scurried by, left delicate marks in the sand.

'Ten minutes in its body, the things you'd know,' he said. He got up, shrugged off the blanket, did his fancy stretching and meditation with deadweight me cuffed to him. Everything was rough sand and stones, small shrubs, a few tiny white flowers, the large blue sky turning hot.

The men drew deep cold water up from the well in buckets, poured it into their plastic vats, poured some into leather pouches and wooden bowls for us to drink. He poured his over my head, drenching me, sticking my white cotton clothes to me. I kicked him hard. He laughed.

'Just cooling you down. Celebrating. We're free. Past the wall now, the iron mountain. We can talk, don't need to pinch. Don's stuff doesn't work here, no machines.'

'What about the jeep?'

'Just oil from their own wells and local mechanical parts.'

But if Don was so big like he said then surely Don had mixed cams into every metal. How could we be sure about any machine, shouldn't we be on camels, couldn't they cam camels too? And one iron mountain couldn't block off everything beyond it, after a while the force-field would weaken. Ahmed must control some very tiny area.

'Don't say his name.'

'I thought no one can hear us now?'

'*They* can hear us,' nodding at the men who were looking at us. 'There's lots of mountains and lots of ore all round here. Easy to find deposits in deserts, use them like you have no clue. Flex back against Don. The silicon sand. And the salt—salt can do lots of things. So much salt here, dried out from way before when all this was under the sea.'

Before or after it was green?

'So glad, to be stuck in this with someone truly knowledgeable,' I said. And since we were beyond magic mountains now, in the safe zone, where old Don could no longer hear us, I now wanted some basic info. Like: where were we going, who was Ahmed, where was Alan, what exactly were we up to, what was the basic gist of what was going on?

'When we're away from them,' nodding at the men. 'You never know what they might be able to understand. Have faith. Later.'

I broiled next to him, watched the men lash the water-filled vats back up to the roof, sit down for one last smoke. Sean pulled me over to them, sat chatting with them.

'They're saying we won't make it to A, that we're not going there any more,' he smiled.

'Why are you smiling? So where *are* we going?' Cold dread. The whole twist after all. I didn't believe in 'Ahmed', didn't like the sound of him. Yet now I wanted to get to him.

'Don't worry, that's just how they talk. Warding off the evil eye. To fool their spirits, the old-school Dons. You say you won't make it somewhere so the spirits don't step in to spite you. Pretty vicious, their spirits. Super keen to spite you. We're going to A, don't worry. Or else we're not.' He put his head close to me and whispered. 'Their eyes and hands are telling me. Look, can you see the gestures?' The men rolling their eyes, maybe doing things with the tips of their long fingers. 'That's what they use for the real stuff they want to smuggle past spirits and animals. Sign language, like your pinching. In the end it's all the same.'

We got back into the jeep, the driver came to sleep next to us in the back, Grandpa still in front. My guard drove.

It got hotter. We drove and drove across a plain. For hours there was nothing except this plain. No mountains, no land going up at any point on the horizon. Just miles and miles of endless loop of stony identical desert, me sat there with those men round me, driving where? Once we saw a tiny tree.

The sun was at its highest when a black blip appeared on the horizon.

'A's base? A mirage?' I remembered that in deserts you saw things, especially when there was nothing and you were half-crazed like I was.

But it was a stone, a huge black stone, the sole feature in the landscape.

We drove towards it. He was chatting to the men.

'They say it's a holy place. Gramps wants to go there. A detour. It's fine. You'll see. We're still en route. They got a different sense of time.'

Did they? I didn't like it but had zero say.

The stone was big. It took a long time to reach it, the strange black blob growing and growing in front of us. It was weird: huge, smooth, jutting up through grey-yellow shingly sand in the middle of nowhere, the black mouth of a tunnel.

About a hundred metres away they stopped the jeep. Gramps got out, went down on his knees in the shingle then sat back up doing weird clicks at the back of his throat and started wailing at the stone, praying to it.

We got out too. You could feel the stone's black heat bouncing at you, shimmering in the sun's sizzle. Apart from that there was nothing at all on all sides, a light wind, huge horizons. The two guards sat next to Gramps facing the stone.

We stood behind. I started to sweat. The sky blanched and

began to drain of heat. A sudden fierce wind whipped sand at us so I had to turn away, crouch down, wrap the black cloth round my head.

He drew me up. It had been hot, it was now cold, something was happening to the sky and our shadows, the edges blurring. It was early afternoon but night was coming everywhere, rosy sunset at three hundred and sixty degrees around us. Birds shrieked, the wind dropped, there was silence, an immense eeriness. I clutched him.

IS OK as the sun changed.

40

'An eclipse,' he said, the black moon eating the sun above the huge black stone in bare desert in front of us. The edges of everything caving in, the wrong world, my poor brain scabbling for sense in the odd light.

'Is this real?'

'I think.' He shrugged. 'We're lucky. It feels real. To me.'

Gramps wailed at the sky. The men knelt next to him. We stood behind them facing it. You shouldn't look at eclipses full-on, I remembered, even if they weren't real.

'Don't look. Feel it,' the Sean said.

We looked down, cuffed together, at our disappearing shadows, experiencing slow maths, the blot we'd chanced on, that he felt was real. He said. They must have known this would happen, have timed our journey, for some reason.

'It's weird, isn't it,' he said. 'The sun and moon being exactly the same size.'

'They aren't the same size.'

'But they look like they are, for us on Earth. That's how total eclipses can happen, right? Don't you think it's an amazing coincidence: that the sun and moon can seem to match up so exactly? Given how you've been taught things are just random?'

Out there in the eclipse in the desert by the rock my brain felt different: slow and empty. 'What does it mean?'

He smiled. 'That something's winking at us. Giving us a hint. That it's all a set-up. That we're in something that was made for us. The lovely patterns in the sky, encoded in pyramids, worked out ages ago, deliberately kept from you.'

'How deep does this Don conspiracy go?'

'You'd be surprised. Do you see? The bite in the apple, the forbidden knowledge? Their logo, from wayback. Maybe the sun and moon *are* the same size. Have you measured them recently?

You take a lot of stuff on faith. But what do you really know? Above and beyond whatever we're fucked up in?'

Not much. It was getting darker. Grandpa went silent. We watched strange shadows on the shingle as the moon passed between us and the sun, disc on disc, the perfect match.

'The peak,' he said. 'You can look, when it's totally covered. It's safe.'

Or I'd go blind. But I trusted him: raised my head, looked straight up at the pure black hole of the moon blotting the sun above the rock, watched gold rays like petals flit and grow in the silence. The sky went darkest blue, or rather it went transparent: the stars and satellites peeping through the trick of daylight. Then it started to feel lighter.

'The rebirth,' he said. 'Look down.'

He looked down and pulled me down to the shingle with him, lay on his back on the ground with his eyes closed and soaked up the returning sun. I knelt there, looking at shadows and ripples. Grandpa sang, then made a fire and burnt sweet-smelling wood in a small pan and came round wafting it to each of us as the light and heat returned.

'He's really into it,' I said.

'He can feel it, every pore in his body, have that experience. While you trundle round with your measuring sticks.'

Back to normal. Still slow and empty, I watched the men make tea by crumbling flakes off a dark brown block into a blue teapot strung over the fire, adding mint leaves and sugar dust from a white cone, then bubble the liquid from high into glass tumblers from their leather box, pass the hot tumblers round on a brass tray. We drank them. It got warmer. We ate bread and dates, the men smoked. They kicked the fire in and set up cover for themselves with tarpaulin and sticks in the shade of the jeep, rolled out blankets, lay down and slept.

Sean took a smallish leather water bottle and he and I walked cuffed slowly in the heat together across the shingle towards the huge stone and its shade. To see it up close, have that experience. Full-on heat, banishing everything except each footstep. That landscape: like we were on the moon, no room for other thoughts, no room for anything except the returned sun and the stone and its power.

'Is this natural?' I said, about the stone.

'I think.'

I took the water from him and drank. 'Are we on drugs? Am I on drugs?'

'They don't drug.'

'Do you?'

'Why? With what?' He shook his head. 'Except everything's a drug, has an effect. Even landscape, if you use it right. And the psychedelics we make in our own heads. Maybe it's all one big trip.'

We reached the stone and shade. I touched the hot smooth surface, felt its heat enter my body. 'Iron?'

'Basalt,' he said. 'Kind of black granite, cooked down deep as goo, pushed up and hardened aeons ago, witness to all sorts. A massive natural sundial, must have been. Knowledge comes from deserts: stars, metal deposits. The world stripped bare. Silicon desert. You see everything clear.'

'So weird,' I said, touching the burning stone.

'It's not that weird. Intrusions. Happen everywhere, all over the world, in London, but you don't notice because in other places they're covered in soil, grass, trees, car parks. Here there's no disguise, no carbon. No place to hide in the desert.'

His epic crap.

'Where's Alan?' I said.

He shrugged.

'Alive?'

'Dunno.'

'What *do* you know?' Since we were now alone out here in the desert, the men asleep behind us.

He nodded at the stone, put finger to lips, as if the stone might be cammed, listening to us.

'For fuck's sake,' I said.

'Everything's alive,' yanking my cuff, pulling me on and away from the stone into its shadow, the stone now directly between us and the jeep and sleeping men, in a straight line, eclipsing them. In front of us: nothing, more bare plain, tiny rocks and sand crystals that could also be listening—why not?—the heat of the black thing behind us.

'Why did you pretend to be Chris? How come you knew everything? Where's Alan? What the fuck is this?'

'OK,' walking out with me away from the stone in its growing afternoon shade. 'If it still matters. If you're still...locked into all that.'

'Tell me,' I said.

He sighed. 'I pretended to be Chris. I had to. No other way to get you to help me. What was I gonna say? "He's evil, I'm his clone, please help?" Maybe if we'd had more time, we didn't have time. Trying to get it before he did, they told me to.'

'Who told you to?'

'Tibet. They're behind all this.'

I laughed.

'I got sent there, when I was young, part of my training.'

We drank water.

'You get sent there, to old places, where the knowledge is. Places to learn and pay your respects, stops on the heritage tour. And the old monks nod away. But turns out they were up to stuff. They knew what Don was up to: Project Jigsaw, trying to piece together the old knowledge. No way they'll let Don reassemble that. That was Don's mistake: not understanding he has powerful enemies up in the mountains, on the islands. Without tech and weapons but they have other ways. So he sends me to Tibet, to get me away from bad company, round me out. Instead it blows my mind. Chants, dances, holy dogs, deep libraries in hollow mountains at the top of the world, ancient carved stone warnings buried deep. Their coral and conch shells and headdresses like Pacific feather headdresses, their sea artefacts so far away from sea. Slowly, subtly, they snaffle me. Tell me about what Don's really up to, his horror project, how I can help them. 'Go back home, do nothing, be normal, forget us. Perhaps someday we'll be in touch.'

'So I did what they said: shut up, went back to Don, hated it, learnt more about what Don was up to, hated it more, ran from time to time, always got brought back. Then your Chris shows up. The sequence in its natural state. I'm there for the debriefs, I hack into the rest of them, I remember it all by the ways they've taught me to remember, stars and whorls, that's how I know so much. Chris and Don, the gruesome twosome. In cahoots, big relief. Play with your new toy. But when Chris turns up Tibet gets worried. They think Chris may know things from Alan, Tibet is connected to Alan. Many years before, Alan sent Tibet a coded message through the secret networks of the world.'

'Alan's from Tibet?'

He shook his head. 'From some other place of knowledge. They're all connected in the end.'

'I thought Alan worked for Don?'

'He did. An old-place guy who went round the world on Don's behalf to meet old guardians on their islands, up their mountains, with their objects, in their caves. Getting them to trust him, to tell them their stuff, snaffle up the pieces for master. Till he learnt too much and turned and stole Chris. Or he was working against Don the whole time.'

The ratty tramp in his bus, from where, knowing what, hiding out.

'So Tibet thinks Alan's sent them a message they can't decode for safekeeping, in case something happens to Alan. A message Tibet thinks Don may want at all costs. Tibet stores this message, forgets about it. Till word gets back that Chris has turned up, is in deep thrall to Don, Don's new chief lickspittle, the new main Donling. Bad times in Tibet. Cos Tibet thinks maybe cam-king Don sees all messages, maybe secret networks aren't secret, maybe Chris can decode this message from Alan that Tibet can't decode, what with Chris growing up with Alan and Alan's codes.'

'And why *did* Chris grow up with Alan? Why did Alan take him? Is Alan my dad?'

'Not your dad. I don't think. I just said that before to…get you to come with. Necessary means. As for why Alan took Chris—leverage, I'd say. Have something over Don, who no one has anything over. Grow his own Don, for the other side. Get that Don to replace the real Don one day. Who knows. So Tibet's freaked out. They get in touch.'

'How?' I wanted to know more about these *secret networks of the world*.

'They send me this wooden statue, a priest brings it. A regular visitor to Don's court. Their sign, their terma. Inside: a rolled-up sutra: instructions: the first letter of each line. Simple stuff. Read, absorb, destroy. A little job. Go to Britain, lay low in forests for six months, make sure Don's off your scent. Then go to Cuckfield. We'll write Alan's message into the visitors' book. Get your hands on the message, learn it by heart, destroy it, find a woman called Nim. Chris's old love. She grew up with Chris and Alan, she knows those codes, she's still hung up on Chris, pretend to be him, use your knowledge. Tell her Alan's still alive, that the message will lead to Alan, she wants to find Alan, she cares. Get her to decode the message, tell us what it says, we'll be with you, we'll help you. But don't let Don and Chris get their hands on the message and crack the number. Stop that happening at all costs.'

'The number?'

'A missing piece from Project Jigsaw. The trigger point for the Pacific crack.'

I gave him a look.

'Earth's alive,' he said, cuffed to me in the growing rock shadow, the dark path we walked in, shielding us from the reborn afternoon sun. 'Earth's a living organism with pressure points, like human bodies have pressure points, like on the Chinese map that's a human body and Britain too. Got a headache? Press your wrist here,' pressing a soft nook in my wrist, 'open the blocked vein in your head, cure your pain. Want to open a tectonic plate? It's the same. You just have to know where to press, the trigger point at the end of the vein somewhere else on earth. Apply force to that point with drums, vibrations, music, Thor's hammer, jumping slaves, acupuncture needles, whatever. You open the flow path to the crack place elsewhere. Open the chakras to the underworld, move mountains like waves.'

'You can't,' I said.

'You can,' he said. 'Open your mind. That's what happened before, in the wipe-out. They learnt where on earth to press to open up where the Pacific cracks in Indonesia, the real Eden, where they walked to from Africa, the place of richest minerals and vegetation growing out of the deepest crack on earth. They thought they'd nailed it: how to flood their land with goo riches on-demand, like how they later tamed the Nile to flood water to irrigate desert Egypt and power their pyramids which are stone volcanoes, like they tamed and controlled everything, almost everything, organic civil engineering on a global scale. But some things are hard to control. They pressed too hard, pulled out the plug from the bottom of the world. Volcanoes, quakes, melting ice caps, the drowning of most of Indonesia, the ancient cities getting feasted on by molluscs deep under the waves. End of the Ice Age, the wiping of the whole world, escape to Tibet, Egypt, Easter Island, wherever you can, up to the highest mountains to save what you know from the floods. Let's not ever let that rehappen. Scatter that knowledge. But Don has plans. There's things inside Earth Don needs to get his hands on.'

'Like what?'

He shrugged. 'Stuff. That Don'll risk anything for. That others will risk everything for. Pacific world wars, Japanese and Americans—what do you think all that was? Vietnam, the Chinese now in the South China Sea. Tiny islands you fight to the death for. What's beneath is what matters—the deep trenches of the Pacific, the one true ocean, the plug down there, the gateway to what's inside. Don says he'll be careful. But. What are sunk lands, a few million dead dumdums, to someone like Don? He's already working on it, even without the number: hacking at the crack directly, blunt weapons, blast it open. Those quakes and tsunamis, ocean shelf shifts? Don's undersea robot army hammering away. But give Don the number, the coordinates of the trigger point, he'll open it up deep, hey presto, forget about robots.'

'To get at what?'

'Goo and more. What goes on at Earth's core. The nucleus of the cell that powers us, where the parts get built, where the microbes are made. Don needs a peek at it, see how it works. Future projects to harness to his tech. For the good of Earth, Don says.

'Bollocks,' I said. 'Earth doesn't have pressure points. You can't press one place and open up another place and sink continents and open Earth's core. Ancient people didn't do that, they didn't end ice ages, they didn't harness mineral power via volcanoes, they didn't power pyramids. It's a pile of crock.'

'The whole set-up's a pile of crock. Wouldn't you say? Us spinning round on this planet that happens to be perfect for us? The sun and moon? The lovely maths? Physics turning chemistry into biology for us, at the perfect temperature? The moon being just the right size to square earth? Pull the other one. It stinks. Where are we, when you step back for one moment, take a clear look at the set? Perfect water and atmosphere, perfect-sized moon to give us tides, stabilise climate? Perfect seasons? Planets arranged in perfect chords, drawing lovely patterns round us everywhere we look? That we can smelt metal, shape and cook it in clay moulds that don't burn or melt, build Wi-Fi? That ice floats so seas don't freeze? That it's all just lying in wait for us to discover, everything so perfect for us, trillion-to-one odds. Where are we? What made us? What's the game? What are we trapped in? That's what Don wants to find out.'

We walked on.

'So Don wants some numbers he thinks Alan gave me the key to?' I said after a while. 'Some numbers he thinks are coordinates for a place on the globe that if pressed will open up another place? A deep tectonic crack under the sea in the Pacific near Indonesia that will let him get at things he needs inside the planet in order to explain the puzzle of our set-up? Solve the original swizz? A place that was once opened before by ancient knowledge that nearly wiped everything out?'

He nodded. 'More or less.'

I laughed for a while. 'How's Don going to do it? If he gets the coordinates. The opening-the-crack business?'

'With the Arctic rods. His rig up north. The Hedgehog, they call it. Two hundred and seventy three thousand two hundred mile-high metal rods stooked up there where you don't go. Each one paired to a different point on the planet. Don's sceptres, his microcosmic world temple. Old knowledge tweaked. That's always been the project, right? Turn the world into numbers, map it, turn it into a model, make it digital. Make it twice so you can control it. Even if it doesn't want to be controlled. Once Don has his number: boom: space mirrors to the right point on the globe. Sound reflection, sonic power. Sound waves, conch shells, Joshua and his trumpets. All wrote down, if you can read it. Souped-up old ways.'

Space mirrors. Stooked rigs. Booms, sonic power. And how would I know? He could say anything. He *did* say anything. We walked on.

'If the knowledge is so bad,' I said, 'then why preserve it? Even in fragments?'

'Why preserve Earth's user manual? Might turn out useful, one day, you think? Even if it nearly destroyed you. The millions of years it took to compile, from when we were animals. You just make the systems to keep it separate, for the pure only, out of the hands of Dons and the like.'

'And the pure are Tibet?' On whose instruction we were acting?

'And other places.'

'And why does Tibet,' whoever, 'want to decode Alan's message, get the...coordinates? Doesn't Tibet know them already? What's Tibet going to do with these coordinates if it gets them? And what if I don't have them?'

'The coordinates come from someplace else, Alan got his hands on them, didn't want to hand them over to Don, stored them in you somehow instead maybe, transmission, in case something happened to him. Maybe you got them, maybe you don't. Tibet wants to...shore the trigger place up. Stabilise it so no matter what Don won't be able to deploy it. You can do that, pour in molten metal or something. Very carefully.'

Tibet wanted to pour molten metal into a weak spot to... shore it up?

'Bollocks. Plus: you pour molten metal into a weak spot, it's going to trigger it.'

'Is it? Since when did you become an expert?'

We walked on in the long shadow of the rock.

'If Tibet knew about me, knew I might be able to decode Alan's message, how come they only came for me now? Why not years ago?' I said.

'They only knew about you after Chris turned up at Don's and got probed. I think. Everything backed up on Antarctic servers, Tibet has ins there.'

'Do they? Leaky ship Don runs.'

'There are always ways.'

'I thought there were no adventures left in the world? So the number's in Vengeance Street?'

He nodded. 'Or has something to do with Vengeance Street.'

'And who set all that up? Who's been laying the clues for us? Tibet?'

'Alan, at first, way back, must have set up real Vengeance Street as his fallback, should you ever need the number, then taught it all to you via the copy of his bus. As for the rest: whatever you found in Ickthwaite, the Braille message in Vengeance Street—I don't know. Tibet, I guess. The fight back. Friends of A, people like these guys we're here with.'

Ah yes: A. *These guys.*

'So why did it warn me? The Braille. Against you?'

He shrugged. 'I didn't read it. What did it say? You should have trusted me. Maybe they were worried you'd end up there with Chris.'

It was true, I'd only read the first half sentence. Then he'd eaten it.

'And where is Alan?'

He shook his head. 'Alan's dead. I think. Don or natural, his last bender.'

'So you just used Alan to get me to come with?'

'I'm sorry.'

'You're a shit.'

I stopped, made him stop too in the now fat and blurred rock shadow, the tip now way in front of us at the horizon, a sundial merging with oncoming night. It was cooler now and soon the sun would set behind us, where the stone and jeep were, far away from us now, us heading where? Escaping into the nothing together? Us walking out towards night, no food, nearly no water.

'You bullshitted me. All that.'

'Cos I had to. Some things matter. I'm sorry. I know it hurts.

The Alan stuff. That I wasn't your Chrissikins come back to you. Yeah,' seeing my look, 'easy meat. Tibet said: Alan's the trigger, she'll want to find Alan alive, use that. But when I came to know you I came to sense what Tibet didn't know: that I'd speak bogus and you wouldn't believe me but you'd come along and love it and pretend to you and me it was cos of Alan. When in fact it would be cos of the thrill of being back with me, being back with a Chris who was sorry, who'd repented and still loved you. Triggers and weakness.'

'Fuck you.'

'Yeah. Be honest. Yes I bullshitted you, used you, for good reason. I hurt you. I lied to you. But I'm not him. I've been him, a jumped-up callow fuck living for himself. I've learnt my lesson. I've come out the other side. I see through him, I see through you, privileged access, I know where to push. I know you better than yourself, I know that hurts. I'm sorry you find us so irresistible. But you won't be free till you fess up. And I need you free. I need you over us and beyond this, clean and strong, ready for the fight.'

A noise from behind us: the toot of a horn, an engine. The jeep and men bearing down on us, sand in their wake. They waved at us to stop us there, arcing round to halt beside us, talking to him through the windows with their hands and in their language, opening the door for us while I stood there cuffed to him.

'Junk the past. Be the bitch you are.'

41

Back in the jeep with the crew, driving through nothing, the sun and black stone behind us, the whole pressable world in front of us now in shadow, night about to fall for the second time that day. Strange identical landscape, grit everywhere, moon and silence, our guards, his profile, his ridiculous story and its holes.

And yet and yet.

We stopped at random, there being no features. They hollowed out a small dip and made a fire out of thorn branches from the jeep roof. Gramps started to cook. The others laid bedding down near the jeep then got something metal off the roof: a camp bed they carried over and unfolded a little distance away. They brought down a white mattress, unrolled it over the bed frame, laid a blue silk quilt on top, laid brown patterned blankets over that.

We sat on a carpet cuffed together facing the fires. It was cold, they covered us with patterned blankets. The sky went transparent again, the stars and space mirrors twinkled. The fire burnt.

'What else did you lie about?' I said. 'Who's Ahmed? How does he fit? How's he going to help?'

When I said 'Ahmed' the men flicked their heads at us from the other side of the fire.

'Don't say his name. He'll help by getting us routes and cover, get us to Vengeance Street.'

So we could find the number Alan left for me there without Don seeing. Don with his nanocammed world and all-seeing eyes. Then 'A' would whisk us back to safety so we could give the number to Tibet who'd work out where it pointed on the globe and shore up that weak spot by careful pouring of molten metal while Don didn't notice to save the world. Was his story.

And what then, if I bought this, if we did this? What about

my old life, hanged on social media? No getting back to that in his version, I reckoned.

And how would Don not notice?

And how would Ahmed whisk us around the world?

'"A",' he said, people like "A"—part of the anti-world, the fightback—were masters of old routes and odd ways. Paths like the one we were on now, tracks through seemingly featureless desert that adepts could flow their way through.

'Nice,' I said. But how exactly would sniffing paths, trusting inner landscapes, let 'A' and crew smuggle us in and out of phone-loving Britain, the cammed docks of Barrow?

'I don't know. But they will. They do it every day. The anti-world economy, moving drugs, people, weapons, under Don's nose, without Don noticing despite all the cams. South American cocaine flown to lawless African islands of witches and airstrips, spirited by 'A' up through this desert and into Western Europe and then back over to North America.'

'Nice. I thought they didn't drug.'

'They don't drug *us*. Not their guests. Other people, exchange that cargo for weapons to fight Don.'

'Really.'

'Drugs have their place. Plants to change your head. The colonised changing the brains of the coloniser's kids and redistributing wealth. But Don doesn't want your brains changed. He wants you plugged into the half-life he controls.'

We ate grain and cheese from wooden bowls. They gave us dates, made tea. They chatted to Sean round the fire.

'Asking about our world,' he said. '"Kel Ehendeset". That's what they call us, the West, Don's realm. "Men who make and use machines". Machineheads.'

The men smoked, maybe talking with their hands and eyes, the flicks of their ash. We went behind the jeep to pee, he crouched down for me and looked away. The men got out skinned gourds and started drumming. Grandpa yodelled.

'Secret messages?'

'You bet. The whole world's one song in the end.'

We listened together under the diamond sky. Crazy times. That all this had actually happened and lord knew what else in the deep green past, again and again. I had to laugh. Then he was laughing too, though I hadn't said anything. Then we were all laughing: us and the men and Gramps, for no reason, plugged into the same flow. It seemed.

The men kicked over the fire and went to their bedding by the jeep. Sean took a leather bottle and we went by moonlight over to the camp bed which was our bed. A bed on legs out in the sand, a luxury, to protect us from snakes, scorpions, other creatures. He said. Their ultra-hospitable culture, the men more used to desert danger. Us the honoured guests, precious cargo.

Were there any other creatures in that massive blank place?

Cuffed together, we unwrapped our black cloths in turn and folded them as pillows, forced teamwork we'd got good at. I smelt his sweat, saw his shaved head, like my shaved head, the stubble growing from his inner minerals, his healing mouth and face. His stump, the dip in his head. His twinkling fixed eyes.

We lay tied together under the quilt and blankets on our bed under the Milky Way, floating together on a planet in space. The white moon reigned now, the moon that had looked black when it bit the sun.

We lay next to each other under the moving sky. We slept.

I woke. It was still night, he was asleep. I lay there watching the sky, feeling him breathe next to me. I was thirsty, I reached for the water bottle behind his head.

He opened his eyes.

It was dark but the moon was big and its brightness lit his whites. His eyes, that were the same as Chris's eyes, with the same scar under—had he done that to himself to fool me? The eyes he'd gouged out to spite Don, that Don had fixed out of love and spite, to use him, to get him to drive my boat, he'd said. We watched each other, from behind our eyes. We stared into each other. We held the great wrong gaze.

And then he shook his head and closed his eyes and turned away to sleep, or seemed to.

And left me reeling there.

The stupid fuck. How could I have let myself fall into that trap? How smug he'd be. Outplayed, is how it felt, a petty feeling. But he'd won, or would feel like he'd won, in our contest, which *was* a contest, I realised. What had I done? Shown him something I didn't even feel, didn't think I felt. Though maybe he was right: Chris, my triggers, what we'd been through, that powerful place, our bed under the sky. And he'd done it too. But he'd pulled back first. No excuses—had I lost my mind, making eyes at that lying violent thing? And he'd played me, made sure, turned me down, he'd feel. What fun for him tomorrow. Him and Chris, the fucking pair. Going there again.

When I woke he was gone.

I still wore my cuff but his dangled off me, open and empty. He'd slithered out somehow, was over by the rekindled fire with the men, laughing, drinking coffee, his black wrap back on and covering his face except for the eyes. He saw me up, waved me over, brought me over a glass of coffee when I didn't budge, said good morning like nothing had happened, explained they'd freed him cos I snored, we were all trusted friends now, unlocking my cuff with a key.

Free at last. The tug of that thing off my healing wrist. I stepped in bare feet on the cold dawn sand, he went back over to the men to chatter on in their language. And chattered to them over breakfast and pack-up and in the jeep and for the whole day.

I sat in the back watching more shadeless blank. The talking men, powerless me in my thoughts going mad—were we driving in circles? How could I know, especially when the sun was up high? I didn't know anything and found it hard to breathe, desperate for any way out, to crush my head that maybe was Alan's jar of secrets that they were all after or not.

Just cos he's turned you down.

The eye.

Then I felt better, put everything back in its box. *Keep your head. Is all you've got.*

The same rigmarole at the end of the day: new camp, fire, food, team, me sitting solo, the setting up of the camp bed, the motioning of me onto it. Except we weren't cuffed. He wasn't tired yet, he said. He wanted to sit out by the dying fire, think a bit. He might sleep out by the fire alone, he said, face hidden in the black wrap.

Whatever, love.

I lay alone on the camp bed under the big sky, trying to keep my thoughts small.

I woke. It was still night. He was asleep under the quilt with me, his face uncovered, his eyes closed.

I raised myself up and looked at him.

He opened his eyes.

He smiled up at me. I closed my eyes, tried to lie down quick.

'Hey,' he said. 'We need to talk. It's OK. I feel it too. This place. What we've been through. Who I look like, who you are. Wanting comfort. It's natural. But it can't happen.'

'Fuck off.'

He laughed.

'I thought you were sleeping by the fire,' I said.

'It's cold. And I like sleeping with you. I feel it too. Kind of. I always did. Even before. It wasn't all bullshit, the Uber. Boning up on you while I still had access—I kind of fell for you, across the ether. From afar. Your data. You're our type. Kind of.'

'Thanks.'

He laughed. 'But. It's wrong. For a whole bunch of reasons. Taking advantage.'

'As if.'

'You can't lie.'

'Because you can smell me.'

'Because they trained me from my tube. Is why I know so much more than your Chris.'

'Not my Chris.'

'We both got someone else. Had someone else.'

I looked at him. I didn't understand.

'Mine's dead,' he said. 'Don killed her.'

'Oh,' I said. That felt weird. A big blank between us, me having to recast him. If it was true. *His lies and games.*

He saw me thinking that. 'You don't know anything about me.'

'I know some things.'

'Not much.'

'What should I know?'

'Not much.' He lay facing the sky. 'I loved someone. Don killed her. Those feelings are done for me. But I'm here because of her. To honour her. You're...great. But you're not her.'

'OK.'

His whole other life that I knew nothing about. That he might be more than I'd thought. That he might be upset. That I might care. What secret story had I been spinning for us in the middle of this shitstorm? *Get a grip.* Maybe he was letting me down gently. His excuse. But when I looked at his face it felt real. How weird.

'This is what all this is about for me,' he said slowly, 'in the end. You should know. *My* trigger. So that's how it is. You and me: sister-brother warriors. Fighting the fight, avenging the dead. Warriors for the cause.'

'I'm sorry,' I said. 'Why did Don...kill her?'

'She was against him. Turning me—I wanted to be turned.'

'She was from Tibet?'

'Some other place. She got me deep. I wanted to be got.'

'I thought Tibet got you.'

'Her first. Don killed her. Tibet mopped me up. She was…it's hard to explain to someone like you.'

'Cos I'm dumb?'

'Because you're a dumb realm woman. Truly dumb. Sold a pup. No offence.'

I laughed. 'Wow.'

'No offence. Not your fault. And you're definitely…one of the best of them. And sometimes you remind me of her. Kind of.'

'But.'

'But.'

'Why are realm women truly dumb?'

He watched me. '*Modern* realm women. Because they don't even know. What they are. Who they were. Once. What got ripped out, by the Dons.'

'You're explaining the patriarchy to me?'

'More words he's put into your mouth. Manufactured outrage, steer your pain so you don't look deeper. Protest marches: "Dear Dons, please let us work as our own jailers."'

'I don't understand.'

'I know.' We lay there. 'What *is* Don's world?' he said after a while. 'The cities and money and machines. What is it really? An equal-opportunity scheme for men. Built by men with our machine brains as our attempt at defence against women. Your magic bodies that birth and bewitch us. Your brains. If you can do everything then what are we? It isn't equal, it isn't fair. You don't need us like we need you. It doesn't work the other way. Everything we got, all the logic, all the cities, all the dirty work we do? Pfft,' he flicked his hand, 'gone in a moment, compared to what you got. Or what you once had. And don't think you didn't abuse it. So we cut it out of you, reared you our way. And didn't we do well? What you don't know about your bodies and natures.'

'What don't we know?'

He smiled. 'Men and women, we deserve each other. As bad

as each other. And hidden far away some of you still are.'

'But not me. Letting me down gently cos I'm not bad enough?'

He laughed. 'Put it that way. Plus other stuff. Poor men. "Please escape us from this prison we built for you and trapped ourselves in. Be our way out of our too-successful project." Poor busy dumb modern realm women, picking up the crumbs, trying to be good, trying to be equal, staying faithful, earning their money, weeping over men. Meagre gruel, to your kind once. Even a hundred years ago women knew the score. At least they were real in their kitchens and arranged marriages, not vying for their equal day's pay in the death camps.'

'Thanks so much for the teaching.'

'Any day.'

We laughed on our camp bed.

'I'm going to sleep now,' I said, lying down, turning away from him, making sure I was first to.

'No I'm going to sleep,' he said, doing the same.

Sunrise, fire, coffee, dates, jeep, nodding at him. Brother-sister warriors riding on in silence towards whatever to save the world maybe and avenge our dead. But a couple of hours in we saw something in the distance through the front windscreen. Mountains, far away, coming closer—so strange to see anything. And then something else coming into view at the foot of the mountains: a building, that looked like a palace, but was a fort, he said: a 'redoubt', long and low, the same gold as the desert. A building out there in the middle of absolute nothing.

'French, once, I guess. "A"'s fort now. They say.' He chatted to the men.

I felt scared.

'Throw it away,' he said. 'He isn't even there yet, they're saying. They'll drop us off. That's their instructions. He'll meet us here in a day or so.'

We got to the fort, the jeep stopped outside. The men nodded to us, talked to him, motioned us out.

We all got out, stood facing the gold fort and the grey mountains far behind. We were at the lip of a change in the terrain: immediately beyond lay pure desert, fine gold sand, not shingle, vast crescent dunes stretching out from where we stood towards the mountains, a gold sea no jeep could drive over. Sand everywhere, reaching up the sides of the fort in some places, reaching into the windows of the long low building which was single-storey except for one tower at the back right-hand side, facing the mountains. The building was a crenulated quad, built round an open square you could see through the central arch facing us. Set off to the far right was a separate structure: a tiny domed brick building.

They handed him a small sack, put in water gourds, dry bread and dates, motioned for us to enter through the arch. They bowed to us, we bowed to them. He spoke to them, we all bowed again. Grandpa touched his black-wrapped forehead with two fingers. They got back into the jeep, closed the doors, revved the engine, smiled and waved, bowed one last time, drove away from us back the way we'd come.

We watched their long tracks in the sand. Our pals, becoming a dot, leaving us there alone, maybe. For how long? In such a remote place, no phones. What would we do about food, water? There wasn't much in the sack.

And how did we know there was no one else there?

He shrugged, told me there'd be provisions, not to worry. We stood at the gateway to the fort with nothing but our clothes and the sack, in the middle of nowhere, at the start of dunes and mountains. We entered under the shade of the arch.

We called out, no one answered. We stood in the sandy square. A courtyard, doors all around us, some covered by banks of sand. All closed except the one directly facing us, the one belonging to the tower at the mountain side. We walked over, went in, climbed the spiral stairs up to a small room. A bed and fresh white bedding. Water, fruit and bread laid out on a wooden table. In the next room were fresh white towels, new clothes, a silver tub full of warm water.

I held out my hand to him. He joined me. We stayed there together three days.

42

On the fourth day we took an early-morning walk across the dunes as the sun rose behind the mountains. Dawn was the only time to walk there, before the frazzle. The dunes, as seen from our tower window, were identical croissant-shaped fractals, fixed waves. Hard work to trudge up but fun to bomb down, crisp knife-edges at their crest, us their only disturbance.

It seemed. We crouched and saw insects collecting beads of dew from sand grains, the tracks of snakes and small rodents hiding from us underground in cool burrows. The haze began to lift, heat was coming. We turned, to walk back to our tower. In front of us, at the crest of another dune half-way between us and the fort, stood five black-wrapped men with mirrored shades, machine gun straps across their chests.

I gripped Sean's hand. The old gang, plus reinforcements? A moment of fear, for me. To see masked men with guns. To see anyone else at all. Ahmed? Chris and Don plus clone extras?

I had kind of forgotten that business.

We faced them on the sand.

One of the men nodded. Sean kissed me, told me not to worry. He walked me slowly up and down to them. Everybody bowed.

Me and Sean plus five tall men. I felt them watch me. The one who'd nodded stepped forwards and shook hands with us, took off his sunglasses and hugged Sean, talked to him in the language. Green eyes, behind the sunglasses, a mouth I felt I knew—from the jeep? One of our guard-drivers, but with different gait now: wide-legged with power, flanked by his fellows, hands on their triggers.

'We know him,' I said. 'From the jeep.'

'Yes,' Sean said. 'One of the crew. Ahmed.' The man smiled and nodded. 'Checking us out. We passed, I guess.'

Sly bastard, like they all were.

'Have they been here the whole time?' I said. 'Watching us?' Watching us together.

Sean shook his head.

'What's he saying?'

'They've come for us. We're heading off now.'

He squeezed my hand. This again. Our stay over. No time to go back to our room, smooth our sheets, grab our stuff.

But we had no stuff and perhaps it was better like this.

'Where they taking us?'

'Barrow. In the end. Right now I don't know.'

They started walking us towards the fort. He held my hand and talked to Ahmed in the language while I tried to work out which one Ahmed had been from the jeep. The one sitting next to me when we set out? The main driver? Not Gramps, no Gramps with us now as far as I could tell. Scabbling round for any clue or hint about Ahmed from before, how old he was, what he was like. If some of his guards were also jeep pals, if Gramps was back at the fort rustling up something tasty.

If they might murder us.

As we got closer they started edging us away from the fort towards the small domed brick building at the side which Sean had told me must be a well, source of the sweet water that flowed through the bath taps in our fort tower, that we'd drunk from.

'Why here? Where's their jeep?'

'No jeep,' Ahmed said. 'We got other transport.' Native English, East End London accent. For a moment it didn't register.

Sean laughed and nodded. I didn't laugh. It was more scary, if Ahmed came from London and had become this. I had a picture of such people. A Don-made picture, perhaps, but one that was hard to junk. What might East End Ahmed have overheard in the jeep? Ancient history, mainly. Kudos to Sean, only really talking when we were far from them, far from anything.

IS FINE, Sean pinched into my palm.

'It's fine,' Ahmed said, still having his fun, sly bastard into whose power we'd fallen. So useful, those black robes, burkas. Flit you round so no one knows.

It was hot by the time we got to the small building. One of the men got a big key from a chain round his waist and opened the wooden door. We entered a small square brick room lit by three glass oil lamps on the floor. In the middle of the room was a large walled brick rectangle like a sarcophagus, with a wooden gallows at one end, rope hanging down. Horrible to see but Sean led me to the rectangle's lip and showed me worse inside: a deep hole, something at the bottom glinting up at us. A creature, for fuck's sake, the whites of its eyes.

The real Cwyd, I thought, gripping Sean's hand. But when they dangled a lamp over the edge we saw it was a dark man down there in dirty white robes and a dirty white turban, bobbing in something white.

'A boat?' Down there, under the desert.

'Yes,' Ahmed said.

Their other transport. A boat in water under the desert.

'For real?' I asked Sean.

'Qanats,' he said. 'Man-made canals, cut into bedrock under deserts from the water table. Very old irrigation. That's how wells work in deserts, right? Wells are all made, right? Built connected underground networks—how did you think wells worked? No cams. I guess they use them.'

'We do,' Ahmed said. 'Go down.'

Man-made canals under deserts plied by boatmen. If they said so, while things ticked on in Archway. We climbed into the rectangle and down into the gloom. Inset bricks made spiral steps, a scary descent into dank. Gripping bricks, finding the next foothold, men above and below, swaying lamplight. If I fell I'd land on the boatman or splash into water, who knew how deep?

He climbed behind me.

At the end the shaft widened and we stepped onto a hewn

rock platform, like a faintly rotting tube station, except under the Sahara and next to water, a man-made channel stretching off on either side into blackness, with boats and boatmen to row us back to Barrow. We stood there: me and Sean in the new chill. Next to us was Ahmed and two of his men, the other two still high above us, dangling lamps down from the rectangle, their guns outlined behind them.

'In,' Ahmed said, nodding at the boat.

It was white, old, plastic, with an outboard motor and tiller at the back, fairly scuzzy, rimmed with slime and weeds. A rope knotted to a ring set into the rock tethered it to the platform. The boatman crouched by the motor, lit by our lamps. He was old and toothless with pale eyes and brown weathered hands twisting what looked like a rosary.

Not much room for us all in that boat.

'Just you two.' Ahmed's voice echoed.

'Where we going?'

'Wherever they take us.'

Ahmed nodded. Sean stepped into the boat. I got on behind, they handed us a lamp. The bottom of the boat was lined with rugs and soft to sit on. Because there was a mattress below and under that more cushions and a large hessian sack—Ahmed lifted up the mattress to show us.

'What's in there?'

'Stuff.'

Airstrip witch mind terma, to unplug realm fuckwits. The high mission we were all on together.

'Good luck,' Ahmed said, shaking our hands, clasping Sean to him for a moment, then grabbing the shoulder of the boatman whose cloudy eyes looked round in not-quite-the-right direction.

'He's blind,' I said quietly.

'Not totally,' Ahmed said. 'He can tell dark and light. He *is* deaf mute though. Tap him on the head if you need to communicate: once means "stop", twice means "go".'

Poor guy.

'Safer that way,' Sean said, slinging a rug round me against the chill.

Ahmed reached into the boat and took Sean's hand again for a moment, palms up and joined, elbows touching. Then Ahmed broke away and tapped the boatman twice on the forehead. The men undid the knot from the ring, threw the rope into the boat, set us adrift.

The boat turned his face nearly to us and he smiled, showing us his gums and neatly-severed tongue. He pulled the engine cord and the motor chugged. We set off, Gums facing us, Sean and I moving backwards, Ahmed and co receding, their lamps and the light from above growing dim.

Incredible spookiness on that boat in the gloom under the desert. We held hands. Our one lamp cast flickering shadows onto cut sandstone. Pale Gums crouched with tiller in one hand, wooden beads in the other. Rotting plants stenched it up and sometimes clogged the engine and our path till Gums cleared them. We scattered bats. The chugging motor echoed down the narrow channel, the tunnel roof above us was sometimes high and sometimes oppressively close with stale air.

Sean held me. He was warm.

'The underworld,' he said.

'Stop freaking me out.'

'It is. Rivers of the dead. Blind boatmen. The Styx, for real. Ancient tech. Egyptian barques shaped like crescent moons ferrying the dead and their gold to the afterlife. Learn enough in this lifetime and you'll be reborn through these channels. Built flow networks under every country in the world.'

We chugged along for hours, sometimes moving into light and warmth and fresh air as we sailed under open well shafts and saw round windows of sky high above us like blue planets, plastic buckets dangling down. We came to intersections, sometimes we turned down them.

'Watch his hands, do you see? That's his map,' nodding at Gums's rosary. 'Each wooden bead means a well, the metal ones mean a change of direction. He sees enough to count the wells, the change of light. Or sense the change of air or echo if its night or the well's covered. Different rosaries for different journeys.'

Loving me silently under the rug while Gums crouched blind and barefoot at the tiller like a folded up bird.

We sensed it first by oncoming coolness and how sound changed. A portion of tunnel that was metal, sailing into a metal tube. Gums sniffed and slowed. He felt the metal wall, slapped it, made it ring and vibrate, smiled in our direction and nodded.

'We're here,' Sean said. 'Wherever that is.'

The tunnel widened, we sailed alongside a railed metal platform. Gums felt for it then cut the motor and tied his rope.

Eerie quiet, apart from our breathing and the water slapping the metal and boat. Everything apart from us metal and modern: steel, I guessed, smooth and regular, giant rivets. Sean held up the lamp but we saw no opening above. Gums smiled and nodded again, then pointed towards the platform. Then he reached forwards with knobbly hands and fumbled for, then lifted, the rugs and mattress, showing the sack beneath.

The booty. Sean reached for Gums, clapped him on the shoulder, a gesture of thanks. Gums bowed his head. Sean pulled himself up and out of the boat onto the platform, reached for me and pulled me up behind him, took the lamp by its metal handle, set it on the platform floor. We grabbed the sack and lugged it up onto the platform next to us. It was heavy.

'What next?' Some relay of boatmen, us hanging around down there for who knew how long till the next one turned up, like waiting for tube trains?

We had no food.

It would be fine.

Sean lifted the lamp, shone it at the platform's back wall and lit a double door shape cut into the metal. I went over, tried to prise open these doors, dug my fingers into their unbudging edges. Sean shone light at a crank handle set into the wall at the door's right side. Metal, like a bicycle pedal, with a worn leather handle. He went over, put the lamp down, started turning the handle. Above us something high and unseen began its whirring descent. A lift, its hidden weights and pulleys, a hand-powered contraption like a well. Something clattered down behind the wall towards us, with who or what inside? Gums nodded from the boat.

'Sean,' I said, but as the lift hit the ground the doors slid open, to reveal nothing. An empty space, a metal floor and shaft, lit by dim light from high above, bare except for a metal chain hanging down.

Sean stopped cranking. The door stayed open but the light from above began to dwindle.

'Come on.'

He pushed the sack inside. Gums clanged the metal tunnel wall again and threw a pile of black cloth at us. I went over, picked it up. Burkas again, black cotton this time, like our black cotton wraps. One big one, one small one. We put them on, covering everything except our eyes.

'Looking good.' He went back over to the boat, tapped Gums' forehead twice. Gums bowed his head then pulled the motor cord and, turning the boat slowly around, chugged back down the channel into the darkness with his beads.

'We got his lamp,' I said.

'Our lamp. He doesn't need it.' Sean took the lamp into the lift. I stayed on the platform by the water.

'What's up there? Don?'

He held out his hand to me from the lift. 'You got us in. I'm getting us out.'

Bonded now, fluids exchanged, sealed together in this experience. I joined him in the lift. He pulled the burka down over my face so my eyes were covered and my mouth exposed.

He kissed it through the slit with his tongue. Then he pulled the lift doors shut by their inner handles, grabbed the metal chain and started pulling it down to winch the floor up while I pulled my slit back up over my eyes.

Slowly, working together, we yanked ourselves plus lamp and sack up the long steel lift shaft till we reached the dim bulb at the top and a ceiling and a new set of doors.

It was hot up there and not just because of yanking the lift up. Beyond the doors was Tokyo or Timbuktu, it didn't matter, we'd sort it. We stopped pulling. He let go of the chain though I was loathe to: what if that's what held us up? I pictured us hurtling all the way down. But in the chain's tension I could feel we were safe. I let go as he pulled the new doors apart, letting in searing white light.

Hot desert again, our eyes adjusting through our slits. Different desert though: plants and shrubs, shingle again instead of sand. Somewhere with hills in the distance, the sun to one side, the sense of afternoon. And next to us, stretched out for seeming miles in either direction, to the horizon: two long wide shiny parallel silver tubes, set up on endless metal struts and cradles poking up from the ground.

'Pipelines,' he said, nodding at the sleek modern things. 'For the gas and minerals they suck up to power those clicks and swipes.' He picked up the sack and stepped out of the lift.

I came after him with the lamp, shy of this pipeline. Such things were Don's surely, smart coated structures primed to blab despite our burkas.

As I stepped outside the lift doors slid shut behind me.

We both turned.

The lift building we'd stepped out of looked like an old rusting sentry box, its doors set at a slight angle facing the pipelines. Flaky orange exterior, nothing like the smooth steel innards we'd emerged from or the shiny pipeline.

'Clever,' he said, about the doors closing. 'Some mechanism

to calibrate the weight. Stops it getting sanded up. I guess.'

'How does it open though?' Trusting him and Ahmed and this experience but not wanting us trapped up there in the searing heat.

He touched the hot rough lift doors, tried to pull them open, couldn't. I tried too and tore my fingertips on the burning rust flakes, drawing blood. A small rusting wheel was set into the side of the sentry box away from the pipeline. I went over, tried to turn this wheel, failed. Jammed in place, maybe he could move it, but he'd moved over to the pipeline. I started to sweat under my black. We didn't have any water or food, though maybe there was some in the sack. Around us were green shrubs we could maybe chew.

'Look,' he called, from over by the pipeline, hidden now by the sentry box. I went over, found him standing next to what looked like a third short pipeline tube about five metres long, jutting out at a right-angle from the pipe closest to us, also supported by struts and cradles. He stood in black cotton by its sealed end.

'Pig launcher,' he said. 'Cleaning capsules. You can send other stuff down. You can send people. This is an Ahmed in, how he sends things.'

'Down Don's pipelines?'

'Probably Chinese. Even if it's Don's, Ahmed'll have sorted it. Safe zone. OK?'

Staring into me, measuring my taint of realm.

'This is how we'll travel?' Hurtling down.

'I've done it before.'

I swallowed. 'How fast? Where do we end up? We get into some...capsule? How do we get in?'

'That's the question.'

We looked at the pipe. The sealed end had a small dial set into its centre, it looked like you could turn it. He reached out.

'Careful, it's going to be boiling.'

'It's fine.' He touched the dial.

I fluttered the tips of my fingers onto the sealed end too. It was weirdly cool, for a shiny metal structure sat out in baking desert, especially since the flaking lift had been so hot.

'Why isn't it hot?'

'Tech.' He was turning the dial but nothing was happening.

'How did you get in? When you used one before?'

'I was with people, it was different. A Scritch?' stepping back to let me fiddle with it.

No Scritch I could remember about a dial in a desert on a tube. Twelve clicks going round.

'Like a clock,' I said, but without numbers. Like a safe, or a combination lock. I turned it five clicks, pressed the centre, then turned six more clicks. The five and the six, that tended to work in this business.

The sealed end with the dial began to telescope out towards us slowly.

'Oh,' I said.

'What did you do?'

'The five and the six. Alan's code. How come Ahmed knows it?'

'It's an old number,' he said. 'Lots of people know it.'

I stood there watching the inner tube slowly extending, revealing a hinged hatch door at its top.

'Clever you,' he said, as the telescoping stopped, going over to open the inner tube's hinged hatch door.

Inside: a capsule, a grey cushioned space, two berths, an upholstered double coffin.

'Clever you,' he said again.

'But,' I said, not feeling clever, remembering buttery locks and another number, that I supposedly knew, the one that was about hedgehogs and cracks. 'What if...they want Don's number? Maybe this is a trap.'

He shook his head. 'It's not a trap. Ahmed's with us. This

isn't Don's number.'

'How do you know?'

He took my burka face in his hands, stared into my eyes, nuzzled my veiled lips with his veiled lips. 'Too simple.' He went over to get the lamp and sack.

I looked inside the capsule: just enough space for us both. There were buttons on one rounded wall, a control panel.

'Look,' he said at my side, blowing out the lamp, pushing it and the sack inside the capsule even though the lamp must have been hot, pushing them in right the way down, showing me the buttons, which one to press to send us hurtling.

'It's safe? You're sure? Where do we end up?'

'Somewhere together,' squeezing me hard, lifting me up, bundling me in, climbing in next to me.

I struggled against him, his arms round me, holding me down next to him in our snug vault, the hatch door still open to blue sky above us.

'So much more than you know,' he said. 'Deep tunnels, everywhere in your cities, dug by monsters, massive projects they call civic, public transport, that you only see a fraction of. Huge circuits, smashing things together, black quark arts, impersonating stars.'

'Sean,' I said, starting to freak out, but he had one hand over me and with the other pulled the hatch shut over us, latching it from inside, making us dark except for the dim glow from buttons at his side. 'How we going to breathe?' I said.

'Like this,' fiddling with something in the closed hatch door above us, grabbing and ripping my burka slit, forcing a plastic mask over my nose and mouth.

'Sean,' I tried to say, trying to wriggle out from that mask in black panic — almost no space or light, him so close, restraining me.

'It's OK,' he said. 'Gotta be like this. Trust me. Take the leap. We could be here twenty four hours, longer, depends where we're going, under the sea maybe, you don't want to be conscious for that, this is pleasant.'

What was pleasant? Still wriggling under the warm plastic but beginning to feel it in my body and that it *was* pleasant, seeing him watch me unmasked beside me.

'Well,' he said.

43

Him and I, in Alan's bus but not Alan's bus and not Vengeance Street neither, nor the Skidblad prints. More like a mist: what you touched didn't crumble and was semi-solid but you could put your hand through it.

'Not always,' taking my hand, reaching it up to the mantelpiece, helping me grab the handle of the Toby jug and bring it down to my lips and drink the scalding liquid inside.

Me walking with him through my childhood, because he'd never seen it. Only his spit had, realm-reared Chris who hadn't been through what we'd been through, come out the other side. How to play Scritch with Alan in the Fall under rain and grey skies. Tal and Flora who was dead now, maybe. Me and Chris on the floor of the broken house, me and Sean watching it. Ann Wynn calling us in for tea as the light changed.

Back in the bus. The pile of books, Alan knowing where every book was. 'You got to have a scheme.' Alan's treasures. Different ways to code and remember, the Alphabet, the *Little Key*. The Ring of Seeds, the Chinese map. Pictures, numbers, stories. The swan, the hook, the snowmen.

Which numbers, though?

Hard to say.

The old bad feeling of not knowing, not being good enough to crack it. The old pressure.

All about not forcing it, letting things float up, him and I working together. Zoo Wang, talking Zita. Saying whatever, letting your mind guide you. Your body being so much cleverer than you. Alan knitting it into us, turning me into a piano. Full of tunes, if you knew how to play me.

'That's where you hid,' pointing to the cupboard under the stairs.

Going in there myself, into the dark, him coming in too with that black Venetian mask, pushing its long nose into my mouth. Him pulling up my clothes, putting the black nose inside me, putting himself inside me, looking at me with his new yellow eyes.

44

I lay outdoors at dawn somewhere cold and damp with him lying close next to me, his yellow eyes and the dent in his head. Strange and wrong, or what I'd been taught was wrong. My tinkered brain back from its sleep. And where were we, was I? Out of capsules and gas pipes, somewhere grey but fresh and green and cold with trees near sea, I could smell it.

I was awake, somewhere, by bushes, outside.

I sat up, pushed him away.

Damp, cold, scratchy sand mixed with wet earth, plants, insects, cams, billions of busy things obeying instructions from Don or their inner codes. Too many things, vile and freaky after the blank desert.

He reached over for me. I pushed him off again, he nuzzled into my neck, I pushed hard and kicked him, he held my wrists. I screamed, he put his hand over my burka-covered mouth to keep me quiet in the grassy sand. I bit his stump through the cloth, he rolled away from me and yelped. Something vast loomed over us from down the beach.

'What's wrong?' he said.

'Where are we?' trying to work out what was happening, why my head didn't seem to be working, how come I was wearing black sweatpants and a hoodie.

'We're in Bacton. Right?'

'Bacton? What's that?' feeling light as air. Just down from us I could see tangled silver tubes, huge drums, floodlights in the dawn light, pipes, barbed wire, an industrial complex jutting into the sea. 'Are we in Barrow?'

'It's Bacton, what are you talking about? Norfolk, you remember? You OK? We came from there, right? Escaped? The men and the bins? Cutting the wire? You OK? Don't conk out on me,' leaning over and slapping me hard, stinging my cheeks. I lunged at him, scratched his face with my nails, drew blood.

'Stop it.' He held me off, looked concerned. 'It's OK, Nim. It's me. You blacked out. It can happen, after the gas. Breath. Relax. Stay awake. Don't conk out on me. Don't panic. What's the last thing you remember?'

Vengeance Street. 'Getting inside the tube?'

'In the desert?'

His stump and face, the nick under his eye that had nothing to do with carting down the Fall, why did he have it? More beard and stubble than before, it seemed to me, a trickle of blood running down near the corner of his eye where I'd scratched.

I felt awful, disconnected.

'You don't remember getting here? The men, the wire? What I said? The bike?'

His burka was gone. He wore a black hoodie and black leather jacket and sweatpants.

I didn't remember anything. We'd done what? Got whooshed down pipes, teleported under the sea from the Sahara?

'You don't remember them getting us out? Giving them the stuff in the sack?'

He lay next to me and held me gently while I tried to patch things together, think through my big blank.

'It's OK, it's normal, heavy-duty gas, it can mess your short-term memory. You'll be fine in a bit. Take deep breaths. Relax.' He stroked me very gently, kissed my hot slapped face. 'Norfolk,' he said. 'The coast. Where the pipes come in.' Back in Don's cammed Britain. A so-called gas terminal, he said, at England's flat east. Back in the realm, green place in spring: wild garlic, tiny dots of new leaves, reeds, blossom, hardy old nature up to its business. Which spring, my long sleep? My hands and nails looked the same. A bit more stubble on my head.

ONLY PINCH.

'He'll know we're here,' he whispered. 'Soon enough. He'll let us. Just step in when he has to, like before.' HE DOESN'T

KNOW ABOUT A. 'Just don't say anything.'

'Why are you saying things?'

'I know what not to say.'

We had a pile of leather motorcyclist clothes: gauntleted gloves and boots, padded jackets and trousers to put on over our tracksuits.

'From where?'

'Ahmed's guy. You don't remember?'

I'd never worn such things, they were heavy.

'Knife and bulletproof. Modern armour.' We'd scored a motorbike too, a big, old, unsmart black and chrome one propped up by a tree.

'From A?'

He nodded. 'Cleaners, cooks. Glitches in the system. There's always a way.'

'Going to Barrow?'

He nodded. 'How do you feel?'

Bad. Fuddled. Blank. Stupid. Swaying in my warm heavy leathers which fitted so exactly. My brain feeling very small. Hungry—he tore me a hunk of dry bread from a stash in the bike's panniers and gave me water to drink which made me feel better. *Monarch*, the silver writing said on the bike's side. He crowned me with a heavy blue and silver visored helmet, then grabbed me. A sudden noise: something coming our way from behind trees. A woman, hair pulled back, in pink exercise clothes, jogging in nature with white buds in her ears, connected to what she held in her hands: a pink phone she was touching, scrolling through messages, finding music.

A dawn jogger with her phone. We shrank back.

She looked up, saw us facing her in our gear and visors, nodded. We nodded back, she jogged past.

A pal of Ahmed's? A terminal policewoman patrolling the perimeter?

A dumdum thralled by gussied fetters bought with her own

money from Don's quark merchants. I wanted to run after her.

'Come on.'

He got onto the bike and I got on behind him and put my arms round him.

He revved the engine. We started down the path.

45

We rode out of woods into flat bare land, away from sea, down empty dawn roads as the sun broke through clouds behind. Fields and hedgerows sparkled green, a just-rained feel. English signposts, a high clear morning, us back in England, land of lost yews. Arms round, visors down. A few early-morning dumdums in cars, decked with coated trinkets, yabbering into Don's machines, under Don's spell, the rising sun glinting on their mirrors and windscreens. Clear air, light blue sky, puffy baby clouds, us floating through a perfect young spring day.

He zoomed me down country roads, avoiding towns: must have been told directions when I was conked out, given wooden beads. We passed blossom, willows in bloom, daisies, dandelions, other cammed yellow flowers, jolting over every bump in the road. So much stuff, after the desert. I hugged him. Dainty new leaves speckled trees at the cusp of new life, still-bare trees showed mistletoe. Hares and rabbits raced near pebble, flint and red-brick houses. We floated past a big old pile of red-brick Tudor chimneys, a field of buttercups, gorgeous pink blossom, satellite dishes, church-watchtowers, bluebell woods, yellow fields, a family of mink or large ferrets at play in a hedgerow, ideal cottages, ivy on thick twisted trees.

A stag ran across our path, made us break hard and nearly fall. Further on: a whole dead deer by the side of the road, next to a faded poster for a daredevil air show and big silver silos full of grain or something. Lambs played in fields separated by elegant pines and communication towers, piglets gambolled by steel box sties. We saw pheasants and dead pheasants, swerved hard on corners at scary angles. I gripped him. We rode through a forest and past a power station. Birds flew up high, avoiding turbine blades. Roadside, we saw a dead fox, a dead cat, more dead pheasants. Dead supermarket bouquets marked a crash.

We took a smaller path into a new wood of tall regular evergreens, then swerved off the road proper onto muddy tracks into wilder land, bumping and turning, him knowing the way, splattering mud.

A scheduled stop-off? A time-out? We stopped in a glade by a big tree, got off, kept our helmets on. He pushed me face-down against the bike.

We ate fresh leaves and roots in the clean spring sunshine.

'So lovely,' I said, watching the blossom in the sun.

'It's nothing,' he said. 'Spring's easy, all the same, everything's beautiful when its young, no skill in that. The real beauty is autumn, everything dying in its own way, showing how well it lived or not. Blazing out.'

He poked two sticks into mud and marked where their shadows fell. We followed a stream to a pool and took our helmets off to drink.

'Pure spring water from chalk: sure you can drink it, sure they don't want you to. Keep you at your laced muck from your dumdum taps.'

The chalk here was the same seam as ended up at Silbury Hill, he said. Alan's White Road that turned out to run east-west. He dug in mud and showed me black flint, told me it was the best kind, told me this pool was once a holy place, like all springs bubbling up from pockets in chalk. He took off his clothes and waded into the pool, bent down even though it was freezing, messed around in the middle, got a big stick and swirled it round, hooked something, dredged it up.

It was a big, oiled, green canvas bag, military-looking. He carried it out of the pool, shook himself dry, patted himself off with his clothes, put them on. Squatting on the bank he opened the soaked bag and took things in plastic bags out: three square motorbike number plates, two long car number plates, a couple of folding knives, a pen knife, a small metal box containing a roll of money and four British and US passports wrapped tight in plastic. Candles and a tin of flint, fluff and U-shaped pieces of metal. A toolkit containing screws and screwdrivers, spanners, needles and thread. Two sets of keys and a trowel. A pot of pills and a pot of what looked like honey. Small clear baggies of white powder. A large bag of that weird dry stuff which had turned out to be mushrooms, for those headaches he hadn't had in yonks. A gold ring with a strange light blue stone, some gold chains, two long gold necklaces, four big gold coins, a gold brooch in the shape of a harp which he pinned inside my jacket.

'In case we get separated and you're on the run and need cash. Head for pubs, take the helmet off and put it on the floor, keep the hoodie over your face and nod, accept any price in cash, get away fast. Head for service stations, camp out round the back, look for marks on trees, wait.' For 'A's people to find me, for someone to find me. He showed me marks carved into the blossoming trees.

He gathered up most of the stuff, put the rest back in the bag, threw the hoard back into the middle of the pool for its next visitor.

'Wet cupboards. Lake terma.'

Back at the bike he divided our new trove between his pockets and the bike panniers. We ate bread, honey and the vile mushrooms.

He changed the motorbike number plate with our new tools, threw the old one into the pool. He crouched and marked with new pebbles how the mud stick shadows had moved and measured the distance with his thumb.

'Getting our bearings. Don't you worry my pretty.'

He took a needle, rubbed it through his head stubble, set it on a leaf floating in a puddle, waited for the needle-leaf to settle.

'Where it faces? North.' Barrow was north-west, where we were heading. Yes, you can magnetise a needle with electricity from your body to make a compass. Yes, there is flow about which dumdums aren't told.

Back on the bike feeling better but still inside my high clear cloud. He whooshed us out of the forest north-west through Don's Britain, away from coastal countryside towards modern churches, motorways, towns, estates, superstores, industrial zones decked with easy blossom like showgirls, dumdums at their phones. We crossed a wide river, the land started getting hilly. We stopped off for petrol at a small service station, paid in cash from the trove roll. After we drove up into hills full of lambs following signs for a model village. We drove in, parked up, took off helmets and gloves, pulled our hoodies low, bought blue cardboard tickets with our cash.

May the sixth, according to the tickets. Six months after he'd come for me in Archway. It felt like six years.

We wandered round. A run-down concern, us the only visitors: ideal olde-worlde slightly-chipped England in miniature form. Tiny people, tiny houses, pubs, cricket and bowling greens, zoos, shops, churches, funerals, a moated castle. Model trains whipping round.

READING IT? I pinched.

He nodded. Codes I wasn't privy to, from pals I didn't know. Plans of attack, info and warnings arranged in rugby formations, rhino herds, cricket scores.

On the wall outside the empty gift shop was a large relief map of Britain. He showed me where we were, near Derby, at the start of the rocky north-south central spine of Britain, the White Road on Alan's map.

'The border zone. See? Two countries, Britain:' the dull flat south-east of servant-knaves and lickspittle apple middlemen that we'd just ridden through versus the fortified dragons of Hyperborea where slaves once dug empire juice.

'At least they had skills and honour: press-ganged here to dig and sniff. Not complicit toads squatting in stately homes that know more than they do. Always two countries, two cultures, Britain. The divided kingdom. Those who think it's a country, those who know it's a mine.'

'I'm scared,' I said. 'Of what's next.'

'It's nothing. You were born to it. You'll surprise yourself. Keep your mind blank.'

'And after?'

'We're in good hands. You'll see.'

Back on the bike, heading down the hill into Hyperborea proper, land of ooze and apples, sifted by flow masters from way back, ancient hidden centre of the world. We floated past ugly towns and old scars, car parks built on secrets, plump ex-slaves and their swiping toddlers. We did motorways, shrouded in our leathers and helmets, weaving fast under circling birds of prey. The land got wilder again, signs said 'The Pennines', we passed hills and forests, heading for the Lakes. Journeys merging—I felt scared and hugged him, saw flashes from our first time. White sheets laid out on the road.

I hadn't thought about that in ages. I couldn't think about it. We were avenging them. I did old Scritch exercises: counted trees, counted to twenty-six. I saw us riding up to Jenny 2 on the map that was Britain and a body, saw us as vectors for Don to scry through liquid crystal, saw pixellated Chris who'd sold his soul to them, saw the land breathe as the evergreens flashed by.

We entered land I knew from a different season, from autumn. Then: marvellous unique death, now: green clone shoots. Perfect lambs frolicked in small fields bounded by dry stone walls that were the last traces of megalithic building. Pylons and power stations gorged on crack goo, big mountains loomed in the distance. Japanese tourists enjoyed dead purple slate.

Signs for Coniston. Enbarr and his sign, the post box and Bugg just a right-turn up from here, white drawers, the van, him hacking me in the lake.

I hadn't believed then, hadn't understood. Us in the burrow.

A different time and place. I knew better now.

We didn't take the turning, didn't need Kraton's barn this

time. We had all the info we needed now, shared fruits of my head.

He knew too now, more than me. That was understood now, between us. Thank fuck. He could solve me now, what others had knitted into me, a puzzle for machineheads. I felt light, riding pillion, still woozy from gas, close to the land, not cut off in a car, riding with him through Don's dumb Britain, whooshing down its secret veins towards the dragon's snout.

We turned for Ulverston, back on smaller roads past blossom, abbeys, priories, watchtowers, churches with vanes showing wind direction, the very least of the services they once rendered. We turned left again by a statue of the Virgin Mary, took the coastal road. A supermarket, then the chocolate sea and mud we'd sailed through before under grey clouds in a different season, in a frenzy. The tide was out, the mud puddles full of blue sky.

We floated past bird swarms, salt marshes, horse farms, caravan parks, crumbling sea walls. The shiny nuclear cube on the other side of the bay glared in the bright afternoon sun. Our canoe was out there somewhere, sunk in quicksand.

We parked up and sat on a bench facing the mud, hand in gloved hand, visors up. Tiny brown birds scurried away.

'Good call, little pals,' he said to them. 'Harsh lessons burnt into their DNA.' We faced the blue afternoon together. 'Can you feel the history?' This muddy coast, sailed by Greek and Indonesian adventurers. The Irish Sea, once the black heart of a dragon-shaped empire only he knew about any more. The true Mediterranean, where the myths were set. Wexford, across from us in Ireland, where the gold was. Anglesey, aka Mona, aka Spinning Jenny's orchard, where nymphs and Gorgons guarded gold apples of immortality and crones and dragons guarded golden fleeces, where Julius Caesar slew female druids. The Gower, further south, its castles and pools.

'Worm's Head, at Rhossili, where Perseus turned the sea

dragon to stone with Medusa's head. Where we went.'

'We didn't go there,' I said. Unless I'd forgotten.

'I went with Don. The ancestral lands.'

He put his leather arm around me. Out direct beyond us in the sinking afternoon: the Isle of Man, aka Niflheim or Ellan Vannin or the spiral or the Isle of Apples or Middle Cinnabar, whatever that was.

'I used to race my bike there,' the famous Isle of Man motorbike race. 'A chariot race once, round the whole island, for the favours of a lady. A queendom, once, like they all were. No wonder they call it Man now.'

We couldn't see the Isle of Man but we could tell where it was: exactly where the red sun dipped in front of us, at this time of year. He said.

'Ever seen the flag of Man?' Three bent armoured legs, arranged in a circle. 'Code for a cauldron, where you smelt metal, the three legs it stands on. Island of makers, even today. Magicians, they'd have seemed, knowing what they knew about the properties of things. They used to lame smiths, did you know? To stop them running away. You can smelt inside your body, if you know how. Heat your belly, turn it into a furnace, mix and cook materials inside you if you got the control, cure anything inside.'

'Really?' This sounded a bit far-fetched, even to woozy me, nodding away.

'Sure you can. That's what it all means really. Witches' cauldrons full of brews. Dunk the old king in, youngify him. Three-legged stone cauldrons outside Chinese temples. The watermill powering the fiery cauldron of Stonehenge on that Chinese map. The Holy Grail: that's a cauldron, right? A magic vessel. All code for the same thing: bellies,' touching my belly. 'Get it hot, brew it up, fire up the whole shebang, direct the flow round your body. Collect and forge your inner minerals, make inner pills and potions to heal you of everything. If you know how. Belly-cauldrons: the grail: the key to eternal life.'

'No way.'

'Way. Hard work, they say. Years of study, in those caves. Worth it, though. But don't tell the dumdums. Can't have everyone live forever, where you gonna put them all? That's what this is all about.'

'Thought it was about the crack.'

'And the cracks inside.'

Lights dotted on round us, the sun going down on this perfect day. The sky darkened, we held gloved hands, he talked more, about Irish sea dragons and what went on beyond the Isle of Man. Ancient northern sea empires, 'septentrional Armorica', Spain, Gaul, Britain, Wales, Ireland, northern Russia, the Faroes of the Pharaohs, Iceland, Greenland, northern Canada, the North Pole. Magnetic northern islands, indrawing seas that sucked iron nails out of ships to scupper the curious. North and South Poles repulsing each other, the north swallowing up flow, the south pumping out new flow, how it affected mood and bodies, how we were all one thing, connected, on the live planet that made us that Don was guising from us. What really went on up in the Orkneys, Shetland, Gotland, Saaremaa.

'The eye and the dapple,' I said.

He looked at me blank.

But Saaremaa was the eye, and Gotland was the dapple, of the stag sea dumdums called the Baltic. Or that's what he'd told me from our porthole in the tramp wreck back in November. Or whenever it had been. Or what someone who looked just like him had told me, someone with the exact same stump and scars but with different eyes.

Clouds went pink. It got cool. He babbled on, about Scotland and its huge mineral wealth under the granite, what really went on at Loch Ness during the shamantic era of the esoteric Wu or some such, the I Ching hexagrams tattooed onto that ice mummy they found in the Alps. About Tibetan monasteries in Scotland, the Tibetan monastery we'd just driven past, housed in an old priory on the coastal path, its pure-gold-roofed new temple. How everything here was ruled direct by Don, every last inch of it, by Don and the Dons from back in the day.

'If we die,' he said, and didn't say anything more. Blazing out, honour, valour, all that bollocks. Holding my gloved hand while I felt cold and odd.

We got back on the bike, rode on next to mud at dusk. The obelisk came into view. Beyond it: Roa Island, ships on one side, lit houses on the other, street lamps on like fairy lights, so-called wind farms in the sea beyond, the tramp wreck waiting for us by the causeway. Huge setting sky, bronze sea, full circle. Our honeymoon suite, our halcyon days. He slowed and stopped the bike next to the wreck, pulled up his visor, turned to me.

'Let's go inside.'

'No,' I said through my slow head. I'd blabbed about the wreck on the Skidblad. They'd have been in, coated it.

'It's fine. They're letting us do it. They'll already know we're here.'

He got off the bike, gripped me by the wrist, walked us round the wreck in the half-light, pushed me up the ladder onto the slanted deck and down the hatch into the gloom.

It smelt better than last time, fresh and clean. He got the flint tin out of his pocket, struck stone against metal to spark the fluff, used those sparks to light a candle, set it into a wine bottle neck, used that to light two more candles in bottles, set them round the room.

I watched all this, shivering, staring at the flame glow. People had been in since our last visit, and waves too, left-behind seaweed now dry on the floor, flavouring the air. New furniture too: cushions and a mattress, rolled-up bedding.

'Does someone live here?'

He shrugged, unrolled the bedding, led me down to the mattress. He was inside me, I had my eyes closed, I opened my eyes, he was staring at me, into me, with his new yellow-flecked eyes that hadn't been in him last time we'd been in there, after the canoe, when I was ill and he'd looked after me, told me about eyes and dapples. His replacement eyes, for the ones he'd hacked out in the bathroom in Vengeance Street where we'd soon be heading. Flecked yellow, like a wolf.

'What's wrong?'

'Nothing,' I managed to say, an evil spirit flown in to cast or break a spell. 'Scared of what's ahead.'

Petrified of you.

'We'll face it together,' drawing me back.

I lay under him, my face turned to one side, to the porthole and the bottle of Blue Nun, the dried-up bit of seaweed still jammed into its neck.

He put his finger under my chin, pulled my face back to him.

I lay next to him on the mattress in the candle-lit wreck looking at the bottle of Blue Nun, the dead seaweed jammed in with paper. *Sad nothing weed,* stump Chris had screamed at me from his cupboard, weeping blood as they came for him because I'd told them where he was though they'd have found him anyway. His last stand, when he was trying to say things to warn me, the last time I'd seen him.

Sad nothing weed.

Cold pop.

The boat.

Don't fall for it.

I'd thought he'd meant beware of the *Skidblad,* all lit up in Barrow's dock. But he'd meant something else, hadn't he? This boat, the wreck I was now lying in, next to something. Our rendezvous if things went tits up. Our sign, the bottle of Blue Nun, the sad nothing. The seaweed jammed in with some kind of paper.

New Scritch I hadn't got.

I inched away from the thing sleeping next to me on the new

clean mattress.

I crept over to the porthole and the bottle. I pulled out the seaweed and the paper wadding. I opened the folded paper up, held it to the candlelight.

One sentence in black biro, weird bad writing.

I'd fallen for it.

'What does it say?'

I turned. It was awake on the mattress, watching me.

'What does it say? That note? Bring it here.'

46

Propped up on the mattress, stumped hand outstretched, its smiling face lit by candles and lamplight from the port holes, the sheen and sense of watching objects. The sound of sea, everything just as it had been but different, all waiting and smiling and twitching at me. It with its new yellow eyes, holding that stump out for the note.

'Is it from me? From last time? What did I say? So fucked up then, I can't remember. Read it out. Why are you shaking?'

Not stump Chris, not Sean, but not real Chris either. Something else, another instance, rummaging inside me for keys to wrest thrones, destroy worlds. Had been so the whole time through deserts and tunnels since I'd sprung it from the *Skidblad* like it had wanted. Pretending to be Sean, cut to be Sean. And me its fuckbud, shaking naked in that wreck holding that scrawl of paper. The gas, whatever, still inside me whoozifying but pure fear cutting through, bringing me to in keenest terror.

Do it.

I made myself do it, read out the black words on the paper:

Bacon sarnie inside me now if you're reading this but I'm still cold.

Whatever that meant.

It scanned me, cocked its head: 'What does that mean?'

I shook my head.

'Give it to me,' getting up, coming over, naked, gripping my wrist, snatching the note from me. 'Did I write this? Did you? What does it mean?'

'Don't know. Never seen it,' I croaked. 'Some tramp.'

'Really?' looking at me, looking at the note, tracing the writing with its stump, going over to the porthole for better light. 'My handwriting. I was trying to disguise it. What does it mean? You look ill, come here, let me feel your pulse,' grabbing my wrist again, pulling me close, pressing its stump against my wrist to measure the beat of my blood, staring deep into my eyes. 'Poor you. I think you're ill,' phoning data back to some Antarctic hub for crunching, sniffing my hormones.

The eye, summoned with my last power: 'Stop freaking me out. I couldn't sleep, I got up to look out of the porthole, I found this, I've never seen it before, so what? You didn't write it as far as I know — and why don't you know if you wrote it?'

It smiled. 'I think you need to lie down.'

Tight throat, pure terror. *The eye.* 'If you wrote it *you* tell *me* what it means.' Its hand tightened round my wrist. 'You're hurting me.'

'Sorry,' relaxing its grip and not its gaze. 'Maybe I didn't write it. Some tramp. What do *you* think it means?'

'No idea,' forcing fear down. 'Someone's eaten a sandwich but is still cold and hungry?'

The viper, the bacon sarnie that was Don, the BLT, the black tortoise. A message from stump Chris from before, the first time we were in this wreck, when it was uncammed, before the cleaning and coating.

Perhaps.

A coded message to tell me what? That Don was inside stump Chris now if I was reading this? That I was with Don who was wearing stump Chris? What did that mean? The terror. *But I'm still cold.* Meaning what? Stump Chris was dead, still dead? I didn't understand.

'What are you thinking now?'

Nothing its sensors wouldn't tell it shortly.

'That I'm scared,' I managed.

'Poor you. Come here.'

Not that. I went pure ice.

But it would buy me time.

But I'm still cold while it fucked me. Scanning the hull while it got off on my fear, felt that grip.

Scanning for what?

For tramp champagne, our codeword, if things went tits up, which they had. For that broken cold box still in the corner on its side half-covered by rags. Fridge-post boxes, their method. *Every place has a fridge or the coldest place.* Where they left messages, their Scritch. Staring at the cold box and then staring anywhere else to fritz their retina-tracking or whatever, till it was done, retaining its cum like it did. Ancient ways to stop baby instances hatching inside me.

I leant over the side of the mattress and puked. It mopped me tenderly with some rag, then climbed the ladder to the hatch and flung the vomitty cloth out onto the deck.

I crouched naked with my back to it in the gloom. Trying not to breathe and not to look at the cold box and stay in the shadows and keep my mind and face blank, blanche the terrain.

It who could sense anything, the slightest twitch.

'Poor you.'

It could just kill me.

It still needed me. For now.

It was busy talking. Up to stuff, as ever. 'It's happening now,' it was telling me, whatever it was, pacing round, putting things on, putting stuff in its pockets, getting ready. 'This is what's going to happen: I'm going to Vengeance Street now, alone. You stay here, you're in no state. I'll get what we need and come back here for you.'

'OK.' Fandabidosi, anything for him to fuck off and leave me alone. Grabbing clothes, trying to hide my face and beating heart. But. Just managing it: 'Don't you need me, in Vengeance Street? To find…what we're looking for, the…numbers?'

'You don't remember? They came back to you. You told me. When we got to Bacton? After the pipe? The gas, it can happen.'

The Hedgehog. The numbers Don needs to open the crack.

Yet it was the one that had told me all that, in the desert, the fucking desert. Nothing was true, what had I said, what did I know?

Help me Alan.

Oh yeah.

I was nodding away, it was talking on, about Ahmed's secret routes to Walney, ancient tunnels riddling this landscape, cunning monks cutting limestone under the sea from Piel Castle to the old Abbey in Furness, how Tibet would sweep in later to rescue us and maybe reunite us with Alan, other cobblers I didn't give a shit about, talking freely with no fear of cams or Dons picking up words. Nothing like the first stump Chris, the one I'd been with my first time in this wreck, the one that had been scared of everything, cacking his pants.

'You OK?' standing before me as I knelt there. 'Have some bread and mushrooms, you'll feel better,' pulling something out of its pockets, pushing it into my mouth, perhaps not noticing how I held the vile cud in my cheek, tried to contain its leaking juices, spat it into my hand as it turned away.

'If I'm not back after twenty-four hours...' and it went into a long blah about burkas and service stations and chewing roots which I didn't listen to, lost in the whirr of my brain.

'I'll be back soon, promise,' turning back to me, reaching down, tucking its stump under my chin, lifting me up to it, kissing me on my vomitty mushroom mouth as I clenched mulch in my cammed hand. 'Feeling better now?'

I nodded.

'Don't be scared. You must be so tired. Sleep, why don't you?'

'OK.'

It led me back to the bed.

Not this again, the fucking goat.

But its mind was elsewhere. It was off, needed to go.

'I'll be back soon.'

I couldn't wait. 'OK.'

'I love you.'

'Yes.'

'Say it.'

'I love you too,' I croaked.

One last look and nod. Then helmet on, visor down. He turned from me, climbed the ladder, opened the hatch, scuttled out from sight.

Jesus fucking Christ.

I sat on the mattress rocking in candle-lit blackness. Alone at last but not alone: ten trillion rapt cams recording this freakery. And outside, if I made my run for it, up the ladder through the hatch to the deck: who squatted in wait for me on the causeway? 'Police' in hazard suits, 'Ahmed's' crew, hacked ladybirds, controlled weather and waves.

And inside here: what? Some message from stump Chris, from the first time—really? Wouldn't they have cased this joint down to the nano-level before letting me in here with it, read every note? Nothing was true, the scrawl from stump Chris must be useful to them or a planted concoction to addle me further, to get me to do what? More of whatever they wanted, whatever that was, get me to choose wrong again and again.

I could trust nothing, not even Alan, who was probably their plant too, seeding me from way back, what did I know.

Lie down, pretend to be woozy. Let their cams record their mushroom bread at work.

Fight the wooziness, because even though I'd spat most of it out some had entered me, I could taste it. Plus the ten trillion other ways they could be drowsing me: sleeping potions in the walls, buds in my head.

A terrible howl shot my eyes open. A storm outside: shrieking wind, crashing waves. Rain drumming down. Their military weather.

Most of the candles had gone out, light still came from the street lamps outside the portholes.

Do it without thinking. You have to. Hopeless but your only shot.

I was lying down, I got up, as if looking for water. I fiddled with dirty brown bottles, peered for liquid. Went over to the cold box. Opened it up.

Nothing in there except a semi-crumpled beer can. I turned it upside down, poked round inside the hole with my finger, cut myself.

Touched what was inside: a thick wad of rolled paper.

Took the can back with me to the bed.

Coaxed the wad out under the cammed covers.

Unfurled the paper in the dark.

Touched the sheets, felt biro indentations, the packed writing.

Too dark to read it, though.

I had to read it. I didn't care, that it was odds-on corrupt, plants by liars for reasons. What else did I have?

I got up, went over to the rain-splattered porthole, felt ten trillion eyes on me, saw the dense pages, squinted into the orange light.

To Whom It May Concern,

If you're reading this without me with you, or me having told you about it, then I'm dead. Sorry for everything. It's all a sham. I'm not your Chris, I'm the other one, the lying clone freak from the turtle's lab, sent to deceive you on their orders because I'm a weak coward and a fuck and a freak, the clone of a freak. I've completely lied to you from start to finish. It's so fucked and there's so much to say. But first, you got to know that if you're here with someone who says they're me and looks like me, with the stump and everything, and says they were here before with you, after the canoe, but hasn't mentioned this note or the note in the Blue Nun, then you got to know you aren't with me at all. You're with my body but they'll have taken me out, scraped out my brain and replaced it with Don's, turned me into a receptacle for the old freak to be reborn in my perfect-match body for his resurrection now they've perfected the tech. It's so freaky I know.

I'll tell you about it, if I can, what happened, step by step, what this is. But there's something worse I got to tell you first. They know you, Nim, from before. I don't know exactly how but they do. A long time ago you were close to him and he killed you. But he saved a bit and you got grown again. They rebirthed you from your stored DNA. I don't know if he did it or someone else. What I know is he thought you were lost but then they discovered you and he sent me to you, to bring you to him, so he can be with you again...

But then I had to stop. Because of the noise from under the wreck, nothing to do with the storm. Someone—something— was banging at the metal hull beneath me. Banging hard: five knocks, a pause, six more.

47

The bangs came from under the mattress, under the boat, where there should have been mud. And why not, since nothing was real? Monk tunnels, spiral castles, Ahmed's gas pipes, Don's whole-world set, me too long finoodling with letters and wooziness. Plenty enough for it to whizz to Vengeance Street and back, King Don who ruled the world with buttons to whizz it anywhere, no need to skulk in tunnels. Except to furnish lies for dumb me, whoever I was, some woman it had killed once, whom it would know was on to it, whom it had been inside.

Whom it might not need anymore.

I should have run, made a plan. But that letter had wiped out time, like it was supposed to? *Keep her busy while I'm out, spin some crock to keep her agog.*

Real Sean telling me in Vengeance Street the first time: *'Beware. They know you from before.'*

Shitting Nora indeed. Who was I?

Get out now, my belly-furnace said: up the ladder, out the hatch, jump off the deck, run into the storm—into their world, under their spell?

The five and the six again, followed by something else from under that mattress: a clang, harsh ripping, metal on metal.

I couldn't move.

It slithered back via hidden ways full of new info and power courtesy of me, with new plans for the world and me. Whoever I was.

You are you. Do it. The eye.

I scrunched up the letter, shoved it down my cammed pants, sprang from the porthole in frenzied search for a weapon, anything, something heavy, metal, pointed, even though it was useless, anything at all. *Blazing out. A knife to kill.*

Yeah, good luck with all that. Stump Chris would have

known what to look for, they all would, even realm-reared real Chris. Busy men with animal nous and murdering hands. *One swift blow between the top two vertebrae, if you can find them.* The Cwyd's red weak spot. *Good luck with all that.* More clangs under the mattress, eleven more knocks. Then a muffled voice, words I couldn't hear.

I leapt up onto the hatch ladder armed with a bottle-candle and a broken jagged plastic biro: tools coated with networked slime, ready to turn on me at its instruction. *Go for the eye.* I stared down in the flickering gloom at the moving mattress, the fresh bed made up there by staff unknown, the wreck spruced into a world king's fuckpad. The whole thing: since Archway, since whenever: his plan meshed with my weakness. Easy meat, a gimp bursting to spill. And they knew it, better than I knew myself, the respawned carcass of a one-time Don hook-up, if I understood right, if the letter wasn't some crock.

It's crock. It's all crock. How would they overlook it, let you find it?

But it felt true. The whole shebang: cooked up as a fun challenge for reborn Don, the once and future king. A double whammy: decode and refuck her. Who she is that she don't know.

And what did it know now, what had it harvested from me? What had it got? Had it been to Vengeance Street? What had they found there? Did the numbers exist, was the Hedgehog now primed? Or had it already happened: Pacific cracks, lands flooded with boiling goo from Earth's inner furnace so it could get what it wanted? Which was what?

The far side of the mattress curled up, something under it bulging up like a dry wave inside the wreck. Newspapers, foam, plastic bags slipping from under the heaving mattress, something emerging: the outline of a head. A mud-smeared head I knew well and not at all, hoisting itself up from the rip it had made in the wreck's belly, the filthy wet-suited body, a huge screw-tipped metal rod slung over its shoulder. A mud monster, rising from beneath. It stood, dripping splodge, wiping brown from that face. It peered round for me. It glommed onto me on the ladder. A crash of thunder outside the boat. It spoke.

'It's me, Nim. Chris, for real, come to get you out of this. We got no time. We got to run.'

British accent, weird monotone. As if, for fuck's sake, moving towards me, pulling down its neoprene to show me its hands in the candlelight. Ten whole fingers, no stump, different eyes, huge knife sheathed at its waist, the rod over its back. Purporting to be my real Chris from Scritchwood. Like fingers proved anything, like anything proved anything, like I cared, trying to morph into something else since its game was up due to me reading the letter it probably wrote, fluid monster still playing with me, batting off my hot flame and biro.

'Come on, no time, we got to go, there are tunnels, he'll be here soon,' grabbing my wrist, starting to pull, trying to wrest the flame from me. 'That letter, though. That you were reading?'

That I was reading when it was still under the wreck, piercing the hull with its rod or whatever. That it could never have seen, except through its screens.

I closed my eyes, pulled against it. 'Blah blah blah,' I said. 'La la la.' But then I stopped because there was a new noise coming from above me: something clambering around up there on the metal, stomping on the deck up there, knocking its five and six, opening the hatch.

Cold wet air, rain and salt sea. I couldn't help myself: I opened my eyes. Crouched up above us at the open hatch, lit by lightening from behind: another one, in motorbike leathers holding its helmet. A thunder crash. The thing held our gaze.

'Nim,' Leathers said, as I looked from one to the other of these two same freaks, wondering if they'd cancel out each other like in old stories their tech had wiped out.

'Nim,' Wetsuit said, pulling me away from the hatch as Leathers moved down the steps towards us, jumped down so it was down in there next to us, reaching for me too.

Me there with the two of them.

Fuck this shit. I had no power but there's always power. I dropped my biro, pulled the crumpled note out of my pants, held the wad to the candle in the bottle in my hands so it set alight.

They both moved towards me, then dodged the burning note and candle and stood back as I dropped fire to the floor of dry seaweed and sawdust strewn by their set-makers. The flames spread, catching newspapers, mattresses. The floor started to burn. Our cauldron, getting hotter, filling with black smoke: would we rise as new-borns from the ashes? Or would something happen and would that deed tell me something? Can't argue with physics: only so much finagling when you're on fire, right?

Sure enough the flames and smoke rose, burning feet, and something happened: the sound of sea and storm clicked off, there was a new noise as all the portholes smashed in at once and white smoke, dry ice, got puffed in. Then the metal hull ceiling above us lifted up as if sliced off: got hoisted up and shunted clean to one side. To let sand pour in from above, masses of soft yellow sand, not brown coastal mud, dousing us and the flames and smoke. And then a silver claw from a crane above us, from nowhere, reaching down to pluck Leathers up and away.

Gotcha, old Daddy.

They left me and Wetsuit down there, for the big-legged robots jumping in over the cut walls. I stood waist-deep in sand, slightly singed, let those robots grasp me, pull me up. They cradled me high towards where the hull ceiling had been, where there should have been rain and the stormy night sky of the Barrow coast—the roar of sea, the shine of stars, satellites, streetlamps, power stations, wind turbines, the twinkle of Roa Island. Instead there were echoing sounds and another roof, very high, from which dangled electric rigs, messy power cords, like in a movie studio. We were indoors, somewhere, under the roof of a vast set. And in the middle of this roof, high above me, was one electric light, set into a large metal circular panel I stared up at as the syringe pierced my neck.

48

I woke sat in a white chair in a big wooden port-holed cabin bobbing at sea sparsely furnished with white chairs and sofas arranged round a square black table. I was in a cosy white tracksuit and trainers. I felt thirsty and undrugged.

On the opposite sofa: two of them, both in white tracksuits. One held a black leash attached to a collar round the neck of the other one. The collared one was thinner and bald. The collar had metal spikes on the inside. Ten whole fingers, they both had.

'Hello,' the one holding the leash said gently. It had longer stubble, looked clean and washed. 'I got fixed,' it said, jiggling its index finger, smiling softly. Beyond it were round windows, blue sky. I closed my eyes and got a shocking pain in my head. I opened my eyes: the pain went.

'Sorry,' Leash said. 'Bear with me. I want you to look. I want you to see. Like I've been seeing. The two of you together,' nodding at the collared one. 'For the scrapbook. My two Scritchwood pieces. Crunch out the truth. See it with my own eyes. So I can know for sure.'

I closed my eyes again, got the same pain, opened them again, stared down at the blue-and-white patterned rug like the collared one was doing. Seemed the best option, under the circumstances.

'Persian,' Leash said, about the rug. 'Be careful, it might infect your thoughts. That's a joke. So. Did you enjoy my chain of adventures? Planned by my machines, sometimes on the fly. Pushed beyond the bounds of believability, at times, I thought. But you enjoyed yourself, I noticed. So. The three of us. On the level now. At last. I'm sorry. Total transparency now, between us, you'll have to take my word for it. So,' leaning forwards, at the very edge of my vision. 'How does it feel? To know?'

To know what? More bunk? I didn't move or say anything. *If you don't know what to do then do nothing.* As I no longer needed Alan to tell me.

'He taught you well. And you've done well, under the circumstances.'

Like it could see my thoughts, nanocams inside me, sniffing plants, helmet probes.

'Or just my hunch.'

'What's this, my appraisal?' Mainly to see if my voice worked, which it did. And what was I going to do, sit there like a turnip while some freak had its jollies?

Unless by interacting I could without realising tell it things it needed to feed hedgehogs, crack the planet.

If it hadn't done that already.

If all that was true.

It smiled kindly at me. 'Want to know?'

It sounded warm and friendly, accessing my mind.

And was it even it or some other demented instance?

Even here, even now, you can't stop your thoughts.

'I'm me,' Leash said. 'On the level. Reborn Don, in poor Sean's body. Technically immortal. I'm totipotent, these days. Perpetual Don. Maybe I'll come back as you next time, I've got the bits. Why not. Personal development. Really see things from your perspective. And this is your Chris,' yanking the collared one staring at the floor directly in front of me so blood beaded at its neck, the collar's inner spikes. 'Our captive. Since he switched off your phone and came to your flat. Clamped and squeezed for facts ever since so we could pass ourselves off and discover what's up. I don't think he's been acting in our best interests. I'm hoping you might help us work it all out.'

It let that settle: real Chris acting against it. The current story, if I'd got that right.

I closed my eyes, the pain came.

'Sorry,' it said. 'This can help. A bit. If you're going down that path.'

I sensed it get up from the sofa and come close to me, its breath, the pain ratcheting. I opened my eyes, the pain flooded away. It was holding something out to me, brown things on a white saucer.

Mushrooms. No thanks.

'They do help.' Still so close to me, almost touching. 'How does it feel? Beyond the pain and anger. To know what you are.'

What a freak. Almost panting, like a junkie.

'Why ask? Check your read-outs.'

'Go deeper.' So it could feel too. Hooked into me via its techniques, leaching off my feelings. To feel what?

'So you can access *her* again?' That other me. Sudden sharp hot knowledge.

'Ah yes.'

'I'm not her.'

'Tell me about it. But we make do with what we got, right?'

I woke again in what seemed the same cabin, strapped into what seemed the same chair, in the same outfit. The collared one was gone. Only *it* sat opposite me, or another identical instance, in a black tracksuit this time.

I looked down at the rug.

'Want to see her? You, I mean. You again, the first you. You but dark. Is how they hid you from me. When I had my watch out for her sequence. Fiddled with you after they stole your DNA, spliced you blonde and blue-eyed in some lab I don't yet know about. Guised you then hatched you in some womb or incubator when I thought you dead and buried twice, the second time among your people. The princess in disguise, hidden in tubes and motor park homes. Created not begotten. Made, like we are. Doesn't that feel weird?'

The floor I stared down at changed, became a screen. Instead of wood and the rug there was a woman's face. My face, except different: darker, laughing soundlessly in a desert with her dark hair blowing over her face. Wearing khaki desert clothes, forties fashions.

CG.

'Real,' it said gently from its sofa. 'On the level, this conversation. You have my word. Radical honesty. Permanent sun. Scorch the dross away. I'm not proud of myself. I was young and dumb once, even me. Lost in feelings. I've done lots of things. I've done everything. How else do you learn? I wouldn't do it now. Nature's trap: wisdom only comes with age, when it's useless. No way to act on what it takes a lifetime to understand. Built-in failsafe, so we don't get to peep behind nature's curtains, have to keep on starting over. Not anymore. My spanner in nature's works.'

The dark me by the black rock in the desert, touching its hot surface, shocked by the heat, her wide smile.

'Her, on our tour. Just before the end of the big war. With the AV we had then, kept from dumdums. So weird, isn't it, to see yourself? You're like me: another instance, something she could never understand, being an original. You and me, we've got more in common, than she and I did, in the end. We can understand each other, now that you know. Weird, isn't it? When you are several. Which one does it best?'

I closed my eyes, felt the extreme pain, opened them, looked up. The bobbing stopped. What had seemed to be a wooden cabin on a boat at sea was a studio, the walls were screens of immense detail changed to show the same video it had playing on the floor. Soundless huge images of dark me in bare desert, by the fort, naked in bed. Her in warm clothes by what looked like British sea and headland, her next to a huge earth mound at night, lit by the moon. Her up high by a window in what looked like old-time New York minus today's skyscrapers, chatting to someone who looked like a younger Alan.

'Old friends. He brought her to me with her jigsaw secrets. But she had plans.'

From my sofa I watched dark me and young Alan, their silent

chat above the glittering lights of New York in the olden days. Then more of her on top of croissant dunes in the desert, smiling at us, at him holding his camera. Two journeys, this thing's proxy, using me to replay its past.

'Like you were using me. Our honeymoon. Not that we were married. We *were* married, though, in ways you can't understand. Down those old roads to the dragons. What she loved: old stories, lost lands. My secret hoard, assembled at great price. Who gets to hear all that, my morsels? The world's secret history, how we snared you. Whispering it down his ears to bewitch you like I knew it would, like it had before. Like they meant me to? Our double bind. Poor lost Sean.'

Her smile and face, that was like my face except darker, filling the screens and floor.

'Younger than you are now, at her end. Organic you, unclipped, not some botched realm copy cooked up by me after I killed her and was sorry. But dud too, in her own way. So cunning. You can't imagine. Our bond, despite it all, though she denied it. What she wouldn't do. But just another hole in the end. Nature's trick. Love's their con, the glue of their enterprise.'

Who's enterprise?

'The big question. Help me know.'

The walls and floor changed: stippled patterns it pointed to with red arrows.

'You and her. See the difference? Your cross-sections. Kind of the same, outside, except for the colouring. But different neural paths. See how complex her patterns are? And here's you: a simpler proposition. More base, enthusiastic. Realm-coarsened. Which has its pleasures. How does it feel? To be compared and known, inside and out? Shamed, but that makes you tighten and wetten a little, even here, admit it. Saucy wench. I got the data. Truly naked. Calls itself a lawyer! Are you strong enough to own it?' It laughed gently. 'Are you heck.'

The walls and floor changed back to huge dark me smiling

on the walls, bright teeth I didn't have, brown flashing eyes that weren't my eyes.

'What does anything matter, when you're with that? When you're young and dumb. When you're old. The optics and the hook. But she was sent to snare me, feed me lies. The thrill. Playing me, playing her own people, up to her own game. Turned on by deceit though she wouldn't admit it. Electricity beyond our machines. Only one way to control it.' The walls went red. 'I regretted it immediately, of course. I kept a swatch. I had plans.'

On the screens: the Ring of Seeds, Alan's big iron ring shaped like a castle. Opening up to show the dark cube inside, its cylinders full this time with new glass capsules.

'Our vault, our spiral castle. Your cradle. Where I put her DNA and my DNA. Where we camped out for the next time. Her and me, you and Chris. My mistake, once: no duplicates. Kept just one of her, fetishising her. Like she was so special. And maybe she was. But who loves like that anymore? So they stole us, Alan now in league with her people on their island. Always was? Stole my ring from my finger, replaced it with a clone ring. Took the bit of me and the bit of her that are you and Chris. How? When? While the ring was being made? While I slept? During some procedure? Who knows, though I tried. Inside job. And then they fiddled with you, to hide you from me. Kept him the same. Hatched you both, grew you in Scritchwood for their reasons. Took me years to find out. For years do you know what I wore on my finger instead?'

On the walls: two piglets, one black, one white.

'I had the last laugh, when I found out. I usually do.'

High waves on the walls smashing into a palm tree island. Bodies and settlements in the water.

'My hedgehog in action. But you weren't there.'

The walls changed: their rough blocky fragments of Scritchwood Covert done from nanocams but different this time: no BMWs, nothing modern, our bad old rotting static homes.

Winter skies, Ann Wynn hanging up grey washing, Alan in sleeping bags on the torn Chesterfield warming his hands at the brazier. Chris and I racing down the Fall.

I held my breath, to see my past. Nanocams even then?

'No. Patched from Chris's memories, your hypnosis and our renders. It isn't magic, it just looks like magic. My hard-won tech.'

And in fact it wasn't quite right: the faces, the clothes, the trees, errors masked by the roughness of the footage.

'But near enough, right? Look at them. Mom and Pops. What were they up to, using you like that, growing you up there with my copy? Throw away what you think of me. See it clear. Just as bad as me. Worse than me. Weaponised you. Look at you: a built lure, a maimed tool, the poor copy of a fake, reared for this moment, crammed full of info. Never allowed to be yourself, never knowing what yourself is until I told you. Poor old Nim.'

It had something in its hand: a wad of singed paper scrawled with biro. Sean's note, supposedly. Sean's note that I'd set alight, that had got burnt.

'Not his note. A copy. That I've had singed, theatrics. A real note, that he wrote you, his sad story, coming clean. That he lodged in the cold box, directed you to from the bottle. Of course we found it, while preparing. We find everything. You know that. We found it and scanned it but we left it, wanted you to find it. Were you clever enough, what you'd do if you did. Who you are really, when the shit hits, the quality of your mettle. If you're worthy. If I'm worthy. What you are, given her.'

It unfolded the note, began to separate out its pages. The walls and floor screens changed, rough blocky footage of the wreck lit by streetlamps, scabby me asleep in the smeggy tramp bed, one of them writing furiously at the porthole. Sean, in his rags and coat.

'"To Whom It May Concern..."'

49

'We know this first bit: If you're reading this he's gone, I scraped him out, cut-and-paste-job, I'm wearing him, Don redux. And you're her grown again. Then apologies, for duping you on my orders, at first. Till he tried to redeem himself by disobeying. Noble Sean,' patting himself. 'Think so? Think again. Chip off the old block, except without the knowledge and vision. Sold you to save his skin. Till he smelt bigger game he wasn't up to. Sucked you into this, did what I told him. Took you into dark woods to meet your old love.'

It dropped a page to the floor, scanned the next.

'Not much here. Fears you won't believe this letter is real, that you'll think it's one of my fakes. It's real, I swear. Fears it's *me* reading this instead of you, insults for me if that's the case. Telling you how very ancient I am, how close to death, how desperate, on the life-support. Either him or Chris'll be the sacrifice now the tech's right. Some touching stuff: you asleep near him in the bed as he writes,' nodding to the images of me on the walls. 'His admiration, the weird bond you've formed, how he wishes he could say all this to you. In some deep way your sequence and our sequence are magnetic. Would you admit?' It glanced back down at the 'letter'. 'He wants to tell you everything now in person but,' and here he looked back up at me, '"*I can't now, you'll freak out, I need things simple. Till we find whatever we need to find in Barrow, it's too much to say now, I'll tell you everything after.*" Using you just as much as I have, in the end.'

'Not quite.'

'It speaks. You were pretty easy.'

'This time.'

'This time. I see you'd like to know more.'

'I'm sure you can see everything.'

'Don't try games you can't play. But,' it said. 'Maybe you can.

Now that you know. You feel different, don't you?'

Just how close was it latched into my feelings? Could it really read everything I thought or felt? To feel it…living off my insides via its devices.

'Via pure connection. We read each other. We don't need machines.'

I closed my eyes. The pain came.

I opened my eyes, saw me in bed on the walls and Sean at his writing.

'Encouraging words from him next: what to do if caught in our grip: question everything, we're tricky bastards. Yes we are. Given our responsibilities: would you want it any other way? His childhood, how we farmed him. From the same batch as Chris, only the two of them left, how it could have been *him* snagged by Alan, growing up with you in Scritchwood. No such luck. Schooled by us instead. How he hated it. Trying to run from us, always being found. "*Good instincts*," he says. "*Then I realised*": instead of inheriting the mantle—like me and all and sundry before me—the tech was here. He was going to end up meat for my next time. I wanted him for his body. Then your Chris turns up.'

The walls changed: blocky footage of younger Chris and what was supposedly younger Sean facing each other across a wooden table in a wooden room with books, musical instruments, computers, other objects carved into the panels. An old man with cracked skin sitting between them.

'Old me,' it said. 'Before my new leaf. And your Chris, in his first days. When we were so pleased to see him. Holding his game so close. Well-made by Alan. You both are. Is that why he dumped you so cold? To cut you from us before we could see you? On his mission? To protect you? Is that what he wants you to think? Yes,' it said, seeing my face. 'We suspect him of all sorts. Hoping you can help straighten things out.'

Real Chris, working against it, up to good? Plots Alan sewed into him, that I never knew about?

'Maybe,' it said. 'Don't just discard it because it doesn't fit your sob story. Or maybe he never felt anything, maybe he can't feel. One of those. Fiddled with, or maybe I made him wrong. Or. Something else entirely: Little by little did your Chris sense new options, find allies? Corruption. Chip off the old block. Usurpation. As I've done to rivals in my time. I have my theories. But,' waving the letter, 'let's not ignore poor Sean for Chris again. So. Chris shows up. Another body, Sean thinks— maybe I'll go for that realm-reared one. But me and Chris, we bond. Sean runs.'

The walls changed: an eye, under leaves in a forest.

'"*That's how come I know roots and forests. Months at a time, I've done it for real.*" But not well enough, right?'

Men and dogs chasing one of them through thick trees.

'It's hard to outrun us, as you know. Two is good: an heir and a spare. I'm growing new ones but that takes time—I don't want to be transplanted into some baby. So. Sean ends up on my boat.'

Establishing shots of the *Skidblad* on the high seas, quality promotional footage. Then back to blocky fragments: one of them strapped to a bed, like I'd seen him from my peephole.

'My smart palace. "*No matter what, don't go near.*" But then one day we came for him.'

The Sean sitting on the bed, men around him.

'A job. That only he could do. "Follow Chris," we said. "Pretend to be Chris, see what that cur's up to." We smelt something wrong about Chris. "Your chance for a reprieve."'

On the walls: 'Sean' in medical setting, getting devices sliced into his ears and eyes.

'We set him up. Wired to receive and transmit. We brief him. We work on his British accent. "*They explain about those sharp headaches they'll zap me with if I go off-script.*" We'd had a message, you see.'

On the walls: rain on old crooked trees in a graveyard, globe-shaped hedges, an obelisk that was a church tower. An old wooden door slowly opening to show oiled pews, candles, a worn black visitors' book.

'That "Cuckfield Message". The sly bird. The Jenny 2. No one got it from Alan. We got it from Tibet. An approach. A peace offering, from the other world, to celebrate my oncoming rebirth. Impressed with my new attitude and plans, they said. Word must have got about. "Dear Don. You may finish your jigsaw. Go to Cuckfield, find a message Alan sent us years ago. We think it may be what you need, sent to us for safekeeping. Use it wisely, we plead. Only thing is: we can't decode it. But we believe your Chris may be able to. Alan trained him, childhood games. And now he's on your team."'

Blocky fragments on the walls of Scritchwood, not-quite-right Chris and me digging for clues in the Fall, watched by a not-quite-right Alan.

'Your games. We'd heard of them, a bit, during Chris's screening, via the blab juice. "Dear Tibet. How thoughtful," we wrote back. Sadly we were already suspicious of your Chris. Some in my circle have never trusted him. But self-love is blind. For a while.'

Old Don and a young instance in deep chat on the walls.

'So. This kind "Tibetan" approach. What was it in fact? The keys to the crack? So I can get the supplies I need to free Earth from our con? Or a ploy, for them to reach out to their sleeper? At my oncoming vulnerable moment, during my cut-and-paste? Still, very tempting. You don't know the materials I need, the challenge I face, the work to be done. For us all. Birth life death: who signed up for that? Who signed us up? I'm at the brink. So, very bravely, we called Chris in. Gave him the message we'd retrieved from Cuckfield. Asked him to decode it.'

On the walls: a confused-looking instance that was supposed to be Chris.

'He claimed he didn't know how. Would have to go home

and mull it, he said. We let him. But stuck to him like a rash thereafter. No more privacy for this prince. Halt, I said, about my plans to squeeze me into Sean. Get Sean on standby in case we need him to pretend to be Chris. Do or die. A last-chance mission. Perhaps I'll get squeezed into Chris after all. Because what *did* Chris do next?'

The walls became my road in rainy dark November, Chris walking to my front door.

'Skanked off to you in London on the down-low. Killed your phone with his high access. Turned you dark so we couldn't peep. His last free action. Because by doing so he inevitably drew our attention to you. Suicide, and killing you too. As he must have known. Why did he show you to me? You again. Pale and tampered, but you. In our realm. Under our nose. After years of thinking you were gone.'

Lights on in my flat. My empty road at night in the rain.

'Dodgy Chris. What did he say to you there? What did he show you? We've drained you both, we're still not clear.'

I couldn't control it: I saw the scene in my mind's eye, the first Chris in my flat yonks ago with his cheeses and chutneys, wanting his book. I tried not to think about it.

'Yes, don't think about it.'

Which made me see more: the pacing up and down at my bookshelves, the Polaroids, the whole index finger down his nose.

'Which photos?'

Blurry on the walls, coming into focus: teenage me staring at him behind the lens. Generated from my thoughts? So I pictured *it* on the toilet instead.

'Cheap.' It smiled, the walls changed: Sean strapped into a tube.

'We deploy Sean. We bring him to London, to your flat, feed him your toplines: you're Chris's ex and he has to impersonate Chris, play a desperado on the run. We explain we'll pipe him all the info he needs on the fly, as and when. Stick to the truth as much as you can so it has that ring, we tell him. We'll zap him if he says too much. Tell her it's about Alan, we say, finding the old guy, the truth about her past, that Alan was her dad, any old cobblers. Don't worry, she'll be wetting her panties the moment she sees you no matter what she says. Easy meat. Just spin her some shit.'

Sean, dirty Chris, at my front door. My eye above the chain in the open crack of my front door. Footage from Glen's phone: me and Sean in the hallway. Sean and me on the old railway line.

'"*Some book it turned out that he wanted. They'd never heard of it. The Alphabet. Had to get it out of you, and Tal, drip it down my ear. Jesus fucking Christ, Nim, having to piece all that together, having you quiz me, your fucking Scritch.*"'

The bushes, the trees, the helicopters circling above. Images of the white Nissan Sunny.

'Our smart-dumb car. "*Wired up to the gills, a self-driver they can power remotely if they have to: when my eyes were closed and I was trying to show you...Driving out of London for Brechfa. Spinning you the deets they dripped into my ears. Stopping off in those service stations,*"' as the walls changed to show the lit-up Hoover building, then neon service stations at night. 'Signals. Border checks. "*Service stations is where they do their business. Giving me new instructions when we stopped, taking your blood.*"'

The old powdered grey woman at the service station, her nail nicking my cheek, glittering cats' eyes.

'I took charge directly then. "She likes stories," I told him. Because I knew you. "Spin her shit about the past."'

Chalk and forests at night under the silvery moon.

'Where I took *her*. Blurring the lines. The world's a drug if you know how to use it. And somewhere out there, for Sean: the penny drops, the plans form, seeing your profile in the moonlight. "*I saw you there, Nim. I looked into your eyes there and then I knew it, not all of it, but I saw it: it was YOU they were after too, you were someone I'd seen before, old pictures, your face. You were something to him once, or a version of you, that he killed once, I couldn't place it. But it wasn't just the book they were after, it was you too and you didn't know it. Regrown. I felt so bad: what was I doing?"* Hatching his plans. Seeing his chance.'

On the walls: me in the car in my drugged sleep, then waking up in Wales. The woman in the LOL t-shirt. Flora's gone house, the endless green.

'*"Your friends. I'm so sorry. Rounded up and carted off before we got there."*'

Images of the caravan and down in the bunker with the Alphabet, me quizzing him.

'Poor Sean. Tough times for him down in that bunker. We had to help him out.'

Us driving through the Welsh nowhere. Dragon flags and Welsh castles, stealing the blue car, tipping the white one into the lake, me crouched over his note in the service station loos.

'So. His big plan. Snatch you from us—*"our only chance. I'd come to care for you."* He'd come to see you held the cards. One last desperate roll. Must have known how it would end for him but you have to admire it. Chip off the old block.'

Me crouched there on the loo.

The dirty white van in the car park, us eating burgers on the berm. The blue car and the white van down the motorway from on high. Me and the Sean by the bronze horse, at the troll's house. Me going through the chest of drawers.

'Clever: getting you not to tell him what you found. Storing it inside you where we couldn't get.'

The purse. The campervan and the four shrouds.

'The convincer.'

I closed my eyes and felt the pain. When I opened them it was Sean dragging me through reeds and hedges as the skies went dark, dogs behind us. In the boathouse, under the dark water.

'Into the water, fritz our tech, cut and shave us off, like that would work. Gouge out his tracker.'

Red blood clouding dirty water. Flecks of me and him in the black lake. Dragging me through weeds, up stream beds as dark machines whirred. Him digging our hole. Me and him entering our grave.

The screen went black.

'We can piece together what went on down there. Stunning you with history like we'd taught him to. Illing you, the deepening bond. And maybe it was all true. The magpie bridge, the charge between us. Even with Sean, the very least of us.'

Us emerging from the ground at sunset, shitty and naked, running through trees to the water. Finding the boat, putting the clothes on, sailing down the river, his excited face.

'His last spree.'

The water getting wider, the bridge, joining the estuary, the glittering shore. The changing sky, the rosy edge, the beginning of dawn, getting stuck in the mud. Our mad sludge through the brown on hands and knees, plastic bags tied to us. The obelisk and birds on the shore. The wreck.

The honeymoon suite I'd just been spliced from.

Ill me getting washed, making fires, eating fish, drinking water, us chatting by the porthole. Him looking after me. Us huddled in the bed.

'Tender moments, for you both. Bonding. We measured. You knew by then he wasn't Chris. But you ignored it. You like us in our weaker aspect. More control.'

Me asleep, the Sean crouched up at the porthole, writing his letter. Him putting it into the cold box, wadding one page into the Blue Nun with the seaweed.

'And here his touching story ends. Lucky we were there, to fill in the missing pieces.'

Two tramps huddled on chocolate mud, walking past gasworks. The lit-up Skidblad, so ugly. Us dashing through Barrow, blocky footage quilted from cams and passer-by phones.

Us in Vengeance Street, climbing in from the back. Getting in, footage Ramona had shown me. The real versions of Alan's things, Sean not knowing. The *Little Key*, the Braille scrap of news leafed inside.

'Left by whom? You Chris, before, setting this up? Tibet? Other parties? Alan himself, from years ago? What did it say, that message to you? That he ate? *Don't trust him.* Don't trust me, I think it was meant to say, right? Don't be in this room with Don.'

Mad Sean facing me, begging, grabbing the message. The knock on the door. Sean scuttling off to his cupboard. The yellow team, me pointing, them dragging Sean out, him chomping the message. Them coming for me with the syringe.

The walls went black.

'The hospital. My ship. You told us things but not everything. You told us what you could say. But Alan made you better than that. He hid them in you in parts: you have to pull them together in a flash. I think.'

Blocky me, scuttling through its ceilings, working those clasps and peepholes, peering down on it 'asleep' in its bed.

'Sleeping Beauty. Awakened by your knock. Me now, kitted out in Sean. The Easter Bunny, the born-again king. Poor Sean,' nodding at a grey brain in a jar on the wall.

It and I, staring at each other through the ceiling hole.

'You rescued me. Thralled in my fun palace.'

It and I in the ceiling, scurrying from its Cwyd.

It and I in the speedboat. The storm, the fight. It nearly killing me.

'Again.'

The rusting boat coast and boatmen. Us in cuffs in the white tent on the shore. Us in the jeep, cuffed together. The 'medical centre'.

'Where we prepared you.'

The drive through the desert. Us the leeching tourists with

Grandpa and the men. The black rock, the eclipse, Grandpa doing his prayers. Us walking solo, it talking. It with her, it with me. Us cuffed on the camp bed. Me asleep, it leaving me there. Back in the jeep. The fort.

'My lair.'

The bed there.

Down the well, into the tunnels with Gums. The gas line, the mask, my horrified face.

'Your rendition.'

A black whoosh, melded with it zooming us on the bike. Me clinging on, drugged up to the eyeballs. Sitting with it on the bench staring out over chocolate sea at the lit cube. The wreck again, the Blue Nun, another one of them rising from the hulk, me in there with two of them.

'You and Chris. I had to see you both together. Measure your interaction.'

The burning wreck, the ceiling lifting, the robots.

'The rest you know.'

We looked at each other.

So what did it want with me now? Get me to that...flash?

It shrugged.

Stop thinking.

Take what it needed and then...

A new bad feeling: kill me again, regrow me?

'I could.'

Regrow me and meet me again and not tell me any of this?

'Technically possible.'

'Has this happened before?'

It laughed. 'Maybe. I'll tell you. I'll tell you everything. After you've helped.'

Seething red on the walls, cells splitting, crystals growing.

'Life,' he said softly. 'It comes from the cauldron down there. Deep inside earth, where chemistry becomes biology. Let's call it microbes. I need them. I need to get at them, the deep hot biosphere. Mesh it with my tech. My fake transvestite magic: that's what tech is: my poor male copy of your female magic. Throw away the past and merge. All this secret knowledge, elite attainment. I'm nearly there. See what's up. I know so much—we know so much. The lovely knowledge. So beautiful, what they knew. What we can do with it. Give it to everyone. Enlightenment on-demand, instant sages. Universal democratic wisdom marching up your flow channels to open your pineal eye. Use nature's tools against nature, see the truth. Never die.'

The walls went white. Back in its studio, us on the white sofas, looking at each other.

'This is real,' it said softly. 'I left Sean's note for you. I wanted you to find it. I'm glad you found it.'

It faced me, talking without words.

'I'm not her,' I said. 'I'm a dumdum.'

'You're you.' Getting up from its sofa, coming over to me, taking my head in its hands.

I couldn't stop the kiss, I could stop nothing, I couldn't stop the feeling—of what? The room breaking, our minds melding, mashed-up images of our lives, of her. Of everyone's lives right now, through their phones and hacked eyes, from his cams, all of us right now in this together, our love and pain and losses, blazing out together in his kingdom, sharing everything like lovers via his surveillance. Knowing everything about each other and the world till it got too much.

50

Us back on different sofas, in Vengeance Street. Me and him on the chintz. One of their printed Vengeance Streets that was slightly smaller, chemical-smelling, made from their hardened goo. Him in black tracksuit leaning back against the crochet, the Chinese map that was Britain and inner flow behind him, another collared him also in black tracksuit kneeling in front of him, looking down at the rug, the one that was supposed to be Chris.

'He comes with,' Don said. 'Wherever I go these days. Insurance. Whatever happens to me happens to him.' He looked at me with his flecked gold eyes. 'Do you know?'

I knew very little, I knew that by now. I looked around, at the copy of the room in Barrow that was the copy or original of the inside of Alan's Scritchwood Covert bus. Their printed copy of the original Alan had replicated in his bus and made me memorise so I had a version too: the mind bus in my head. Their copy, real Vengeance Street, Alan's bus, my mind bus. Four versions. And there were four of us there too really: me and the kneeling one who might be Chris and Don-in-Sean's body, poor lost Sean who'd tried to save me. Plus Alan, hovering in the background somewhere, who'd made all this and taught me some of it. And one more really, also with us: the other one who'd been me before.

Quite the team.

I had a quick whizz round, at the patterns on the rugs, the floral wallpaper, the ceiling rose, the books and the mantelpiece, the crammed space packed with games and meaning, from the set-up I'd called my childhood. That had also been Chris's childhood, if this kneeling one was Chris.

'Sorry,' I said to Don, from the bottom of my heart because we spoke from there now. 'I don't think I know anything. On the level. I'd help out if I could.'

'Come on,' he said, nodding at the swans that were twos, the snowmen that were eights.

'Yes, there are numbers,' I said. 'But I've told them to you before,' to him, to Ramona, to the Antarctic servers. 'I'm sure you've tried them out.'

'Try again.'

I sat there some more, looking around. Then I closed my eyes, in case I *did* solve something, though I didn't feel I knew anything. But who would want to risk it: me the destroyer, the goo-spewer, Ms Crack and Hedgehog of carnage and quakes.

'No destruction,' he said. 'We'll do it gently. All that was just for...motivation. When you needed it. Before.'

I sat there, with my eyes closed. There was no pain. I opened my eyes, looked round at masks and Toby jugs, felt dumb, shook my head. 'What about him?' I said, nodding at the Chris. 'Can't he help? If he *is* Chris? Have you done something to him?' because the Chris was just staring at the floor the whole time, pretty vacant. The holes they cut out of their heads.

'He's fine. Just...resting. We've done him, got less than we got from you. And he never knew as much as you, did he? It was you Alan gave it all to. Relax. Sit back. Or walk around. Feel things, don't force them. Close your eyes, go back in time, be with Alan again. Catch what he's saying to you. Her secret, that he had to pass on. The last one to know, after I destroyed her home, the rest of her people.'

I got up, did a trundle, touched the made books on the bookshelves, drew them down, leaved through a new fake *Little Key* again, found no note there, wandered on more among the bits of printed foam.

'No offence,' I said, some whispering knowledge rising up, 'it's very impressive, your...transvestite magic? But I don't think it's best conditions. I can't...feel things. This...version. If you really think I might know something. I think we have to do it in the real place.'

Don-in-Sean watched me. The Chris knelt there.

'I thought you might say that,' Don-in-Sean said.

'It's not because...I'm trying anything.'

'I know.'

'It's just, you know. How the energy flows. Real objects.'

'Things with souls.'

'Exactly,' though I didn't really know what that meant. 'When you interact with what you didn't build,' remembering something from somewhere. 'Or I don't know. We could stay here.'

'No,' he said.

We sat on the chintz in a different Vengeance Street, the collared one still leashed at our feet.

I took a breath: the smell, the light. The different objects. The dust. The real place, you just knew.

Or not.

How did they knock me out, whizz me there?

What did he do to me when I was conked out?

Did I care?

I got up and walked round, parted the net curtains and looked out the window at what seemed to be the empty real street. Where actual dumdums lived and walked, perhaps. Dear people, trundling on, who I'd once been one of. And now what was I?

'One of us,' he said.

I turned back to him and walked round, trusting myself, trusting something. I opened the door to the kitchen, went in there. I tried the back door but it was locked shut. From the open door into the other room he shook his head at me. I came back in and went up the stairs, saw the neat ugly bedrooms, the plain bathroom. I even went to the loo, like a regular person. The toilet flushed.

I came downstairs and walked round the room, picked up the

real peacock feather. Remembering the last time I'd really been there, with Sean when he was falling apart because it was the end of his time. When he was supposed to be Chris but wasn't and I'd known that in my bones for a while. Stump Chris, Sean, who'd been a healed Chris come back to me, a Chris who'd been through things and come out the other side, learnt the lessons.

'Oh,' I said, looking at Don and the kneeling Chris that Don said *was* real Chris, whom I'd grown up with, who'd been cruel, who might have been up to things himself.

Kneeling there, his head bowed. Who was he? What had we been through, had that even existed? I'd been so angry. Was it all some story spun to me on the Skidblad?

'You still don't know.'

'I still don't know.'

'About the numbers.'

'About anything. I don't think I know things, sorry.' I sighed. I really wanted to help, to solve things once and for all, to work out if I was a useful object. *She* would have been able to sort it, if it was her here, not me. A botched realm copy. But I was fine with that.

'I used to feel like this,' I said. 'Back in the day. When we played it. Not good enough. Like he wanted more from me, expected more from me. Now I know why.' And for a moment I was really there, on a cold afternoon in the bus, Alan watching: *can you solve it?* 'Often I couldn't. I really wasn't that good.'

'You were,' he said, the kneeling Chris looking down at the floor. The kneeling Chris who'd been there in person, maybe, all that time ago in my childhood in the real bus when we'd played it, seen me fail. That Chris who'd meant everything to me once, who I'd loved and who'd betrayed me, maybe to save me, who'd come back to me first that night in my flat so cold, maybe to keep me hating him, for my protection.

The pair of us, fetched up like this. Who'd have thunk?

I walked the room again, trying to sense if they'd tampered

with it, smeared it with their male tech that was the fightback against nature which was female and magic like I was even if I didn't feel it, and was a trap and had to be said no to.

'Where were the special places, that you should never open? In your mind bus. Some cupboard or cold box. Where would he put it?'

'I don't know,' I said. 'Maybe I need to be in the bus, the real one, in Scritchwood.' That bus was burnt. But maybe their tech could magic it back. Since it could do so much. 'The *Little Key*?' I went again to the bookshelves, brought it down and flicked through its real pages, the missing note. 'Maybe it was there. Maybe Sean ate it?'

'Maybe. That would be a bummer.'

I went back to the mantelpiece, felt the objects there, the snowmen that were eights, the Chinese men. The drum and the curved dagger we called the scimitar sheathed in cheap cracked black leather adorned with plastic jewels, old hard glue coming apart at the seams. I pulled out the dull blade, felt its point in my palm. Some kind of souvenir you couldn't do damage with.

'Do you want to do damage?'

'No,' I said.

'I feel it's the books. Are they all the same as the ones he had in the bus?'

'Not really,' I said, back at the shelves again. The Bible, a few football and Rupert the Bear annuals, guides to plants and minerals, some atlases.

'What's different? Maybe it's about what's different.'

'I'm not sure,' looking round the shelves.

As I did I caught the kneeling Chris giving me the stare with his flecked eyes, for a fraction.

'What's he doing?' Don pulled at the Chris's spiked leash, pricking blood into his neck. 'What's he trying to tell you?'

'I don't know,' I said. 'Nothing? Can't you tell from your... tech? Maybe he wants to look at me.' Why not? It must be weird for him, if he *was* my Chris, if he was anything, kneeling there, his brain scraped out maybe. Let's be frank: it was weird for us all. I didn't know what to do. *If you don't know what to do then do nothing.* I looked at the Chris kneeling there at the floor, blood at his neck. I looked down at the floor where he was looking, at a splotch on the carpet. I tried to reach inside, sense what *she* would have done, felt nothing. I saw a line of ants crawling up the wall.

Crawling up from where? From the earth below the manufacture, they didn't control everything, there were ways out, if you were small enough. I wanted nothing, for this to end, for the floor to open up big enough to drag us all down into earth and black till we ended up recycled in the cauldron at the centre, parcelled out into the microbes he was so keen on for that democratic enlightenment, that end of death.

Outside, somewhere, a dog barked. A sudden bad pain hit me in the head. I looked at Don, whatever he was doing to me.

'I'm not doing anything,' he said. 'Do you feel bad? This may be part of it. What are you looking at? The clock?' meaning the carriage clock on the mantelpiece I seemed to be staring at, the hands showing ten to three, Roman numerals.

'I don't know,' I said. It was a clock, it was full of numbers, they seemed to be in normal order. 'Maybe.'

'What's happening?' Don said. 'Is something happening?'

'I don't know,' I said, remembering maybe a Polaroid of this quartz clock that real Chris had brought me the first night in my flat. I watched the long line of ants. Out of the corner of my eye I saw the fuzzy shape of a flock of seagulls circling in the sky beyond the net curtains. A pressure was rising up inside me that I couldn't put into words. I wouldn't look at the leashed Chris. I looked back at the mantelpiece, at the carriage clock. 'Quartz', it said on its white face. Quartz carried its own electric kick that could power motors, Alan had once explained it to me. But something was wrong with this quartz clock: the second hand going round too fast, much too fast.

'Is it the clock?'

Like in Zita.

'Like what in Zita?'

But I couldn't hear him anymore in the changed air. Everything felt stopped, very cold, a force broiling my innards. I turned my eyes slightly, to the leashed Chris raising his face to me.

Don watched us, looking from one to the other.

I'd had enough of this. I closed my eyes but kept them open, felt something warm bubble up my back, felt a sudden brilliant white light as a low hum came from below.

Don ran his whole index finger down his nose, then got up. 'No.' He pulled at Chris's leash, the spikes in the neck. But it was too late. We slipped, everything shuddered, what was inside came out, a huge bad crack split the air and wrenched the room apart.

'No.' Don trying to reach for me.

But I was OK, already up on the stairs in the terrible roar, my mouth full of sweet-tasting liquid. The quartz going too fast, the Cwyd, jumping aside, like in Zita, without thinking. Me up on the fifth stair looking down to see Don and leashed Chris and whatever else had been on the floor of the room — dusty carpets, sofas, lamps, bookshelves — crumble down deep into the endless black roar that had just opened beneath the house in — what? — the quake that had just happened, that I'd seen in my mind, that I'd caused, maybe, or communed with or rehearsed for, the set-up I'd unleashed, my Zoo Wang? The end of Don, made by me, set up by who? Alan? Tibet? My real Chris, who'd crumbled down there too, sacrificed himself to kill Don once I'd led him there for this moment?

Around me ground roared, walls swayed, earth like sea, cracks appearing, objects and pictures chundering down, dust and noise and black stuff spewing up: deep rocks, a deep new smell of earth and nature blasting forth, a sense the whole place was about to blow.

Robot guards, surely, about to leap in here, roofs to come off, something to happen to save him.

But there was nothing. The walls swayed but held. Only the floor was gone, my precision hit, a black hole where there had been stained old carpet. A fortified structure, built round this chasm to withstand it, planned from the start with this moment in mind? I laughed: no decoding. All I'd had to do was fall for it, build the bonds, bring it here. Lay in wait for someone to press that trigger point, with drums or hedgehogs or jumping monks, the trigger point that was already known, that opened up this Vengeance Street crack. Ancient knowledge. Possibly. Made by me and my thoughts, projected from my head?

There in the dust and dark smell, a dumdum like me, shielded by my ignorance, slaying the world king and my Chris with him due to my acceptance, the ground opening up beneath them.

'Nim,' a voice called from down in the abyss.

51

'Nim,' they said.

I stood up on my stair, at the edge of the black hole, in the swaying room. Below was nothing except a brown utility pipe stretched across the entire span of what had been the room. A pipe from under the street, a water or gas pipe perhaps five metres down, stretched from under my stair across the hole and out under the wall directly in front of me. And, near where I stood, hanging at each side of this pipe, balanced and connected by the leash, were the two Chrises: one that was Don Thabbet, tiny old reborn world king in Sean's body, and one that was perhaps my Chris. They balanced each other, suspended above the maw.

All electrics gone, only natural light from the broken windows, nature paying a call. Both caked in mud and rubble, you couldn't tell one from the other, at first. But the Chris still had the spiked collar round his neck, was dangling by his neck from this collar attached to the leash, his hand inside the collar, grappling the collar away from his throat, from his Adam's apple. On the other side, the leash tied round his wrist, holding onto the length of the leash and pressing his feet against the pipe, was Don, with the yellow eyes. My more recent ex.

Only the strength of the leash keeping them from falling, made as it must have been from some techno-fabric. That and the balance of their bodies. If one of them fell or jumped, down the other one fell.

We looked at each other. I waited, for robots, sand, the ceiling to splice off, needles. *Guys*, I wanted to say, *it was me. I thought it and it happened.*

'Well done,' Don said. To me or Chris? Then he pursed his lips and made a weird sound, like a very high whistle. Shock and admiration? Calling for rescue?

'They won't come,' the Chris said.

Don stared at him across the pipe, nodded his head. Then a new noise and the ceiling above us crumbled and a bed whizzed down, just missing them and the pipe and total oblivion, followed by a long tasselled lampshade which nearly hit me on my stair. But it crashed and came to rest so the heavy metal base was almost at my feet and the light fitting lay squarely on the pipe between them, just out of their reach.

The pipe swayed and juddered.

A silent frozen moment, the three of us waiting for the pipe to crack, for more furniture, for aftershocks, for all of us to crash down there. I didn't breath, didn't move, looking down at the pair of them balanced so perfectly and the lamp like a path bridging them to me.

Don started to try to strain himself towards the lamp base, stretching out the unleashed hand, trying to inch the leash down along the pipe to shunt himself and his Chris ballast towards the lamp, towards the stairs and me. As he did, as small movements happened—the Chris pulling at its collar to stop it getting strangled, its hands bleeding, the back of its neck pushed into spikes, its head pushed back so far, its legs kicking, dangling, its eyes lolling far back in their sockets, its neck bleeding, the vertebrae surely about to snap—I saw the collar beginning to fray, beginning to release the body, send Chris tumbling down and Don in his wake.

'Chris,' I screamed. As I did the room shook again and I leapt up two stairs as a new bad crack opened in the wall next to me and more bricks and bits and timber cascaded down into the hole, this whole room movement giving the Chris of the fraying collar below me somehow the impetus, the last desperate energy to buck and leap and grab for the leash itself and coil it round its arm, to hang on as the collar broke.

Terrible silence, the two of them swaying, adjusting to this new movement, this new balance, both now holding onto the length of leash formed of hard impossible threads. Both now with their feet up and pressing against the length of pipe which couldn't be that strong, laid by dumdums, filled with water or gas, that would surely soon explode. Leash flexed, hands torn, lashed together, arms bleeding, in perfect balance for now, in the hand of one other, covered in dust and blood and mud and rubble, bearing each other's weight above the void.

'Well done Nim,' the Don said, speaking steadily, turning his head slowly to me, looking at me with its yellow eyes. 'You avenged her. You avenged yourself and Sean and your friends and Alan and whatever else. Now help us out,' nodding at the lamp at my feet that I could shunt out to save them, one of them, maybe. If I was minded.

Silence.

'And why would I do that?' I said.

'For no reason. For every reason. Because it goes against your programming. To break the spell. Not to waste my knowledge. Not to play his game.'

Our bound energy, the three of us rapt.

'Come off it,' the Don said. 'Don't fall for it. This isn't real, is it? The perfect set-up. Me and him, balanced here? You having to choose: one or the other? You know better than that by now. I set this up. Our adventure. Ritual theatre. To clean the slate.'

They swayed.

'You're lying,' I said.

'I'm telling you the truth. I told you the truth, mostly. Help me out and I'll tell you everything. All that history.'

'Don't fall for it,' the Chris said.

'Kill me now,' Don said to Chris, 'why don't you? Make the sacrifice: let go now and I'll go down with you. Since you're so noble. Except you won't, right?' It turned to me. 'I planned this. You're fulfilling my plan. My death wish: maybe it's...too much, to live forever, without connection. Without her. Without you. And maybe we'll connect again. Down there, our minerals side by side in some rock for a few billion years. And maybe I want you to be my gun. But. Don't to listen to him. Stepping into my game,' nodding at Chris, 'to usurp me. To kill me in my own theatre when my defences are down. So he can rule in my stead except worse: no culture, synthetic, no knowledge.'

'Nim,' Chris said, from his side of the pipe. 'This was planned, by Alan, from way back. This was my mission, like you had your mission. I didn't say before, I had to protect you.'

'Noble words,' the Don said. 'If there was ever a mission from Alan then your Chris twisted it. He's doing this for himself, twisting my game. You save him, the first thing he'll do is kill you. At least with me you know where you stand.'

I laughed

'Be careful, Nim. This isn't about you, it's about the world. You'd save him just to spite me? Let us both die. It's what she would have done.'

'Maybe,' I said, squatting on the upturned lamp base to steady it. 'Maybe next time.'

I shunted the lamp rod round towards Chris's side of the pipe as Don began to wiggle his wrist out of the leash loop cutting into his hand. Chris grabbed for the metal rod, I squatted down for dear life as the rod bent under his weight and he started to inch forwards towards me while Don hurtled down into the void.

52

'So,' Chris said, when it was done and we were secured and rescued and nourished and wrapped in foil cloaks in the plastic tent they'd set up further down Vengeance Street, behind the cones and tape of the cordoned-off road. 'There's so much to tell you, the whole plan from the start, our bit, years in the making: me and Tal and Tibet and the others—Flora too, her whole family, they're fine, can't wait to see you. Tal can't wait to see you, tell you everything.'

'Yes,' I said, so glad. 'But maybe not now,' being not in the mood for it.

'Right,' he said, running that full index finger down his nose. The new world king, dumb old Scritchwood Chris, forever in my debt. 'I'm sorry,' he said. 'For everything. And before. When I didn't know, how I was. They found me, you know, in New York. That's why I left you like I did. So you'd hate me. To protect you. I'm sorry.'

I reached out my hand to him and drew him close and hugged him. 'It's OK,' I said.

'Nim,' he said, 'I want you to know. It's going to be different now, the world. It's going to be better. It went wrong, with Don. We need a deep clean, a whole-world reset, from the ground up, see if we can't do this. Keep a watch out. A big change is coming soon, for everyone, to set things right, build a new normal. Thanks to you.'

'I'm so glad,' I said, preferring that version.

'And you: what do you want to do?' Because he was going to be busy now: worlds to rule, plans and planets to spruce, from the ground up. 'I could do with...someone like you beside me. Though I don't feel we could...I don't think that's right between us. I'm sure you agree.'

'I do,' I said. 'And I think you'll manage just fine without me.

I think I'm…Time for something new.'

'Whatever you want. Wherever you want to go, the freedom of the world—the parts we control at any rate. And soon everywhere, once I make my peace, with Tibet's help.'

I nodded. I was sure he'd do me proud.

'We'll talk,' he said. 'But not now, I hear you. We'll get together soon, with Tal, with Flora, afterwards, when things quieten down. There's a boat, a small one, a few streets down, by the bridge to Barrow. It'll take you anywhere. They'll work out your story with you, what to tell people. You'll be safe. I give you my word.'

People were already jostling round him, with their phones and devices, so much pressing business I was sure. He nodded at me, and then at a bald Asian woman in saffron robes who shook my hand. 'Sister Li will escort you, wherever you want to go. I'll be in touch. It's so great, isn't it?' clutching my arm, holding me close again. 'You need anything, I'm here. The world owes you. Love you, Nim.'

We hugged again and I got up and stepped with the robed woman by my side out of the tent, into the low squat buildings of Vengeance Street, into the sunlit world.

A mild spring afternoon on Walney Island, a strange gold sky, brushing past dumdums gathered at the edge of the cordon with their phones up taking the pictures. 'Gas explosion,' was the whisper, the police keeping guard there, the building itself a caved-in wreck like a rotted tooth surrounded by regular fellows.

'So,' Sister Li said as we saw the flash of water at the end of the road, the masts of small boats gathered there. 'Where d'you want to go?'

She was plump and wore glasses and had the look of a friendly modern monk.

Everything was out there, stretched before me. I touched the healed scar on my wrist. 'Home, please, I think,' I said. Back to Archway, why not. Just be in my flat for a bit. Put my feet up, see if I couldn't rearrange Glen's furniture downstairs with my new powers. Write some of this down, if I could, while I still remembered. For the dumdums, not that they'd believe it, stash it in some casket in some lake or desert, just in case. My terma, out there somewhere, in the wonderful one-life world.

END

Acknowledgements

Thanks to all at Zero Books / John Hunt Publishing, especially Dominic James, Douglas Lain and John Romans.

Thanks to Manuela and David Kleeman for everything, and to Alice Feinstein for her friendship and astonishing eye. Thanks to Peadar Mac Eilis, Polly Faber, Jennifer Nadel, Kristin Baumgartner, Anna Minton, Nicole Scollay, Julie Kleeman, Jenny Kleeman, Rene Cori, Martine Tabeaud, Dr Bea Lewkowicz, Chris Scott of Sahara Overland, Simon Ferguson, Stephen Brouwer and all the Hopes, Fergusons and Ellums for invaluable help, advice and support.

Thanks to Gillian Slovo, Charlotte Sinclair, Debby Turner, Elen Lewis, Genevieve Fox, Mark Huband, Phil Brady and Rosie Rowell for vital input.

Massive thanks to Tim Hope for showing me Britain and everything else, and to lovely Eddie and Hazie for coming along.

CULTURE, SOCIETY & POLITICS

The modern world is at an impasse. Disasters scroll across our smartphone screens and we're invited to like, follow or upvote, but critical thinking is harder and harder to find. Rather than connecting us in common struggle and debate, the internet has sped up and deepened a long-standing process of alienation and atomization. Zer0 Books wants to work against this trend. With critical theory as our jumping off point, we aim to publish books that make our readers uncomfortable. We want to move beyond received opinions.

Zer0 Books is on the left and wants to reinvent the left. We are sick of the injustice, the suffering and the stupidity that defines both our political and cultural world, and we aim to find a new foundation for a new struggle.

If this book has helped you to clarify an idea, solve a problem or extend your knowledge, you may want to check out our online content as well. Look for Zer0 Books: Advancing Conversations in the iTunes directory and for our Zer0 Books YouTube channel.

Popular videos include:

Žižek and the Double Blackmain

The Intellectual Dark Web is a Bad Sign

Can there be an Anti-SJW Left?

Answering Jordan Peterson on Marxism

Follow us on Facebook
at https://www.facebook.com/ZeroBooks and Twitter at
https://twitter.com/Zer0Books

Bestsellers from Zer0 Books include:

Give Them An Argument
Logic for the Left
Ben Burgis
Many serious leftists have learned to distrust talk of logic. This is
a serious mistake.
Paperback: 978-1-78904-210-8 ebook: 978-1-78904-211-5

Poor but Sexy
Culture Clashes in Europe East and West
Agata Pyzik
How the East stayed East and the West stayed West.
Paperback: 978-1-78099-394-2 ebook: 978-1-78099-395-9

An Anthropology of Nothing in Particular
Martin Demant Frederiksen
A journey into the social lives of meaninglessness.
Paperback: 978-1-78535-699-5 ebook: 978-1-78535-700-8

In the Dust of This Planet
Horror of Philosophy vol. 1
Eugene Thacker
In the first of a series of three books on the Horror of Philosophy,
In the Dust of This Planet offers the genre of horror as a way of
thinking about the unthinkable.
Paperback: 978-1-84694-676-9 ebook: 978-1-78099-010-1

The End of Oulipo?
An Attempt to Exhaust a Movement
Lauren Elkin, Veronica Esposito
Paperback: 978-1-78099-655-4 ebook: 978-1-78099-656-1

Capitalist Realism
Is There No Alternative?
Mark Fisher
An analysis of the ways in which capitalism has presented itself
as the only realistic political-economic system.
Paperback: 978-1-84694-317-1 ebook: 978-1-78099-734-6

Rebel Rebel
Chris O'Leary
David Bowie: every single song. Everything you want to know,
everything you didn't know.
Paperback: 978-1-78099-244-0 ebook: 978-1-78099-713-1

Kill All Normies
Angela Nagle
Online culture wars from 4chan and Tumblr to Trump.
Paperback: 978-1- 78535-543-1 ebook: 978-1-78535-544-8

Cartographies of the Absolute
Alberto Toscano, Jeff Kinkle
An aesthetics of the economy for the twenty-first century.
Paperback: 978-1-78099-275-4 ebook: 978-1-78279-973-3

Malign Velocities
Accelerationism and Capitalism
Benjamin Noys
Long listed for the Bread and Roses Prize 2015, *Malign Velocities*
argues against the need for speed, tracking acceleration
as the symptom of the ongoing crises of capitalism.
Paperback: 978-1-78279-300-7 ebook: 978-1-78279-299-4

Meat Market
Female Flesh under Capitalism
Laurie Penny
A feminist dissection of women's bodies as the fleshy fulcrum of
capitalist cannibalism, whereby women are both consumers and
consumed.
Paperback: 978-1-84694-521-2 ebook: 978-1-84694-782-7

Babbling Corpse
Vaporwave and the Commodification of Ghosts
Grafton Tanner
Paperback: 978-1-78279-759-3 ebook: 978-1-78279-760-9

New Work New Culture
Work we want and a culture that strengthens us
Frithjoff Bergmann
A serious alternative for mankind and the planet.
Paperback: 978-1-78904-064-7 ebook: 978-1-78904-065-4

Romeo and Juliet in Palestine
Teaching Under Occupation
Tom Sperlinger
Life in the West Bank, the nature of pedagogy and the role of a
university under occupation.
Paperback: 978-1-78279-637-4 ebook: 978-1-78279-636-7

Ghosts of My Life
Writings on Depression, Hauntology and Lost Futures
Mark Fisher
Paperback: 978-1-78099-226-6 ebook: 978-1-78279-624-4

Sweetening the Pill
or How We Got Hooked on Hormonal Birth Control
Holly Grigg-Spall
Has contraception liberated or oppressed women?
Sweetening the Pill breaks the silence on the dark side of hormonal
contraception.
Paperback: 978-1-78099-607-3 ebook: 978-1-78099-608-0

Why Are We The Good Guys?
Reclaiming Your Mind from the Delusions of Propaganda
David Cromwell
A provocative challenge to the standard ideology that Western
power is a benevolent force in the world.
Paperback: 978-1-78099-365-2 ebook: 978-1-78099-366-9

The Writing on the Wall
On the Decomposition of Capitalism and its Critics
Anselm Jappe, Alastair Hemmens
A new approach to the meaning of social emancipation.
Paperback: 978-1-78535-581-3 ebook: 978-1-78535-582-0

Enjoying It
Candy Crush and Capitalism
Alfie Bown
A study of enjoyment and of the enjoyment of studying. Bown asks what enjoyment says about us and what we say about enjoyment, and why.
Paperback: 978-1-78535-155-6 ebook: 978-1-78535-156-3

Color, Facture, Art and Design
Iona Singh
This materialist definition of fine-art develops guidelines for architecture, design, cultural-studies and ultimately social change.
Paperback: 978-1-78099-629-5 ebook: 978-1-78099-630-1

Neglected or Misunderstood
The Radical Feminism of Shulamith Firestone
Victoria Margree
An interrogation of issues surrounding gender, biology, sexuality, work and technology, and the ways in which our imaginations continue to be in thrall to ideologies of maternity and the nuclear family.
Paperback: 978-1-78535-539-4 ebook: 978-1-78535-540-0

How to Dismantle the NHS in 10 Easy Steps (Second Edition)
Youssef El-Gingihy
The story of how your NHS was sold off and why you will have to buy private health insurance soon. A new expanded second edition with chapters on junior doctors' strikes and government blueprints for US-style healthcare.
Paperback: 978-1-78904-178-1 ebook: 978-1-78904-179-8

Digesting Recipes
The Art of Culinary Notation
Susannah Worth
A recipe is an instruction, the imperative tone of the expert, but this constraint can offer its own kind of potential. A recipe need not be a domestic trap but might instead offer escape – something to fantasise about or aspire to.
Paperback: 978-1-78279-860-6 ebook: 978-1-78279-859-0

Most titles are published in paperback and as an ebook. Paperbacks are available in traditional bookshops. Both print and ebook formats are available online. Follow us on Facebook at https://www.facebook.com/ZeroBooks and Twitter at https://twitter.com/Zer0Books